Splatterpunks

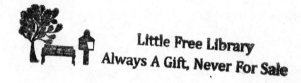
EXTREME
HORROR

Splatterpunks

EXTREME HORROR

EDITED BY
PAUL M. SAMMON

ST. MARTIN'S PRESS NEW YORK

Design by Jaye Zimet.

Library of Congress Cataloging-in-Publication Data
Splatterpunks : extreme horror / Paul Sammon, ed.
p. cm.
1. Horror tales, American. I. Sammon, Paul.
PS648.H6S65 1990   813'.0873808—dc20   90-8641

ISBN 0-312-04581-6 (pbk.)
ISBN 0-312-05201-4 (cloth)

First Edition: December 1990
10 9 8 7 6 5 4 3 2 1

ACKNOWLEDGMENTS

To bad taste

There Are No Limits
    —ad copy for *Hellraiser*

CONTENTS

PERSONAL
ACKNOWLEDGMENTS

I used to sneer at the varied thank you's that traditionally clutter these pages. After all, I thought, in all my youthful wisdom, wasn't the *author* or the *editor* primarily responsible for bringing out a book?

Little did I know . . .

First and foremost, I'd like to extend my appreciation to the *Splatterpunks* contributors; your collective craziness is what this book is all about. I'd also like to thank Gordon Van Gelder and Stuart Moore of St. Martin's Press, guys who were always there when I needed them. And a tip o' the hat to Joe Lansdale, for putting up with the innumerable bitching sessions.

Finally, my sincere gratitude to the three people most responsible for *Splatterpunks*:

To Lori Perkins, agent and confidant extraordinaire; next time, let's do a book on tapioca!

To John Skipp, whose courageousness is matched only by his honesty; it's not a movement!

And to Sherri Sires Sammon, soulmate, wife, lifelong companion; you can put away the voodoo doll.

Paul M. Sammon

INTRODUCTION

There have always been outlaws.
Then;
The Marquis de Sade. William Burroughs. Baudelaire.
Now;
Clive Barker. John Skipp. Joe R. Lansdale.
These are the renegades, the edge walkers, the dwellers in the abyss; uncompromising artists whose inner eyes see bitter truths.

They are the dark magnets to which we are drawn, attractors/repulsors who understand the allure of outrageousness. They are the epitome of black humor, stand-up comics for the apocalypse. And their fiction sweeps across the page like hot actinic searchlights, probing the darkest corners of our souls.

They are, in a word, splatterpunks.

What *is* a splatterpunk?

Imagine a new word for an old attitude, one which knows no restraints, bows to no god, recognizes no boundaries.

Imagine energy, and imagination, and freedom from convention.

Imagine a book which distills these qualities into the essential contradictions of human nature; light and dark, yin and yang.

You have just imagined *Splatterpunks*.

Contained herein are seventeen singular voices, voices that sing against repression and taboo. And be warned; like Reagan's guns-for-hostages deal, *Splatterpunks* is not for the squeamish.

The stories you are about to read have been composed in the true outlaw spirit; they operate beyond the law. Consider—where else can you find butchers working the late-night shift on the New York City Transit Authority? Only herein. How about mutant shit-eating babies? We've got it. Corpse fucking? Of course! Incest, racism, rape, animal cruelty, serial murders, exploitation of the dead—just turn the page.

But please, not only for the shock value. For these stories carry profound subtexts, harrowing insights into our own sick and shining twentieth century. Within every evisceration you will find humor's darkest entrails; beside every seemingly adolescent gross-out, the most serious adult concerns.

So walk softly, and carry a big stick. You have entered the dark lands, where horror wrestles with art. And you need carry but three provisions:

A sense of humor.

A sense of courage.

And a portable radio, turned up *loud*, preferably to maximum rock 'n' roll.

Ready?

Good.

We're waiting for you . . .

Paul M. Sammon

Splatterpunks

EXTREME
HORROR

Night They Missed the Horror Show

JOE R.
LANSDALE

Joe R. Lansdale has a very personal sense of the geography and culture of his home state, the Republic of Texas, an unrestrained talent for disturbingly accurate depictions of all-too-believable cruelty and macabre vindictiveness, and a feel for characterization which is utterly convincing and frighteningly involving.

That's part of the bio-blurb from Lansdale's first hardcover selection of short stories (1989's *By Bizarre Hands*, published by Mark V. Ziesing), and only part of the story; Joe Lansdale also happens to be one of the most promising writers working in fiction today, a Major Talent poised on the edge of Major Breakthroughs.

Coming up through the ranks of such "little" magazines as *Last Wave*, *Modern Stories*, and *Hardboiled*, Lansdale cracked the pro ranks a few years ago and hasn't looked back since. He's equally (and prolifically) adept at mysteries (*Cold in July*, on which he is doing a screenplay for mainstream film director John Irvin), westerns (*The Magic Wagon*), science fiction ("Tight Little Stitches in a Dead Man's Back"), and black comedy (*The Drive-In*, a cult classic which reads like Joe Bob Briggs meets *Lord of the Flies*).

But what we're concerned with here is Lansdale's horror output. And nobody—*nobody*—makes readers as uncomfortable as Joe Lansdale. Maybe it's his rattlingly good sense of place, the feeling that Lansdale really knows his fictional mean streets. Maybe it's the explicit violence which organically unfolds from his characters' all-too-familiar weaknesses. Maybe it's his astoundingly enthusiastic fondness for bad taste. Or maybe it's just Joe's drop-dead sense of humor; Lansdale is one of the funniest, and wickedest, American writers practicing today.

Don't call him a splatterpunk, though. "I'm Joe Lansdale and I'm not part of any movement," Joe has said. "I like publicity for my fiction, of course, but I ain't no splatterpunk and dislike the label. I like to be thought of as my own label."

Fair enough. Lansdale's many talents and generic diversity indicate a writer who should certainly *not* be nailed into a single, constricting box. But Joe occasionally writes splatterpunk-like stories, and this is definitely the category under which "Night They Missed The Horror Show" falls. This Bram Stoker Award–winning entry is one of the toughest selections in this book; beneath its incredible surface impact lies a deeply felt rejection of racism, sexism, and plain old redneck stupidity.

And even with Lansdale's rejection of the label, "Night They Missed the Horror Show" remains one of the few altars before which all true splatterpunks bow.

(For Lew Shiner. A story that doesn't flinch.)

If they'd gone to the drive-in like they'd planned, none of this would have happened. But Leonard didn't like drive-ins when he didn't have a date, and he'd heard about *Night of the Living Dead*, and he knew a nigger starred in it. He didn't want to see no movie with a nigger star. Niggers chopped cotton, fixed flats, and pimped nigger girls, but he'd never heard of one that killed zombies. And he'd heard too that there was a white girl in the movie that let the nigger touch her, and that peeved him. Any white gal that would let a nigger touch her must be the lowest trash in the world. Probably from Hollywood, New York, or Waco, some godforsaken place like that.

Now Steve McQueen would have been all right for zombie killing and girl handling. He would have been the ticket. But a nigger? No sir.

Boy, that Steve McQueen was one cool head. Way he said stuff in them pictures was so good you couldn't help but think someone had written it down for him. He could sure think fast on his feet to come up with the things he said, and he had that real cool, mean look.

Leonard wished he could be Steve McQueen, or Paul Newman even. Someone like that always knew what to say, and he figured they got plenty of bush too. Certainly they didn't get as bored as he did. He was so bored he felt as if he were going to die from it before the night was out. Bored, bored, bored. Just wasn't nothing exciting about being in the Dairy Queen parking lot leaning on the front of his '64 Impala looking out at the highway. He figured maybe old crazy Harry who janitored at the high school might be right about them flying saucers. Harry was always seeing something. Bigfoot, six-legged weasels, all manner of things. But maybe he was right about the saucers. He'd said he'd seen one a couple nights back hovering over Mud Creek and it was shooting down these rays that looked like wet peppermint sticks. Leonard figured if Harry really had seen the saucers and the rays, then those rays were boredom rays. It would be a way for space critters to get at Earth folks, boring them to death. Getting melted down by heat rays would have been better. That was at least quick, but being bored to death was sort of like being nibbled to death by ducks.

Leonard continued looking at the highway, trying to imagine flying saucers and boredom rays, but he couldn't keep his mind on it. He finally focused on something in the highway. A dead dog.

Not just a dead dog. But a DEAD DOG. The mutt had been hit by a semi at least, maybe several. It looked as if it had rained dog. There were pieces of that pooch all over the concrete and one leg was lying on the curbing on the opposite side, stuck up in such a way that it seemed to be waving hello. Doctor Frankenstein with a grant from Johns Hopkins and assistance from NASA couldn't have put that sucker together again.

Leonard leaned over to his faithful, drunk companion, Billy —known among the gang as Farto, because he was fart lighting champion of Mud Creek—and said, "See that dog there?"

Farto looked where Leonard was pointing. He hadn't noticed the dog before, and he wasn't nearly as casual about it as Leonard. The puzzle-piece hound brought back memories. It reminded him of a dog he'd had when he was thirteen. A big, fine German shepherd that loved him better than his Mama.

Sonofabitch dog tangled its chain through and over a barbed wire fence somehow and hung itself. When Farto found the dog its tongue looked like a stuffed, black sock and he could see where its claws had just been able to scrape the ground, but not quite enough to get a toehold. It looked as if the dog had been scratching out some sort of coded message in the dirt. When Farto told his old man about it later, crying as he did, his old man laughed and said, "Probably a goddamn suicide note."

Now, as he looked out at the highway, and his whisky-laced Coke collected warmly in his gut, he felt a tear form in his eyes. Last time he'd felt that sappy was when he'd won the fart-lighting championship with a four-inch burner that singed the hairs of his ass and the gang awarded him with a pair of colored boxing shorts. Brown and yellow ones so he could wear them without having to change them too often.

So there they were, Leonard and Farto, parked outside the DQ, leaning on the hood of Leonard's Impala, sipping Coke and whisky, feeling bored and blue and horny, looking at a dead dog and having nothing to do but go to a show with a nigger starring in it. Which, to be up front, wouldn't have been so bad if they'd had dates. Dates could make up for a lot of sins, or help make a few good ones, depending on one's outlook.

But the night was criminal. Dates they didn't have. Worse yet, wasn't a girl in the entire high school would date them. Not even Marylou Flowers, and she had some kind of disease.

All this nagged Leonard something awful. He could see what the problem was with Farto. He was ugly. Had the kind of face that attracted flies. And though being fart-lighting champion of Mud Creek had a certain prestige among the gang, it lacked a certain something when it came to charming the gals.

But for the life of him, Leonard couldn't figure his own problem. He was handsome, had some good clothes, and his car ran good when he didn't buy that old cheap gas. He even had a few bucks in his jeans from breaking into washaterias. Yet his right arm had damn near grown to the size of his thigh from all the whacking off he did. Last time he'd been out with a girl had been a month ago, and as he'd been out with her along with nine other guys, he wasn't rightly sure he could call that a date. He wondered about it so much, he'd asked Farto if he thought it qualified as a date. Farto, who had been fifth in line, said he didn't think so, but if Leonard wanted to call it one, wasn't no skin off his dick.

But Leonard didn't want to call it a date. It just didn't have the feel of one, lacked that something special. There was no romance to it.

True, Big Red had called him Honey when he put the mule in the barn, but she called everyone Honey—except Stoney. Stoney was Possum Sweets, and he was the one who talked her into wearing the grocery bag with the mouth and eye holes. Stoney was like that. He could sweet talk the camel out from under a sand nigger. When he got through chatting Big Red down, she was plumb proud to wear that bag.

When finally it came his turn to do Big Red, Leonard had let her take the bag off as a gesture of goodwill. That was a mistake.

He just hadn't known a good thing when he had it. Stoney had had the right idea. The bag coming off spoiled everything. With it on, it was sort of like balling the Lone Hippo or some such thing, but with the bag off, you were absolutely certain what you were getting, and it wasn't pretty.

Even closing his eyes hadn't helped. He found that the ugliness of that face had branded itself on the back of his eyeballs. He couldn't even imagine the sack back over her head. All he could think about was that puffy, too-painted face with the sort of bad complexion that began at the bone.

He'd gotten so disappointed, he'd had to fake an orgasm and get off before his hooter shriveled up and his Trojan fell off and was lost in the vacuum.

Thinking back on it, Leonard sighed. It would certainly be nice for a change to go with a girl that didn't pull the train or had a hole between her legs that looked like a manhole cover ought to be on it. Sometimes he wished he could be like Farto, who was as happy as if he had good sense. Anything thrilled him. Give him a can of Wolf Brand Chili, a big moon pie, Coke and whisky and he could spend the rest of his life fucking Big Red and lighting the gas out of his asshole.

God, but this was no way to live. No women and no fun. Bored, bored, bored. Leonard found himself looking overhead for space-ships and peppermint-colored boredom rays, but he saw only a few moths fluttering drunkenly through the beams of the DQ's lights.

Lowering his eyes back to the highway and the dog, Leonard had a sudden flash. "Why don't we get the chain out of the back and hook it up to Rex there? Take him for a ride."

"You mean drag his dead ass around?" Farto asked.

Leonard nodded.

"Beats stepping on a tack," Farto said.

They drove the Impala into the middle of the highway at a safe moment and got out for a look. Up close the mutt was a lot worse. Its innards had been mashed out of its mouth and asshole and it stunk something awful. The dog was wearing a thick, metal-studded collar and they fastened one end of their fifteen-foot chain to that and the other to the rear bumper.

Bob, the Dairy Queen manager, noticed them through the window, came outside and yelled, "What are you fucking morons doing?"

"Taking this doggie to the vet," Leonard said. "We think this sumbitch looks a might peaked. He may have been hit by a car."

"That's so fucking funny I'm about to piss myself," Bob said.

"Old folks have that problem," Leonard said.

Leonard got behind the wheel and Farto climbed in on the passenger side. They maneuvered the car and dog around and out of the path of a tractor-trailer truck just in time. As they drove off, Bob screamed after them, "I hope you two no-dicks wrap that Chevy piece of shit around a goddamn pole."

As they roared along, parts of the dog, like crumbs from a flakey loaf of bread, came off. A tooth here. Some hair there. A string of guts. A dew claw. And some unidentifiable pink stuff. The metal-studded collar and chain threw up sparks now and then like fiery crickets. Finally they hit seventy-five and the dog was swinging wider and wider on the chain, like it was looking for an opportunity to pass.

Farto poured him and Leonard up Cokes and whisky as they drove along. He handed Leonard his paper cup and Leonard knocked it back, a lot happier now than he had been a moment ago. Maybe this night wasn't going to turn out so bad after all.

They drove by a crowd at the side of the road, a tan station wagon and a wreck of a Ford up on a jack. At a glance they could see that there was a nigger in the middle of the crowd and he wasn't witnessing to the white boys. He was hopping around like a pig with a hotshot up his ass, trying to find a break in the white boys so he could make a run for it. But there wasn't any break to be found and there were too many to fight. Nine white boys were knocking him around like he was a pinball and they were a malicious machine.

"Ain't that one of our niggers?" Farto asked. "And ain't that some of them White Tree football players that's trying to kill him?"

"Scott," Leonard said, and the name was dogshit in his mouth. It had been Scott who had outdone him for the position of quarterback on the team. That damn jig could put together a play more tangled than a can of fishing worms, but it damn near always worked. And he could run like a spotted-ass ape.

As they passed, Farto said, "We'll read about him tomorrow in the papers."

But Leonard drove only a short way before slamming on the brakes and whipping the Impala around. Rex swung way out and clipped off some tall, dried sunflowers at the edge of the road like a scythe.

"We gonna go back and watch?" Farto said. "I don't think

them White Tree boys would bother us none if that's all we was gonna do, watch."

"He may be a nigger," Leonard said, not liking himself, "but he's our nigger and we can't let them do that. They kill him they'll beat us in football."

Farto saw the truth of this immediately. "Damn right. They can't do that to our nigger."

Leonard crossed the road again and went straight for the White Tree boys, hit down hard on the horn. The White Tree boys abandoned beating their prey and jumped in all directions. Bullfrogs couldn't have done any better.

Scott stood startled and weak where he was, his knees bent in and touching one another, his eyes big as pizza pans. He had never noticed how big grillwork was. It looked like teeth there in the night and the headlights looked like eyes. He felt like a stupid fish about to be eaten by a shark.

Leonard braked hard, but off the highway in the dirt it wasn't enough to keep from bumping Scott, sending him flying over the hood and against the glass where his face mashed to it then rolled away, his shirt snagging one of the windshield wipers and pulling it off.

Leonard opened the car door and called to Scott, who lay on the ground. "It's now or never."

A White Tree boy made for the car, and Leonard pulled the taped hammer handle out from beneath the seat and stepped out of the car and hit him with it. The White Tree boy went down to his knees and said something that sounded like French but wasn't. Leonard grabbed Scott by the back of the shirt and pulled him up and guided him around and threw him into the open door. Scott scrambled over the front seat and into the back. Leonard threw the hammer handle at one of the White Tree boys and stepped back, whirled into the car behind the wheel. He put the car in gear again and stepped on the gas. The Impala lurched forward, and with one hand on the door Leonard flipped it wider and clipped a White Tree boy with it as if he were flexing a wing. The car bumped back on the highway and the chain swung out and Rex clipped the feet out from under two White Tree boys as neatly as he had taken down the dried sunflowers.

Leonard looked in his rearview mirror and saw two White Tree boys carrying the one he had clubbed with the hammer handle to the station wagon. The others he and the dog had knocked down were getting up. One had kicked the jack out from under Scott's car and was using it to smash the headlights and windshield.

"Hope you got insurance on that thing," Leonard said.

"I borrowed it," Scott said, peeling the windshield wiper out of his T shirt. "Here, you might want this." He dropped the wiper over the seat and between Leonard and Farto.

"That's a borrowed car?" Farto said. "That's worse."

"Nah," Scott said. "Owner don't know I borrowed it. I'd have had that flat changed if that sucker had had him a spare tire, but I got back there and wasn't nothing but the rim, man. Say, thanks for not letting me get killed, else we couldn't have run that ole pig together no more. Course, you almost run over me. My chest hurts."

Leonard checked the rearview again. The White Tree boys were coming fast. "You complaining?" Leonard said.

"Nah," Scott said, and turned to look through the back glass. He could see the dog swinging in short arcs and pieces of it going wide and far. "Hope you didn't go off and forget your dog tied to the bumper."

"Goddamn," said Farto, "and him registered too."

"This ain't so funny," Leonard said, "them White Tree boys are gaining."

"Well speed it up," Scott said.

Leonard gnashed his teeth. "I could always get rid of some excess baggage, you know."

"Throwing that windshield wiper out ain't gonna help," Scott said.

Leonard looked in his mirror and saw the grinning nigger in the backseat. Nothing worse than a comic coon. He didn't even look grateful. Leonard had a sudden horrid vision of being overtaken by the White Tree boys. What if he were killed with the nigger? Getting killed was bad enough, but what if tomorrow they found him in a ditch with Farto and the nigger. Or maybe them White Tree boys would make him do something awful with the nigger before they killed them. Like making him suck the nigger's dick or some such thing. Leonard held his foot all the way to the floor; as they passed the Dairy Queen he took a hard left and the car just made it and Rex swung out and slammed a light pole then popped back in line behind them.

The White Tree boys couldn't make the corner in the station wagon and they didn't even try. They screeched into a car lot down a piece, turned around and came back. By that time the taillights of the Impala were moving away from them rapidly, looking like two inflamed hemorrhoids in a dark asshole.

"Take the next right coming up," Scott said, "then you'll see a little road off to the left. Kill your lights and take that."

Leonard hated taking orders from Scott on the field, but this was worse. Insulting. Still, Scott called good plays on the field, and the habit of following instructions from the quarterback died hard. Leonard made the right and Rex made it with them after taking a dip in a water-filled bar ditch.

Leonard saw the little road and killed his lights and took it. It carried them down between several rows of large tin storage buildings, and Leonard pulled between two of them and drove down a little alley lined with more. He stopped the car and they waited and listened. After about five minutes, Farto said, "I think we skunked those father rapers."

"Ain't we a team?" Scott said.

In spite of himself, Leonard felt good. It was like when the nigger called a play that worked and they were all patting each other on the ass and not minding what color the other was because they were just creatures in football suits.

"Let's have a drink," Leonard said.

Farto got a paper cup off the floorboard for Scott and poured him up some warm Coke and whisky. Last time they had gone to Longview, he had peed in that paper cup so they wouldn't have to stop, but that had long since been poured out, and besides, it was for a nigger. He poured Leonard and himself drinks in their same cups.

Scott took a sip and said, "Shit, man, that tastes kind of rank."

"Like piss," Farto said.

Leonard held up his cup. "To the Mud Creek Wildcats and fuck them White Tree boys."

"You fuck 'em," Scott said. They touched their cups, and at that moment the car filled with light.

Cups upraised, the Three Musketeers turned blinking toward it. The light was coming from an open storage building door and there was a fat man standing in the center of the glow like a bloated fly on a lemon wedge. Behind him was a big screen made of a sheet and there was some kind of movie playing on it. And though the light was bright and fading out the movie, Leonard, who was in the best position to see, got a look at it. What he could make out looked like a gal down on her knees sucking this fat guy's dick (the man was visible only from the belly down) and the guy had a short, black revolver pressed to her forehead. She pulled her mouth off of him for an instant and the man came in her face then fired the revolver. The woman's head snapped out of frame and the sheet seemed to drip blood, like dark condensation on a window pane. Then Leonard couldn't see anymore because another man had appeared in the doorway, and like the first he was fat. Both looked like huge bowling balls that had been set on top of shoes. More men appeared behind these two, but one of the fat men turned and held up his hand and the others moved out of sight. The two fat guys stepped outside and one pulled the door almost shut, except for a thin band of light that fell across the front seat of the Impala.

Fat Man Number One went over to the car and opened Farto's door and said, "You fucks and the nigger get out." It was the voice of doom. They had only thought the White Tree boys were dangerous. They realized now they had been kidding themselves. This was the real article. The guy would have eaten the hammer handle and shit a two-by four.

They got out of the car and the fat man waved them around and lined them up on Farto's side and looked at them. The boys still had their drinks in their hands, and sparing that, they looked like cons in a lineup.

Fat Man Number Two came over and looked at the trio and smiled. It was obvious the fatties were twins. They had the same bad features in the same fat faces. They wore Hawaiian shirts that varied only in profiles and color of parrots and had on white socks and too-short black slacks and black, shiny, Italian shoes with toes sharp enough to thread needles.

Fat Man Number One took the cup away from Scott and sniffed it. "A nigger with liquor," he said. "That's like a cunt with brains. It don't go together. Guess you was getting tanked up so you could put the ole black snake to some chocolate pudding after while. Or maybe you was wantin' some vanilla and these boys were gonna set it up."

"I'm not wanting anything but to go home," Scott said.

Fat Man Number Two looked at Fat Man Number One and said, "So he can fuck his mother."

The fatties looked at Scott to see what he'd say but he didn't say anything. They could say he screwed dogs and that was all right with him. Hell, bring one on and he'd fuck it now if they'd let him go afterwards.

Fat Man Number One said, "You boys running around with a jungle bunny makes me sick."

"He's just a nigger from school," Farto said. "We don't like him none. We just picked him up because some White Tree boys were beating on him and we didn't want him to get wrecked on account of he's our quarterback."

"Ah," Fat Man Number One said, "I see. Personally, me and Vinnie don't cotton to niggers in sports. They start taking showers with white boys the next thing they want is to take white girls to bed. It's just one step from one to the other."

"We don't have nothing to do with him playing," Leonard said. "We didn't intergrate the schools."

"No," Fat Man Number One said, "that was ole Big Ears Johnson, but you're running around with him and drinking with him."

"His cup's been peed in," Farto said. "That was kind of a joke on him, you see. He ain't our friend, I swear it. He's just a nigger that plays football."

"Peed in his cup, huh?" said the one called Vinnie. "I like that, Pork, don't you? Peed in his fucking cup."

Pork dropped Scott's cup on the ground and smiled at him. "Come here, nigger. I got something to tell you."

Scott looked at Farto and Leonard. No help there. They had suddenly become interested in the toes of their shoes; they examined them as if they were true marvels of the world.

Scott moved toward Pork, and Pork, still smiling, put his arm around Scott's shoulders and walked him toward the big storage building. Scott said, "What are we doing?"

Pork turned Scott around so they were facing Leonard and Farto who still stood holding their drinks and contemplating their shoes. "I didn't want to get it on the new gravel drive," Pork said and pulled Scott's head in close to his own and with his free hand reached back and under his Hawaiian shirt and brought out a short, black revolver and put it to Scott's temple and pulled the trigger. There was a snap like a bad knee going out and Scott's feet lifted in unison and went to the side and something dark squirted from his head and his feet swung back toward Pork and his shoes shuffled, snapped, and twisted on the concrete in front of the building.

"Ain't that somethin'," Pork said as Scott went limp and dangled from the thick crook of his arm, "the rhythm is the last thing to go."

Leonard couldn't make a sound. His guts were in his throat. He wanted to melt and run under the car. Scott was dead and the brains that had made plays twisted as fishing worms and commanded his feet on down the football field were scrambled like breakfast eggs.

Farto said, "Holy shit."

Pork let go of Scott and Scott's legs split and he sat down and his head went forward and clapped on the cement between his knees. A dark pool formed under his face.

"He's better off, boys," Vinnie said. "Nigger was begat by Cain and the ape and he ain't quite monkey and he ain't quite man. He's got no place in this world 'cept as a beast of burden. You start trying to train them to do things like drive cars and run with footballs it ain't nothing but grief to them and the whites too. Get any on your shirt, Pork?"

"Nary a drop."

Vinnie went inside the building and said something to the men there that could be heard but not understood, then he came back with some crumpled newspapers. He went over to Scott and wrapped them around the bloody head and let it drop back on the cement. "You try hosing down that shit when it's dried, Pork, and you wouldn't worry none about that gravel. The gravel ain't nothing."

Then Vinnie said to Farto, "Open the back door of that car." Farto nearly twisted an ankle doing it. Vinnie picked Scott up by the back of the neck and seat of his pants and threw him onto the floorboard of the Impala.

Pork used the short barrel of his revolver to scratch his nuts, then put the gun behind him, under his Hawaiian shirt. "You boys are gonna go to the river bottoms with us and help us get shed of this nigger."

"Yes sir," Farto said. "We'll toss his ass in the Sabine for you."

"How about you?" Pork asked Leonard. "You trying to go weak sister?"

"No," Leonard croaked. "I'm with you."

"That's good," Pork said. "Vinnie, you take the truck and lead the way."

Vinnie took a key from his pocket and unlocked the building door next to the one with the light, went inside, and backed out a sharp-looking gold Dodge pickup. He backed it in front of the Impala and sat there with the motor running.

"You boys keep your place," Pork said. He went inside the lighted building for a moment. They heard him say to the men inside, "Go on and watch the movies. And save some of them beers for us. We'll be back." Then the light went out and Pork came out, shutting the door. He looked at Leonard and Farto and said, "Drink up, boys."

Leonard and Farto tossed off their warm Coke and whisky and dropped the cups on the ground.

"Now," Pork said, "you get in the back with the nigger, I'll ride with the driver."

Farto got in the back and put his feet on Scott's knees. He tried not to look at the head wrapped in newspaper, but he couldn't help it. When Pork opened the front door and the overhead light came on Farto saw there was a split in the paper and Scott's eye was visible behind it. Across the forehead the wrapping had turned dark. Down by the mouth and chin was an ad for a fish sale.

Leonard got behind the wheel and started the car. Pork reached over and honked the horn. Vinnie rolled the pickup forward and Leonard followed him to the river bottoms. No one spoke. Leonard found himself wishing with all his heart that he had gone to the outdoor picture show to see the movie with the nigger starring in it.

The river bottoms were steamy and hot from the closeness of the trees and the under- and overgrowth. As Leonard wound the Impala down the narrow, red clay roads amidst the dense foliage, he felt as if his car were a crab crawling about in a pubic thatch. He could feel from the way the steering wheel handled that the dog and the chain were catching brush and limbs here and there. He had forgotten all about the dog and now being reminded of it worried him. What if the dog got tangled and he had to stop? He didn't think Pork would take kindly to stopping, not with the dead burrhead in the floorboard and him wanting to get rid of the body.

Finally they came to where the woods cleared out a spell and they drove along the edge of the Sabine River. Leonard hated water and always had. In the moonlight the river looked like poisoned coffee flowing there. Leonard knew there were alligators and gars big as little alligators and water moccasins by the thousands swimming underneath the water, and just the thought of all those slick, darting bodies made him queasy.

They came to what was known as Broken Bridge. It was an old worn-out bridge that had fallen apart in the middle and it was connected to the land on this side only. People sometimes fished off of it. There was no one fishing tonight.

Vinnie stopped the pickup and Leonard pulled up beside him, the nose of the Chevy pointing at the mouth of the bridge. They all got out and Pork made Farto pull Scott out by the feet. Some of the newspaper came loose from Scott's head exposing an ear and part of the face. Farto patted the newspaper back into place. "Fuck that," Vinnie said. "It don't hurt if he stains the fucking ground. You two idgits find some stuff to weight this coon down so we can sink him."

Farto and Leonard started scurrying about like squirrels, looking for rocks or big, heavy logs. Suddenly they heard Vinnie cry out. "Godamighty, fucking A. Pork. Come look at this."

Leonard looked over and saw that Vinnie had discovered Rex. He was standing looking down with his hands on his hips. Pork went over to stand by him, then Pork turned around and looked at them. "Hey, you fucks, come here."

Leonard and Farto joined them in looking at the dog. There was mostly just a head now, with a little bit of meat and fur hanging off a spine and some broken ribs.

"That's the sickest fucking thing I've ever fucking seen," Pork said.

"Godamighty," Vinnie said.

"Doing a dog like that. Shit, don't you got no heart? A dog. Man's best fucking goddamn friend and you two killed him like this."

"We didn't kill him," Farto said.

"You trying to fucking tell me he done this to himself? Had a bad fucking day and done this."

"Godamighty," Vinnie said.

"No sir," Leonard said. "We chained him on there after he was dead."

"I believe that," Vinnie said. "That's some rich shit. You guys murdered this dog. Godamighty."

"Just thinking about him trying to keep up and you fucks driving faster and faster makes me mad as a wasp," Pork said.

"No," Farto said. "It wasn't like that. He was dead and we were drunk and we didn't have anything to do, so we—"

"Shut the fuck up," Pork said sticking a finger hard against Farto's forehead. "You just shut the fuck up. We can see what the fuck you fucks did. You drug this here dog around until all his goddamn hide came off . . . What kind of mothers you boys got anyhow that they didn't tell you better about animals?"

"Godamighty," Vinnie said.

Everyone grew silent, stood looking at the dog. Finally Farto said, "You want us to go back to getting some stuff to hold the nigger down?"

Pork looked at Farto as if he had just grown up whole from the ground. "You fucks are worse than niggers, doing a dog like that. Get on back over to the car."

Leonard and Farto went over to the Impala and stood looking down at Scott's body in much the same way they had stared at the dog. There, in the dim moonlight shadowed by trees, the paper wrapped around Scott's head made him look like a giant papier-mâché doll. Pork came up and kicked Scott in the face with a swift motion that sent newspaper flying and sent a thonking sound across the water that made frogs jump.

"Forget the nigger," Pork said. "Give me your car keys, ball sweat." Leonard took out his keys and gave them to Pork and Pork went around to the trunk and opened it. "Drag the nigger over here."

Leonard took one of Scott's arms and Farto took the other and they pulled him over to the back of the car.

"Put him in the trunk," Pork said.

"What for?" Leonard asked.

"Cause I fucking said so," Pork said.

Leonard and Farto heaved Scott into the trunk. He looked pathetic lying there next to the spare tire, his face partially covered with newspaper. Leonard thought, if only the nigger had stolen a car with a spare he might not be here tonight. He could have gotten the flat changed and driven on before the White Tree boys even came along.

"All right, you get in there with him," Pork said, gesturing to Farto.

"Me?" Farto said.

"Nah, not fucking you, the fucking elephant on your fucking shoulder. Yeah, you, get in the trunk. I ain't got all night."

"Jesus, we didn't do anything to that dog, mister. We told you that. I swear. Me and Leonard hooked him up after he was dead . . . It was Leonard's idea."

Pork didn't say a word. He just stood there with one hand on the trunk lid looking at Farto. Farto looked at Pork, then the trunk, then back to Pork. Lastly he looked at Leonard, then climbed into the trunk, his back to Scott.

"Like spoons," Pork said, and closed the lid. "Now you, what-sit, Leonard? You come over here." But Pork didn't wait for Leonard to move. He scooped the back of Leonard's neck with a chubby hand and pushed him over to where Rex lay at the end of the chain with Vinnie still looking down at him.

"What you think, Vinnie?" Pork asked. "You got what I got in mind?"

Vinnie nodded. He bent down and took the collar off the dog. He fastened it on Leonard. Leonard could smell the odor of the dead dog in his nostrils. He bent his head and puked.

"There goes my shoeshine," Vinnie said, and he hit Leonard a short one in the stomach. Leonard went to his knees and puked some more of the hot Coke and whisky.

"You fucks are the lowest pieces of shit on this earth, doing a dog like that," Vinnie said. "A nigger ain't no lower."

Vinnie got some strong fishing line out of the back of the truck and they tied Leonard's hands behind his back. Leonard began to cry.

"Oh shut up," Pork said. "It ain't that bad. Ain't nothing that bad."

But Leonard couldn't shut up. He was caterwauling now and it was echoing through the trees. He closed his eyes and tried to pretend he had gone to the show with the nigger starring in it and had fallen asleep in his car and was having a bad dream, but he couldn't imagine that. He thought about Harry the janitor's flying saucers with the peppermint rays, and he knew if there were any saucers shooting rays down, they weren't boredom rays after all. He wasn't a bit bored.

Pork pulled off Leonard's shoes and pushed him back flat on the ground and pulled off the socks and stuck them in Leonard's mouth so tight he couldn't spit them out. It wasn't that Pork thought anyone was going to hear Leonard, he just didn't like the noise. It hurt his ears.

Leonard lay on the ground in the vomit next to the dog and cried silently. Pork and Vinnie went over to the Impala and opened the doors and stood so they could get a grip on the car to push. Vinnie reached in and moved the gear from park to neutral and he and Pork began to shove the car forward. It moved slowly at first, but as it made the slight incline that led down to the old bridge, it picked up speed. From inside the trunk, Farto hammered lightly at the lid as if he didn't really mean it. The chain took up slack and Leonard felt it jerk and pop his neck. He began to slide along the ground like a snake.

Vinnie and Pork jumped out of the way, and watched the car make the bridge and go over the edge and disappear into the water with amazing quietness. Leonard, tugged by the weight of

the car, rustled past them. When he hit the bridge, splinters
tugged at his clothes so hard they ripped his pants and underwear
down almost to his knees.

The chain swung out once toward the edge of the bridge and
the rotten railing, and Leonard tried to hook a leg around an
upright board there, but that proved wasted. The weight of the
car just pulled his knee out of joint and tugged the board out of
place with a screech of nails and lumber.

Leonard picked up speed and the chain rattled over the edge
of the bridge, into the water and out of sight, pulling its connection after it like a pull toy. The last sight of Leonard was the
soles of his bare feet, white as the bellies of fish.

"It's deep there," Vinnie said. "I caught an old channel cat
there once, remember? Big sucker. I bet it's over fifty feet deep
down there."

They got in the truck and Vinnie cranked it.

"I think we did them boys a favor," Pork said. "Them running
around with niggers and what they did to that dog and all. They
weren't worth a thing."

"I know it," Vinnie said. "We should have filmed this, Pork,
it would have been good. Where the car and that nigger lover
went off in the water was choice."

"Nah, there wasn't any women."

"Point," Vinnie said, and he backed around and drove onto
the trail that wound its way out of the bottoms.

The Midnight Meat Train

CLIVE BARKER

Clive Barker burst out of nowhere in 1984 with *Clive Barker's Books of Blood*, volumes One through Three. Originally planned as a single volume, these first three *Books* were graphic, intense, and sexually explicit. Not only did they recognize the full spectrum of previous horror fiction but, unheralded, they broke away from that tradition by mounting a full-frontal assault on the status quo. Barker's method of attack was simplicity personified; nothing was suggested, all was allowed.

Mixing stylistic elements from the films of David Cronenberg, Dario Argento, and George Romero, displaying literary influences stretching from Ramsey Campbell and Graham Greene to S&M bondage magazines, the *Books of Blood* were the foundation upon which Barker subsequently built a one-man empire (helped along by three more *Books of Blood*; novels like *Weaveworld, Cabal, The Damnation Game*, and *The Great and Secret Show*; numerous comic book adaptations; and films like *Hellraiser* and *Nightbreed*, which Barker both wrote and directed).

Since 1984 this charming, articulate, Paul McCartney look-alike has hit commercial pinnacles shared only by the likes of James Herbert and Stephen King. By displaying excellent craftsmanship, a hyper-hallucinatory imagination and an unabashed glee for over-the-top sex and violence, Barker remains a steady compass for a twisted clutch of like-minded fictioneers.

Interestingly, like fellow countryman Graham Greene, Barker's output falls into two categories: entertainments and serious works (I hesitate to use the word *art*; even Greene relies on the terms *Entertainments* and *Novels*). To find a serious Barkerian work, simply seek out "In the Hills, the Cities," a Borges-like novella involving intervillage warfare which Barker has supplied with a carefully planned substructure to support its towering, fantastic weight.

Then there are the entertainments, like "The Midnight Meat Train."

"The Midnight Meat Train" mixes splatter-film techniques with a subtle incorporation of H. P. Lovecraft's "Old Ones" mythology. The result is a rather nasty satirical swipe at New York City's ongoing fear of its own subway system. Be warned, however, for we're about to get—uh—"meaty" here, and Barker has obviously studied a dog-eared copy of *Gray's Anatomy*.

Finally, there's also a sturdy historical function behind "The Midnight Meat Train." For this carnographic exercise perfectly captures that historic moment when, via the arrival of Clive Barker, splatter-punk's favorite English role model first chewed his way (laterally) through traditional horror's womb.

Leon Kaufman was no longer new to the city. The Palace of Delights, he'd always called it, in the days of his innocence. But that was when he'd lived in Atlanta, and New York was still a kind of promised land, where anything and everything was possible.

Now Kaufman had lived three and a half months in his dream city, and the Palace of Delights seemed less than delightful.

Was it really only a season since he stepped out of the Port Authority Bus Station and looked up 42nd Street towards the Broadway intersection? So short a time to lose so many treasured illusions.

He was embarrassed now even to think of his naivete. It made him wince to remember how he had stood and announced aloud: "New York, I love you."

Love? Never.

It had been at best an infatuation.

And now, after only three months living with his object of adoration, spending his days and nights in her presence, she had lost her aura of perfection.

New York was just a city.

He had seen her wake in the morning like a slut, and pick murdered men from between her teeth, and suicides from the tangles of her hair. He had seen her late at night, her dirty back streets shamelessly courting depravity. He had watched her in the hot afternoon, sluggish and ugly, indifferent to the atrocities that were being committed every hour in her throttled passages.

It was no Palace of Delights.

It bred death, not pleasure.

Everyone he met had brushed with violence; it was a fact of life. It was almost chic to have known someone who had died a violent death. It was proof of living in that city.

But Kaufman had loved New York from afar for almost twenty years. He'd planned his love affair for most of his adult life. It was not easy, therefore, to shake the passion off, as though he had never felt it. There were still times, very early, before the cop sirens began, or at twilight, when Manhattan was still a miracle.

For those moments, and for the sake of his dreams, he still gave her the benefit of the doubt, even when her behavior was less than ladylike.

She didn't make such forgiveness easy. In the few months that Kaufman had lived in New York her streets had been awash with spilt blood.

In fact, it was not so much the streets themselves, but the tunnels beneath those streets.

"Subway Slaughter" was the catchphrase of the month. Only the previous week another three killings had been reported. The bodies had been discovered in one of the subway cars on the AVENUE OF THE AMERICAS, hacked open and partially disembowelled, as though an efficient abattoir operative had been interrupted in his work. The killings were so thoroughly professional that the police were interviewing every man on their records who had some past connection with the butchery trade. The meat-packaging plants on the waterfront were being watched, the slaughterhouses scoured for clues. A swift arrest was promised, though none was made.

This recent trio of corpses was not the first to be discovered in such a state; the very day that Kaufman had arrived a story had broken in *The Times* that was still the talk of every morbid secretary in the office.

The story went that a German visitor, lost in the subway system late at night, had come across a body in a train. The victim was a well-built, attractive thirty-year-old woman from Brooklyn. She had been completely stripped. Every shred of clothing, every article of jewelry. Even the studs in her ears.

Even more bizarre than the stripping was the neat and systematic way in which the clothes had been folded and placed in individual plastic bags on the seat beside the corpse.

This was no irrational slasher at work. This was a highly organized mind: a lunatic with a strong sense of tidiness.

Further, and yet more bizarre than the careful stripping of the corpse, was the outrage that had then been perpetrated upon it. The reports claimed, though the Police Department failed to confirm this, that the body had been meticulously shaved. Every hair had been removed: from the head, from the groin, from beneath the arms; all cut and scorched back to the flesh. Even the eyebrows and eyelashes had been plucked out.

Finally, this all-too-naked slab had been hung by the feet from one of the holding handles set in the roof of the car, and a black plastic bucket, lined with a black plastic bag, had been placed beneath the corpse to catch the steady fall of blood from its wounds.

In that state, stripped, shaved, suspended and practically bled white, the body of Loretta Dyer had been found.

It was disgusting, it was meticulous, and it was deeply confusing.

There had been no rape, nor any sign of torture. The woman had been swiftly and efficiently dispatched as though she was a piece of meat. And the butcher was still loose.

The city fathers, in their wisdom, declared a complete closedown on press reports of the slaughter. It was said that the man who had found the body was in protective custody in New Jersey, out of sight of enquiring journalists. But the coverup had failed. Some greedy cop had leaked the salient details to a reporter from *The Times*. Everyone in New York now knew the horrible story of the slaughters. It was a topic of conversation in every deli and bar; and, of course, on the subway.

But Loretta Dyer was only the first.

Now three more bodies had been found in identical circumstances; though the work had clearly been interrupted on this occasion. Not all the bodies had been shaved, and the jugulars had not been severed to bleed them. There was another, more significant difference in the discovery: it was not a tourist who had stumbled on the sight, it was a reporter from *The New York Times*.

Kaufman surveyed the report that sprawled across the front page of the newspaper. He had no prurient interest in the story, unlike his elbow mate along the counter of the deli. All he felt was a mild disgust, that made him push his plate of overcooked eggs aside. It was simply further proof of his city's decadence. He could take no pleasure in her sickness.

Nevertheless, being human, he could not entirely ignore the gory details on the page in front of him. The article was unsensationally written, but the simple clarity of the style made the subject seem more appalling. He couldn't help wondering, too, about the man behind the atrocities. Was there one psychotic loose, or several, each inspired to copy the original murder? Perhaps this was only the beginning of the horror. Maybe more murders would follow, until at last the murderer, in his exhilaration or exhaustion, would step beyond caution and be taken. Until then the city, Kaufman's adored city, would live in a state somewhere between hysteria and ecstasy.

At his elbow a bearded man knocked over Kaufman's coffee.

"Shit!" he said.

Kaufman shifted on his stool to avoid the dribble of coffee running off the counter.

"Shit," the man said again.

"No harm done," said Kaufman.

He looked at the man with a slightly disdainful expression on his face. The clumsy bastard was attempting to soak up the coffee with a napkin, which was turning to mush as he did so.

Kaufman found himself wondering if this oaf, with his florid cheeks and his uncultivated beard, was capable of murder. Was there any sign on that overfed face, any clue in the shape of his head or the turn of his small eyes that gave his true nature away?

The man spoke.

"Wannanother?"

Kaufman shook his head.

"Coffee. Regular. Dark," the oaf said to the girl behind the counter. She looked up from cleaning the grill of cold fat.

"Huh?"

"Coffee. You deaf?"

The man grinned at Kaufman.

"Deaf," he said.

Kaufman noticed he had three teeth missing from his lower jaw.

"Looks bad, huh?" he said.

What did he mean? The coffee? The absence of his teeth?

"Three people like that. Carved up."

Kaufman nodded.

"Makes you think," he said.

"Sure."

"I mean, it's a coverup isn't it? They know who did it."

This conversation's ridiculous, thought Kaufman. He took off his spectacles and pocketed them: the bearded face was no longer in focus. That was some improvement at least.

"Bastards," he said. "Fucking bastards, all of them. I'll lay anything it's a coverup."

"Of what?"

"They got the evidence: they're just keeping us in the fucking dark. There's something out there that's not human."

Kaufman understood. It was a conspiracy theory the oaf was trotting out. He'd heard them so often; a panacea.

"See, they do all this cloning stuff and it gets out of hand. They could be growing fucking monsters for all we know. There's something down there they won't tell us about. Coverup, like I say. Lay you anything."

Kaufman found the man's certainty attractive. Monsters on the prowl. Six heads: a dozen eyes. Why not?

He knew why not. Because that excused his city: that let her off the hook. And Kaufman believed in his heart, that the monsters to be found in the tunnels were perfectly human.

The bearded man threw his money on the counter and got up, sliding his fat bottom off the stained plastic stool.

"Probably a fucking cop," he said, as his parting shot. "Tried to make a fucking hero, made a fucking monster instead." He grinned grotesquely. "Lay you anything," he continued and lumbered out without another word.

Kaufman slowly exhaled through his nose, feeling the tension in his body abate.

He hated that sort of confrontation: it made him feel tongue-tied and ineffectual. Come to think of it, he hated that kind of man: the opinionated brute that New York bred so well.

It was coming up to six when Mahogany woke. The morning rain had turned into a light drizzle by twilight. The air was about as clear-smelling as it ever got in Manhattan. He stretched on his bed, threw off the dirty blanket, and got up for work.

In the bathroom the rain was dripping on the box of the air conditioner, filling the apartment with a rhythmical slapping sound. Mahogany turned on the television to cover the noise, disinterested in anything it had to offer.

He went to the window. The street six floors below was thick with traffic and people.

After a hard day's work New York was on its way home: to play, to make love. People were streaming out of their offices and into their automobiles. Some would be testy after a day's sweaty labor in a badly aired office; others, benign as sheep, would be wandering home down the avenues, ushered along by a ceaseless current of bodies. Still others would even now be cramming onto the subway, blind to the graffiti on every wall, deaf to the babble of their own voices, and to the cold thunder of the tunnels.

It pleased Mahogany to think of that. He was, after all, not one of the common herd. He could stand at his window and look down on a thousand heads below him, and know he was a chosen man.

He had deadlines to meet, of course, like the people in the street. But his work was not their senseless labor, it was more like a sacred duty.

He needed to live, and sleep, and shit like them, too. But it was not financial necessity that drove him, but the demands of history.

He was in a great tradition, that stretched further back than America. He was a night-stalker: like Jack the Ripper, like Gilles de Rais, a living embodiment of death, a wraith with a human face. He was a haunter of sleep and an awakener of terrors.

The people below him could not know his face; nor would care to look twice at him. But his stare caught them, and weighed them up, selecting only the ripest from the passing parade, choosing only the healthy and the young to fall under his sanctified knife.

Sometimes Mahogany longed to announce his identity to the world, but he had responsibilities and they bore on him heavily. He couldn't expect fame. His was a secret life, and it was merely pride that longed for recognition.

After all, he thought, does the beef salute the butcher as it throbs to its knees?

All in all, he was content. To be part of that great tradition was enough, would always have to remain enough.

Recently, however, there had been discoveries. They weren't his fault, of course. Nobody could possibly blame him. But it was a bad time. Life was not as easy as it had been ten years ago. He was that much older, of course, and that made the job more exhausting; and more and more the obligations weighed on his shoulders. He was a chosen man, and that was a difficult privilege to live with.

He wondered, now and then, if it wasn't time to think about training a younger man for his duties. There would need to be consultations with the Fathers, but sooner or later a replacement would have to be found, and it would be, he felt, a criminal waste of his experience not to take on an apprentice.

There were so many felicities he could pass on. The tricks of his extraordinary trade. The best way to stalk, to cut, to strip, to bleed. The best meat for the purpose. The simplest way to dispose of the remains. So much detail, so much accumulated expertise.

Mahogany wandered into the bathroom and turned on the shower. As he stepped in he looked down at his body. The small paunch, the greying hairs on his sagging chest, the scars, and pimples that littered his pale skin. He was getting old. Still, tonight, like every other night, he had a job to do . . .

Kaufman hurried back into the lobby with his sandwich, turning down his collar and brushing rain off his hair. The clock above the elevator read seven-sixteen. He would work through until ten, no later.

The elevator took him up to the twelfth floor and to the Pappas offices. He traipsed unhappily through the maze of empty desks and hooded machines to his little territory, which was still illuminated. The women who cleaned the offices were chatting down the corridor: otherwise the place was lifeless.

He took off his coat, shook the rain off it as best he could, and hung it up.

Then he sat down in front of the piles of orders he had been tussling with for the best part of three days, and began work. It would only take one more night's labor, he felt sure, to break the back of the job, and he found it easier to concentrate without the incessant clatter of typists and typewriters on every side.

He unwrapped his ham on whole wheat with extra mayonnaise and settled in for the evening.

It was nine now.

Mahogany was dressed for the night shift. He had his usual sober suit on, with his brown tie neatly knotted, his silver cufflinks (a gift from his first wife) placed in the sleeves of his immaculately pressed shirt, his thinning hair gleaming with oil, his nails snipped and polished, his face flushed with cologne.

His bag was packed. The towels, the instruments, his chain-mail apron.

He checked his appearance in the mirror. He could, he thought, still be taken for a man of forty-five, fifty at the outside.

As he surveyed his face he reminded himself of his duty. Above all, he must be careful. There would be eyes on him every step of the way, watching his performance tonight, and judging it. He must walk out like an innocent, arousing no suspicion.

If they only knew, he thought. The people who walked, ran, and skipped past him on the streets: who collided with him without apology: who met his gaze with contempt: who smiled at his bulk, looking uneasy in his ill-fitting suit. If only they knew what he did, what he was, and what he carried.

Caution, he said to himself, and turned off the light. The apartment was dark. He went to the door and opened it, used to walking in blackness. Happy in it.

The rain clouds had cleared entirely. Mahogany made his way down Amsterdam towards the subway at 145th Street. Tonight he'd take the AVENUE OF THE AMERICAS again, his favorite line, and often the most productive.

Down the subway steps, token in hand. Through the automatic gates. The smell of the tunnels was in his nostrils now. Not the smell of the deep tunnels of course. They had a scent all of their own. But there was reassurance even in the stale electric air of this shallow line. The regurgitated breath of a million travellers circulated in this warren, mingling with the breath of creatures far older; things with voices soft like clay, whose appetites were abominable. How he loved it. The scent, the dark, the thunder.

He stood on the platform and scanned his fellow travellers critically. There were one or two bodies he contemplated following, but there was so much dross amongst them: so few worth the chase. The physically wasted, the obese, the ill, the weary. Bodies destroyed by excess and by indifference. As a professional it sickened him, though he understood the weakness that spoiled the best of men.

He lingered in the station for over an hour, wandering between platforms while the trains came and went, came and went, and the people with them. There was so little of quality around it was dispiriting. It seemed he had to wait longer and longer every day to find flesh worthy of use.

It was now almost half past ten and he had not seen a single creature who was really ideal for slaughter.

No matter, he told himself, there was time yet. Very soon the theater crowd would be emerging. They were always good for a sturdy body or two. The well-fed intelligentsia, clutching their ticket stubs and opining on the diversions of art—oh yes, there'd be something there.

If not, and there were nights when it seemed he would never find something suitable, he'd have to ride downtown and corner a couple of lovers out late, or find an athlete or two, fresh from one of the gyms. They were always sure to offer good material, except that with such healthy specimens there was always the risk of resistance.

He remembered catching two black bucks a year ago or more, with maybe forty years between them, father and son perhaps. They'd resisted with knives, and he'd been hospitalized for six weeks. It had been a close fought encounter and one that had set him doubting his skills. Worse, it had made him wonder what his masters would have done with him had he suffered a fatal injury. Would he have been delivered to his family in New Jersey, and given a decent Christian burial? Or would his carcass have been thrown into the dark, for their own use?

The headline of the *New York Post*, discarded on the seat across from him, caught Mahogany's eye: "Police All-Out to Catch Killer." He couldn't resist a smile. Thoughts of failure, weakness, and death evaporated. After all, he was that man, that killer, and tonight the thought of capture was laughable. After all, wasn't his career sanctioned by the highest possible authorities? No policeman could hold him, no court pass judgement on him. The very forces of law and order that made such a show of his pursuit served his masters no less than him; he almost wished some two-bit cop would catch him, take him in triumph before the judge, just to see the looks on their faces when the word came up from the dark that Mahogany was a protected man, above every law on the statute books.

It was now well after ten-thirty. The trickle of theatergoers had begun, but there was nothing likely so far. He'd want to let the rush pass anyway; just follow one or two choice pieces to the end of the line. He bided his time, like any wise hunter.

Kaufman was not finished by eleven, an hour after he'd promised himself release. But exasperation and ennui were making the job more difficult, and the sheets of figures were beginning to blur in front of him. At ten past eleven he threw down his pen and admitted defeat. He rubbed his hot eyes with the cushions of his palms till his head filled with colors.

"Fuck it," he said.

He never swore in company. But once in a while to say fuck it to himself was a great consolation. He made his way out of the office, damp coat over his arm, and headed for the elevator. His limbs felt drugged and his eyes would scarcely stay open.

It was colder outside than he had anticipated, and the air brought him out of his lethargy a little. He walked towards the subway at 34th Street. Catch an express to Far Rockaway. Home in an hour.

Neither Kaufman nor Mahogany knew it, but at 96th and Broadway the police had arrested what they took to be the Subway Killer, having trapped him in one of the uptown trains. A small man of European extraction, wielding a hammer and a saw, had cornered a young woman in the second car and threatened to cut her in half in the name of Jehovah.

Whether he was capable of fulfilling this threat was doubtful. As it was, he didn't get the chance. While the rest of the passengers (including two Marines) looked on, the intended victim landed a kick to the man's testicles. He dropped the hammer. She picked it up and broke his lower jaw and right cheek bone with it before the Marines stepped in.

When the train halted at 96th the police were waiting to arrest the Subway Butcher. They rushed the car in a horde, yelling like banshees and scared as shit. The Butcher was lying in one corner of the car with his face in pieces. They carted him away, triumphant. The woman, after questioning, went home with the Marines.

It was to be a useful diversion, though Mahogany couldn't know it at the time. It took the police the best part of the night to determine the identity of their prisoner, chiefly because he couldn't do more than drool through his shattered jaw. It wasn't until three-thirty in the morning that one Captain Davis, coming on duty, recognized the man as a retired flower salesman from the Bronx called Hank Vasarely. Hank, it seemed, was regularly arrested for threatening behavior and indecent exposure, all in the name of Jehovah. Appearances deceived: he was about as dangerous as the Easter Bunny. This was not the Subway Slaughterer. But by the time the cops had worked that out, Mahogany had been about his business a long while.

It was eleven-fifteen when Kaufman got on the express through to Mott Avenue. He shared the car with two other travellers. One was a middle-aged black woman in a purple coat, the other a pale, acne-ridden adolescent who was staring at the "Kiss My White Ass" graffiti on the ceiling with spaced-out eyes.

Kaufman was in the first car. He had a journey of thirty-five minutes' duration ahead of him. He let his eyes slide closed, reassured by the rhythmical rocking of the train. It was a tedious journey and he was tired. He didn't see the lights flicker off in the second car. He didn't see Mahogany's face, either, staring through the door between the cars, looking through for some more meat.

At 14th Street the black woman got out. Nobody got in.

Kaufman opened his eyes briefly, taking in the empty platform at 14th, then shut them again. The doors hissed closed. He was drifting in that warm somewhere between awareness and sleep and there was a fluttering of nascent dreams in his head. It was a good feeling. The train was off again, rattling down into the tunnels.

Maybe, at the back of his dozing mind, Kaufman half-registered that the doors between the second and first cars had been slid open. Maybe he smelt the sudden gush of tunnel air, and registered that the noise of wheels was momentarily louder. But he chose to ignore it.

Maybe he even heard the scuffle as Mahogany subdued the youth with the spaced-out stare. But the sound was too distant and the promise of sleep was too tempting. He drowsed on.

For some reason his dreams were of his mother's kitchen. She was chopping turnips and smiling sweetly as she chopped. He was only small in his dream and was looking up at her radiant face while she worked. Chop. Chop. Chop.

His eyes jerked open. His mother vanished. The car was empty and the youth was gone.

How long had he been dozing? He hadn't remembered the train stopping at West 4th Street. He got up, his head full of slumber, and almost fell over as the train rocked violently. It seemed to have gathered quite a substantial head of speed. Maybe the driver was keen to be home, wrapped up in bed with his wife. They were going at a fair lick; in fact it was bloody terrifying.

There was a blind drawn down over the window between the cars which hadn't been down before as he remembered. A little concern crept into Kaufman's sober head. Suppose he'd been sleeping a long while, and the guard had overlooked him in the car. Perhaps they'd passed Far Rockaway and the train was now speeding on its way to wherever they took the trains for the night.

"Fuck it," he said aloud.

Should he go forward and ask the driver? It was such a bloody idiot question to ask: where am I? At this time of night was he likely to get more than a stream of abuse by way of reply?

Then the train began to slow.

A station. Yes, a station. The train emerged from the tunnel and into the dirty light of the station at West 4th Street. He'd missed no stops.

So where had the boy gone?

He'd either ignored the warning on the car wall forbidding transfer between the cars while in transit, or else he'd gone into the driver's cabin up front. Probably between the driver's legs even now, Kaufman thought, his lip curling. It wasn't unheard of. This was the Palace of Delights, after all, and everyone had their right to a little love in the dark.

Kaufman shrugged to himself. What did he care where the boy had gone?

The doors closed. Nobody had boarded the train. It shunted off from the station, the lights flickering as it used a surge of power to pick up some speed again.

Kaufman felt the desire for sleep come over him afresh, but the sudden fear of being lost had pumped adrenalin into his system, and his limbs were tingling with nervous energy.

His senses were sharpened too.

Even over the clatter and the rumble of the wheels on the tracks, he heard the sound of tearing cloth coming from the next car. Was someone tearing their shirt off?

He stood up, grasping one of the straps for balance.

The window between the cars was completely curtained off, but he stared at it, frowning, as though he might suddenly discover X-ray vision. The car rocked and rolled. It was really travelling again.

Another ripping sound.

Was it rape?

With no more than a mild voyeuristic urge he moved down the seesawing car towards the intersecting door, hoping there might be a chink in the curtain. His eyes were still fixed on the window,

and he failed to notice the splatters of blood he was treading in.
Until—

—his heel slipped. He looked down. His stomach almost saw
the blood before his brain and the ham on whole wheat was
halfway up his gullet catching in the back of his throat. Blood.
He took several large gulps of stale air and looked away—back
at the window.

His head was saying: blood. Nothing would make the word go
away.

There was no more than a yard or two between him and the
door now. He had to look. There was blood on his shoe, and a
thin trail to the next car, but he still had to look.

He had to.

He took two more steps to the door and scanned the curtain
looking for a flaw in the blind: a pulled thread in the weave would
be sufficient. There was a tiny hole. He glued his eye to it.

His mind refused to accept what his eyes were seeing beyond
the door. It rejected the spectacle as preposterous, as a dreamed
sight. His reason said it couldn't be real, but his flesh knew it
was. His body became rigid with terror. His eyes, unblinking,
could not close off the appalling scene through the curtain. He
stayed at the door while the train rattled on, while his blood
drained from his extremities, and his brain reeled from lack of
oxygen. Bright spots of light flashed in front of his vision, blotting
out the atrocity.

Then he fainted.

He was unconscious when the train reached Jay Street. He was
deaf to the driver's announcement that all travellers beyond that
station would have to change trains. Had he heard this he would
have questioned the sense of it. No trains disgorged all their
passengers at Jay Street; the line ran to Mott Avenue, via the
Aqueduct Race Track, past JFK Airport. He would have asked
what kind of train this could be. Except that he already knew.
The truth was hanging in the next car. It was smiling contentedly
to itself from behind a bloody chain-mail apron.

This was the Midnight Meat Train.

There's no accounting for time in a dead faint. It could have
been seconds or hours that passed before Kaufman's eyes flickered
open again, and his mind focussed on his newfound situation.

He lay under one of the seats now, sprawled along the vibrating wall of the car, hidden from view. Fate was with him so far, he thought: somehow the rocking of the car must have jockeyed his unconscious body out of sight.

He thought of the horror in Car Two, and swallowed back vomit. He was alone. Wherever the guard was (murdered perhaps), there was no way he could call for help. And the driver? Was he dead at his controls? Was the train even now hurtling through an unknown tunnel, a tunnel without a single station to identify it, towards its destruction?

And if there was no crash to be killed in, there was always the Butcher, still hacking away a door's thickness from where Kaufman lay.

Whichever way he turned, the name on the door was Death.

The noise was deafening, especially lying on the floor. Kaufman's teeth were shaking in their sockets and his face felt numb with the vibration; even his skull was aching.

Gradually he felt strength seeping back into his exhausted limbs. He cautiously stretched his fingers and clenched his fists, to set the blood flowing there again.

And as the feeling returned, so did the nausea. He kept seeing the grisly brutality of the next car. He'd seen photographs of murder victims before, of course, but these were no common murders. He was in the same train as the Subway Butcher, the monster who strung his victims up by the feet from the straps, hairless and naked.

How long would it be before the killer stepped through that door and claimed him? He was sure that if the slaughterer didn't finish him, expectation would.

He heard movement beyond the door.

Instinct took over. Kaufman thrust himself further under the seat and tucked himself up into a tiny ball, with his sick-white face to the wall. Then he covered his head with his hands and closed his eyes as tightly as any child in terror of the Bogeyman.

The door was slid open. Click. Whoosh. A rush of air up from the rails. It smelt stranger than any Kaufman had smelt before: and colder. This was somehow primal air in his nostrils, hostile and unfathomable air. It made him shudder.

The door closed. Click.

The Butcher was close, Kaufman knew it. He could be standing no more than a matter of inches from where he lay.

Was he even now looking down at Kaufman's back? Even now

bending, knife in hand, to scoop Kaufman out of his hiding place, like a snail hooked from its shell?

Nothing happened. He felt no breath on his neck. His spine was not slit open.

There was simply a clatter of feet close to Kaufman's head; then that same sound receding.

Kaufman's breath, held in his lungs 'til they hurt, was expelled in a rasp between his teeth.

Mahogany was almost disappointed that the sleeping man had alighted at West 4th Street. He was hoping for one more job to do that night, to keep him occupied while they descended. But no: the man had gone. The potential victim hadn't looked that healthy anyway, he thought to himself, he was an anaemic Jewish accountant probably. The meat wouldn't have been of any quality. Mahogany walked the length of the car to the driver's cabin. He'd spend the rest of the journey there.

My Christ, thought Kaufman, he's going to kill the driver.

He heard the cabin door open. Then the voice of the Butcher: low and hoarse.

"Hi."

"Hi."

They knew each other.

"All done?"

"All done."

Kaufman was shocked by the banality of the exchange. All done? What did that mean: all done?

He missed the next few words as the train hit a particularly noisy section of track.

Kaufman could resist looking no longer. Warily he uncurled himself and glanced over his shoulder down the length of the car. All he could see was the Butcher's legs, and the bottom of the open cabin door. Damn. He wanted to see the monster's face again.

There was laughter now.

Kaufman calculated the risks of his situation: the mathematics of panic. If he remained where he was, sooner or later the Butcher would glance down at him, and he'd be mincemeat. On the other hand, if he were to move from his hiding place he would risk being seen and pursued. Which was worse: stasis, and meeting his death trapped in a hole; or making a break for it and confronting his Maker in the middle of the car?

Kaufman surprised himself with his mettle: he'd move.

Infinitesimally slowly he crawled out from under the seat, watching the Butcher's back every minute as he did so. Once out, he began to crawl towards the door. Each step he took was a torment, but the Butcher seemed far too engrossed in his conversation to turn around.

Kaufman had reached the door. He began to stand up, trying all the while to prepare himself for the sight he would meet in Car Two. The handle was grasped; and he slid the door open.

The noise of the rails increased, and a wave of dank air, stinking of nothing on earth, came up at him. Surely the Butcher must hear, or smell? Surely he must turn—

But no. Kaufman skinned his way through the slit he had opened and so through into the bloody chamber beyond.

Relief made him careless. He failed to latch the door properly behind him and it began to slide open with the buffetting of the train.

Mahogany put his head out of the cabin and stared down the car towards the door.

"What the fuck's that?" said the driver.

"Didn't close the door properly. That's all."

Kaufman heard The Butcher walking towards the door. He crouched, a ball of consternation, against the intersecting wall, suddenly aware of how full his bowels were. The door was pulled closed from the other side, and the footsteps receded again.

Safe, for another breath at least.

Kaufman opened his eyes, steeling himself for the slaughterpen in front of him.

There was no avoiding it.

It filled every one of his senses: the smell of opened entrails, the sight of the bodies, the feel of fluid on the floor under his fingers, the sound of the straps creaking beneath the weight of the corpses, even the air, tasting salty with blood. He was with death absolutely in that cubbyhole, hurtling through the dark.

But there was no nausea now. There was no feeling left but a casual revulsion. He even found himself peering at the bodies with some curiosity.

The carcass closest to him was the remains of the pimply youth he'd seen in Car One. The body hung upside-down, swinging back and forth to the rhythm of the train, in unison with its three fellows; an obscene dance macabre. Its arms dangled loosely from the shoulder joints, into which gashes an inch or two deep had been made, so the bodies would hang more neatly.

Every part of the dead kid's anatomy was swaying hypnotically. The tongue, hanging from the open mouth. The head, lolling on its slit neck. Even the youth's penis flapped from side to side on his plucked groin. The head wound and the open jugular still pulsed blood into a black bucket. There was an elegance about the whole sight: the sign of a job well-done.

Beyond the body were the strung-up corpses of two young white women and a darker-skinned male. Kaufman turned his head on one side to look at their faces. They were quite blank. One of the girls was a beauty. He decided the male had been Puerto Rican. All were shorn of their head and body hair. In fact the air was still pungent with the smell of the shearing. Kaufman slid up the wall out of the crouching position, and as he did so one of the women's bodies turned around, presenting a dorsal view.

He was not prepared for this last horror.

The meat of her back had been entirely cleft open from neck to buttock and the muscle had been peeled back to expose the glistening vertebrae. It was the final triumph of The Butcher's craft. Here they hung, these shaved, bled, slit slabs of humanity, opened up like fish, and ripe for devouring.

Kaufman almost smiled at the perfection of its horror. He felt an offer of insanity tickling the base of his skull, tempting him into oblivion, promising a blank indifference to the world.

He began to shake, uncontrollably. He felt his vocal cords trying to form a scream. It was intolerable: and yet to scream was to become in a short while like the creatures in front of him.

"Fuck it," he said, more loudly than he'd intended, then pushing himself off from the wall he began to walk down the car between the swaying corpses, observing the neat piles of clothes and belongings that sat on the seats beside their owners. Under his feet the floor was sticky with drying bile. Even with his eyes closed to cracks he could see the blood in the buckets too clearly: it was thick and heady, flecks of grit turning in it.

He was past the youth now and he could see the door into Car Three ahead. All he had to do was run this gauntlet of atrocities. He urged himself on, trying to ignore the horrors, and concentrate on the door that would lead him back into sanity.

He was past the first woman. A few more yards, he said to himself, ten steps at most, less if he walked with confidence.

Then the lights went out.

"Jesus Christ," he said.

The train lurched, and Kaufman lost his balance.

In the utter blackness he reached out for support and his flailing arms encompassed the body beside him. Before he could prevent himself he felt his hands sinking into the lukewarm flesh, and his fingers grasping the open edge of muscle on the dead woman's back, his fingertips touching the bone of her spine. His cheek was laid against the bald flesh of the thigh.

He screamed; and even as he screamed, the lights flickered back on.

And as they flickered back on, and his scream died, he heard the noise of the Butcher's feet approaching down the length of Car One towards the intervening door.

He let go of the body he was embracing. His face was smeared with blood from her leg. He could feel it on his cheek, like warpaint.

The scream had cleared Kaufman's head and he suddenly felt released into a kind of strength. There would be no pursuit down the train, he knew that: there would be no cowardice, not now. This was going to be a primitive confrontation, two human beings, face to face. And there would be no trick—none—that he couldn't contemplate using to bring his enemy down. This was a matter of survival, pure and simple.

The door handle rattled.

Kaufman looked around for a weapon, his eye steady and calculating. His gaze fell on the pile of clothes beside the Puerto Rican's body. There was a knife there, lying amongst the rhinestone rings and the imitation gold chains. A long-bladed, immaculately clean weapon, probably the man's pride and joy. Reaching past the well-muscled body, Kaufman plucked the knife from the heap. It felt good in his hand; in fact it felt positively thrilling.

The door was opening, and the face of the slaughterer came into view.

Kaufman looked down the abattoir at Mahogany. He was not terribly fearsome, just another balding, overweight man of fifty. His face was heavy and his eyes deep-set. His mouth was rather small and delicately lipped. In fact he had a woman's mouth.

Mahogany could not understand where this intruder had appeared from, but he was aware that it was another oversight, another sign of increasing incompetence. He must dispatch this ragged creature immediately. After all, they could not be more than a mile or two from the end of the line. He must cut the little man down and have him hanging up by his heels before they reached their destination.

He moved into Car Two.

"You were asleep," he said, recognizing Kaufman. "I saw you."

Kaufman said nothing.

"You should have left the train. What were you trying to do? Hide from me?"

Kaufman still kept his silence.

Mahogany grasped the handle of the cleaver hanging from his well-used leather belt. It was dirty with blood, as was his chain-mail apron, his hammer, and his saw.

"As it is," he said, "I'll have to do away with you."

Kaufman raised the knife. It looked a little small beside the Butcher's paraphernalia.

"Fuck it," he said.

Mahogany grinned at the little man's pretensions to defense.

"You shouldn't have seen this: it's not for the likes of you," he said, taking another step towards Kaufman. "It's secret."

Oh, so he's the divinely inspired type is he? thought Kaufman. That explains something.

"Fuck it," he said again.

The Butcher frowned. He didn't like the little man's indifference to his work, to his reputation.

"We all have to die sometime," he said. "You should be well pleased: you're not going to be burnt up like most of them: I can use you. To feed the fathers."

Kaufman's only response was a grin. He was past being terrorized by this gross, shambling hulk.

The Butcher unhooked the cleaver from his belt and brandished it.

"A dirty little Jew like you," he said, "should be thankful to be useful at all: meat's the best you can aspire to."

Without warning, the Butcher swung. The cleaver divided the air at some speed, but Kaufman stepped back. The cleaver sliced his coat arm and buried itself in the Puerto Rican's shank. The impact half severed the leg and the weight of the body opened the gash even further. The exposed meat of the thigh was like prime steak, succulent and appetizing.

The Butcher started to drag the cleaver out of the wound, and in that moment Kaufman sprang. The knife sped towards Mahogany's eye, but an error of judgement buried it instead in his neck. It transfixed the column and appeared in a little gout of gore on the other side. Straight through. In one stroke. Straight through.

Mahogany felt the blade in his neck as a choking sensation, almost as though he had caught a chicken bone in his throat. He made a ridiculous, half-hearted coughing sound. Blood issued from his lips, painting them, like lipstick on his woman's mouth. The cleaver clattered to the floor.

Kaufman pulled out the knife. The two wounds spouted little arcs of blood.

Mahogany collapsed to his knees, staring at the knife that had killed him. The little man was watching him quite passively. He was saying something, but Mahogany's ears were deaf to the remarks, as though he was underwater.

Mahogany suddenly went blind. He knew with a nostalgia for his senses that he would not see or hear again. This was death: it was on him for certain.

His hands still felt the weave of his trousers, however, and the hot splashes on his skin. His life seemed to totter on its tiptoes while his fingers grasped at one last sense . . . then his body collapsed, and his hands, and his life, and his sacred duty folded up under a weight of grey flesh.

The Butcher was dead.

Kaufman dragged gulps of stale air into his lungs and grabbed one of the straps to steady his reeling body. Tears blotted out the shambles he stood in. A time passed: he didn't know how long; he was lost in a dream of victory.

Then the train began to slow. He felt and heard the brakes being applied. The hanging bodies lurched forward as the careering train slowed, its wheels squealing on rails that were sweating slime.

Curiosity overtook Kaufman.

Would the train shunt into the Butcher's underground slaughterhouse, decorated with the meats he had gathered through his career? And the laughing driver, so indifferent to the massacre, what would he do once the train had stopped? Whatever happened now was academic. He could face anything at all; watch and see.

The tannoy crackled. The voice of the driver:

"We're here, man. Better take your place, eh?"

Take your place? What did that mean?

The train had slowed to a snail's pace. Outside the windows, everything was as dark as ever. The lights flickered, then went out. This time they didn't come back on.

Kaufman was left in total darkness.

"We'll be out in half an hour," the tannoy announced, so like any station report.

The train had come to a stop. The sound of its wheels on the tracks, the rush of its passage, which Kaufman had grown so used to, were suddenly absent. All he could hear was the hum of the tannoy. He could still see nothing at all.

Then, a hiss. The doors were opening. A smell entered the car, a smell so caustic that Kaufman clapped his hand over his face to shut it out.

He stood in silence, hand to mouth, for what seemed a lifetime. See no evil. Hear no evil. Speak no evil.

Then, there was a flicker of light outside the window. It threw the door frame into silhouette, and it grew stronger by degrees. Soon there was sufficient light in the car for Kaufman to see the crumpled body of the Butcher at his feet, and the sallow sides of meat hanging on every side of him.

There was a whisper too, from the dark outside the train, a gathering of tiny noises like the voices of beetles. In the tunnel, shuffling towards the train, were human beings. Kaufman could see their outlines now. Some of them carried torches, which burned with a dead brown light. The noise was perhaps their feet on the damp earth, or perhaps their tongues clicking, or both.

Kaufman wasn't as naive as he'd been an hour before. Could there be any doubt as to the intention these things had, coming out of the blackness towards the train? The Butcher had slaughtered the men and women as meat for these cannibals, they were coming, like diners at the dinner gong, to eat in this restaurant car.

Kaufman bent down and picked up the cleaver the Butcher had dropped. The noise of the creatures' approach was louder every moment. He backed down the car away from the open doors, only to find that the doors behind him were also open, and there was the whisper of approach there too.

He shrank back against one of the seats and was about to take refuge under them when a hand, thin and frail to the point of transparency, appeared around the door.

He could not look away. Not that terror froze him as it had at the window. He simply wanted to watch.

The creature stepped into the car. The torches behind it threw its face into shadow, but its outline could be clearly seen.

There was nothing very remarkable about it.

It had two arms and two legs as he did; its head was not abnormally shaped. The body was small, and the effort of climbing into the train made its breath coarse. It seemed more geriatric than psychotic; generations of fictional man-eaters had not prepared him for its distressing vulnerability.

Behind it, similar creatures were appearing out of the darkness, shuffling into the train. In fact they were coming in at every door.

Kaufman was trapped. He weighed the cleaver in his hands, getting the balance of it, ready for the battle with these antique monsters. A torch had been brought into the car, and it illuminated the faces of the leaders.

They were completely bald. The tired flesh of their faces was pulled tight over their skulls, so that it shone with tension. There were stains of decay and disease on their skin, and in places the muscle had withered to a black pus, through which the bone of cheek or temple was showing. Some of them were naked as babies, their pulpy, syphilitic bodies scarcely sexed. What had been breasts were leathery bags hanging off the torso, the genitalia shrunken away.

Worse sights than the naked amongst them were those who wore a veil of clothes. It soon dawned on Kaufman that the rotting fabric slung around their shoulders or knotted about their midriffs was made of human skins. Not one, but a dozen or more, heaped haphazardly on top of each other, like pathetic trophies.

The leaders of this grotesque meal line had reached the bodies now, and the gracile hands were laid upon the shanks of meat, and were running up and down the shaved flesh in a manner that suggested sensual pleasure. Tongues were dancing out of mouths, flecks of spittle landing on the meat. The eyes of the monsters were flickering back and forth with hunger and excitement.

Eventually one of them saw Kaufman.

Its eyes stopped flickering for a moment and fixed on him. A look of enquiry came over the face, making a parody of puzzlement.

"You," it said. The voice was as wasted as the lips it came from.

Kaufman raised the cleaver a little, calculating his chances. There were perhaps thirty of them in the car and many more outside. But they looked so weak, and they had no weapons but their skin and bones.

The monster spoke again, its voice quite well modulated, when it found itself, the piping of a once-cultured, once-charming man.

"You came after the other, yes?"

It glanced down at the body of Mahogany. It had clearly taken in the situation very quickly.

"Old anyway," it said, its watery eyes back on Kaufman, studying him with care.

"Fuck you," said Kaufman.

The creature attempted a wry smile, but it had almost forgotten the technique and the result was a grimace which exposed a mouthful of teeth that had been systematically filed into points.

"You must now do this for us," it said through the bestial grin. "We cannot survive without food."

The hand patted the rump of human flesh. Kaufman had no reply to the idea. He just stared in disgust as the fingernails slid between the cleft in the buttocks, feeling the swell of tender muscle.

"It disgusts us no less than you," said the creature. "But we're bound to eat this meat, or we die. God knows, I have no appetite for it."

The thing was drooling nevertheless.

Kaufman found his voice. It was small, more with a confusion of feelings than with fear.

"What are you?" He remembered the bearded man in the deli. "Are you accidents of some kind?"

"We are the city fathers," the thing said. "And mothers, and daughters and sons. The builders, the lawmakers. We made this city."

"New York?" said Kaufman. The Palace of Delights?

"Before you were born, before anyone living was born."

As it spoke the creature's fingernails were running up under the skin of the split body, and were peeling the thin elastic layer off the luscious brawn. Behind Kaufman, the other creatures had begun to unhook the bodies from the straps, their hands laid in that same delighting manner on the smooth breasts and flanks of flesh. These too had begun skinning the meat.

"You will bring us more," the father said. "More meat for us. The other one was weak."

Kaufman stared in disbelief.

"Me?" he said. "Feed you? What do you think I am?"

"You must do it for us, and for those older than us. For those born before the city was thought of, when America was a timberland and desert."

The fragile hand gestured out of the train.

Kaufman's gaze followed the pointing finger into the gloom.

There was something else outside the train which he'd failed to see before; much bigger than anything human.

The pack of creatures parted to let Kaufman through so that he could inspect more closely whatever it was that stood outside, but his feet would not move.

"Go on," said the father.

Kaufman thought of the city he'd loved. Were these really its ancients, its philosophers, its creators? He had to believe it. Perhaps there were people on the surface—bureaucrats, politicians, authorities of every kind—who knew this horrible secret and whose lives were dedicated to preserving these abominations, feeding them, as savages feed lambs to their gods. There was a horrible familiarity about this ritual. It rang a bell—not in Kaufman's conscious mind, but in his deeper, older self.

His feet, no longer obeying his mind, but his instinct to worship, moved. He walked through the corridor of bodies and stepped out of the train.

The light of the torches scarcely began to illuminate the limitless darkness outside. The air seemed solid, it was so thick with the smell of ancient earth. But Kaufman smelt nothing. His head bowed, it was all he could do to prevent himself from fainting again.

It was there; the precursor of man. The original American, whose homeland this was before Passamaquoddy or Cheyenne. Its eyes, if it had eyes, were on him.

His body shook. His teeth chattered.

He could hear the noise of its anatomy: ticking, crackling, sobbing.

It shifted a little in the dark.

The sound of its movement was awesome. Like a mountain sitting up.

Kaufman's face was raised to it, and without thinking about what he was doing or why, he fell to his knees in the shit in front of the Father of Fathers.

Every day of his life had been leading to this day, every moment quickening to this incalculable moment of holy terror.

Had there been sufficient light in that pit to see the whole, perhaps his tepid heart would have burst. As it was he felt it flutter in his chest as he saw what he saw.

It was a giant. Without head or limb. Without a feature that was analogous to human, without an organ that made sense, or senses. If it was like anything, it was like a shoal of fish. A thousand snouts all moving in unison, budding, blossoming, and withering rhythmically. It was iridescent, like mother of pearl, but it was sometimes deeper than any color Kaufman knew, or could put a name to.

That was all Kaufman could see, and it was more than he wanted to see. There was much more in the darkness, flickering and flapping.

But he could look no longer. He turned away, and as he did so a football was pitched out of the train and rolled to a halt in front of the Father.

At least he thought it was a football, until he peered more attentively at it, and recognized it as a human head, the head of the Butcher. The skin of the face had been peeled off in strips. It glistened with blood as it lay in front of its Lord.

Kaufman looked away, and walked back to the train. Every part of his body seemed to be weeping but his eyes. They were too hot with the sight behind him, they boiled his tears away.

Inside, the creatures had already set about their supper. One, he saw, was plucking the blue sweet morsel of a woman's eye out of the socket. Another had a hand in its mouth. At Kaufman's feet lay the Butcher's headless corpse, still bleeding profusely from where its neck had been bitten through.

The little father who had spoken earlier stood in front of Kaufman.

"Serve us?" it asked gently, as you might ask a cow to follow you.

Kaufman was staring at the cleaver, the Butcher's symbol of office. The creatures were leaving the car now, dragging the half-eaten bodies after them. As the torches were taken out of the car, darkness was returning.

But before the lights had completely disappeared the father reached out and took hold of Kaufman's face, thrusting him round to look at himself in the filthy glass of the car window.

It was a thin reflection, but Kaufman could see quite well enough how changed he was. Whiter than any living man should be, covered in grime and blood.

The father's hand still gripped Kaufman's face, and its forefinger hooked into his mouth and down his gullet, the nail scoring the back of his throat. Kaufman gagged on the intruder, but had no will left to repel the attack.

"Serve," said the creature. "In silence."

Too late, Kaufman realized the intention of the fingers—

Suddenly his tongue was seized tight and twisted on the root. Kaufman, in shock, dropped the cleaver. He tried to scream, but no sound came. Blood was in his throat, he heard his flesh tearing, and agonies convulsed him.

Then the hand was out of his mouth and the scarlet, spittle-covered fingers were in front of his face, with his tongue, held between thumb and forefinger.

Kaufman was speechless.

"Serve," said the father, and stuffed the tongue into his own mouth, chewing on it with evident satisfaction. Kaufman fell to his knees, spewing up his sandwich.

The father was already shuffling away into the dark; the rest of the ancients had disappeared into their warren for another night.

The tannoy crackled.

"Home," said the driver.

The doors hissed closed and the sound of power surged through the train. The lights flickered on, then off again, then on.

The train began to move.

Kaufman lay on the floor, tears pouring down his face, tears of discomfiture and of resignation. He would bleed to death, he decided, where he lay. It wouldn't matter if he died. It was a foul world anyway.

The driver woke him. He opened his eyes. The face that was looking down at him was black, and not unfriendly. It grinned. Kaufman tried to say something, but his mouth was sealed up with dried blood. He jerked his head around like a driveler trying to spit out a word. Nothing came but grunts.

He wasn't dead. He hadn't bled to death.

The driver pulled him to his knees, talking to him as though he were a three-year-old.

"You got a job to do, my man: they're very pleased with you."

The driver had licked his fingers, and was rubbing Kaufman's swollen lips, trying to part them.

"Lots to learn before tomorrow night . . ."

Lots to learn. Lots to learn.

He led Kaufman out of the train. They were in no station he had ever seen before. It was white-tiled and absolutely pristine; a station-keeper's Nirvana. No graffiti disfigured the walls. There were no token booths, but then there were no gates and no passengers either. This was a line that provided only one service: The Meat Train.

A morning shift of cleaners were already busy hosing the blood

off the seats and the floor of the train. Somebody was stripping
the Butcher's body, in preparation for dispatch to New Jersey.
All around Kaufman people were at work.

A rain of dawn light was pouring through a grating in the roof
of the station. Motes of dust hung in the beams, turning over
and over. Kaufman watched them, entranced. He hadn't seen
such a beautiful thing since he was a child. Lovely dust. Over
and over, and over and over.

The driver had managed to separate Kaufman's lips. His mouth
was too wounded for him to move it, but at least he could breathe
easily. And the pain was already beginning to subside.

The driver smiled at him, then turned to the rest of the workers
in the station.

"I'd like to introduce Mahogany's replacement. Our new
butcher," he announced.

The workers looked at Kaufman. There was a certain defer-
ence in their faces, which he found appealing.

Kaufman looked up at the sunlight, now falling all around him.
He jerked his head, signifying that he wanted to go up, into the
open air. The driver nodded, and led him up a steep flight of
stairs and through an alleyway and so out onto the sidewalk.

It was a beautiful day. The bright sky over New York was
streaked with filaments of pale pink cloud, and the air smelt of
morning.

The streets and avenues were practically empty. At a distance
an occasional cab crossed an intersection, its engine a whisper;
a runner sweated past on the other side of the street.

Very soon these same deserted sidewalks would be thronged
with people. The city would go about its business in ignorance:
never knowing what it was built upon, or what it owed its life
to. Without hesitation, Kaufman fell to his knees and kissed the
dirty concrete with his bloody lips, silently swearing his eternal
loyalty to its continuance.

The Palace of Delights received the adoration without comment.

Film at Eleven

JOHN
SKIPP

John Skipp is one-half of the high-amp horror duo Skipp and (Craig) Spector, splatterpunk's backbeat boys. "Backbeat" because Skipp and Spector have injected splatterpunk with its most tasty element—rock 'n' roll.

Two well-known members of The Splat Pack, Skipp and Spector usually write as a team; they're also practicing musicians who bring the best elements of the rock culture—energy and confrontation—to their work. In such books as 1986's *The Light at the End* (vampires in the subway), 88's *The Scream* (rock really *is* the devil's music), and 89's *Book of the Dead* (the ultimate zombie anthology), Skipp and Spector's prose drums along with a very fast beat. Their fiction is cadenced, cinematic, and socially concerned, commenting on everything from the urban nightmare to America's recent (and ongoing) attack on personal freedoms.

Skipp and Spector—or The Boys, as they're jointly known—are also the most passionate of the splatterpunks. They write straight from their hearts, and spleens, and nuts; thankfully, their intellects are hotwired to their emotions. For example, here's Skipp explaining what splatterpunk, to him, is all about (excerpted from the 1988 *Midnight Graffiti* article by Jessie Horsting titled "The Splat Pack: Horror's Young Writers Spill Their Guts"):

What this gang of horror writers is doing is similar to what comedians like Richard Pryor did for stand-up comedy. They were people that weren't afraid to talk about their dicks and who aren't afraid to be outrageous and crazy because they knew it would serve them well. It's more of an attitude than just an exercise in seeing how much blood, how many gross-outs you can get on a page. The idea is to ground the paranormal, to give credibility, to make it organic and upsetting. We're trying to cut through the somnambulism—there's something stultifying about late Twentieth-Century American culture that wants to turn you into a good little drone.

The drone attitude is tackled head-on in "Film at Eleven," a rare solo outing from John Skipp focusing a dark, angry look on the battered wife syndrome. More important, "Film at Eleven" directly addresses the most serious, oft-heard criticism leveled at splatterpunk—that it's essentially misogynistic.

In Lucius Shepard's otherwise tough-minded essay "Waiting for the Barbarians" (found in the winter 1989 issue of *Journal Wired*), Shepard unfortunately aligns himself with this (knee-jerk) criticism by stating that splatterpunks should "stop slashing the throats of women with big chest problems and go after the throats that need slashing."

"Film at Eleven" certainly slashes the right throats.

However, as Skipp ironically points out, where—and when—does the slashing stop?

It started out like just another Thursday in Hell.

She awoke in her bed at eight A.M. The air was thick with heat and sweat. Dale was naked and snoring beside her, his fists unfurled in sleep. She heard the screen door at the front of the house scream open, then slam shut. Tiny footsteps hit the sidewalk and receded into the world.

Nikki was safe: for now, at least.

And Dottie Neff was alone.

With him.

She let the day's pain seep back into her body gradually, let her memory piece together what it could. Sleep had put a buffer between Wednesday's Hell and the new one abornin', but that mercy fried quickly in the sweet light of day. Then the damage began to itemize itself, meticulous but in no particular order.

This morning brought the skull-ache first. It centered on the jaws, the temples, and the space immediately behind her eyes. By the time her brain began to throb, the rest of her body was catching up: the wrenched left arm, the throbbing nipples, the pummeled pussy, all on fire. Before she even began to move, the entire inventory had been laid out.

Then she remembered poor ol' Buzz Royer, which reminded

her of the plan, and the ghostly sweet taste of freedom came
flooding back to warm and haunt her.

It didn't make Hell go away, of course; when she moved, the
pain got instantly worse. "Oh, God," she moaned, but she did
so quietly. There was much to do in the next hour or so; the last
thing she wanted was to wake up Dale. Not with that flavor so
close to her tongue.

Not when she was so close.

Her feet edged off the side of the bed and wobbled to the floor.
The rest of her followed, wobbling naked toward the open bedroom door. He had not bothered to close it before launching into
last night's hate-making ritual. So Nikki, as usual, had heard it
all.

But for the last time, Dottie silently swore. *Baby, I promise.
Today we say goodbye . . .*

She shuffled into the hallway and headed for the back of the
house. There was a full-length mirror on the bathroom door at
the end of the hall. She saw herself in it, could not look away.

The woman who stared back was thirty-two, five foot six, one
hundred and sixty-nine. She had big brown eyes with tiny pupils
and dark puffy bruises around them. A styleless mop of mud-
brown hair, limp as roadkill, crowned her head. There was no
tone to the pale white flesh, just bulge and stoop and sag. In
fact, there was nothing to commend this woman at all. Except.

Except that she was ready.

And that, with every step she took, she seemed to grow . . .

june 17

dear oprah winfrey,

i don't know how to start this. i've never written to a big star
like yourself before! i never thought i had anything that important
to say, you know? but i watch your show all the time, and it
moved me so much. your so brave and strong and funny. i just
wish that i was like you. i think you are the greatest woman in
the whole world. i really mean that.

but the problem is i'm not like you at all. i don't have any
guts. i think the bravest thing i ever did was writing you this
letter, and i bet i don't even have the nerve to mail it.

you see, i have problems. most of them are my fault, i know,
but i just don't know how to get around them. when i think about
how messed up my life has gotten, sometimes it doesn't seem
like theres any hope at all. it's just too complicated. do you know
what i mean?

but then i watch your show, and i get hope. i see all these women overcoming all these incredible things, just being so honest and open about their feelings, and i wish that i could do that, but i can't.

sometimes it gets me really scared, like when you had on the rapists for two days, or those people who wrote books about murderers like son of sam. and sometimes you make me laugh, like when you had on burt reynolds or mel gibson and that black man. and then sometimes you really just make me think, like when you had shirley maclaine. i mean, that stuff was just so far out, i didn't know *what* to think!

but most of the time, it makes me cry. (not that i need any help, thank you!) its just that i see so much of my own life, things that help me explain whats going on in my own life, and i don't know why but most of the time it just makes me more confused.

i geuss the reason i'm writing today is because you just had on that woman doctor susan forward again. you know, the one who wrote *men who hate women and the women who love them?* i had never heard the word misojony before, but i'll never forget it now, because my boyfriend is just like that. he puts me down all the time he doesn't let me have any friends. when i try to make myself look pretty, like i buy a new dress or put on makeup or get a haircut or something, he says things like what the blank is *that* suppose to be, anyway? i swear it drives me crazy sometimes.

the problem is that i think i could fight him except for my mind doesn't work too well. my doctor, doctor himmler, says that i get seizures in my brain, in the frontal lobe. thats why my thoughts race around so crazy. the drugs he gives me help alot, 1600 mgs. of lithium and 500 mgs. of a new drug called tegretol, which he says suppresses the convulsions. but i still can't get a handle on what i'm doing, and besides my boyfriend is even more messed up than me. he's got a different doctor than me, and he gets lots of percodans and this cough syrup that i think is called hycutus, and all i know is that it has a lot of codeine in it, and it makes him so crazy and mean once he gets going that a lot of times i'm afraid for my life.

the worst part is that i've got a little daughter. her name is nichole, but i call her nikki. she's only six years old, and she doesn't understand whats happening, but i know that she hates dale and i think she hates me for letting him live here, and i would throw him out except i'm afraid he wouldn't leave, he'd just beat me worse and maybe hurt nikki too. i dont think that i could live if he ever did anything to nikki.

so you see what my problem is. i dont know what to do. i dont even know what i'm writing you for except that if you were on my side i know i could do anything. i geuss that its too much to ask, sense i'm just somebody off of the streets, but if i was on your show one day, i swear to god i'd spill my guts, and maybe somebody would know how bad i hurt and help me, and maybe other women who are in the same situation could get help. thats the most beautiful thing about your show. you find out that your not alone. thats the most beautiful thing that anyone could ever give a person.

i love you, oprah, and i hope you read this letter. if you cant every write back, i understand. i wish you all the happiness in the world, and thank you for what you've given me.

all my love,
⋅ dorothy abigail neff.

MARK AS EXHIBIT A

After she had thrown up and taken her pills, control began to set in. She could feel it as a cool power running taut down her spine. She could feel it in her movements, the assuredness of them, the sense that she was moving herself and not just being dragged along behind. She was drawing on parts of herself that hadn't seen light in a long long time. But they were still there. And they still worked.

She checked herself out in the bathroom mirror. The swelling on her face was expansive and colorful. It would look great on the Channel 8 News Break, she felt quite sure. A picture's worth a thousand words . . .

. . . *and of course that took her back to poor Buzz Royer, the beetle-black flatness of his eyes in those, his final moments on-screen. There was something in the way that he parted his lips to swallow Death: not like an invasion, but like a lover's tongue* . . .

. . . and then she was back in the bathroom, and the clock was ticking.

8:11.

Time to move.

She had started out okay enough. Dad was a $50,000-a-year sales manager for York Caterpillar. Mom was up to her bouffant hairdo in garden clubs and church activities. They loved her just fine, albeit always from a distance. They taught her to be well-mannered, obedient, and clean, and above all to put on a happy face.

Dottie had mediocred her way through school, never seeing the point and not entirely wrong in that. She was bright enough, but it was hard to whip up much enthusiasm. The important thing was to make nicey-nice, to not make waves, and to keep on smilin'. There were always friends, and there were always parties, and someday there'd be a man who would take care of her in style.

But then the recreational drugs had begun to get serious roughly one year after graduation; time began to slide by on a moist trail of cheap wine, overpriced Colombian, angel dust, and ludes. It was the early seventies, and the mighty counterculture of the previous decade had shot its mighty wad. Left behind in archeological splendor were the sex, the drugs, the rock 'n' roll, the threadbare middle-class rebellion; but its lofty values were nowhere to be found, either driven underground or sputtered off into the ozone.

It was an empty time to be young and white in America: and while some covered for it with a brave new cynicism, the Dotties of the world huddled en masse toward the center, where they had no fucking idea as to what was going on. Fake it. Hang out. Don't worry about tomorrow, it'll take care of itself. Don't bother building for it, either. Just gimme another hit.

Her parents responded by throwing her out, after all the hand-wringing and shouting was through. She spent the next few years doing a retro tapdance of her father's footsteps, selling hot pretzels, silly shoes, and the last of the great black-lite posters as the different jobs shuffled her from one York Mall emporium to the other. The party was dimming, but so was her soul; despite a gnawing dissatisfaction, life appeared to go on.

By the time she met her one true love, she was almost twenty-seven years old. His name was Barry Strasbaugh, and he was tall and skinny, with a nose like a large kosher dill; but he treated her sweetly, and he had a steady job, and she knew for a fact that he wasn't fucking around behind her back.

Most of all, he did not try to change her. He accepted her for what she was. There was no greater gift than that.

She accepted it, and gave him all her love in return.

A year of considerable happiness followed, the dream not decaying until after the marriage, roughly five months into her first to-term pregnancy. That was when her inability to cut back on the drink and smoke and pills began to erode his patience. The fact that his habits remained unchanged was quite beside the point, he felt. After all, he wasn't the one who was pregnant.

By the time Nicole arrived, Barry was yelling most of the time, and Dottie had made the big leap to tequila, vodka, and gin. Little Nikki was tiny indeed—a month premature, at five pounds seven ounces—and there was some doubt as to whether she would live. But after three insurance-free and financially devastating weeks in the hospital, their daughter was released into the world of hurt.

It was good of Barry to wait for the baby before he started to slap Dottie around. At that point, he didn't know what else to do. It didn't help matters, but it gave him something to do with his hands when he wasn't busy drinking, playing cards with the boys, or test-driving tanks out at Bowen-McLaughlin.

The marriage lasted for nearly three years. During that time, she made seven trips to the hospital: two mild concussions, one slightly more serious one, a fractured rib, a badly sprained ankle, a stomach ulcer, and one rather lengthy stay in Three Northeast, the psychiatric wing of York Hospital. It was during that sojourn that Barry took his leave for good, bestowing Nikki's sickly presence on Dottie's long-suffering parents.

Under the expert care of the astoundingly named Dr. Himmler, Dottie went through six weeks that verified her residence in Hell. She remembered very little of her stay, except in snatches that could just as easily have been dreams. She remembered long stretches of questions and answers, where next to none of the words made sense. She remembered A.A. meetings and sessions with priests. She remembered someone giving her injections in her feet. She remembered a number of strange locations: a slum where crumbling doorways were being rebuilt, a room where lots of teenagers were milling around, a place distinguished by white walls and a steady rocking motion. She remembered waking up to a sharp pain in her rectum, then fading out again.

At the end, she was diagnosed as suffering from irregular brain seizures. This was not good news. Dr. Himmler, however, had just the thing for her: more drugs. He also set her up on the public dole through the Pennsylvania Department of Mental Health, which paid for everything from her house to her food stamps to her drugs and doctor's appointments. She left the hospital in a cerebrally passive state, free of every nasty habit but smoking and the inability to hold a concrete thought for more than three minutes at a time.

Time heals, and Dottie's seemed to stretch forever; so when six months down the road found her both drinking and thinking again, nobody was too surprised. Though she couldn't find a steady job, or hold it if she did: there was a series of off-the-books housecleaning assignments that kept her in margaritas and occasional clothes for Nikki. For a while, life was almost bearable again.

And then, one night at the Gaslight Tavern, she met Dale. And Hell resumed in earnest . . .

july 20

dear oprah,

its been a while since my last letter. since then, things have gotten much worse, sometimes dale takes as many as twelve percodans at a time, and if he isnt hitting me then he's passed out in bed. he got fired from his job at borg warner. and the money i get from the state isn't enough to keep us all alive. sometimes he goes out and tries to bum some, but his family and friends gave up on him a long time ago, just like mine did with me. i geuss i can't blame them, but its still so hard.

i keep trying to think of something that will make this important, something that makes it different from every other sob story you ever heard. i can't. if there was anything special about me, i probably wouldnt be in this mess.

no, maybe i'm wrong. i'm sitting here writing this, and suddenly its all making sense somehow. i'm not just an ordinary person, because ordinary people dont sink this low. i'm a *very* special person, in a very strange way. i'm god's own special fuckup, you'll pardon my french. i'm as fucked up as a person can be.

its like, everybody is born with thier own special guardian angel, you know what i mean? and you live and you live, but every time it comes down to the point of the disaster, he's there for you. he sees you thru it, and he kinda gives you a little pat on the head and says its okay, dottie. you made a couple wrong turns there, but i still love you.

now you still have yours. thats real clear. i watch you up there on the tv screen, and its perfectly obvious that you know why you were born. you laugh and you cry and you ask all the right questions, and you bring millions of us together five days a week to help us remember why god bothered to make us in the first place. its the little voice of the angel in your ear going remember me? come on! we got places to go and people to see!

but i lost mine, i swear to god, and now i dont know what to do. its like i went this way and he went that, and the next thing we knew we were out in the wilderness with thousands of miles between us and no way back, because there is no way back, everybody always told me you cant go back and i cant help but beleive them now because i'm totally totally lost.

so what can i think? i'll tell you what. i think i was supposed to lose it. i think that i'm suppose to be an example of what *not* to do, you know what i'm saying? i feel like a soldier thats marching off to war, and he knows hes going to die, and he knows that theres no way out of it, and the only thing he can figure is that theres a bigger picture somewhere, and he'll be one of the details, one of the bodies in a pile on a page in a textbook on history that somebody will make thier little kids read so that maybe they wont make the same mistake, theyll hold on to that angel and theyll never let go until its time to die and they fly away forever. could that be what its like?

i dont know. tell the truth, i probably never will. i cant stop thinking that if i got on your show, and fifty million people were watching, that maybe my guardian angel would see and get back to me in time.

but i didn't have the guts to send my last letter, so i bet i wont send this one either. sometimes i dont think i'll see my angel again until i die, and all that makes me want to do is die faster. you know what i mean?

i dont know what i mean. i have convulsions in my brain. how are you suppose to think with convulsions in your brain? so maybe i'm not so wrong after all. what do you think?

i love you, oprah, i'm sorry.

love,

dorothy abigail neff.

MARK AS EXHIBIT B

Most of the hardest work had already been done the last night, before Dale staggered home and raped and beat her. She had had her shit that much together. And so much of it was simple opportunism: the piles of clothing strewn about, the loose newspaper, the cheap furniture and carpet and paneling that constituted her home.

Plus one other little thing . . .

From there, it was largely a matter of strategic placement and timing. Yes, timing was clearly of the essence; that, and the purchase of three cans of lighter fluid. From there, all that remained was getting dressed.

And making a phone call.

And doing it up.

Dottie slid into the green halter top and frayed cutoffs that she had left in the living room the night before. There was no shortage of footwear by the side of the front door. She opted for the tawny brown leather thongs.

As she put them on, she thought, *These are the clothes that you're going to die in.* The thought didn't bother her nearly as much as she felt it should have. Funny thing about that. When she thought about Buzz Royer, with his jet-black suit and ridiculous striped tie and balding pate, she felt a burst of ugly pity that was quickly subsumed by the knowledge that he'd died just as he lived. And if that meant he was a fool, then at least he died consistent, he didn't try to be somebody else as he went out.

She hoped to achieve at least that much honesty.

All the way down Lehman Street, she was astounded by how *bright* everything was. Not just the sun, which had been scorching the poor long-suffering earth with record heat for the last ten days. It was everything: the crisp green and brown of tree and lawn, the white and brick and tan of the houses that lined the street, the multi-colored cars and flowers, the blue and white of the sky. She felt as if a thick swath of tinted film had been lifted from before her eyes. It was almost like tripping, euphoria and all.

There was a pay phone in the back of Jim & Nina's Pizzeria. The massive air conditioner on the wall above kicked the 110 degrees around the little room with gargantuan futility, but its pointless roar more than shielded her words from the ears of the counter girl. Dottie unraveled the moist strip of paper from her back pocket, slipped a quarter in the slot, and dialed.

Seven rings later, a man's voice informed her that she had reached the Channel 8 news department.

"I'd like to report a fire," she said.

august 7

dear oprah,

if your reading this, i must be dead. dont feel bad. i certainly dont. death cant be any worse than living has been, and i have a feeling that its gonna be a whole lot better.

but i want you to know what happened, because i want you to understand. then maybe you can do a show without me, but people will still get the story, and maybe others wont have to do what i did just to let the world know that they cant take it anymore.

it all started yesterday, when i was watching tv. during the morning, my station is channel 2 from baltimore. it shows you at nine, then phil donohue at ten (i like him, but hes not like you. i geuss its because hes not a woman. sometimes i feel like hes talking down to me, and i get enough of that from dale.) anyway, and then the wheel comes on at 11, and i love pat sajak, i think hes so funny. so i watch straight through to 11:30, and by then dale usually wakes up long enough to choke down some food before passing out again.

but yesterday, just as they were going into the bonus round, they cut in with a special news report, you probably heard about it. this man named buzz royer shot himself in the head in front of national tv at a press conference. i dont know if you saw it, but it was pretty amazing.

i mean, here was this poor man, and you could just see how bad he was hurting inside. i think they had caught him stealing money from the government, he was state treasurer or something. anyway, he was in some deep shit, you could tell right away.

so there he was, standing behind his little podium, and all of a sudden he pulls this gun out of this manila envelope, and everybody starts yelling, and he sticks it in his mouth. and the next thing you know theres this horrible noise and he disappears behind the podium, and before i had a chance to think it was over.

but you know what i thought when i got the chance?

i thought *i can do that*.

i mean, it was over so quickly. the worst part must have been the press conference. thinking about it. talking to all these people as if he was going to be around to have a drink with them later, pretending that he didn't know that it was all over but the shooting. (bad pun. i'm sorry.)

but pulling the trigger, that only took a second. a second and it was over. i mean, you couldnt even see him, thats how over it was. and i thought god, if thats all it takes, then what the hell am i waiting for anyway?

the worst part, of course, is thinking about nikki. but i cant help but feel that shell be happier with her real father, or maybe with my parents, or even if somebody has to adopt her. at least she wont be stuck with me and dale any more. and at least i know that i got her away before dale did anything.

god, if only you coulda see how dale treated me back when we met. people warned me about him, but i couldn't believe it because he seemed like such a sweet guy. we used to go out drinking and to parties, and then we would come home and make love and just talk for hours and hours. back then he used to listen to what i had to say. i think he was like me, just so blown away by the idea that someone could actually love him that he would have given anything just to be with me. i know thats how i felt.

but then, once he had me, everything changed. it was like he was scared to be without me, scared that anyone else would find me attractive (ha ha!), scared that i would leave him. and then it got to the point where we would go to a party and he couldnt even drink beer or hed upchuck, but he always had that bottle of cough syrup with him. did you ever see someone just sit there and swig cough syrup? at first its almost funny, and then you realize how sick it is.

its like that woman doctor said. self-esteem, pure and simple. just like the overeaters, the shoplifters, the adulterers. and even the rapists and murderers ive seen on your show. it always seems to come back to that. if he had any self-esteem, he wouldnt have to put me down. but he doesnt. i think that the only person he hates more than me is himself, and if he could just admit that, maybe he wouldn't have to hate either one of us.

of course, if i had any, i wouldnt put up with him either.

i guess i should tell you that dale was a singer. i hear that he was really great, tho hed stopped pretty much by the time i met him. he said he always knew he was gonna be a star, but then he never left town, and after a while he started losing his hair, and his back started to give him trouble, and i guess he just got tired. but something must have died when he decided to give up, because everyone says that hes been fucked up ever since.

oh well. at any rate, i'll be gone some time tomorrow morning, by way of the old buzz royer alternitive. dale and the rest of the world can straighten out their own god damn act. not that i blame him or anybody else. you get born, things happen, and eventually you die. thats just the way it goes.

i love you, oprah. i wish you all the best. hope to see you on the other side, even tho i wonder if we will wind up in the same place. you know what they say about suicide, after all.

but i believe that if i can hear my angels voice at all, hes telling me that its time to go now.

goodbye.

love,

dorothy abigail neff.

MARK AS EXHIBIT C

Dale Snyder woke to smoke and heat and the fog inside his brain. His first reaction was one of muddled alarm: his washed-out red, white, and blue eyes flew open; he began to cough; he fell backwards off the bed. There were a hundred and eighty pounds of him, spanning an even six feet. They hit the floorboards hard. Even through the drugs, it hurt like a bastard.

"DOTTIE!" he yelled, dragging himself to hands and knees. His voice felt like stars of burning glass in his throat. "WHAT THE FUCK IS GOING *ON* HERE? DOTTIE!"

There was no answer, just a dull rumble of voices from somewhere in the house. Dale struggled to his feet, murkily assessed the state of the room and his own chances of survival. So far, it didn't look too bad. There were no flames in the room; just a fair amount of smoke rolling in under the door. He eyed the open windows for a second; in a pinch, they'd be all he needed for escape.

But first, he wanted to check the rest of the place out. There was a good chance, he reasoned now, that Dottie had simply fucked something up. She never cooked, so that couldn't be the problem; most likely, she had dumped a hot ashtray into the trash, or maybe passed out with a lit cigarette. Whatever it was, the dumb cunt was about to become very sorry there was no fucking doubt about that.

His toes caught on last night's discarded underwear, and he slipped them on awkwardly; he didn't want to be caught with his balls hanging out if the fire trucks showed up. Then, his confidence bolstered, he made his wobbly way toward the door.

The knob was room temperature. That was good news, at least. He fitted his sweaty palm around it and twisted. It opened, no problem; the fleeting paranoia that she might have been trying to burn him alive vanished as quickly as it had flitted across his mind . . .

. . . *and his mind was a madhouse, he hated to admit it but it was the fucking truth and had been for quite some time, this early in the morning it was a wonder that he could think at all, much less motorvate himself across the floor, and though he knew it was absurd he couldn't shake the idea that she had planned this, she had something up her sleeve, it would have been better if he really had killed her last night, or the night before that, or maybe even a year ago, instead of just beating her around all the time; it would have been better if he'd listened to the voice that never never wanted to stop . . .*

. . . and then he was in the hallway, and it was both better and worse than he had expected. The stretch between front door and back was relatively clear of everything but smoke; but there were licks of orange light in the kitchen, casting inverse shadows.

And the living room wall was lined with flame.

He stood there, indecisive, in the broiling hallway heat. The noise of voices was clearer now, clearly coming from the front. Maybe it was firemen. Maybe it was pigs. He was surprised to hear women's voices, but these days you never knew.

Then the laughter began, and the theme music kicked in, and Dale's vision went as red as the reflections on the wall before him.

It was the fucking TV.

It was the fucking TV, and Dottie was probably passed out in front of it, curled up in the old brown ottoman with her big tits scraping the air, her wide mouth open, and her already useless brain turned to punk wood by smoke inhalation. It made him crazy just thinking about it.

And that was the weird thing. He knew he should be gearing up to save her, to grab her ass up and cart her off to salvation. The good guy side of his brain knew just what to do, rationale complete down to the little tin Good Citizenship medal affixed to his righteously thudding chest.

But there was another voice in his head: one that slid more easily through the codeine and percodan murk. It was the one that could describe, in tiny detail, what her face would look like as it was held down to the flames. Her eyelids would be shut, of course, but he was willing to bet that the balls beneath would start to sizzle something fierce once those little flaps of skin baked away. Her hair would be a bicentennial celebration of colorful sparks by then; and with all the goddam fat in her cheeks, the odds in favor of a unquenchable grease fire were good, very good indeed . . .

. . . and the good guy voice told him to shut up, reminded him of why he hadn't killed her yet or taken out a little frustration on her bitch of a daughter; and that reason was the law and the way it had of taking things into its own long arms. The law could fuck up your life forever. The law could bust right in through the door. All dipshit morality aside, the law was a very good reason to play nicey-nice and just keep smiling.

But the pictures were too clear.

He started thinking about his hands, what would happen to them if he held her down in the flames that long. *Damage*: that was what. Serious damage. Maybe it would be better if he kicked her into the flames; on the other hand, where was the fun in that? You wanted to see. You wanted to feel . . .

There was a half-sane voice in his head, more biology than logic. It moved him forward, along the wall that was not burning. It moved him to the lip of the living room, bid his head poke around the corner and survey the scene.

It could not believe what it bade his eyes see.

Because she was not frying in the ottoman, though the ottoman was burning up a storm. She wasn't even fucking asleep. She was just *standing* there, by the open front door, with nothing but screen door separating her from the great outdoors. In her left hand, she clenched her pocketbook tightly.

In her right hand, she held his gun . . .

. . . and they hadn't come, they still hadn't come, nearly fifteen minutes later and still the Channel 8 news team had yet to appear. She had run the three blocks back from Jim & Nina's, hastily checked to see that Dale was still out of it, and then doused strategic portions of the house with lighter fluid. The first match had been the hardest to light, but once things got going, it was hard to stop.

Which was why the place was now getting hotter than hell.

Which was why she wished they would please God hurry.

She didn't hear the footsteps behind her until it was far too late. Between the crackle of flame and the laugh of Oprah Winfrey, she didn't have a chance. The grip on the gun barrel had twirled her around before she could start to turn on her own.

An illusion of control vanished in an instant.

As her boyfriend began to scream. . .

. . . and then he was hitting her, backhanded slaps to the face, the way he usually started. She fell back against the door, and it started to open, and before he could catch her she had hit the concrete step outside, her purse flying off into the yard. She made a bad sound in landing, and her eyes unfocused, but it did not occur to him that she might not be able to hear what he had to say next.

"WHAT THE FUCK IS THE MATTER WITH YOU!" he bellowed. He bent over her, and the hand holding the gun came back across her lips, moving fast. He felt something give, and marveled at the sensation: he had never taken out teeth before, or made flesh tear to quite that extent. She coughed, and the blood sprayed back at him; he caught it on his tongue, and the taste wasn't bad.

"YOU HEARD ME, YOU COW!" he screamed again, and her eyes seemed to struggle toward focus. He was smiling now, he couldn't help it, he had gone too far and there was no question of turning back, so he abandoned himself to the will of the voice, the voice that did not want to stop, the voice that said *now, baby, now* . . .

. . . as the van pulled up to the curb and made its screeching halt. Dottie saw it upside-down, a vision that fought its way through the blankness. She saw the words *CHANNEL 8* stenciled across its side, saw the two figures scurrying out the doors, saw the video camera that one of them hoisted to its shoulder . . .

. . . and she realized that this was it, except that maybe it wasn't, the gun was no longer in her hand and she was choking on something hard and sharp, and the part of her brain that was not going into unprecedented spasms suffered a sudden and keen sense of loss as she was hoisted upright, and her eyes went back to seeing nothing again . . .

. . . and Dale put two and two together. It did not spell four. It spelled something better. For the first time in too long to count, he thought that maybe Dottie *had* something there, she wasn't just the utterly stupid twat that she'd led him to believe she was. Maybe she'd gotten a glimpse of what it takes to hit the big time after all.

You start a fire. The news team comes.

You die in public.

A star is born.

"This is *great!*" he gushed. "This is fucking perfect! You stupid fucking bitch, you UNDERSTAND!"

It was the chance of a lifetime.

Now it was simply a matter of making it all pay off.

He had dragged her inside, where the flames were mounting. Those pretty old pictures of her still remained. He saw a can of lighter fluid, and the scenario was complete. He let her drop.

Picked up the can.

Spritzed her good.

And kicked her into the flames.

She came up quickly, animate and ablaze. She did a quick spin and collapsed at his feet. He flipped her over with his foot, and her face was on fire; the black hole of her open and screaming mouth was the only thing unlit. "*Wee HAH!*" he enthused. "*Thank* you, baby!"

Then he kicked her sparkling ass out into the yard.

The camera missed nothing within its range. It locked on the crawling, burning body. The door opened again, and the skinny balding crazy man in the white BVDs came staggering out of the house, waving a gun, yelling something that the mike couldn't quite pick up. The gun was aimed and fired; a red explosion cascaded down from the flaming belly.

Still the body continued to crawl, close enough now to distinguish as a woman. It reached out its hand to the camera lens, stretching fingers of fire from ten yards away. Then the man fired again, and its head came apart in black smoking chunks.

The camera's perspective began to back away, its operator's voice drowning omigod, omigod. Too late. The man was running now, eyes huge and smiling triumphantly as he screamed, "OH NO YA DON'T! MY NAME IS DALE SNYDER, AND I'M A FUCKING STAR . . . !"

Then the man began to sing, aiming his gun at the camera. When the camera moved, he fired again.

MARK AS EXHIBIT D

Two things:

When the pain was gone, the angel was waiting on the other side. It patted her on her little head and said *it's okay, Dottie. You made a couple of wrong turns, but I still love you.*

Then it sent her back to do it again.

Until she got it right.

And meanwhile, back in Hell, there was a film at eleven: substantially edited down, of course.

For the sake of the children.

And the meek in spirit.

Red

Richard Christian
Matheson

He's probably heard this so many times that he's sick of it, but here goes anyway.

Richard Christian Matheson is a prolific, drop-dead handsome guy whose father is the legendary master of print, screen, and television, Richard Matheson.

There. Now that *that*'s out of the way, let's see what Ellen Datlow, fiction editor of *Omni Magazine*, has to say about R. C.: "Richard Christian Matheson's prose is elegant, yet spare. He is undoubtedly the master of the contemporary horror short-short story. His potent, subtle horror sneaks up on the reader and its echoes linger long after the story has ended."

Very true . . . but Datlow failed to mention that R. C. is *also* one of the most talented writers/producers working in Hollywood today.

Matheson has written and/or produced more than three hundred episodes for such American television programs as "Simon and Simon," "The Incredible Hulk," and "Amazing Stories" (he went on to become either head writer, executive story consultant, and/or producer on over twenty other prime-time series, including "Quincy," "Hunter," "Stingray," and "A-Team"). But wait—there's more. Besides his television work, R. C. has created and seen filmed a number of theatrical scripts for the likes of Steven Spielberg (*Three O'clock High*), so it's clearly evident that he will someday become a major player within the motion-picture industry as well.

And yet, with this crushing work load, Matheson still manages to produce a steady stream of short, punchy fiction, exemplary works of contemporary horror that consistently appear in both the amateur and mainstream press.

When, I ask you, does he sleep?

For all his credits, R. C. is perhaps best known to the horror community for his short-short stories, a number of which clearly reflect splatterpunk values. These tiny gems are skillfully written in a condensed style that has not really been successfully attempted since the 1950s and 1960s heyday of Fredric Brown (another short-short genius who, in the 1954 classic "Answer," has a character ask a newly developed supercomputer if there's a God; the computer answers, "There is now").

Not that Matheson is a splatterpunk. His close friendship with a number of the leading splat writers (including David J. Schow) probably led to a mistaken identification with the splatterpunks early on. But now R. C. is quite clear in stating that he's not a member of The Splat Pack. Still, he continues to produce splatterpunk-like works, including "Goosebumps," "Where There's a Will" (cowritten with his father), and "Red."

Those fortunate enough to have met R. C. in the flesh know him to be a kind, genuinely gentle man. Those emotions are reflected in "Red"—but don't confuse sensitivity with sentimentality. For while "Red" is probably the least explicit, most subtle story in this book, the end result is like a timebomb going off inside your head.

He kept walking.

The day was hot and miserable and he wiped his forehead. Up another twenty feet, he could make out more. Thank God. Maybe he'd end it all. He picked up the pace and his breathing got thick. He struggled on, remembering his vow to himself to go through with this, not to stop until he was done. Maybe it had been a mistake to ask this favor. But it was the only way he could think of to work it out. Still, maybe it had been a mistake.

He felt an edge to his stomach as he stopped and leaned down to what was at his feet. He grimaced, lifted it into the large canvas bag he carried, wiped his hands, and moved on. The added weight in the bag promised more, and he somehow felt better. He had found most of what he was looking for in the first mile. Only a half mile more to go, to convince himself; to be sure.

To not go insane.

It was a nightmare for him to realize how far he'd gone this morning with no suspicion, no clue. He held the bag more tightly and walked on. Ahead, the forms who waited got bigger; closer. They stood with arms crossed, people gathered and complaining behind them. They would have to wait.

He saw something a few yards up, swallowed, and walked

closer. It was everywhere and he shut his eyes, trying not to see how it must have been. But he saw it all. Heard it in his head. The sounds were horrible and he couldn't make them go away. Nothing would go away, until he had everything, he was certain of that. Then his mind would at last have some chance to find a place of comfort. To go on.

He bent down and picked up what he could, then walked on, scanning ahead. The sun was beating down and he felt his shirt soaking with sweat under the arms and on his back. He was nearing the forms who waited when he stopped, seeing something halfway between himself and them. It had lost its shape, but he knew what it was and couldn't step any closer. He placed the bag down and slowly sat crosslegged on the baking ground, staring. His body began to shake.

A somber-looking man walked to him and carefully picked up the object, placing it in the canvas bag and cinching the top. He gently coaxed the weeping man to stand and the man nodded through tears. Together, they walked toward the others, who were glancing at watches and losing patience.

"But I'm not finished," the man cried. His voice broke and his eyes grew hot and puffy. "Please . . . I'll go crazy . . . just a little longer?"

The somber-looking man hated what was happening. He made the decision. "I'm sorry, sir. Headquarters said I could only give you the half hour you asked for. That's all I can do. It's a very busy road."

The man tried to struggle away but was held more tightly. He began to scream and plead.

Two middle-aged women who were waiting watched uncomfortably.

"Whoever allowed this should be reported," said one, shaking her head critically. "The poor man is ready to have a nervous breakdown. It's cruel."

The other said she'd heard they felt awful for the man, whose little girl had grabbed on to the back bumper of his car when he'd left for work that morning. The girl had gotten caught and he'd never known.

They watched the officer approaching with the crying man whom he helped into the hot squad car. Then the officer grabbed the canvas bag, and as it began to drip red onto the blacktop, he gently placed it into the trunk beside the mangled tricycle.

The backed-up traffic began to honk, and traffic was waved on as the man was driven away.

A Life in the Cinema

Mick Garris

Mick Garris's "A Life in the Cinema" first appeared in *Silver Scream*, a seminal collection of movie-oriented stories edited by David J. Schow.

Schow's choice of Garris was particularly relevant. Better yet, it was typecasting; not only did Mick give Schow his *Silver Scream* manuscript during a preview screening of *Hellraiser*, but, like the title of his story, Garris's life *is* the cinema.

When I first met Mick in 1980, he was working for Avco-Embassy (Joseph E. Levine's old company, now defunct) on David Cronenberg's *Scanners*. We became friendly; Garris subsequently moved to Universal, where he was directly responsible for that company's hiring me to promote their first *Conan* picture (leading to my occasional practice of publicizing films at horror/comic book/science fiction conventions; it's belated, but thanks, Mick).

Garris then soon found himself working for the likes of Steven Spielberg on *The Goonies* and John Landis for the videocassette-only release of *Coming Soon*, a compendium of Universal horror–science fiction trailers. Around this time Mick also appeared, with his wife Cynthia, as a Rick Baker–created zombie in Michael Jackson's *Thriller* video.

Unfortunately, just when Garris became first-season story editor for "Amazing Stories," Spielberg's TV anthology, we somehow drifted apart. Not for any particular reason, either; sometimes these things just happen. In any event, this was bad timing on my part, because I wasn't around later to congratulate him on an even more successful career.

Mick Garris is now a bona fide member of the Hollywood film community. He's directed *Critters 2* (1988), wrote the initial screenplay for *The Fly II*, and is currently directing *Psycho IV*. He's also expanding his fictional career; Mick's short story "Joy" was recently published in the Spring 1990 issue of *Midnight Graffiti*. Upcoming projects include the film *Red Sleep*, based on a screenplay cowritten by Garris and Richard Christian Matheson, one to be directed by John Landis.

All by way of saying that with his background of hard-won film experience, you can believe the frantic environment Mick portrays in "A Life in the Cinema." Here's a tale of special effects, desperate deal making, and a shit-eating mutant baby that goes way beyond what you might expect from someone who named his company Nice Guy Productions.

But with that self-same infant, Garris has invented a potent symbol for the self-degradation lurking just beneath the bright, shining surface of the Hollywood Dream Machine.

Not to mention the monsters that go with the territory.

The Mexican woman's freak baby might have been the worst thing ever to happen to her, but it could have been the best thing in the world to ever happen to me.

I'd much rather show it than tell it, but that's just not the way things work out in this town. You hear all that shit about only being as good as your last picture, and all those other hoary old saws about the Industry-with-a-capital-I, but that's ancient Hollywood masturbatory storytelling. If you're smart, you get your next picture set up before the last one comes out. You're as good as your last *two*.

I guess.

It started with film school. We didn't have the kind of money you need to go to USC and use all that stuff Steven and George bought for them, but I did get a scholarship at UCLA. So you make do, right?

It was *great*! I mean, just imagine having all that equipment to use for nothing! Sure, most of the study work had to be done on video, but the thesis was always shot on film, with sync sound, even optical titles. I shot mine in 35mm 'scope and Dolby stereo.

One good thing about UCLA is the agent connection. You make a good film or write a good script, and every door in Century City suddenly opens up to you. It's like dogs smelling a bitch in heat. Make a short film on your own, and even if it's *Raiders of the Lost Ark*, nobody's ever going to see it unless it comes from film school.

So that's what happened. It took me a year and a half to finish *Words Without Voices*, but it was worth it. I badgered my way into incredible locations, built weird, wonderful sets that represented every dreamscape you could imagine (and many you couldn't, I'm sure), got a full orchestral original score, and made my 24-minute epic.

If you know lighting, manipulation, composition, and you throw away the zoom lens, directing's easy.

After copyrighting the film in *my* name, and not the school's (they weren't going to make money off of my talent), I submitted it to film festivals around the world, and started collecting ribbons. First place at AFI Fest, first place at USA Film Festival, honorable mention in Seattle (fuck 'em. Who cares about Seattle?).

And then, you learn about taking meetings. I got calls from ICM, William Morris, CAA, Triad, the whole catalogue. The hungry young guys have the most hustle, but the old Jewish farts have the connections and the clients. Maybe you wouldn't want to eat with them, but they know how to get a deal greenlighted. I learned quick that it's the agent, not the agency, that makes the difference. The old guys are never too eager to take on the new clients, but some of them can be convinced. Eventually.

All of them wanted me to leave a cassette of my film—can you imagine that? I shot it in Panavision, spent weeks on the stereo mix, and they're going to glance at it through phone calls on a nineteen-inch screen. *I* know these lazy bastards all have screening rooms, so I insisted that they run the film in 35. I was nice about it and everything, but very persistent, so they'd know they were dealing with an artist.

Well, I got the pick of the litter. I made a couple of mistakes, first, like everybody does. One of these ten-percenters got real excited about getting me a "Miami Vice" meeting; as if I would even consider television drek. Another one thought getting me a sequel would speed things up. Right. Do *Police Academy* 7 and Hollywood spreads its legs. Then, who knows? Maybe *Hardbodies* 4!

So finally, old Rosen at CAA and I reach an understanding. I mean, you don't want to watch this toothless clown take meals, but he knows how to throw his ninety-eight pounds around. We don't want to make development deals, he says, we want to make *movies*. No TV, no cable. Theatrical features only. *My* scripts, no options. Pay *and* play.

It's good cop/bad cop time. I'm taking meetings in high-altitude offices on every lot, with Sean and Mike and Len and Jeffrey and all the big boys, discovering how easy all of this can be. Thank God for film school. These guys love to talk about how there's such a void left by Preston Sturges and Alfred Hitchcock and how there's never been an American equivalent to *The Bicycle Thief*, and all that other dinosaur shit I flunked in Film History 101. And then I talk Carpenter, Dante, Hooper, and my gods. They like that, but only if you talk *Poltergeist* and not *Lifeforce*, *Halloween* and not *The Thing*. The supreme measure of art is box office.

So I pitch them my movies, and listen to their reactions. They give me their "thoughts," and I get all excited about some of their ideas, as though they just made my story better than I ever could have alone. Then I hang back and consider their "notes" a few moments, before telling them why those ideas don't work. They get a feeling of give and take, that I'm willing to listen to their suggestions, and yet that I'm strong enough to defend my own ideas. They like me.

My job is to charm them, then Rosen gets to be the asshole. But that's okay, he's used to that. He *likes* that. He wheels and deals, gets the studios fighting over me, the price goes into the stratosphere, and I get to make my movie in Burbank.

Now there's an experience. At UCLA, you've got everybody and his grandmother thrilled to death to be a part of a movie (tell them it'll be on cable and you can hose any of the women who took their clothes off for free on camera). Everybody works twenty hours a day, just for the sake of making your movie. Commitment, creativity, drive: everybody wants to help out.

But the studio experience is something else again. First, there's the unions; you've never seen so many people to do so few things. You kick out a plug, a union electrician has to plug it in. You're just about to shoot the crucial shot you and the cameraman (excuse me—*cinematographer*) have been setting up for the last three hours, and the assistant director calls lunch. Of course, everybody dicks around when they get there, so you can't start on time, but there is no going over, or you're into triple golden time.

And then there's the twenty-seven teamster drivers who are assigned to the show, sitting on their asses in their air-conditioned station wagons, waiting around at $2,500 a week in case somebody needs a Diet Dr. Pepper at the Company Store.

But that's the least of it. That shit I can understand. These guys make a living, they do their work, and they get paid. The

Suits are worse. I mean, I wear a tie on the set; when you can still get into Disneyland on a Junior ticket, and shaving is an exercise in wishful thinking, you do anything you can to direct from a position of power. But these fuckers in their Armanis with their cigars and soft voices are the reason why all the movies you see are shit. Okay, here's how they think. What's "good" mean to you. Quality? Great. You and I think alike. But "good" to these guys is "familiar." Good is somebody else's hit. God forbid you make something unique, with an original vision. No, they want the "heart" of *E.T.*, the "visual kineticism" of *Star Wars*, the "pacing" of *Beverly Hills Cop*, the "gloss" of *Top Gun*, shit like that. All they know how to sell is what they know how to sell. And that, not very well.

So once we're in preproduction, there are the fights. They want storyboards, and I don't work with storyboards. We hire a storyboard artist to keep them happy, knowing full well I'm never going to look at the fucking little cartoons once I'm on the set.

Then there's casting. Oh, God, you wouldn't believe the names they want in my movie. If it were up to me—believe me, it wasn't—I'd cast all unknowns. I want you to see the characters I've created, not famous actors in the roles. But no. I write the scientist role patterned on an old high school biology teacher of mine, and they want Tom Cruise. Tom fucking Cruise to play a biogeneticist! For the social worker they can get Kelly LeBrock . . . but they'd have to give her husband executive producer credit. Ultimately, it doesn't matter who I want, because with money and schedule and billing and studio problems, nobody is available anyway. At least not until you get down to the bottom of the list. Dreg city.

And then, of course, there is the wonderfully creative hand of Mr. Flotsam, our esteemed producer. He "developed" this "package," and his involvement is primarily to bring in Tangerine Dream for the music, and he gets a presentation credit for that. For that he should get a black eye! This film demands a full orchestra, and I get three fucking synthesizer programmers who can't even speak English.

Somehow, we get into production. Once the train starts, there is no stopping it. ILM is already shooting plates for the effects shots, the dailies are coming in, the Suits are bitching about diffusion and coverage and boom shadows. They haven't the slightest idea how a movie is made. All I can say is Trust Me. I know what I'm doing. You're going to love it when it's cut. Of course, that's not enough for them. They're insisting on more coverage at the same time they're bitching about going over schedule and budget. And this isn't *Howard the Duck* or *Ishtar*—this is just a lousy ten million bucks they're talking about!

Okay, I admit I can be a bit tyrannical on the set. But do you blame me? My name is on the line. Written and directed by. Me. Nobody notices the accountant's name. Nobody cares about editor, or *cinematographer*, or the atmosphere, or matte artist. Nobody gives fuck one about costume design. So, yeah. If it's going to get done, it's going to get done right . . . even if it means a little more time and money. What are they going to do, fire me and replace me, twenty days in on a thirty-five day shoot?

So maybe a couple of *thespians* cried . . . it's the performance that counts, not how you get it. The only thing anybody can judge is what's on the screen. And actors! They'll do *anything*! Unless they're "names," of course. Then the fucking prima donnas won't even give you so much as a little nipple.

You've never seen a less cooperative group of people. I never set out to win a popularity contest; I just wanted to make my film.

So we made it. It wasn't that much over budget; I mean, it wasn't *Heaven's Gate,* or anything like that. So they sneaked my cut, like the Director's Guild requires. The preview cards were okay—not as good as we hoped, but okay. And it wasn't made for the carbohydrate crowd anyway. This is a sophisticated film, and they preview it for the horny-handed machinists and their toothless girlfriends in Long Beach. Brilliant. So the studio, of course, recut it and completely fucked the whole thing up, and tested their abortion in San Diego—my hometown! Thanks, guys. Somehow the trades found out about the San Diego sneak, and they crucified us. I mean slit us up the middle and yanked out the entrails. Those guys like nothing more than shitting on an artist. If they know so much about making movies, let them try it! Fuck critics. If you ever met a critic, you wouldn't want to eat with him, either.

So much for flavor of the month. It plays the art house graveyard in four major markets, no TV support, no radio, just some print ads in the hip weekly papers that nobody pays for anyway. It plays in the 50-seat house at the Herpes Cineplex, and even Rosen doesn't answer my calls anymore. My one solace is that it killed Annamarie Longines's career in features. She got a sitcom last season, but it was gone after three weeks. They put it up against Cosby. I gloated.

Okay, so the Brothers Warner (or, at least, their corporate equivalent) give me the boot. So what? There's six or seven other majors. Yeah, right, except that with the executive circle jerk that goes on, the VP assigned to your picture will be at Universal next week; his girlfriend is being hosed by an exec at Columbia who's now at Tri-Star until his father-in-law makes him exec VP at Disney to keep him from telling about the episode in the private jet with the male lead in their new picture.

So the old gray fag gets protection, and I get a chainsaw right in the career.

CAA dumped me, the development deals undeveloped, and before I know it, I'm sniffing around New World, Atlantic, New Line, and the other independents. I'm hosing this 43-year-old Jewish American Princess agent who wants me to call her Mama. You should see the claw marks on my back. She's got an office with no secretary in Pacoima or some god-awful place in the Valley, but the phone never rings. Never. She's hardly worth spilling my precious bodily fluids over. Or your time. Sorry.

She calls in a few favors, getting me meetings with Rehme and Corman and the other guys. I go in, tie and all, and it's inevitably the same song: "I'm sorry, Mr. Corman was called out of town at the last minute. But he personally asked Mr. Third-string Pimpleface Nobody to hear your pitch."

Needless to say, my pitches were never home runs. The galling thing is that these guys are constantly hiring first-time directors—guys who've only made videos of their kids' birthday parties before they wind up getting ten grand to do these veg-o-matic killer thrillers that gross 67 million. I've done a studio picture, for Christ's sake, and get the bottom rung shoved up my ass.

By now my beach condo had flown to repossessionland. Ditto my 941. I met Rebecca in a corridor at DEG; I think we were both thinking of fucking the same producer. Her dream was jumping from soaps to features; personally, I thught she only made widescreen by doing hard-core, but who am I to say so? Shacking up in Rebecca's West Hollywood apartment meant that I could dump Mama as a fuckmate, but keep her on the string as an agent.

Rebecca also had a car.

By now, I'm starting to think TV sitcom work ain't so bad. The door has slammed in my face so hard that "Charles in Charge" starts to seem pretty goddamn funny.

I had to get out, go somewhere, anywhere. Get away from the TV.

Rebecca was out on an interview, so I jumped the bus downtown. It's not what you think. Downtown LA has no orange trees, no limos or movie stars, nothing you'd ever want to send pictures of to Mom. Just corporate highrises, and a crumbling, decaying but lively city center, virtually 100% Latino: street vendors hustling in Spanish, salsa blasting from cheap, torn speakers, outlet stores, huge, fantastic old movie palaces now dowdy and rotting, showing three Spanish-language hits for two bucks, 24 hours a day. It's much more like Mexico City than the center of an American metropolis.

All I can do is wander and watch, chewing churros as the cops make the winos perambulate along. Gulping fresh Mexican juice from the vendors while a pimp opens his whore's face in a piss-scented doorway. I like it here; the street's like a 360-degree Sensurround movie.

One of the things I like best is the collapsible green magazine rack on every corner. They're filled with weird Mexican adult comic books, bosomy romance pulps, and unbelievably bloody wrestling magazines—really great stuff. They cost next to nothing . . . and are worth every centavo. Even if you don't speak Spanish, like me.

But this time I found more than masked wrestlers in bondage.

The old woman minding the stand had a basket in the shade, which she kept rocking with her foot. I saw the blanket in the basket squirm; she noticed me looking, and moved in front of it.

"*Muchacho?*" I asked, because I had nothing else to say.

"*Muchacha.*"

Like it really mattered if it was a boy or a girl. A baby's a baby, right? They all look like Alfred Hitchcock, anyway.

Then the kid started to cry, this weird, soft mewling sort of sound. I sneaked a peek over the Santo magazine. The crying got louder, but the old lady wouldn't move. She just kept watching me like she was mad at me or something. I can't help it; I watch stuff. All the time. I guess I'm nosy . . . but show me a filmmaker who isn't a voyeur, and I'll show you a TV hack.

The kid's catlike bellow was a primal screech by now, and even the old lady could no longer pretend to ignore it. She picks up the baby and lifts her blouse to release a stretched, hanging blob of a tit. She carefully lifts the edge of the baby blanket, and springs a leaking, incredibly long and erect nipple into the begging mouth.

She turns to see me watching her, and our eyes lock. I can't look away, and her grim face defies my stare.

Finally, the infant has taken its fill, and releases its hold on her breast. The leaking prong of her nipple springs up, and is quickly tucked away, after splashing drops of lactose on the baby's face.

As she wiped its face, I caught my first glance of it.

This was no child. I didn't know what it was, but it was nothing I'd seen before. It was slippery looking, completely hairless, with dark, rubbery skin. It looked more like a human than any other kind of animal, but just barely. It seemed like it had been burned or something, except that its skin was wet, oily. It had lips like a fish, large and gasping, breathing like a rich fat man puffs on a Havana, wet and floppy.

I tried to get a better look, but she kept shielding it from me, covering it with the blanket and blocking it from view with her girth. I tried to wear as much sympathy as I could get on my face, a mask of soft, gentle caring. I had to see this kid more closely.

Talk was useless; she couldn't speak English, and Spanish is Greek to me. But I reached out with Allstate-sized helping hands to touch the baby. She was hesitant and defensive, but when she saw I had no intention of hurting or making fun of the thing, she let me lift the blanket, still watching my face the whole time.

Close up, with time to really see it, this freak baby was incredible. I knew immediately that I was back in business. And if you judge this thing the way you do a real baby, it *was* a girl. I had Rebecca's rent money in an envelope in my back pocket, and gave it to the old woman. I'm not sure why. I guess I just had to touch it. This thing would make the most incredible story ever; it all rushed through my mind in the time it took for the lights to flash around the marquee of the Million Dollar Theatre: all the words that had been shoved down my throat from the critics and the development meetings.

Heart. Story. Character. All that shit.

I just wanted to hold the thing, feel its reality, touch it. But I didn't just want to do some latex life story. *Words Without Voices* had soured me on special effects. This thing was *real*, and *that*'s what I had to show the world. No state-of-the-art Rob Bottin special effect could ever hope to compete with the beating-

heart, coursing-blood reality of this slippery, shifting-irised creature squirming in the blanket in my hands.

This baby was my movie.

I couldn't tell how old it was; how do you judge the age of
something you've never seen before? It couldn't have been more
than a couple months. When it realized that somebody new was
holding it, its eyes locked onto mine, and we were both transfixed.
The muddy irises seemed to swirl like whirlpools, clearing and
changing to blue, then becoming so clear that I swear I could see
the brain behind them. I could feel its heartbeat rippling through
my hands as I stared into its cortex, distantly hearing it mewl,
and seeing music deep within. Not like musical notes, but actually
seeing the music itself. I don't know how else to explain it, except
to compare it to the acid trips my stepfather always talks about.

This kind of eye contact seemed to tire the kid out, and the
huge eyes filled with dead brown mud again, then slowly drifted
closed. When I looked up, Mamacita was vamoosed.

Not that I minded. She had a chance to dump the freak, and
jumped at it. If I had to sell year-old wrestling magazines to
farmworkers on a streetcorner, I'd probably have done the same
thing.

But I lucked out. I had this incredible treasure in my hands;
I would get another chance to thrill the world. And a month's
rent for Rebecca's West Hollywood digs would pay for the old
bitch's flop for five years. Later I would realize that she got the
better end of the deal.

Rebecca was freaked but fascinated by the little slug in the
bassinette in the kitchen. I decided to leave the details out of the
story until later—especially the part about the rent money. I'd
deal with that when the Arab came around asking for it.

"You said you always wanted a baby," I told her. She was not
amused. But I knew how to handle her. She wouldn't have any
trouble dealing with the freak if she knew she'd get at least a
featured role in the picture at scale-plus-ten. We quickly discovered how simple the care and feeding of the little monster
was; it sucked on anything and everything that found its way
into its disgusting little smacking lips. Once Rebecca was leaning
over it to get a good look, and the little sucker went for her breast
right through the shirt. I tried to joke her into suckling it, but
her sense of humor has its limits.

I named it Asta.

I gave Mama in Pacoima the heave-ho, and set about scaling

every bridge I ever burned. I bullied, badgered, and blackmailed my way into meetings everywhere in town, from the sleaziest Troma to the most musclebound Paramount. At first it was always the third-stringers, like before; the studios are cautious. You can get the meetings; they don't want to close the door on anybody who might make a hit movie for somebody else, and not be able to get them back. The guy who flops with *THX 1138* at Warners might go on to do *Star Wars* at Fox. The door is shut, but not locked.

Anyway, I've got meetings with sons of mucky-mucks at *other* studios, and we talk "Heart" and "Story" and "Character," and we shoot box office shit, and then I bring up The Idea. It's always the same reaction: "Yeah, but it's been done. The unfortunate baby is really more a Movie-of-the-Week, don't you think? But I'd be glad to put you in touch with our TV people." And that's supposed to signal the end of the meeting.

I won't let go. We talk *Elephant Man* and *Mask* and *E.T.* and all that other heartfelt mutant crap, and my eyes go misty and caring and gentle. They start to get uncomfortable. I tell them how The Idea could be done so cheaply, and how much I learned by the last experience. Then I shrug like it's obviously brick wall time, and I say thank you, and walk out like a broken man. But they can't see my smile.

Before the door closes all the way, I pretend to spot the box I have sitting in the reception area, like I forgot about it. And before Mr. Pimple can finish punching up his next phone call, I scoop it up and swing around to face him, with Asta in my arms under a Smurf baby blanket. "Oh, by the way . . . you want to see it?"

Of course he's too busy, and he has no idea that what I'm talking about is real, and he wants me the hell out of his office. Fruitless meetings never end. So I don't give him a chance to answer. I rush up, put the thing under his nose, and pull back the Smurf.

The guy shits his pants. He wants to know if the guys who did *Nightmare on Elm Street Part 3* made it, and I have to say over and over, no, it's real.

They don't believe me. I hold it closer, so close they can smell the acrid urine-stink that seeps from its skin, and invite them to touch her. Every single one I ever asked has declined.

It's amazing how quickly I get access to the ladder. I meet Sonny's boss, then her boss, then his boss, then his boss, and finally it's the rarefied penthouse office of Daddy himself.

At this point, Rosen's calling me back; he's caught wind of the tarbaby story, and he wants to break some backs at the majors. I don't blame the guy for dropping me; after all, I was poison. And Rosen doesn't give a shit about relationships or being my pal. He's a businessman. Right. He yanks mine and I squeeze his, and we both come dollars. He knows I know he can negotiate the hell out of my deals, so I give him the nod. It's old home week, and he's got the studios beating each other up for the baby story.

Praise Jesus.

We set the deal up in Culver City. I'm writer, producer, and director; no presentation credit, but I'm not crying. We want to keep the budget low, shoot in some right-to-work state in the South, and I finally get to cast my talented unknowns, and throw Rebecca a three-line bone. Now that I'm producing, I can see the wisdom of keeping costs low, so that it's tougher for the studio to hide the profits if the film does business. We're talking a below-the-line of maybe three-point-five. And most of the above-the-line is me.

I decided early not to allow the cast and crew to see the kid until we actually shot the birth scene. I knew the reality of their reactions would make the scene really sing. I couldn't wait.

Everybody loved the script: even the Heart and Story and Characters. But wait until they saw Pee Wee. I was worried that during three or four months of preproduction, Asta might grow out of her weirdness. The freakishness might just be a stage. I held my breath every morning before checking under that Smurf blanket. But the thing wasn't changing at all.

In truth, I *did* learn a lot from the Warners experience. I'm prepared this time, I become the cast and crew's best pal, actually let them make suggestions, and pretend to consider them for a moment before I turn them down to do it my way. They like that.

Everything is going fine. We've run a day or two over schedule, but stay under budget, so the Suits are happy. They like the dailies, love the coverage and what we call the Look of Show.

I couldn't be happier. During breaks, I'm rocking my Winnebago with Cindy, my superstar discovery, chewing her implants and filling her with my goo. But the headier foreplay is thinking about the birth scene, scheduled for the Monday of week four.

Everybody's asking to see the puppet, who made the baby, when are we going to see the poor little thing. I just smile, playing the wise man with the secret.

B Day.

Crew call is 7 A.M., and I get there an hour early. Asta's been a little fussy, but seems okay. She's comfortable and well fed; I've got her in a basket that once held Snookie's Cookies.

Everybody's excited about the big scene. We'll be shooting Asta for the next three weeks, but this is her debut. I want to shoot the freak in continuity, just in case it changes at all during production. The locations that feature it are limited, so it's easy to shoot those scenes in order.

So we've got Cindy Starlet's belly as padded as Dr. Ellenbogen stuffed her breasts, and she's on her back, hyping up. For authenticity's sake she has been taking Lamaze classes at the clinic. Whatever works.

Rebecca's in the corner studying her line, looking sexy in her nurse outfit. She has no idea about me and Cindy, not that it matters if she did. I can afford my own place now.

Vilmos has just about finished lighting. I rush off and bring in the basket from my Winnie, and keep it hidden from view as I move onto my mark. I'm doing my cameo as the doctor who delivers the thing, so I'm in total control. I even gave myself a crucial close-up.

I'm mildly surprised to see that Cindy isn't wearing anything under the hospital gown. She winks, knowing I'm the only one in a position to know, and I give her little curls a tickle. She tries not to react in front of the others.

Then I bring Asta up onto the table, covered in her little blanket. Still, nobody but me has seen the thing, and my heart is pounding through the stethoscope hanging from my ears.

I place the baby thing between Cindy's legs (I like putting things between Cindy's legs). I'm the only one who can see Asta, and I enjoy watching it move wetly up against Cindy's private parts. Cindy tries not to react to the rippling wet pressure. Then, the inquisitive little beggar's lips seek out something that resembles a nipple down there, and starts to suckle.

"Quiet! Rolling!" Cindy can scarcely breathe . . . but she isn't about to blow the shot.

"Speed!" I can't believe what only I can see, but manage to stifle my laughter, and gently try to move it away from Cindy's happy button. I guess I'm sensitive that way.

"Slate it!"

"Settle! Okay, Cindy . . . Action!"

And the camera makes its slow, relentless push in to the table. Cindy and I have spray sweat on our brows; I notice Rebecca watching me sneak a private grope under Cindy's sheet. But she won't bitch while the camera is rolling. It's perfect. Drama, tension, Cindy really making me believe she's delivering a difficult baby. Maybe this method shit isn't so bad; she was probably really dilating under there.

The camera is almost on top of us now, she's spasming with pain, and I'm struggling heroically to save the baby. Special effects releases the wash of fluid from hoses run through the table, and I lift Asta from between Cindy's thighs, holding the thing up in the blue light directly in front of the camera.

Asta played it beautifully, letting loose with that long, weak tremolo, spooking everyone on the stage into bug-eyed silence. I kept it rolling for a full two extra minutes, and when I finally yelled "Cut!" cast and crew alike burst into spontaneous applause. I bowed, holding the thing up in front of them, and Hollywood welcomed me home.

When I was sure that there was no camera bobble or sound problem, there was no way I was going to tempt fate. The take was perfect, and we wouldn't do another for Prudential.

I cleared the gawkers away, and set up for the closeup. Asta was no trouble at all under the lights. It just lay there, as if waiting for direction. Vilmos asked me if I wanted to use a doll for a stand-in to set the lights, and like a supreme dick, I said no. No doll is going to have the same reflective qualities of this kid's weird flesh. And it didn't seem to mind, anyway.

Well, I don't know how the word got out so quick, but Welfare showed up on the set before we even ran through the close-up. They were furious, screaming child abuse. There's some law about not being able to have an infant under stage lights for more than thirty seconds, and there must be a state welfare worker and a nurse and a teacher present at all times, or some shit like that.

I tell them there's no child here, that it's special effects. Or an animal. They want to know where the wrangler is. Right. Freak wrangler. By then, we're all yelling, so the A.D. calls a break, and everybody else is glad to sneak away.

While the Welfare bitch and I are getting close to fisticuffs, the second A.D. gently taps my shoulder. What he whispers makes the whole argument moot. After biting his head off for butting in, I push him aside and rush over to the now-dark delivery table, where Asta is lying. I try to stand in the way, but the bitch in the gray suit is right behind me, wanting to see.

I let her.

Because the little freak wasn't moving, or breathing, or eating, or smelling, or fucking *living*.

Inside my head, there were fireworks, suicide, guns, and cacophony. But I stood stock still, my face a blank, vapid wall of I-told-you-so. While the woman was trying to puzzle out the rapidly rubberizing little torso on the table, I slowly turned to look her in the eye, and using all my power, said softly, "Is this really something that concerns you?"

We both turned to see what it was not: a glass-eyed, latex-skinned dummy prop. I remember being astonished at how phony it looked with its lights out; devoid of life it looked like a castoff from *Ghoulies* or something.

"There's your baby," I gloated, and she split, pissed off, even disappointed.

I called a wrap, and while everybody started to get ready for the next day's shoot, I took the little body and retired to the Winnebago. Cindy was waiting for me, looking all smiley and coquettish about the secret gumming she got under the sheet. I threw her out. She looked all upset and hurt, but fuck her. This was the end of my career.

I locked the door, and sat the little creep on the table and stared at it. The thing now looked ridiculously fake, its skin drying and looking like inner tube rubber—even down to the white dust of powder. The eyes were sightless, soul-less, clear glass windows to a dark room.

Before I knew it, Rebecca was knocking on the door, but I just ignored her. She gave up quickly; she must not have been as pissed as I thought she would be.

I started yelling at the little pile of shit on the table, backhanding it to the floor. I'm sorry now, but you've got to comprehend the stress I was under. This little fucker was the key to everything I'd worked so long and hard for, and now all that was smoke. Fuck!

Suicide was an alternative, but I'm too much of a coward to pull the trigger, and not enough of a coward not to go quickly. But as I stared into its ugly rubber mug, a simpler choice came to mind. We had the most important shot in the can already. The establishing shot of the monster was there. I could use the whole take. We'd already moved in to a good tight shot anyway, and there was no way the audience wouldn't buy it. Shot properly, maybe one of these effects tyros could help me pull off the rest of the show. Looking at the thing now, with its wick extinguished, the difference between life and latex was obvious . . . but there was no other way out.

We shut down the production for a few weeks while we sent out emergency bids to Stan Winston and Chris Walas and some non-union guys. When I showed them the kid the next day, they all thought it was nice, but a little simplistic in design. They all wanted to know who made it, and why didn't I just use them? I told them I'd made it myself, based on a dream I'd had, but I needed someone who could articulate and manipulate it better than I could. It had to be exactly the same look, I told them, only with more life.

After the bids came in, we went with a local Texas kid who cost us a third of the big boys, and was willing to work thirty-hour days for the honor.

As I was waiting in the screening room to see the birth scene, I held my breath. All the big cheeses were there for the dailies; they knew it was the most important moment in the picture. I had only seen it on the Moviola so far. But it was perfect. Everything in perfect focus, no bobbles, and the kid looked great. Unbelievable. When the Suits all gasped at the reveal, I started to breathe easy. By now, they all assumed that this thing had always been a special effect, anyway, and were almost glad to shut down for a couple weeks to keep the quality up.

All we had to do was hook them with the real baby footage, and they'd buy the rubber surrogate.

I went home that night feeling almost relaxed. New place, no furniture in it yet: just a bed, a hi-fi VCR, and a projection TV. And a wicker basket with Asta in it. Once the latex clone was finished, I promised to give the thing a decent burial out back . . . but only if the rubber one was perfect.

I didn't have to shoot the next day, so I had my own mini-movie-marathon: *It's Alive*, *Rosemary's Baby*, and *Taboo IV*, which put me to sleep, but with a raging erection.

It was an engorgement that would not subside in slumber, but rather kept time with my heartbeat until the door opened late that night. I opened my eyes. Unexpectedly, delightfully, Rebecca and Cindy entered in a shaft of light that penetrated the sparse, diaphanous nightclothes they wore. However unlikely, they seemed the best of friends, and got even friendlier when they joined me in the kip.

Our acrobatics were like a letter to *Penthouse*, and featured every erotic combination you could imagine . . . and six or seven more. It was a release I hadn't felt since preproduction began.

I had a mouth at either end of me, and the two of them brought me to the most devastating, sphincter-clenching orgasm of my life!

But on the second jolt, I woke up, my little friend pumping, my eyes rolled back in abandoned ecstacy.

As the waves of orgasm died down, I gradually resumed consciousness. I opened my eyes for real . . . and almost threw up. That slippery fucking maggot kid from the cookie basket was between my legs, impaled on my divining rod taken so deeply down its throat that I must have fertilized its stomach. The thing was ravenously sucking my milk until I was dry. Its skin was slippery again, oily and alive, as it slid hungrily over my flesh.

Barely conscious at four in the morning, and dazed from the force of the orgasm, I could only stare through slitted, puffy eyes at the monstrosity devouring me. The incredible suction slackened as it sensed there was no more juice to be had, and I weakly backhanded the thing. It didn't even react; gathering my strength in disgust, I hit out with full force, knocking the piece of shit against the wall, where it hit with a splat before sliding stickily and lifelessly down the wall.

I stood up, my head throbbing with every heartbeat, and walked dizzily across the room, following my still-extended wand until I was right over Asta. There was a trail of blood on the wall, as if pointing at the gooey little heap that lay on the floor. Guilt, disgust, and horror welled up in the pit of my stomach, and lurched out of my mouth and onto the dead heap.

First with the stage lights and now, literally, with my own hands, I had killed the thing again.

I jumped into my sweats, and scooped the horrid pile into a plastic bag, then carried it out into the yard. There was no moon, which was fine with me, so I took the mess and buried it deep behind the barbecue pit. Blood-blisters on my hands, I rushed back into the barren house.

I stayed in bed the whole next day, just thinking about the little monster. There was no innocence there. This was no child, no infant. In the months I had been in possession of it, there had been no sign of growth or maturity or change. The thing is what it is, not what it's going to be. What that is, I don't know, but I soon would make an educated guess.

All I know is that day I was as fucked up as I've ever been—my ecstasy had been linked end-to-end with extreme revulsion. I'd been blown by the ghost of a monster baby. Not recommended. And then the fucking toilets backed up. I know that may seem mundane in this perspective, but it has everything to do with it. When I tried to flush, there was merely a gurgle, and I knew at once the damned machine was playing with its food. The lid was lowered and the plumber called.

I forgot about it until I had to go again that afternoon. Ready for relief, I lifted the lid, only to see that fucking squirmer Asta settled in the bowl, basking in dinner. I tried to flush it down to greet the legendary sewer 'gators, but the plumbing just backed up, spewing fouled water onto the bathroom floor.

Again, in anger, humiliation, and disgust, I beat the shit out of it, mangled the tortured little body, and killed it a third time. Big fucking deal. It would be back . . . no matter how often, or distant, or deeply I buried the thing.

The old Mexican woman knew I was her salvation the first time she saw me. I know that now. I must have destroyed the baby two dozen times by now, but it'll keep coming back. To feed.

I can only imagine how long its last host continued to lactate and suckle the parasite that had claimed and controlled her. It's like giving a stray cat a dish of milk—you'll never shake the fucking thing. My lust to own it was the closest thing to love it ever felt, and now we're paired. Mated. For life.

It comes, each day after I kill it, to partake of my body's castoffs—my cells, my essence. It sweats my saliva, lives on my excreta, rejuvenated by my spermatozoa.

God help me if it tastes my blood.

In the months since we shot the birth scene, sleep has been only a distant dream that comes fleetingly. The phone used to ring before I pulled it out, and many people have come to the door and given up trying to find me. Whenever my defenses drop, it comes home to ravage me. I fade into exhausted sleep, knowing I'll wake to find it devouring me, my sex slid deep into its female region, another slippery appendage behind and inside me, taking, not wasting anything, not even tears.

This thing will live as long as I do. Maybe longer.

I had to have the little fucker to exploit. It was the strongest emotion I could feel, and now I'm paying up. I know of one sure way to end the torment. I can't believe I've put it off so long. Asta may be indestructible, but I am not. I have only a single regret.

I know I'll never make another movie.

Less Than Zombie

DOUGLAS E.
WINTER

Douglas E. Winter is a tall, elegant fellow whose eyes start sparking at the merest mention of Dario Argento.

No stranger to the worlds of horror or splatterpunk, Doug's fiction, interviews, and criticism have appeared in such magazines as *Harper's Bazaar* and *Saturday Review* as well as newspapers like the *Washington Post* and the *Philadelphia Inquirer*.

Winter initially drew attention as the first serious critic of Stephen King, and his biographical/critical study *Stephen King: The Art of Darkness* is generally considered the definitive book on that subject. Doug also produced a more broad-based critical survey of the horror field, *Faces of Fear*, has written a dense novella titled "Splatter: A Cautionary Tale" (which mixes censorship, politics, and gore films), and is the editor of the excellent horror anthology *Prime Evil*.

Doug's day job involves the field of jurisprudence (as a lawyer in the firm of Bryan, Cave, McPheeters and McRoberts), but don't let this seeming contradiction fool you. Rumor has it that Winter has litigated airline disasters, and we *know* what ground zero at those tragedies look like. In any event, Douglas E. Winter is a respected fixture on the convention circuit, maintains a rabid affection for splatter films (hence the love of Argento; we occasionally exchange cassettes of our favorite "moist" movies), and stoutly resists the idea of splatterpunk being either a genre or movement. "For that matter," Doug says, "I resist the idea of horror itself being a genre. Horror is an *emotion*."

Doug also resists being thought of as a splatterpunk. In fact, as he wrote in a letter to me, " 'Less Than Zombie' was written as an anti-splatterpunk story, not in the negative sense, but in the sense that I have used the concept of 'Antihorror' as a critique of horror, one which continues the dialogue about the directions that horror should go . . . rather than defining where it's been."

"Antihorror" is Winter's intriguing word for reminding us that the term *horror* itself is a restrictive one; what Antihorror examines and confronts are exactly those conventions to which the horror story has succumbed.

In a story like "Less than Zombie," we are dealt Antihorror with a vengeance. Beyond the obvious parody of Bret Easton Ellis's *Less Than Zero* (and a fine send-up it is, too, with a devilishly bang-on recreation of Ellis's style), "Less Than Zombie" is a sad confirmation of humanity's basic lack of same. The youthful protagonists in Doug Winter's disturbing morality tale crystalize one of splatterpunk's basic contentions: that the old horrors are tired, or irrelevant. The old monsters aren't really that important anymore.

The *real* monsters are us.

People are afraid to live on the streets of Los Angeles. This is the last thing I say before I get back into the car. I don't know why I keep saying this thing. It's something I started and now I can't stop. Nothing else seems to matter. Not the fact that I'm no longer eighteen and the summer is gone and it's raining and the windshield wipers go back and forth, back and forth, and that Skip and DJ and Deb will soon be sitting with me again. Not the blood that splattered the legs of my jeans, which felt kind of hot and tight, as I stood in the alley and watched. Not the stain in the arm of the wrinkled, damp sweater I wear, a sweater that had looked fresh and clean last night. All of this seems meaningless next to that one sentence. It seems easier to hear that people are afraid to live rather than Skip say "This is real" or that song they keep playing on the radio. Nothing else seems to matter but those ten, no, eleven words. Not the rain or the cold wind, which seemed to propel the car down the street and into the alley, or the faded smells of marijuana and sex that still flow through the car. All it comes down to is that the living are dying and the dying are living but that people, whether alive or dead, are still fucking afraid.

It's actually the weekend, a Saturday night, and the party by this guy named Schuyler or Wyler was nothing and no one seems to know just where Lana is having her party and there's nothing much else to do except go to a club, go to a movie, go to the Beverly Center, but there aren't any good bands playing and everyone's seen all the movies and we went to the Beverly Center last night so I've been driving around and around in the hills overlooking Sunset and Skip is telling me that we've got to score some crystal meth. DJ does another line and he's running his finger over his teeth and gums and he asks Skip whatever happened to his friend Michael and Skip says "Really?" and DJ laughs and Skip pushes in my Birthday Party tape and twists up the volume and Nick Cave starts to scream.

I light a cigarette and remember something, a dream maybe, about running down the streets of Los Angeles, and I pass the cigarette to Skip and he takes a drag and passes it back to Jane and Jane takes a drag and passes it back to Skip. DJ lights a cigarette of his own and just ahead a billboard reads Your Message Here and beneath it is an empty space. A car is stopped at the next light, a silver Ferrari, and when I pull up next to it, I turn my head to see two guys inside wearing sunglasses and one of them looks at me and I look back at him and he starts to roll down his window and I drive fast out of the hills and back into the city. The rain is pouring harder and the sidewalks are empty and the streets shine like black mirrors and I start thinking about last summer and I make a couple of wrong turns and end up back on Sunset.

Summer. There is nothing much to remember about last summer. Nights at clubs like Darklands, Sleepless, Cloud Zero, The End. Waking up at noon and watching MTV. A white Lamborghini parked in front of Tower Records. The Swans concert, DJ pissing in the aisle at the Roxy in the middle of "Children of God." A prostitute with a broken arm, waving me over on Santa Monica and asking me if I'd like to have a good time. Breakfast at Gaylords, Mimosas with Perrier-Jouet. Lunch with my mother at the Beverly Wilshire and then driving her to LAX for the red-eye back to Boston. Dinner with Deb and her parents at R.T.'s, blackened mahimahi, Cobb salad, Evian water, and feeling Deb up under the table while her father talked about the Dodgers. The new S.P.K. Album. Going to Palm Springs with Skip over Labor Day weekend and getting fucked up and watching a lizard crawl along a palm tree for about an afternoon. Jane's abortion. Monster billboards of Mick Jagger grinning down on Hollywood Boulevard like the skull of a rotting corpse. Clive getting busted, DWI and possession, and his father getting him off and buying him a new 380SL. Hearing the Legendary Pink Dots on AM radio. And, oh yeah, the thing with the zombies.

It's ten P.M. and I'm sitting at the bar in Citrus with Skip and DJ and Jane and the television down at the end is turned to MTV but the sound is off. I order a Stoly straight up and DJ orders a Rolling Rock and Jane orders a Kir and Skip orders a champagne cocktail and Jane changes her mind and orders a champagne cocktail. We look at the menus for a while but we're not very hungry since we did a half a gram at this guy Schuyler's or Wyler's party so we sit at the bar and we talk about new videos and this girl I don't know comes up to me and thanks me for the ride to Bel Air. Jane digs in her purse and I think she takes some Quaaludes and I look down the bar and out the window and I see nothing at all. "What are we going to do?" I ask no one in particular. "What are we going to do?" Skip asks back and he gives me a matchbook and shows me the handwritten address on the back, some place in the Valley, and he tells the bartender that we'll take the check.

I drive to Jane's house. Nobody's home. Jane forgets the security code and Skip is telling her to try typing the year, it's always the year, and she types one nine eight nine into the little box and the red light goes green and the front door's open and we're inside. We walk through the darkness of the hall to get to the kitchen and there's a note on the table with the telephone number of the hotel where her mother and father, or her mother and her mother's lover, are spending the holidays. There's a stack of unread newspapers and a can of Diet Coke and an empty box of Wheat Thins and then the three videotapes.

"Deal with it" Skip says and he picks up the videotapes and he walks into the living room and he starts on the vodka and tries to turn on the television. I sit on the floor with DJ and Jane, and her parents have one of these big-screen TVs, forty-five inches maybe, with a pair of videotape machines on top, and Skip finds the right buttons and the first tape is rolling. I think that maybe DJ got the tapes or probably Jane, she was at Claremont for a while and had a friend who knew some guy whose brother worked one time at a video store, a film student, and this guy stuck them away when the lists came out, and Jane maybe balled him and got the tapes, so we're watching them, all in a row, three of them, lying on the floor of this high-ceilinged living room with this antique furniture and this print by Lucian Freud and Jane keeps telling us that she's seen all these movies before even though she hasn't. Skip is sitting with the remote control in his hand and he doesn't say a word, he keeps flicking the fast forward, jumping ahead to the best scenes, and the first one is called *Dawn of the Dead* and right away this zombie's head gets blown apart by a shotgun blast and this other zombie gets its head chopped off and the next one is just called *Zombie* and the last one I can't remember much about except the part where this doctor blew away this little girl, she was a zombie, and he put the pistol almost right to her head and the pieces of head and brains and blood went spraying away across the inside of an elevator and just for a moment you could see right through the space where her brain used to be and I look at Jane right after this happens but she isn't looking at me, she's looking at Skip and DJ, and I guess she knows what she wants, don't we all?

An hour later, there's no more vodka and there's no more beer and the television is turned to MTV and Jane just lays there on the floor of her parents' living room, staring at the ceiling, while DJ fucks her for about the third time. Skip is on the telephone in Jane's bedroom, trying to score some meth from a dealer in the city, and after a while I'm in there with him, looking at the poster of The Doors and the poster of The Smiths and listening to him say "Deal with it" over and over before he slams the telephone back onto the cradle and rolls his eyes at me and looks at the posters and says "Strange days and strange ways" and then he starts to smile and I think I get it.

The telephone rings and Skip answers and it's Deb. Skip sighs and waves me to the phone and I say hello and she says hello and asks me what I want for Christmas and can she talk to Jane. I tell her I don't know and that Jane can't talk right now and she says that's okay, she's coming over, don't go, she'll be right there and I say okay and good-bye and she says good-bye. I watch Skip go through the drawers of Jane's desk. He stuffs a pack of cigarettes and a lighter into his pocket and hands me a

Polaroid picture and it's Jane when she was a little girl and she's standing in front of a fat birthday cake with eight blue-and-white candles and she is smiling a big smile and I don't tell him that that's me standing next to her, the little blond kid with the burry haircut and the thick black glasses. He isn't looking at the photograph anyway, he's looking at me, and all he says is "You faggot" and then he has his hands on the buckle of my jeans and he's pulling me onto the bed on top of him.

Afterward, we smoke a couple of cigarettes and I follow Skip back downstairs. DJ has found another bottle of beer somewhere and he's sitting on the couch watching MTV. Jane is still lying on the carpet, staring at the ceiling, and the fingers of her right hand are moving, clutching into a fist, flattening, then clutching into a fist again. Skip walks over to her and unzips his jeans and says that Deb is on her way and doesn't anybody know how we can score some meth. Jane's right hand flattens, then curls into another fist, then flattens again, and she looks up at Skip and says "Well?" and DJ looks up from the television and says "Well what?"

Another video flashes by. Another. Then another. Love and Rockets has no new tale to tell by the time Deb shows up. She's wearing a silk blouse and a brown leather miniskirt that she bought at Magnin's in Century City. "Love you" she says to no one at all. She kisses DJ on the cheek and sticks out her tongue at Skip and Skip acts like he doesn't notice and keeps on fucking Jane. She says hello to me and I say hello back and she tries on my sunglasses. She walks across the room and starts searching through a stack of CDs. She holds up an old album by Bryan Ferry, puts it down, and picks up one by This Mortal Coil. She says "Can I play this?" and when nobody answers, she slides it into the player and punches a few buttons and cranks the stereo up loud. DJ is watching MTV and Skip is watching MTV while he's fucking Jane and Jane is still looking at the ceiling and I'm trying not to look at Deb. She is singing along with Elizabeth Fraser, swaying back and forth in a kind of dance. "I dreamed," she is singing, "you dreamed about me." Then she sits down in front of the fireplace and slips a joint out of the pocket of her skirt and she takes off my sunglasses and squints her eyes and she looks a long time at the joint before lighting it. "Song for the

Siren" winds down and there's a moment of silence and Skip is
pulling himself off Jane with a sound that is hot and wet.

"Next" he says, and he looks first at Deb, then at me.

I dream, but I dream about me. I see myself walking through
the streets of downtown Los Angeles and the day is cloudy and
the sun goes out and it starts to rain and I start to run and I see
myself start to run. In my dream I am chasing myself, running
past the Sheraton Grande, past the Bonaventure, past the Arco
Tower, and for a minute I think I am going to catch up but the
streets are slippery with rain and I fall once, twice, and when I
stand again I can't see anyone but this teenager at the opposite
corner of the intersection and when I look again it's me, a younger
me, and he's fifteen years old and he turns away and starts to
run and I start chasing him and now he's thirteen years old and
he runs and I run and now he is eleven years old and he is getting
younger with each step, younger and smaller, and now he's nine
years old and he's eight years old and he's seven years old and
I've almost caught him and he's six years old and he turns into
this alley and I'm right behind him and he's four years old and
it's a dead-end street and he's three years old and he can just
barely run and I catch him and he's two years old and I pull
him up into my arms and I'm at the end of the alley and he's
one year old and I'm standing on the porch of our house, the
house where I grew up in Riverside, and he's six months old and
I'm knocking on the door and I can hear footsteps inside and
he's three months old and my mother is coming to the door and
I can't wait for her to see me and he's just a baby and he's getting
smaller and he's disappearing and the door is opening and my
mother is looking out and he's gone and I'm gone and then there's
nothing. Nothing at all.

It's midnight. Still raining. Jane's parents live in the Flatlands,
next door to the French actor in that new CBS sitcom, and his
dog is barking as we get in the car and Skip shows me the matchbook and the handwritten address and gives me some directions.
I drive toward Westwood and take a right onto Beverly Glen and
somewhere in the hills I stop at a liquor store for some cigarettes
and a bottle of Freixenet and then I'm back at the wheel and
I'm driving onto Mulholland and into the Valley and onto the
Ventura Freeway and I look at Skip and he acts like he's smiling,

his left hand keeping beat on his leg and it's right on target, one two three four, one two three four, but I don't know the song on the radio, I've never heard it before. I look into the rearview mirror and I see that Deb is all over Jane and I see that DJ is watching them and I see that Deb's tongue is in Jane's mouth and I look at Skip and I see that he is watching me while I'm watching DJ who is watching Deb and Jane and I still don't know the name of that song.

Skip taps me on the shoulder and we're coming up on the exit and he has just popped something into his mouth and he downs it with the last of the Freixenet. He drops the black bottle onto the floor and opens his palm to me as if to say "Want some?" and I look at the little yellow pill and I wonder if I could use some Valium. The music is loud with guitars, it sounds like the Cult, and Skip is pounding out the big electric beat on the window, harder and harder, and spiderwebs are running across the glass and he hits the window one more time and it shatters and he shows me his hand. Little cuts run along his knuckles but he hasn't started bleeding and the song ends and the commercial begins and he turns the volume back down. We go to the Lone Star Chili Parlor in Hidden Hills and sit there drinking coffee and wait a while because we're early and then we go back to the car.

The Valley at two A.M. Van Nuys Boulevard out farther than I thought it went. The moon is curled and shiny and I pull into the parking lot and for some reason Skip seems nervous and we pass the empty theater twice and I keep asking him why and he keeps asking me if I really want to go through with this and I keep telling him that I do. Jane is digging around for something in her purse and Deb is saying "I want to see" and DJ is trying to laugh and as soon as I step out of the car and I look at the line in the shadows, I tell him again.

The mall is no Galleria, not even a mall, just a hollow horseshoe, a curve of little shops, the theater, a drugstore, a pizza place, a karate club, and lots of empty windows lined with whitewash and old newspapers and printed signs that say COMMERCIAL SPACE. There's a chubby kid sitting in a lounge chair in front of the theater, wearing Vuarnets and reading *The Face* and taking ten dollars from each person who wants to go inside. He doesn't even look up as we walk by. DJ pays him and Deb takes my hand and we're inside and the hallway is lined with torn movie posters and shattered glass and spray paint and Skip nods at me and points to the handwritten sign that reads Club Dead.

The lobby looks something like an attic and it's dark and crammed with furniture. Some guy at the back, the manager maybe, is dealing dollar bills to a pair of policemen. He nods at Skip and he nods at me and he lets us through and this girl in the corner winks at me and tries to smile, pale white lipstick and her tongue licking out, and she knows Skip and she says something that I can't hear and Skip gives her the finger.

Inside the lights are bright and it takes my eyes a while to adjust. The place is crowded but we find a table and five chairs and DJ orders a round, four Coronas and a Jack Daniels, straight up, for Deb. "Black Light Trap" is playing over the sound system and the bar is lined with boys trying to look interested in anything but what's about to go down. No one is looking at Jane, plain Jane. Some are looking at Deb and some are looking at these other girls smoking clove cigarettes and standing or sitting in little groups. Skip points out his friend Philip, standing in the back and wearing sunglasses and a black Bauhaus T-shirt.

I get up from the table and go to the bar and then outside with Philip and it's raining and I can hear Shriekback from inside singing that we make our own mistakes and I score from Philip and then I go to the bathroom and lock the door and stare at myself in the mirror. Somebody knocks on the door and I put my foot back against it and say "Deal with it" and lay out three lines and do them and take a drink from the faucet and decide I need a haircut.

It's hot back in the theater and I hold my Corona up to my face, my forehead. There's a man sitting at a table next to us whose eyes are closed so tight that he is crying. The girl he's sitting with is tugging at the crotch of her Guess jeans and drinking a California Cooler and she's fourteen if she's a day. When the man opens his eyes, he looks at his Rolex and he looks at the stage and he looks at the girl and for some reason I'm relieved.

That's when the music goes down and the lights dim and there's some applause, scattered, and the music revs up again, something by Skinny Puppy, and at long last it's showtime. There are video screens set in a line over the stage and I look up and they shoot on one by one and it's a clip, just a short sixty seconds or so, from one of the films we saw, a grainy bootleg copy of a copy of a copy with subtitles in some foreign language, Spanish I think, and the zombies are loose inside a shopping mall and Skinny Puppy is pounding on and the singer's voice is barking deep down trauma hounds and the film clip jumps and now it's from some place back east, you can tell by the trees, and this is from television, from the news last summer, before they stopped talking, before the lists came out, and these soldiers are sweeping through a little town and the buildings are burning and the air is filled with smoke and they're moving house to house and they're blasting the doors and firing inside and now there's a pile of bodies and it's on fire and now it's that commercial, that public service announcement, whatever, and the Surgeon General is saying that the dead are alive, they're coming back to life, but we're killing them again, it's okay, it's all right, and somebody told me he's dead, all those guys are dead, and now the film clip jumps again and the colors roll over and over and the picture steadies and there's a test pattern. Skip says "This is it" and a new picture fades in and then this real tinny music, more like muzak, and it's a video, a home video, something shot with a Handycam maybe, and the picture is a basement or a garage, just bare walls, gray concrete, and after about a minute shadows start walking across the walls and then the first one's out on stage.

The music is gone and there's nothing but silence and a kind of hum, the tape is hissing, and the camera goes out of focus and the picture breaks up and then it's back in focus and she is looking at the camera. She's recent, blond and tall and sort of cute, and she's wearing a Benetton sweatshirt and acid-wash 501 jeans and it's hard to believe she's dead.

"This is real" Skip says to me and he turns to DJ and Deb and Jane and he says "For real." It's quiet in the club, quiet except for the hissing tape, and on the tape the girl is staring at the camera for a long time and nothing else happens. The floor behind her is covered with plastic trash bags and what looks like newspaper and there's a thin wooden cot and there's a worktable in the corner and I wonder why there's a power saw on the table and it does seem warm and I reach for my Corona and the bottle is empty and I look around for the waitress and everybody is watching the screen so I do too. This guy comes into the picture with a coil of rope and he's wearing this black hood and she sees him or hears him and she starts to turn his way and she stumbles and her legs are caught, there are chains on her ankles, and now there's another guy and he's wearing a ski mask and he's coming up behind her and he's carrying a chain and something like a harness, a leather harness, and I look at Deb and Deb looks at me and now they're hitting the girl with the chain and she falls to the ground and they're hitting her some more and now the rope is around her and the harness is over her face and I look at Deb and Deb is touching herself and I look back at the video and they're cutting her clothes and now they're cutting her and I look at Deb and Deb looks at me and she reaches to touch me and now they loop the rope around her neck and Deb's hand is moving up my leg and now the first guy is gone and Deb's hand is moving and now he's back and Deb is squeezing me and he's got a hammer and he swings it once and he swings it twice and Deb is squeezing me harder and now the rope is fastened over-head and someone in the audience says "Yeah" and Skip's arm circles Jane and he pulls her close and says "For real" and now they are yanking the rope and the noose is tightening and her feet are off the floor and Deb's hand is moving and squeezing and I tell her to slow down and she stops and says to hold on a minute and I try and I look back at the screen and now they have a set of hooks and Deb's hand is moving again and the hooks connect to chains and her hand is moving faster and the chains go taut and faster and there's a sound like a scream and faster and her head is bent back and faster and now they have a dildo and faster and they're fitting it with nails and faster and faster and faster now they have a boy, faster a little naked boy, and faster now they have a blowtorch and faster now they have a power drill and faster now they have and now they have and now they and now they and now and now and now the picture is gone and my crotch is wet and Deb reaches over and hands me a napkin.

It's four A.M. and it's getting cold and we're still sitting in the club and Skip is picking lint from my sweater and telling me that he wants to leave. The Clan of Xymox fades to Black and it's a wonderful life, the singer is singing, it's a wonderful, wonderful life. Jane is vomiting in the corner and the lights are dark and red and for a moment I think it looks like blood. DJ is turned away, watching two boys wet-kissing in the shadows beyond the stage and taking deep pulls on another Corona. Deb is out back fucking this guy from U.S.C., bleach-blond and tan and wearing a white Armani sweater. Skip is telling me that we ought to leave real soon now. The music clicks off and it's smoke and laughter and broken glass and the sound of Jane spitting up and then the live band saunters onto the stage and the band is called 3 but there are four of them. The bass player has a broken right hand and Skip says "The bass player has a broken right hand" and slides a clove cigarette from his shirt pocket. The four-man band called 3 starts playing a speed metal version of "I Am the Walrus" and Deb is standing in front of me and she kisses me and tells Skip she's ready and Skip is saying that we have to leave and DJ is pulling Jane by the arm and Jane is still bent over and I wonder if I should ask if she's okay and my eyes meet Skip's and he cuts them to the exit and the next thing you know, we're gone.

Skip says Jimmy has a camera and I drive over to Jimmy's house, but Jimmy, somebody remembers, is either dead or in Bermuda, so I drive to Toby's place and this black kid answers the door wearing white underwear and a hard-on. A lava lamp bubbles red in the living room behind him. "Toby's busy" the black kid says and shuts the door. I take the Hollywood Freeway to Western Avenue but it's not right and I take the Holywood Freeway to Alvarado but it's not right and I drive downtown and I take an exit, any exit, and I see the Sheraton Grande and I see the Bonaventure and I see the Arco Tower and I think it's time to run. Skip says to stop but it's still not right and I turn the corner and now it's right and so I stop and Skip tosses Jane out the door and she's facedown in the gravel and it sounds like she's going to vomit again.

"You didn't have to do that" somebody says but I don't know who. DJ is sitting up in the backseat and he pulls his arm from around Deb and shrugs and looks down at Jane. Skip starts to laugh and it sounds like choking and he turns up the radio and it's the New Order single and Jane is crawling away from the car. Skip is pulling something from under his jacket and his door slams and I check the rearview mirror. I look at the reflection of Deb's eyes for a moment and I don't say anything more.

The car is stopped in the middle of the street, at the mouth of an alley, and I see now that it's the alley from my dream, a hidden place, a perfect place, and Jane is crawling away from the car and Skip is walking toward her and he's taking his time and there's something in his hand, something long and sharp, and it glows in the glare of the headlights and his shadow is streaking across the brick walls of the alley and I think I've just seen this. Skip is standing over her and I see Jane start to say something and Skip is shaking his head as if he's saying no and then he's bending down toward her and she just watches as he cuts her once, then again, and she rolls onto her back and he flicks the knife past her face and she doesn't blink, doesn't move, and now the back door slams and DJ and Deb are out of the car and walking down the alley and now I'm walking down the alley and when we get there Skip shows us the knife, a thick military job, and Jane is bleeding on her arms and hands and a little on her neck and DJ says "Make it like the movie" and Skip says "This is the movie." He looks at DJ and he looks at Deb and he looks at me and he looks at Jane and he slides the knife into her stomach and the sound is soft and she barely moves and there isn't much blood at all, so he slides the knife into her stomach again, then into her shoulder, and this time she shudders and her back arches up and she seems to moan and the blood bubbles up but it isn't very red, it isn't very red at all. Deb says "Oh" and Skip tosses the knife aside and Jane rolls onto her stomach and I think she's starting to cry, just a little, and he looks around the alley but there's nothing there, garbage cans and crumpled papers and the burned-out hulk of an RX-7, and he finds a brick and he throws it at her and she curls up like a baby and DJ picks up the brick and throws it and Deb picks up the brick and throws it and then it's my turn and I pick up the brick and throw it and hit her in the head.

We kick her for a while and then she starts to crawl and there still isn't much blood and it's the wrong color, almost black I guess, and it isn't very shiny and it's just like dripping, not spraying around or anything, and she is almost to the end of the alley and the street ends and there's a curb and there's a sidewalk and there's a wall and there's a light from somewhere beaming down and she crawls some more. Her head is in the gutter and Skip looks at DJ and he is saying "This is real" and he pulls at Jane's hair and her head is bent back and her mouth is open and he's dragging her forward and then he's pressing her face against the curb and her upper teeth are across the top of the curb, her lips are pulled back into a smile and it looks like the smile in the Polaroid, Jane is eight years old, and her head is hanging there by those upper teeth and I look at Skip and I look at DJ and I look at Deb and Deb is looking down and she's smiling too and Skip is saying "Real" and he puts his boot on the back of Jane's head and he presses once, twice, and that smile widens into a kiss, a full mouth kiss on the angle of concrete, and then he stomps downward and the sound is like nothing I have ever heard.

The sound is on the radio. I'm listening to the radio and it echoes along the alley and it plays song after song after song. I'm sitting on the curb with Skip and DJ and Deb, and DJ is smoking another cigarette and the stubs are collecting at his feet and there are seven or eight of them and we've been here an hour and it's nearly light and we've been waiting but now it's time to go.

"Okay, Jane" Deb says and she is standing and she is jabbing Jane with her foot and she is saying "We gotta go." Skip is standing and DJ is standing and Deb is looking at her Swatch and she says "Get up" and then she says "You can get up now." She is jabbing Jane with her foot and Jane isn't moving and Skip is wiping his knife and looking at Jane and DJ is smoking his cigarette and looking at Jane and I'm just looking at Jane and then I think I know. No, I do know. I'm sure I know.

"She's coming back, right?" Deb is saying and she's looking at Skip and she's looking at DJ and then she's looking at me. "Bret?" she is asking me and she is crossing her arms and she isn't smiling now. "She's coming back, isn't she?" Deb is saying "I mean, we're all coming back, right?" Skip is putting the knife in his pocket and DJ is finishing his cigarette and I am standing and she is saying "Right?"

People are afraid to live on the streets of Los Angeles. This is the last thing I say as I walk away from Skip and DJ and Deb and get back into the car. I don't know why I keep saying this thing. It's something I started and now I can't stop. Nothing else seems to matter.

I sit behind the wheel of the car and I watch the windshield wipers go back and forth, back and forth, back and forth, and the city blurs, out of focus, beneath the thin black lines. I want to say that people are afraid of something and I can't remember what and maybe it's nothing, maybe it's a dream and I am running, I am running after something and I can't remember what,

I can't remember the dream, and the windshield wipers go back
and forth, back and forth. People are afraid of something and
in my dream I am running and the radio is playing and I try to
listen but it is playing the song I do not know. The windshield
wipers go back and forth. The doors open and close and then I
drive away.

Rapid Transit

**WAYNE
ALLEN
SALLEE**

Karl Edward Wagner, distinguished editor of DAW Books's *The Year's Best Horror Stories* series, once wrote: "Wayne Allen Sallee is not another King/Barker/Jason/Freddie clone. He is an original writer, and his pen is dipped in pain. One wonders just how far he can go."

So far, *very* far. An incredibly prolific contributor to the small-press horror magazines (*Grue, New Blood, 2 A.M.*), Sallee has written more than seven hundred poems and a bazillion short stories (all right, actually only about seventy. OK?). And Wagner is most correct in pointing out that Sallee's pen is dipped in pain; pain is the recurring theme, the overall rationale, in most of Sallee's stories.

Don't believe me? All right, here are the titles of just two Wayne-works: "The Pain Detail" and "PainGrin." How about the fact that Sallee wears a watch with the words *Pain Killer* on its face? Maybe I should also point out that he's had first-hand experience with agony; Wayne was recently struck by a car (according to Sallee, "My writing arm looked like a skin baggie filled with Kibbles and Bits.")

Now do you believe?

Wayne Allen Sallee is based in Chicago, and often uses that windy, sprawling city as a backdrop for his fiction. Like the best of the splatterpunks, he tends to focus on real-world horrors. His characters are ordinary fathers, roommates, and little kids. But when these plain folks are confronted with unsettling true-life situations and cocooned in uncomfortable atmospheres, the squirm factor in a typical Sallee offering tends to jump toward the stratosphere.

Sallee has written a number of splat-like stories, including "Threshold" (about mutant children) and "Lullaby and Goodnight" (deformity). But "Rapid Transit" seems to be the one tale most Sallee aficionados hunger for. Part of the "Dennis Cassady Trilogy" (which concludes with "Take the A Train" and "Bleeding Between the Lines"), "Rapid Transit" is nominally concerned with the effects of random urban violence on an innocent bystander. In its lower depths, this examination of the murkiest depths of human pathology indicates just how well Sallee understands the potential madness lurking within all of us.

By the way, Sallee tells me that what he practices is "psychological horror." But he doesn't mind being called a splatterpunk, either.

Thank you, Wayne!

Thank you!

Waiting for the Douglas El on the final day of Indian summer, Dennis Cassady saw the woman slowly and relentlessly knifed to death in the field below the platform. He had been standing, unaware, for several minutes, thinking about whether or not he should take the weekend off and boogie up to Fallon Ridge to catch the remainder of the World Series on big screen TV (since, let's not kid ourselves, if he lived to be frigging ninety, the chances of seeing the games at Wrigley Field . . . hell, the Cubs will always be looking at a sweep of the playoffs like a fourteen-year-old pimply necked kid with one hand buried deep in his pants drooling over the Playmate of the Month), and not until he looked down the tracks for the elevated train did he notice her. She had not made a sound. He was standing behind a billboard that advertised a brand of cigarettes. The billboard showed a woman with beautiful red lips and matching fingernail polish looking through a pair of binoculars at a package of cigarettes. The legend below the ad read: TRUE. YOU FOUND IT. He realized with a sudden twinge of morbid fascination, which went sliding down his back like an ice cube on a hot day, that he had a perfect view.

The woman's jeans—he was sure that she had to be in her mid-twenties—her jeans were pulled down to her knees, and blood was running in fine rivulets down one thigh. The Western Avenue sodium vapor lamps cast a violet haze on the field, the kind of haze you see at dusk during the summer if rain is on the way, and it made the blood appear livid and oily.

Her breasts were large, but he could not tell if she was attractive: her face was twisted in fear, eyes widened, nostrils flared, blond hair matted with dirt. All of this surrounded a black pit of a mouth from which no sound came. Cassady's eyes drifted back to her spread legs and perfect thighs, they really were perfect, except for that ugly stream of blood that largely resembled a doctor's El Marko outline of some old bag's varicose vein.

The twinge he had initially experienced became stronger; he felt as if his entire body was starting to fall asleep. It ran across him in waves, like that time he had been hypnotized at Massie's and his friend Frank Haid had sat by and laughed. The mesmerist extraordinaire—he called himself that; the guy was really just a two-bit showoff in a bouffant toupee—had said to Cassady, "You are getting sleeepy. You feel a *ting*ling in your fingers, a *ting*ling in your toes . . ." and shit like that. The guy had sounded like a queer, and Cassady had ended up hypnotized into "becoming" Neil Diamond, kissing old women and running the microphone cord up and down his crotch.

But he wasn't falling asleep. He felt both excitement and curiosity at what was happening below him, how things were going to turn out. He felt the same way as do people who lead boring lives, when they slow down their cars at the scene of an auto wreck, or mill about the aftermath of a Haddon Street grocery store robbery, just to see how many times the fifty-year-old Polish immigrant was shot after his till had been emptied, and to maybe get their faces on the five o'clock news.

He didn't need his face on the news; not at all.

Cassady thought about that Don McLean song that he and Sarah had listened to in high school. *I feel the trembling tingle of a sleepless night . . .*

Only the girl in the song had chestnut-colored hair *that fell across her pillowcase.*

The field below was in the process of becoming the early stages of a project of which Cassady knew nothing about. A lime green construction shack with MYERS AND SONS, WINNETKA printed in three-dimensional blue on its side stood at the far end of the field. Beyond that, the monolithic overpass of the Burlington Northern's railroad tracks ran beneath the el about twenty feet to the west; the two sets of ties cut the field off effectively and almost completely. He heard the man below him grunt. The sound of a car with a dead battery being turned over.

Maybe the woman will be lucky and the guy really *will* have a dead battery, Cassady thought, then she won't end up in some Division Street abortion clinic telling the doctor: "Yes, it was my boyfriend, and, yes, I know I should have come in sooner, but —" "—you were embarrassed," the doctor would finish. "Right? Well, now, don't worry, just rest your feet in these stirrups. The hose won't hurt *too* much . . ."

The people who worked at the building on the south side of the el, from nine until six-thirty, made picture frames. Moonlight splashed across several third-floor windows; he could vaguely make out a small bottle of Jergens hand lotion, a miniature sentry that seemed to stare at him from the window sill. All of the windows seemed to stare at him.

A nearly deserted CTA bus advertising NOBODY DOES IT BETTER: CHANNEL TWO NEWS AT 5, 6, AND 10 split the night, droning by within ten feet of the two figures in the field. The driver's eyes mirrored the unblinking darkness of the building's windows, as they stared straight ahead toward the north side and better neighborhoods.

The man—Christ! Cassady had paid hardly any attention to him at all—looked up as the bus hissed on. He had a full and unshaven face, white hairs spotting his beard. Broad shoulders pushed out from a checkered shirt, and his soiled shirttails were dangling out of the open fly of his Wrangler jeans. The man was wearing a pair of red Keds basketball sneakers that made squishing noises as he shifted his weight in the muddy tire tracks on the ground. His teeth were crooked.

Cassady was captivated at the clarity with which he saw things. It was as if he was sitting in the sixth-row aisle seat in the Hub Theater, secure in the darkness, stuffing popcorn into his mouth as some B-movie starlet is hacked at by some B-movie slasher in a B-movie with Spanish subtitles.

The woman kicked at the man, who was still looking toward the street. He stumbled backward, howling. More out of surprise than anger. The woman staggered to her feet, her jeans still bunched at the knees. The two moved in a drunken pavane, the man trying to regain his balance, his arms flapping at the air; the woman attempting to turn away, her mouth now resembling a gaping wound.

Later Cassady would remember everything that followed as happening with a cruel slowness, as if the field had been invisibly flooded with glycerine. Everything that followed, *everything*— ripple of muscle, ripping of flesh, blinking of eyes, expanding and contracting of lungs as air was inhaled and scream was expelled—it all happened in slow motion, separate frames in a great motion picture. He could almost see himself breathing in slo-mo.

The man came forward again, a knife suddenly in his left hand—Cassady thought of a stiletto his father, a retired Monroe Street cop, had shown him once; when he flicked the release button a six-inch blade jumped out uncaringly, capable of slicing flesh and bone alike, press it into somebody's back *snnikt!* and their spinal cord is severed like so much butter—and he heard the slow whirring of the Hub movie projector again.

The woman took three steps backward before falling to the ground with a wet thud. A streetlamp near the corner flickered twice and went out. The man's arm descended in jagged flashes, as if a piece of film was being slowed down and then speeded up spasmodically, or maybe the scene below had been poorly edited and hastily shipped out for viewing to reap whatever profits could be made. The huge knife ripped twice into the woman's right breast.

Blood, a rich purple color in the streetlamp's haze, flowered across her blouse. A third thrust, this one accompanied by a miserable sucking sound (as if the knife had entered the exact same hole as the previous stab), and the purplish blood sprayed out in all directions; it had the effect of a garden hose being turned on with a thumb over its nozzle. The man was drenched, his pants and shirt streaked shiny in places, and the ejaculation of blood drove him into an even greater frenzy.

Then, only then, did the woman scream. It was the sound of something trapped, like a child camping with his parents who wanders into a fox trap, which snaps around his tiny leg, crushing tiny bone. A rabbit staring into the muzzle of the shotgun. A mother who answers the phone angrily at two in the morning, starting to say "Can't you at least call if—" and being interrupted by the police officer.

Her arms wrapped frantically around her chest, clamping her life back in.

As her scream skittered down the empty streets into the gutters and alleys, the man punched her below the right eye, and Cassady heard her nose break. It was muffled, like the sound of a pretzel being bit in half inside your mouth. Her skin began to swell, darkening her mascara, which had already began to run, minutes before. Not from tears, but from the man's spittle.

He pulled her hair and her head snapped brutally forward, and then he casually let it drop back with a dull crack. All of this of course happening in slow motion, the moonlight washed through the woman's blond hair as her head fell back, and Cassady thought of a line from a Richard Lovelace poem: *Shake your head and scatter day . . .* What an absurd—

The woman screamed again.

The sound slapped Cassady's awareness with the same intensity of his radio alarm going off to WBBM's Hot Hits each morning. After the initial onslaught of the Go-Gos or Toni Basil singing about Mickey, whatever dream-thoughts still slumbered in his head disappeared when he dipped his soft contacts in icy tap water before putting them in, and he was left staring at reality: reflected in the bathroom mirror of a shabby two-room flat, the face of a twenty-seven-year-old man who looked older than he really was.

Cassady looked in the mirror in front of him and saw the knife high in the air. *This is really happening!* he thought. *I can still save her!* As he moved backward, quickly and quietly, past the *Creepshow* billboard that some half-assed Rembrandt had retouched in marker so that the cockroach coming out of E. G. Marshall's mouth was instead a giant black penis, past the small blue sign that gave the hours of arrival and departure for the Douglas trains, and he was finally at the phone and the man wasn't coming after him and the phone felt cold in his hand and there were initials carved into the wood of the bench next to him that said JUICE L'S LAVON and LATIN KINGS RULE and he dialed 911 and—

All of this happened in little over three seconds in Dennis Cassady's mind. He was rooted where he stood like a corpse to its grave. He badly wanted to urinate.

The man dropped the knife straight into the woman's mouth. It fell o god it fell ever so slowly. Straight down, like the swan dive of an Olympic swimmer. It fell, and Cassady saw the veins sticking out in the man's wrists, he held the knife so tightly. Knuckle white. Like her eyes. White and huge, the one that had been beaten purple looked as if it had been painted into its socket.

And the knife fell, and there were images of that "60 Minutes" show on slow-motion filming and that shot of the drop of milk falling with the camera recording every 1/1000th of a second with the drop so gracefully falling into the dish and the splattering milk formed a tiny crown and one tiny globe stood balanced in dead center with a thin tongue of white reaching to pull it back down.

Cassady would later remember dreaming of the sound that the knife made when it ripped through the woman's tongue. It was like the sound the dentist's air hose makes when it is in your mouth and you have to swallow. Violet blood flew out of the mutilated mess that had been her mouth a moment before. The smell of blood filled the air and worked its way into Cassady's mouth. He tasted copper, and his own bile, deep in his throat.

The woman hitched out a cough. Another, convulsively. The man sliced her throat from ear to ear. He was smiling. The wind caught the sharp odor of pickles and onions from the Wendy's up on Twenty-fifth. Black pools welled up in the sockets of the woman's still staring *o god why couldn't he have just raped me and masturbated in my face instead of KILLING me* eyes. One hand clawed lifeless etchings into the mud. The man replaced the knife through his belt loop into an invisible holster, its blade grinning wickedly, and—

He walked away. He simply walked away. Twenty minutes had passed, according to the flashing neon Seiko sign down the block.

The train pulled in several minutes after the red basketball sneakers had shrank first to a pinpoint and then to nothing in the darkness. Cassady walked disjointedly down the aisle of the last car, his ankle-length trenchcoat slapping against the seats. He was surprised that it was crowded, filled with simpering suburbanites intent on following Governor Thompson's orders: *Because of the rail strike, leave work a little early or stay awhile longer, so we can all spread the rush hour out more, and hopefully, etcetera, etcetera.* And hopefully I'll be reelected in 1987 was what he *didn't* say on the TV spot.

And so, no doubt about it, everybody piles onto the 7:03 out of Cicero-Berwyn. Cassady nearly tripped over a toad of a man sitting virtually on top of the doors. Thin, a scarecrow of a man in a three-piece suit. Sunken shoulders, bony knees and ankles touching, eyebrows perched atop black plastic frames from Sears Optical. Neck muscles protruding from an ill-fitting collar twitched together in a mad fugue. A Cermak Road businessman working late. He smelled of Brut 33 cologne.

In the last seat, next to the conductor's booth, a pregnant black woman gazed out at the rooftops passing just below eye level. A small boy with huge brown eyes and a Walter Payton T-shirt sat tugging at the woman's faded blue sweatshirt, vying for supremacy over the dirt on the tenements for his mother's attention. Their clothes said off-the-rack Zayre's blue-light special, and their faces had 18th and Hoyne written in every sad wrinkle, and in the dirt under their fingernails as well.

Cassady was able to get a seat in the back of the car. He slid down next to a man in work boots reading (most likely with some degree of difficulty, he thought) the new Robert Ludlum novel. Across from him sat two elderly women, one with a purple babushka wrapped around her head, both of their faces buried deep in *The National Enquirer*.

"*My*, my, that Prince Andrew going out with that Koo actress what appeared nekked in those movies," the purple babushka said. The cloth was wrapped so tightly around her head that her eyebrows were pulled back on her forehead, like Mr. Spock's on "Star Trek." Her withered hand touched her cheek in actual concern. "What *is* this world coming to?"

Look around you and see, lady, Cassady thought. See if anybody cares that some woman was cut to pieces tonight and you all passed her right on by and *I saw it happen!*

None of you even bothered to look out of the window. Too damn caught up in your own damn lives and your own damn problems. Somebody could have seen the—her—body.

Hell, nobody was even looking at him.

Down the aisle somewhere, a kid had his Sony Walkman turned on too loud, and John Cougar was singing about Jack and Diane sucking down chilidogs outside a Tastee-Freez. Go for it, Jacky-boy.

Cassady shut his eyes.

. . . *say, hey, Diane, let's go off behind a shady tree* . . .

How about an el overpass, Jacky-boy; that'll do the trick. Cassady could almost hear the sound of his own thoughts. He had an insane urge to laugh, loud and without reason. A madman's laugh.

What could he have done, anyway? His ears rang.

. . . *oh, yeah, life goes on* . . .

You talking to me, Jacky-boy? Cassady's mind was a black hole, and except for the song, every single sensory feeling—the cold metal he rested his hands on, the smell of a pipe three seats up, even the old ladies' murmurings—was sucked into his brain and pulled into swirling blackness at thought speed. It was like when you are walking down a street, maybe thinking about the girl you're seeing, and you don't even realize that you're walking or that your legs are moving up and down at each curb, and you turn down the right street without looking at the sign and you only know that when she wears her red headband it drives you crazy . . .

Outside, away from his mind, shadowed buildings passed by at breakneck speed. The floor of the car vibrated with the tempo of the rails underneath. Except for the armchair-espionage spy next to him and the two mental cases across the aisle, everybody sat with vacant stares, their heads bobbing in rhythm with the motions of the car, like empty beer cans floating in the water off

Oak Street Beach, their eyes staring noncommittally at their reflections, washed black by the night beyond the rhomboid-shaped windows.

Inside, Cassady saw the woman's face and the man's face, with its twisted grin, grotesquely out of proportion, as if an egg beater had been stuck in the middle of their faces, funhouse faces leering like the ones at the beginning of "Rod Serling's Night Gallery" . . .

    . . . *long after the thrill of livin' is gone* . . .

Go to hell, Jacky-boy.

The train made a hissing sound as it slowly pulled into the Central Park Station, jolting Cassady's awareness as abruptly as a cop's nightstick jabs the wino on the park bench out of his drunken slumber. Cassady found that he had been staring at the "Life in These United States" signs lining the car, furnished by the *Reader's Digest* for your reading enjoyment.

He was one of a handful of people who were either poor enough or stupid enough to get off the train, the quality of the neighborhood being what it was, sprawled beneath him in two-dimensional decay, gang slogans—VICE LORDS, BLACK GANGSTERS—in carnival colors sprayed on every shuttered building. He stood alone, hands gripping the railing, the wood rough on his fingers, and let the wind that carried the copper smell of blood into his nose twenty blocks east blow gently through his hair.

He looked down at his hands. They were strong, able hands; nails neatly trimmed. He began to examine a small scab on his right hand, just below the knuckles, a product of a careless slip of the razor while shaving. Methodically, like an old man whittling wood, he scratched at it until a tiny sliver flaked off. He stared at the ugly red skin underneath. Stretching the skin taut with his other hand, he watched a small bubble of blood rise to the surface. The blood was thick; Cassady felt the sharp sting of nausea begin a slow pulse in his nose. Black patches grabbed at the corners of his eyes and his stomach heaved. Now he was running down the steps two at a time, dumbly thinking that every time his feet hit the stairs and then the concrete, his socks were sliding further down his calves.

He felt his throat getting all gummy, and he knew it wouldn't be long before he threw up, like the time he had downed a pint of Yukon Jack on Vic Raciunas's dare and gave his erstwhile friend's AMC Pacer a new set of seat covers. That had been outside of Lorenzo's, a Greek lounge on Halsted Street, where the owners called everybody "my friend" and the whole block smelled like gyros. Cassady wished to fuck that he was there right now.

He fumbled for his front door key, his bladder doing a fast boogaloo. Blood poked through the scab again. The light in the foyer reflected off of it, making it look like spittle in a baby's mouth. He retched all over himself.

It rained the next day. Cassady threw up several times in the morning; the taste of bile stayed in his mouth. He could taste it when he belched. He stared vacantly out of his window at life progressing down Cullerton and Ridgeway. Faces stood in doorways, kept dry by yesterday's racing forms, waiting for the rain to stop so their daily crap games could begin. A hunkered down old man, the rain seemingly beating him into the ground, waited patiently for the Ogden Avenue bus, his eyes gently watching two young boys who did not know what rheumatoid arthritis was splash playfully in the puddles. The sky did not have a horizon: it was a bowl of smokestack gray that was smacked down on everything, and as the afternoon died into early evening, the rain quickened, ripping its way through the trees, tearing autumn's last remaining leaves and smashing them to the ground in lifeless piles.

Through all of this, Cassady sat and watched as the rain beat against his window and eroded lines onto his reflected face. Behind him, on the Quasar television he had bought hot the previous summer on Maxwell Street, Eddie Haskell was calling the Beaver a little runt.

He was holding a cockroach in his hand. Had been for quite some time. He held it firmly between his thumb and forefinger; its legs hung limp. Cassady raised it to eye level, and the roach met his stare with little disdain. He had found it creeping through his kitchen. *Remind you of someone you know?* a dark voice asked. *NO!* Cassady's mind overrode the dark voice, and his eyes squeezed shut.

When he opened them, a million years after the sight of the knife's grin became too much to bear, he saw that he had ripped one of the roach's legs off. The roach's attitude had not changed.

The tiny leg resting on his right finger resembled a woman's false eyelash. Cassady then tossed the roach behind him, hardly heard it hit the floor. Let it bleed to death, he thought.

Four-thirty. Channel Seven gave the best account of the woman's death. A voluptuous bottle blond read from the prompter that the victim's name had been Quita McLean—"Quita" after the heroine in a Harlequin romance her mother had once read. She would have been twenty-three, and her sister said that she had always cried when the puppies were burned in the barn fire in *Lad: A Dog*. The camera focused on a withered old man who would not stop crying.

After a commercial break, the blond came back on to talk about a hostage situation in a European embassy. One woman had been released because she had told the terrorists that she was pregnant. Would that revelation have stopped Quita McLean from being raped and murdered?

Cassady walked into the kitchen, reaching for a full bottle of Seagram's, thinking that if he was lucky he would get liver failure. Out of the corner of his eye, his hand still on the bottle, Cassady saw his friend limping erratically toward the safety of an empty Jays potato chips box. Taking a dirty fork from the sink, Cassady stepped forward, lunging it into the roach's midsection. It sounded like a taco breaking in half. He kicked it out of the way.

By the time the fast money round came on "Family Feud," Cassady was sprawled in his living room chair like a discarded rag doll. A rusted spring stuck out of the top of the chair, coming closer with each of Cassady's deep breaths to piercing his shoulderblade. The empty bottle lay on the floor beside him, and he dreamt.

". . . as the Beaver." "Mommy, Mommy, Denny was playing with my *Barbie dolls* again!" Jenet, his older sister, was singing, her voice like the broken record it still was. They were sitting at the dinner table and his mother—no, it was Barbara Billingsley, Beaver's mom; no, it wasn't at all, this was getting confusing—turned her head sharply at the revelation. She was wearing a pink housecoat, and a pearl necklace dangled from around her neck. The housecoat was missing several buttons. From the chair he sat in across from his mother, who was now staring at him from behind a fortress of Teflon, Cassady thought that he could not remember June Cleaver ever wearing a housecoat on the show before . . .

His father peered over the edge of his paper in slits. "He took *all* their clothes off, Mommy!" the stupid bitch was saying. Why didn't she just shut the hell up? "*Did not, did not!*" Cassady became a broken record of his own, but his father was already standing, looming over his chair like an ogre, his belt coming off rapidly, making rough sounds as it passed through each loop of his pants. His beer belly fell forward, giving way to gravity now that the belt was not holding it back, and it sort of plopped into his potatoes. The belt made a flapping sound as it hit Cassady in the back, right where the spring in the chair was poking through . . .

Faggot! Lousy faggot! Prissy Denny's playing with Corky the Retard! The words were ritualistically chanted by several male voices whose owners he couldn't see because he was scraping mud out of his eyes. He tasted dirt on his tongue. He blinked his eyes open, and no one was there except Sarah Dunleavy, and wasn't that strange because he hadn't met her until college, long after he and Jimmy Corcoran left the old neighborhood. "Sarah!" his baby voice shrieked. "They hurt me, Sarah!" He felt embarrassed at the smallness of his voice. "C'mere, you," she soothed, cradling his head, which fell away from the rusted spring. He awoke in darkness.

Kee-*rist*! What a Grade A bitch of a nightmare that was! He remembered parts of it, just like certain parts of songs keep floating through your head (*long after the thrill of livin' has gone*) while you're walking down the street or waiting for a local. Sarah, Corky, even a vague image of Sister Veronetta making him recite the Lord's Prayer in kindergarten back at St. Vitus. And the dolls . . .

Shit . . . he sniffed the air. Smelled like—no, he hadn't crapped himself. Smelled like grass. Wet grass, how the inside of a lawnmower bag smells after you've cut the grass when it was damp with dew or rain.

But it was more than that.

He smelled something decaying. *The roach?*

It was dark out—how long had he been sleeping?—and Cassady reached over to turn on the lamp. The tallow light flickered beneath a lampshade that depicted a panoramic view of Niagara Falls, and he screamed.

Cassady's screams echoed through the thin walls and bare floor, but Audrey and Willis Fenton, who were watching "Magnum, P.I." below, didn't hear anything.

Because the scream never made it to reality; it was a sob welled up in his throat like so much phlegm. It was the sound that the woman had made just before the man had let the knife drop into her mouth.

And she was lying on his living room couch.

She was naked. And she was dead. Her skin had become green and cheesy-looking, like a person who had been receiving advanced cancer treatments. Her eyes were open, both sunk down into their sockets, the mucous and membrane running over the sides like badly prepared eggs, leaving dried yellowed pus lining the rims of her eyelids. One eye stared lollingly at the ceiling, the other focused above and to the left of the television, which was sputtering in static. Her hair was white and alive with maggots. The skin was pulled back tightly around her lips, a death grin of dried leather. Mud was caked on her gums and her cheeks. Blood spattered her teeth. Her hands clawed . . .

Cassady felt a sharp tingling in his crotch. At first he thought he had urinated. A pain shot through his testicles. Sharp and quick like when he sometimes rode his ten speed wearing shorts that were too tight, and pumping his legs too fast.

He looked down.

There was movement under his pants.

His testicles drew up. Cassady pulled the pants away from his waist.

A cockroach the size of a half dollar was tangled in his pubic hairs like a fly in a spider's web. Its legs backpedaled madly; with each revolution the skin below Cassady's naval tugged outward in small, flesh-colored tents as the cockroach became more tightly entwined.

It looked up at Cassady, and the shadow of its antennae slashed a huge V across his chest.

Cassady screamed again. This time, it was real.

He awoke in a cold sweat. Shaking. It was evening; the lamp was off. A talk show was on television, Barbara Walters interviewing Bruce Willis about his role on "Moonlighting."

Dennis Cassady did not move from his chair for hours. He sat like someone in the later stages of senility, eyes glassy and vacant, lips quivering. Later, he would tell Sarah what had happened to him. He would tell her everything.

But that evening, he sat.

He scratched at the scab on his hand.

He let it bleed.

While She Was Out

EDWARD
BRYANT

Edward Bryant is not a splatterpunk—his first story appeared in the
Harlan Ellison—edited, sf-tinged anthology *Again, Dangerous Visions*,
and he subsequently wrote a *lot* of science fiction. But lately this
laconic, long-haired citizen of Denver, Colorado, is definitely leaning
toward the horrific.

Among Ed's nine books and hundreds of short stories is fiction
which has appeared in the seminal horror collections *Cutting Edge*,
Dark Forces, and *Book of the Dead* (with its highly recommended
Bryant novella "A Sad Last Love at the Diner of the Damned"). Ed
also specializes in reviewing horror for the magazines *Locus* and *Mile
High Futures*, work which, as he puts it, "sometimes irritates folks."
Bryant has further labored in film and television (as an actor in director
S. P. Somtow's *The Laughing Dead* and as a screenwriter for the new
"Twilight Zone"). "While She Was Out" obviously springs from this
sector of the media. For here we have Bryant's satirical inversion of
a particularly offensive stereotype, one that continues to fuel countless
splatter and slasher films. Amusingly, "While She Was Out" also is
grounded in an actual incident, as Bryant tells us:

> One hot June morning I parked at Denver's Cinderella City
> shopping mall. Doubtless because of the over-heated nature of
> the day, I found myself steamed at the sight of a big old junker
> sedan spread across three parking spaces. Seeing this as the
> opportunity for a little wish fulfillment fantasy play-out, I left a
> note under the wiper blade saying: "Dear Jerk, Thanks for taking
> up all the available space. P.S. Too bad about your gas-line and
> gas tank." About twenty steps from this triumph of petty vindic-
> tiveness, I turned, went back, and tore off the P.S.
>
> So I was chickenshit. Sue me. That was real life.

Another aspect of not-so-real life is addressed in "While She Was Out," and it's a particularly disturbing one—the role of women in horror films. Despite such recent anomalies as the 1990 movie *Blue Steel*—wherein rookie cop Jamie Lee Curtis, the strong, complex protagonist, entangles herself in a disturbing relationship with a serial killer—horror films consistently portray women in the most blatantly superficial terms. Victim, sex object, bitch/witch; the emphasis on female stereotyping in everything from *Frankenstein* to *Ghostbusters 2* is depressingly insistent.

That's why "While She Was Out" is so much fun; here's an instance where splatterpunk serves as antisexist indictment. With its all-too-believable domestic scenario and killer tag line, "While She Was Out" and Edward Bryant have resoundingly turned horror movie clichés upside down. Right on their dick-oriented heads.

Women, this one's for you.

It was what her husband said then that was the last straw.

"Christ," muttered Kenneth disgustedly from the family room. He grasped a Bud longneck in one red-knuckled hand, the cable remote tight in the other. This was the time of night when he generally fell into the largest number of stereotypes. "I swear to God you're on the rag three weeks out of every month. PMS, my ass."

Della Myers deliberately bit down on what she wanted to answer. PXMS, she thought. That's what the twins' teacher had called it last week over coffee after the parent-teacher conference Kenneth had skipped. Pre-holiday syndrome. It took a genuine effort not to pick up the cordless Northwestern Bell phone and brain Kenneth with one savage, cathartic swipe. "I'm going out."

"So?" said her husband. "This is Thursday. Can't be the auto mechanics made simple for wusses. Self defense?" He shook his head. "That's every other Tuesday. Something new, honey? Maybe a therapy group?"

"I'm going to Southeast Plaza. I need to pick up some things."

"Get the extra-absorbent ones," said her husband. He grinned and thumbed up the volume. ESPN was bringing in wide shots of something that looked vaguely like group tennis from some sweaty-looking third-world country.

"Wrapping paper," she said. "I'm getting some gift wrap and ribbon." Were there fourth-world countries? she wondered.

Would they accept political refugees from America? "Will you put the twins to bed by nine?"

"Stallone's on HBO at nine," Kenneth said. "I'll bag 'em out by half past eight."

"Fine." She didn't argue.

"I'll give them a good bedtime story." He paused. " 'The Princess and the Pea.' "

"Fine." Della shrugged on her long down-filled coat. Any more, she did her best not to swallow the bait. "I told them they could each have a chocolate chip cookie with their milk."

"Christ, Della. Why the hell don't we just adopt the dentist? Maybe give him an automatic monthly debit from the checking account?"

"One cookie apiece," she said, implacable.

Kenneth shrugged, apparently resigned.

She picked up the keys to the Subaru. "I won't be long."

"Just be back by breakfast."

Della stared at him. What if I don't come back at all? She had actually said that once. Kenneth had smiled and asked whether she was going to run away with the gypsies, or maybe go off to join some pirates. It had been a temptation to say yes, dammit, yes, I'm going. But there were the twins. Della suspected pirates didn't take along their children. "Don't worry," she said. I've got nowhere else to go. But she didn't say that aloud.

Della turned and went upstairs to the twins' room to tell them good night. Naturally they both wanted to go with her to the mall. Each was afraid she wasn't going to get the hottest item in the Christmas doll departmment—the Little BeeDee Birth Defect Baby. There had been a run on the BeeDees, but Della had shopped for the twins early. "Daddy's going to tell you a story," she promised. The pair wasn't impressed.

"I want to see Santa," Terri said, with dogged, five-year-old insistence.

"You both saw Santa. Remember?"

"I forgot some things. An' I want to tell him again about BeeDee."

"Me, too," said Tammi. With Tammi, it was always "me too."

"Maybe this weekend," said Della.

"Will Daddy remember our cookies?" said Terri.

Before she exited the front door, Della took the chocolate chip cookies from the kitchen closet and set the sack on the stair step where Kenneth could not fail to stumble over it.

"So long," she called.

"Bring me back something great from the mall," he said. His only other response was to heighten the crowd noise from Upper Zambo-somewhere-or other.

Sleety snow was falling, the accumulation beginning to freeze on the streets. Della was glad she had the Subaru. So far this winter, she hadn't needed to use the four-wheel drive, but tonight the reality of having it reassured her.

Southeast Plaza was a mess. This close to Christmas, the normally spacious parking lots were jammed. Della took a chance and circled the row of spaces nearest to the mall entrances. If she were lucky, she'd be able to react instantly to someone's backup lights and snaffle a parking place within five seconds of its being vacated. That didn't happen. She cruised the second row, the third. Then—there! She reacted without thinking, seeing the vacant spot just beyond a metallic blue van. She swung the Subaru to the left.

And stamped down hard on the brake.

Some moron had parked an enormous barge of an ancient Plymouth so that it overlapped two diagonal spaces.

The Subaru slid to a stop with its nose about half an inch from the Plymouth's dinosaurian bumper. In the midst of her shock and sudden anger, Della saw the chrome was pocked with rust. The Subaru's headlights reflected back at her.

She said something unpleasant, the kind of language she usually only thought in dark silence. Then she backed her car out of the truncated space and resumed the search for parking. What Della eventually found was a free space on the extreme perimeter of the lot. She resigned herself to trudging a quarter mile through the slush. She hadn't worn boots. The icy water crept into her flats, soaked her toes.

"Shit," she said. "Shit shit shit."

Her shortest-distance-between-two-points course took her past the Plymouth hogging the two parking spots. Della stopped a moment, contemplating the darkened behemoth. It was dirty gold with the remnants of a vinyl roof peeling away like the flaking of a scabrous scalp. In the glare of the mercury vapor lamp, she could see that the rocker panels were riddled with rust holes. Odd. So much corrosion didn't happen in the dry Colorado air. She glanced curiously at the rear license plate. It was obscured with dirty snow.

She stared at the huge old car and realized she was getting

angry. Not just irritated. Real, honest-to-god, hardcore pissed off. What kind of imbeciles would take up two parking spaces on a rotten night just two weeks before Christmas?

Ones that drove a vintage, not-terribly-kept-up Plymouth, obviously.

Without even thinking about what she was doing, Della took out the spiral notebook from her handbag. She flipped to the blank page past tomorrow's grocery list and uncapped the fine-tip marker (it was supposed to write across anything—in this snow, it had *better*) and scrawled a message:

> DEAR JERK, IT'S GREAT YOU COULD USE UP TWO PARK-ING SPACES ON A NIGHT LIKE THIS. EVER HEAR OF THE JOY OF SHARING?

She paused, considering, then appended:

> —A CONCERNED FRIEND

Della folded the paper as many times as she could, to protect it from the wet, then slipped it under the driver's-side wiper blade.

It wouldn't do any good—she was sure this was the sort of driver who ordinarily would have parked illegally in the handicapped zone—but it made her feel better. Della walked on to the mall entrance and realized she was smiling.

She bought some rolls of foil wrapping paper for the adult gifts—assuming she actually gave Kenneth anything she'd bought for him—and an ample supply of Strawberry Shortcake pattern for the twins' presents. Della decided to splurge—she realized she was getting tired—and selected a package of pre-tied ribbon bows rather than simply taking a roll. She also bought a package of tampons.

Della wandered the mall for a little while, checking out the shoe stores, looking for something on sale in deep blue, a pair she could wear after Kenneth's office party for staff and spouses. What she *really* wanted were some new boots. Time enough for those after the holiday when the prices went down. Nothing appealed to her. Della knew she should be shopping for Kenneth's family in Nebraska. She couldn't wait forever to mail off their packages.

The hell with it. Della realized she was simply delaying returning home. Maybe she *did* need a therapy group, she thought. There was no relish to the thought of spending another night sleeping beside Kenneth, listening to the snoring that was interrupted only by the grinding of teeth. She thought that the sound of Kenneth's jaws moving against one another must be like hearing a speeded-up recording of continental drift.

She looked at her watch. A little after nine. No use waiting any longer. She did up the front of her coat and joined the flow of shoppers out into the snow.

Della realized, as she passed the rusted old Plymouth, that something wasn't the same. *What's wrong with this picture?* It was the note. It wasn't there. Probably it had slipped out from under the wiper blade with the wind and the water. Maybe the flimsy notebook paper had simply dissolved.

She no longer felt like writing another note. She dismissed the irritating lumber barge from her reality and walked on to her car.

Della let the Subaru warm up for thirty seconds (the consumer auto mechanics class had told her not to let the engine idle for the long minutes she had once believed necessary) and then slipped the shift into reverse.

The passenger compartment flooded with light.

She glanced into the rearview mirror and looked quickly away. A bright, glaring eye had stared back. Another quivered in the side mirror.

"Jesus Christ," she said under her breath. "The crazies are out tonight." She hit the clutch with one foot, the brake with the other, and waited for the car behind her to remove itself. Nothing happened. The headlights in the mirror flicked to bright. "Dammit." Della left the Subaru in neutral and got out of the car.

She shaded her eyes and squinted. The front of the car behind hers looked familiar. It was the gold Plymouth.

Two unseen car doors clicked open and chunked shut again.

The lights abruptly went out and Della blinked, her eyes trying to adjust to the dim mercury vapor illumination from the pole a few carlengths away.

She felt a cold thrill of unease in her belly and turned back toward the car.

"I've got a gun," said a voice. "Really." It sounded male and young. "I'll aim at your snatch first."

Someone else giggled, high and shrill.

Della froze in place. This couldn't be happening. It absolutely could not.

Her eyes were adjusting, the glare-phantoms drifting out to the limit of her peripheral vision and vanishing. She saw three figures in front of her, then a fourth. She didn't see a gun.

"Just what do you think you're doing?" she said.

"Not doing *nothin'*, yet." That, she saw, was the black one. He stood to the left of the white kid who had claimed to have a gun. The pair was bracketed by a boy who looked Chinese or Vietnamese and a young man with dark, Hispanic good looks. All four looked to be in their late teens or very early twenties. Four young men. Four ethnic groups represented. Della repressed a giggle she thought might be the first step toward hysteria.

"So what are you guys? Working on your merit badge in tolerance? Maybe selling magazine subscriptions?" Della immediately regretted saying that. Her husband was always riding her for smarting off.

"Funny lady," said the Hispanic. "We just happen to get along." He glanced to his left. "You laughing Huey?"

The black shook his head. "Too cold. I'm shiverin' out here. I didn't bring no clothes for this."

"Easy way to fix that, man," said the white boy. To Della, he said, "Vinh, Tomas, Huey, me, we all got similar interests, you know?"

"Listen—" Della started to say.

"Chuckie," said the black Della now assumed was Huey, "let's us just shag out of here, okay?"

"*Chuckie?*" said Della.

"Shut up!" said Chuckie. To Huey, he said, "Look, we came up here for a vacation, right? The word is fun." He said to Della, "Listen, we were having a good time until we saw you stick the note under the wiper." His eyes glistened in the vapor-lamp glow. "I don't like getting any static from some 'burb-bitch just 'cause she's on the rag."

"For God's sake," said Della disgustedly. She decided he didn't really have a gun. "Screw off!" The exhaust vapor from the Subaru spiraled up around her. "I'm leaving, boys."

"Any trouble here, Miss?" said a new voice. Everyone looked. It was one of the mall rent-a-cops, bulky in his fur trimmed jacket and Russian-styled cap. His hand lay casually across the unsnapped holster flap at his hip.

"Not if these underage creeps move their barge so I can back out," said Della.

"How about it, guys?" said the rent-a-cop.

Now there *was* a gun, a dark pistol, in Chuckie's hand, and he pointed it at the rent-a-cop's face. "Naw," Chuckie said. "This was gonna be a vacation, but what the heck. No witnesses, I reckon."

"For God's sake," said the rent-a-cop, starting to back away.

Chuckie grinned and glanced aside at his friends. "Remember the security guy at the mall in Tucson?" To Della, he said, "Most of these rent-a-pig companies don't give their guys any ammo. Liability laws and all that shit. Too bad." He lifted the gun purposefully.

The rent-a-cop went for his pistol anyway. Chuckie shot him in the face. Red pulp sprayed out the back of his skull and stained the slush as the man's body flopped back and forth, spasming.

"For chrissake," said Chuckie in exasperation. "Enough already. Relax, man." He leaned over his victim and deliberately aimed and fired, aimed and fired. The second shot entered the rent-a-cop's left eye. The third shattered his teeth.

Della's eyes recorded everything as though she were a movie camera. Everything was moving in slow motion and she was numb. She tried to make things speed up. Without thinking about the decision, she spun and made for her car door. She knew it was hopeless.

"Chuckie!"

"So? Where's she gonna go? We got her blocked. I'll just put one through her windshield and we can go out and pick up a couple of sixpacks, maybe hit the late show at some other mall."

Della heard him fire one more time. Nothing tore through the back of her skull. He was still blowing apart the rent-a-cop's head.

She slammed into the Subaru's driver seat and punched the door-lock switch, for all the good that would do. Della hit the four-wheel-drive switch. *That* was what Chuckie hadn't thought about. She jammed the gearshift into first, gunned the engine, and popped the clutch. The Subaru barely protested as the front tires clawed and bounced over the six-inch concrete row barrier. The barrier screeched along the underside of the frame. Then the rear wheels were over and the Subaru fishtailed momentarily.

Don't over-correct, she thought. It was a prayer.

The Subaru straightened out and Della was accelerating down the mall's outer perimeter service road, slush spraying to either side. Now what? she thought. People must have heard the shots. The lot would be crawling with cops.

But in the meantime—

The lights, bright and blinding, blasted against her mirrors. Della stamped the accelerator to the floor.

This was crazy! This didn't happen to people—not to *real* people. The mall security man's blood in the snow had been real enough.

In the rearview, there was a sudden flash just above the left-side headlight, then another. It was a muzzle-blast, Della realized. They were shooting at her. It was just like on TV. The scalp on the back of her head itched. Would she feel it when the bullet crashed through?

The twins! Kenneth. She wanted to see them all, to be safely with them. Just be anywhere but here!

Della spun the wheel, ignoring the stop sign and realizing that the access road dead-ended. She could go right or left, so went right. She thought it was the direction of home. Not a good choice. The lights were all behind her now; she could see nothing but darkness ahead. Della tried to remember what lay behind the mall on this side. There were housing developments, both completed and under construction.

There had to be a 7-Eleven, a filling station, *something*. Anything. But there wasn't, and then the pavement ended. At first the road was suddenly rougher, the potholes yawning deeper. Then the slush-marked asphalt stopped. The Subaru bounced across the gravel; within thirty yards, the gravel deteriorated to roughly graded dirt. The dirt surface more properly could be called mud.

A wooden barrier loomed ahead, the reflective stripes and lightly falling snow glittering in the headlights.

It *was* like on TV, Della thought. She gunned the engine and ducked sideways, even with the dash, as the Subaru plowed into the barrier. She heard a sickening *crack* and shattered windshield glass sprayed down around her. Della felt the car veer. She tried to sit upright again, but the auto was spinning too fast.

The Subaru swung a final time and smacked firm against a low grove of young pine. The engine coughed and stalled. Della hit the light switch. She smelled the overwhelming tang of crushed pine needles flooding with the snow through the space where the windshield had been. The engine groaned when she twisted the key, didn't start.

Della risked a quick look around. The Plymouth's lights were visible, but the car was farther back than she had dared hope. The size of the lights wasn't increasing and the beams pointed up at a steep angle. Probably the heavy Plymouth had slid in the slush, gone off the road, was stuck for good.

She tried the key, and again the engine didn't catch. She heard something else—voices getting closer. Della took the key out of the ignition and glanced around the dark passenger compartment. Was there anything she could use? Anything at all? Not in the glovebox. She knew there was nothing there but the owner's manual and a large pack of sugarless spearmint gum.

The voices neared.

Della reached under the dash and tugged the trunk release. Then she rolled down the window and slipped out into the darkness. She wasn't too stunned to forget that the overhead light would go on if she opened the door.

At least one of the boys had a flashlight. The beam flickered and danced along the snow.

Della stumbled to the rear of the Subaru. By feel, she found the toolbox. With her other hand, she sought out the lug wrench. Then she moved away from the car.

She wished she had a gun. She wished she had learned to *use* a gun. That had been something tagged for a vague future when she'd finished her consumer mechanics course and the self-defense workshop, and had some time again to take another night course. It wasn't, she had reminded herself, that she was paranoid. Della simply wanted to be better prepared for the exigencies of living in the city. The suburbs weren't *the city* to Kenneth, but if you were a girl from rural Montana, they were.

She hadn't expected *this*.

She hunched down. Her nose told her the shelter she had found was a hefty clump of sagebrush. She was perhaps twenty yards from the Subaru now. The boys were making no attempt at stealth. She heard them talking to each other as the flashlight beam bobbed around her stalled car.

"So, she in there chilled with her brains all over the wheel?" said Tomas, the Hispanic kid.

"You an optimist?" said Chuckie. He laughed, a high-pitched giggle. "No, she ain't here, you dumb shit. This one's a tough lady." Then he said, "Hey, lookie there!"

"What you doin'?" said Huey. "We ain't got time for that."

"Don't be too sure. Maybe we can use this."

What had he found? Della wondered.

"Now we do what?" said Vinh. He had a slight accent.

"This be the West," said Huey. "I guess now we're mountain men, just like in the movies."

"Right," said Chuckie. "Track her. There's mud. There's snow. How far can she get?"

"There's the trail," said Tomas. "Shine the light over there. She must be pretty close."

Della turned. Hugging the toolbox, trying not to let it clink or clatter, she fled into the night.

They cornered her a few minutes later.

Or it could have been an hour. There was no way she could read her watch. All Della knew was that she had run; she had run and she had attempted circling around to where she might have a shot at making it to the distant lights of the shopping mall. Along the way, she'd felt the brush clawing at her denim jeans and the mud and slush attempting to suck down her shoes. She tried to make out shapes in the clouded-over dark, evaluating every murky form as a potential hiding place.

"Hey, baby," said Huey from right in front of her.

Della recoiled, feinted to the side, collided painfully with a wooden fence. The boards gave only slightly. She felt a long splinter drive through the down coat and spear into her shoulder. When Della jerked away, she felt the splinter tear away from its board and then break off.

The flashlight snapped on, the beam at first blinding her, then lowering to focus on her upper body. From their voices, she knew all four were there. Della wanted to free a hand to pull the splinter loose from her shoulder. Instead she continued cradling the blue plastic toolbox.

"Hey," said Chuckie, "what's in that thing? Family treasure, maybe?"

Della remained mute. She'd already gotten into trouble enough wising off.

"Let's see," said Chuckie. "Show us, Della-honey."

She stared at his invisible face.

Chuckie giggled. "Your driver's license, babe. In your purse. In the car."

Shit, she thought.

"Lousy picture." Chuckie. "I think maybe we're gonna make your face match it." Again, that ghastly laugh. "Meantime, let's see what's in the box, okay?"

"Jewels, you think?" said Vinh.

"Naw, I don't think," said his leader. "But maybe she was makin' the bank deposit or something." He addressed Della, "You got enough goodies for us, maybe we can be bought off."

No chance, she thought. They want everything. My money, my rings, my watch. She tried to swallow, but her throat was too dry. My life.

"Open the box," said Chuckie, voice mean now.

"Open the box," said Tomas. Huey echoed him. The four started chanting, "Open the box, open the box, open the box."

"All right," she almost screamed. "I'll do it." They stopped their chorus. Someone snickered. Her hands moving slowly, Della's brain raced. Do it, she thought. But be careful. So careful. She let the lug wrench rest across her palm below the toolbox. With her other hand, she unsnapped the catch and slid up the lid toward the four. She didn't think any of them could see in, though the flashlight beam was focused now on the toolbox lid.

Della reached inside, as deliberately as she could, trying to betray nothing of what she hoped to do. It all depended upon what lay on top. Her bare fingertips touched the cold steel of the crescent wrench. Her fingers curled around the handle.

"This is pretty dull," said Tomas. "Let's just rape her."

Now!

She withdrew the wrench, cocked her wrist back and hurled the tool about two feet above the flashlight's glare. Della snapped it just like her daddy had taught her to throw a hardball. She hadn't liked baseball all that much. But now—

The wrench crunched something and Chuckie screamed. The flashlight dropped to the snow.

Snapping shut the toolbox, Della sprinted between Chuckie and the one she guessed was Huey.

The black kid lunged for her and slipped in the muck, toppling face-first into the slush. Della had a peripheral glimpse of Tomas leaping toward her, but his leading foot came down on the back of Huey's head, grinding the boy's face into the mud. Huey's scream bubbled; Tomas cursed and tumbled forward, trying to stop himself with out-thrust arms.

All Della could think as she gained the darkness was, I should have grabbed the light.

She heard the one she thought was Vinh, laughing. "Cripes, guys, neat. Just like Moe and Curley and that other one."

"Shut up," said Chuckie's voice. It sounded pinched and in pain. "Shut the fuck up." The timbre squeaked and broke. "Get up, you dorks. Get the bitch."

Sticks and stones—Della thought. Was she getting hysterical? There was no good reason not to.

As she ran—and stumbled—across the nightscape, Della could feel the long splinter moving with the movement of the muscles in her shoulder. The feeling of it, not just the pain, but the sheer, physical sensation of intrusion, nauseated her.

I've got to stop, she thought. I've got to rest. I've got to think.

Della stumbled down the side of a shallow gulch and found she was splashing across a shallow, frigid stream. Water. It triggered something. Disregarding the cold soaking her flats and numbing her feet, she turned and started upstream, attempting to splash as little as possible. This had worked, she seemed to recall, in *Uncle Tom's Cabin*, as well as a lot of bad prison escape movies.

The boys were hardly experienced mountain men. They weren't Indian trackers. This ought to take care of her trail.

After what she estimated to be at least a hundred yards, when her feet felt like blocks of wood and she felt she was losing her balance, Della clambered out of the stream and struggled up the side of the gulch. She found herself in groves of pine, much like the trees where her Subaru had ended its skid. At least the pungent evergreens supplied some shelter against the prairie wind that had started to rise.

She heard noise from down in the gulch. It was music. It made her think of the twins.

"What the *fuck* are you doing?" Chuckie's voice.

"It's a tribute, man. A gesture." Vinh. "It's his blaster."

Della recognized the tape. Rap music. Run DMC, the Beastie Boys, one of those groups.

"Christ, I didn't mean it." Tomas. "It's her fault."

"Well, he's dead," said Chuckie, "and that's it for him. Now turn that shit off. Somebody might hear."

"Who's going to hear?" said Vinh. "Nobody can hear out here. Just us, and her."

"That's the point. She can."

"So what?" said Tomas. "We got the gun, we got the light. She's got nothin' but that stupid box."

"We *had* Huey," said Chuckie. "Now we don't. Shut off the blaster, dammit."

"Okay," Vinh's voice sounded sullen. There was a loud click and the rap echo died.

Della huddled against the rough bark of a pine trunk, hugging the box and herself. The boy's dead, she thought. So? said her common sense. He would have killed you, maybe raped you, tortured you before pulling the trigger. The rest are going to have to die too.

No.

Yes, said her practical side. You have no choice. They started this.

I put the note under the wiper blade.

Get serious. That was harmless. These three are going to kill you. They will hurt you first, then they'll put the gun inside your mouth and—

Della wanted to cry, to scream. She knew she could not. It was absolutely necessary that she not break now.

Terri, she thought, Tammi. I love you. After a while, she remembered Kenneth. Even you. I love you too. Not much, but some.

"Let's look up above," came the voice from the gully. Chuckie. Della heard the wet scrabbling sounds as the trio scratched and pulled their way up from the streambed. As it caught the falling snow, the flashlight looked like the beam from a searchlight at a movie premiere.

Della edged back behind the pine and slowly moved to where the trees were closer together. Boughs laced together, screening her.

"Now what?" said Tomas.

"We split up." Chuckie gestured; the flashlight beam swung wide. "You go through the middle. Vinh and me'll take the sides."

"Then why don't you give me the light?" said Tomas.

"I stole the sucker. It's mine."

"Shit, I could just walk past her."

Chuckie laughed. "Get real, dude. You'll smell her, hear her, somethin'. Trust me."

Tomas said something Della couldn't make out, but the tone was unconvinced.

"Now *do* it," said Chuckie. The light moved off to Della's left. She heard the squelching of wet shoes moving toward her. Evidently Tomas had done some wading in the gully. Either that or the slush was taking its toll.

Tomas couldn't have done better with radar. He came straight for her.

Della guessed the boy was ten feet away from her, five feet, just the other side of the pine. The lug wrench was the spider type, in the shape of a cross. She clutched the black steel of the longest arm and brought her hand back. When she detected movement around the edge of the trunk, she swung with hysterical strength, aiming at his head.

Tomas staggered back. The sharp arm of the lug wrench had caught him under the nose, driving the cartilage back up into his face. About a third of the steel was hidden in flesh. "Unh!" He tried to cry out, but all he could utter was, "Unh, unh!"

"Tomas?" Chuckie was yelling. "What the hell are you doing?"

The flashlight flickered across the grove. Della caught a momentary glimpse of Tomas lurching backward with the lug wrench impaled in his face as though he were wearing some hideous Halloween accessory.

"Unh!" said Tomas once more. He backed into a tree, then slid down the trunk until he was seated in the snow. The flashlight beam jerked across that part of the grove again and Della saw Tomas's eyes stare wide open, dark and blank. Blood was running off the ends of the perpendicular lug wrench arms.

"I see her!" someone yelled. "I think she got Tomas. She's a devil!" Vinh.

"So chill her!"

Della heard branches and brush crashing off to her side. She jerked open the plastic toolbox, but her fingers were frozen and the container crashed to the ground. She tried to catch the contents as they cascaded into the slush and the darkness. Her fingers closed on something, one thing.

The handle felt good. It was the wooden-hafted screwdriver, the sharp one with the slot head. Her auto mechanics teacher had approved. Insulated handle, he'd said. Good forged steel shaft. You could use this hummer to pry a tire off its rim.

She didn't even have time to lift it as Vinh crashed into her. His arms and legs wound around her like eels.

"Got her!" he screamed. "Chuckie, come here and shoot her."

They rolled in the viscid, muddy slush. Della worked an arm free. Her good arm. The one with the screwdriver.

There was no question of asking him nicely to let go, of giving warning, of simply aiming to disable. Her self-defense teacher had drilled into all the students the basic dictum of do what you can, do what you have to do. No rules, no apologies.

With all her strength, Della drove the screwdriver up into the base of his skull. She thrust and twisted the tool until she felt her knuckles dig into his stiff hair. Vinh screamed, a high keening wail that cracked and shattered as blood spurted out of his nose and mouth, splattering against Della's neck. The Vietnamese boys' arms and legs tensed and then let go as his body vibrated spastically in some sort of fit.

Della pushed him away from her and staggered to her feet. Her nose was full of the odor she remembered from the twins' diaper pail.

She knew she should retrieve the screwdriver, grasp the handle tightly and twist it loose from Vinh's head. She couldn't. All she could do at this point was simply turn and run. Run again. And hope the survivor of the four boys didn't catch her.

But Chuckie had the light, and Chuckie had the gun. She had a feeling Chuckie was in no mood to give up. Chuckie would find her. He would make her pay for the loss of his friends.

But if she had to pay, Della thought, the price would be dear.

Prices, she soon discovered, were subject to change without warning.

With only one remaining pursuer, Della thought she ought to be able to get away. Maybe not easily, but now there was no crossfire of spying eyes, no ganging up of assailants. There was just one boy left, even if he *was* a psychopath carrying a loaded pistol.

Della was shaking. It was fatigue, she realized. The endless epinephrine rush of flight and fight. Probably, too, the letdown from just having killed two other human beings. She didn't want to have to think about the momentary sight of blood flowing off the shining ends of the lug wrench, the sensation of how it *felt* when the slot-headed screwdriver drove up into Vinh's brain. But she couldn't order herself to forget these things. It was akin to someone telling her not, under any circumstances, to think about milking a purple cow.

Della tried. No, she thought. Don't think about it at all. She thought about dismembering the purple cow with a chainsaw. Then she heard Chuckie's voice. The boy was still distant, obviously casting around virtually at random in the pine groves. Della stiffened.

"They're cute, Della-honey. I'll give 'em that." He giggled. "Terri and Tammi. God, didn't you and your husband have any more imagination than that?"

No, Della thought. We each had too much imagination. Tammi and Terri were simply the names we finally could agree on. The names of compromise.

"You know something?" Chuck raised his voice. "Now that I

know where they live, I could drive over there in a while and say howdy. They wouldn't know a thing about what was going on, about what happened to their mom while she was out at the mall."

Oh God! thought Della.

"You want me to pass on any messages?"

"You little bastard!" She cried it out without thinking.

"Touchy, huh?" Chuckie slopped across the wet snow in her direction. "Come on out of the trees, Della-honey."

Della said nothing. She crouched behind a deadfall of brush and dead limbs. She was perfectly still.

Chuckie stood equally still, not more than twenty feet away. He stared directly at her hiding place, as though he could see through the night and brush. "Listen," he said. "This is getting real, you know, *boring*." He waited. "We could be out here all night, you know? All my buddies are gone now, and it's thanks to you, lady. Who the hell you think you are, Clint Eastwood?"

Della assumed that was a rhetorical question.

Chuckie hawked deep in his throat and spat on the ground. He rubbed the base of his throat gingerly with a free hand. "You hurt me, Della-honey. I think you busted my collarbone." He giggled. "But I don't hold grudges. In fact—" He paused contemplatively. "Listen now, I've got an idea. You know about droogs? You know, like in that movie?"

Clockwork Orange, she thought. Della didn't respond.

"Ending was stupid, but the start was pretty cool." Chuckie's personality seemed to have mutated into a manic stage. "Well, me droogs is all gone. I need a new gang, and you're real good, Della-honey. I want you should join me."

"Give me a break," said Della in the darkness.

"No, really," Chuckie said. "You're a born killer. I can tell. You and me, we'd be perfect. We'll blow this popsicle stand and have some real fun. Whaddaya say?"

He's serious, she thought. There was a ring of complete honesty in his voice. She floundered for some answer. "I've got kids," she said.

"We'll take 'em along," said Chuckie. "I like kids, always took care of my brothers and sisters." He paused. "Listen, I'll bet you're on the outs with your old man."

Della said nothing. It would be like running away to be a pirate. Wouldn't it?

Chuckie hawked and spat again. "Yeah, I figured. When we

pick up your kids, we can waste him. You like that? I can do it, or you can. Your choice."

You're crazy, she thought. "*I* want to," she found herself saying aloud.

"So come out and we'll talk about it."

"You'll kill me."

"Hey," he said, "I'll kill you if you *don't* come out. I got the light and the gun, remember? This way we can learn to trust each other right from the start. I won't kill you. I won't do nothing. Just talk."

"Okay." Why not, she thought. Sooner or later, he'll find his way in here and put the gun in my mouth and—Della stood up.—but maybe, just maybe—Agony lanced through her knees.

Chuckie cocked his head, staring her way. "Leave the tools."

"I already did. The ones I didn't use."

"Yeah," said Chuckie. "The ones you used, you used real good." He lowered the beam of the flashlight. "Here you go. I don't want you stumbling and falling and maybe breaking your neck."

Della stepped around the deadfall and slowly walked toward him. His hands were at his sides. She couldn't see if he was holding the gun. She stopped when she was a few feet away.

"Hell of a night, huh?" said Chuckie. "It'll be really good to go inside where it's warm and get some coffee." He held the flashlight so that the beam speared into the sky between them.

Della could make out his thin, pain-pinched features. She imagined he could see hers. "I was only going out to the mall for a few things," she said.

Chuckie laughed. "Shit happens."

"What now?" Della said.

"Time for the horror show." His teeth showed ferally as his lips drew back in a smile. "Guess maybe I sort of fibbed." He brought up his hand, glinting of metal.

"That's what I thought," she said, feeling a cold and distant sense of loss. "Huey, there, going to help?" She nodded to a point past his shoulder.

"Huey?" Chuckie looked puzzled just for a second as he glanced to the side. "Huey's—"

Della leapt with all the spring left in her legs. Her fingers closed around his wrist and the hand with the gun. "Christ!" Chuckie screamed, as her shoulder crashed against the spongy place where his broken collarbone pushed out against the skin.

They tumbled on the December ground, Chuckie underneath, Della wrapping her legs around him as though pulling a lover tight. She burrowed her chin into the area of his collarbone and he screamed again. Kenneth had always joked about the sharpness of her chin.

The gun went off. The flash was blinding, the report hurt her ears. Wet snow plumped down from the overhanging pine branches, a large chunk plopping into Chuckie's wide-open mouth. He started to choke.

Then the pistol was in Della's hands. She pulled back from him, getting to her feet, backpedaling furiously to get out of his reach. She stared down at him along the blued-steel barrel. The pirate captain struggled to his knees.

"Back to the original deal," he said. "Okay?"

I wish, she almost said. Della pulled the trigger. Again. And again.

"Where the hell have you been?" said Kenneth as she closed the front door behind her. "You've been gone for close to three hours." He inspected her more closely. "Della, honey, are you all right?"

"Don't call me that," she said. "Please." She had hoped she would look better, more normal. Unruffled. Once Della had pulled the Subaru up to the drive beside the house, she had spent several minutes using spit and Kleenex trying to fix her mascara. Such makeup as she'd had along was in her handbag, and she had no idea where that was. Probably the police had it; three cruisers with lights flashing had passed her, going the other way, as she was driving north of Southeast Plaza.

"Your clothes." Kenneth gestured. He stood where he was.

Della looked down at herself. She'd tried to wash off the mud, using snow and a rag from the trunk. There was blood, too, some of it Chuckie's, the rest doubtless from Vinh and Tomas.

"Honey, was there an accident?"

She had looked at the driver's side of the Subaru for a long minute after getting home. At least the car drove; it must just have been flooded before. But the insurance company wouldn't be happy. The entire side would need a new paint job.

"Sort of," she said.

"Are you hurt?"

To top it all off, she had felt the slow stickiness between her legs as she'd come up the walk. Terrific. She could hardly wait for the cramps to intensify.

"Hurt?" She shook her head. No. "How are the twins?"

"Oh, they're in bed. I checked a half hour ago. They're asleep."

"Good." Della heard sirens in the distance, getting louder, nearing the neighborhood. Probably the police had found her driver's license in Chuckie's pocket. She'd forgotten that.

"So," said Kenneth. It was obvious to Della that he didn't know at this point whether to be angry, solicitous or funny. "What'd you bring me from the mall?"

Della's right hand was nestled in her jacket pocket. She felt the solid bulk, the cool grip of the pistol.

Outside, the volume of sirens increased.

She touched the trigger. She withdrew her hand from the pocket and aimed the pistol at Kenneth. He looked back at her strangely.

The sirens went past. Through the window, Della caught a glimpse of a speeding ambulance. The sound Dopplered down to a silence as distant as the dream that flashed through her head.

Della pulled the trigger and the *click* seemed to echo through the entire house.

Shocked, Kenneth stared at the barrel of the gun, then up at her eyes.

It was okay. She'd counted the shots. Just like in the movies.

"I think," Della said to her husband, "that we need to talk."

Meathouse Man

GEORGE R. R. MARTIN

Elsewhere in this book you'll find my essay "Outlaws," which posits the notion that there have *always* been splatterpunks (under different names, of course). One relevant example of this theory is the 1960s writings of Harlan Ellison, who in such protosplat stories as "A Boy and His Dog" and "I Have No Mouth and I Must Scream" clearly delineated the attitudes and explicitness to be later linked with splatterpunk fiction.

But splatterpunk is infinitely flexible; it could even be found in seventies science fiction.

George R. R. Martin is, to my way of thinking, one of the best and most consistently satisfying writers in generic fiction today (even though, once again, here's a writer who wants me to tell you that he's definitely *not* a splatterpunk). Martin's work first appeared in the mid-1970s, and since then he's amassed a steady stream of impressive credentials. On the printed page these works include historical vampire novels (the award-winning *Fevre Dream*, a love song to old steam-powered riverboats), first-rate fiction collections (*Songs the Dead Men Sing*), classic short stories (the Nebula Award–winning "Sandkings"), and bizarre series anthologies (the *Wild Cards* alternate universe books).

George's novel *Nightflyers* also was made into a (very bad) motion picture. Then there's his television work; Martin's scripts have appeared on the new "Twilight Zone" series as well as HBO's "The Hitchhiker," although he's received the most TV exposure from the nearly three years he spent writing for the cult favorite "Beauty and the Beast" (starring Linda Hamilton and Ron Perlman; George eventually became supervising producer on the show).

As for "Meathouse Man," this is a deeply felt work, and one of the darkest stories in this book. Martin originally submitted it to Harlan

Ellison as a potential entry in *Again, Dangerous Visions*; Ellison rejected it (and later told me he was sorry he did). Whatever its history, "Meathouse Man" operates on a multitude of levels. On the one hand it's a disturbing illustration of man's rapacious capacity for economic exploitation; on the other a weary, defeated farewell to the childish conceits of innocence and romantic love.

"Meathouse Man" deserves to be resurrected from its relative obscurity. It's an effective history lesson, a prime example of the fact that not all good splatterpunk needs to have been written after the publication of *Books of Blood*.

I hope you enjoy this story; I know you won't forget it.

(I) IN THE MEATHOUSE

They came straight from the ore-fields that first time, Trager with the others, the older boys, the almost-men who worked their corpses next to his. Cox was the oldest of the group, and he'd been around the most, and he said that Trager had to come even if he didn't want to. Then one of the others laughed and said that Trager wouldn't even know what to do, but Cox the kind-of leader shoved him until he was quiet. And when payday came, Trager trailed the rest to the meathouse, scared but somehow eager, and he paid his money to a man downstairs and got a room key.

He came into the dim room trembling, nervous. The others had gone to other rooms, had left him alone with her (no, *it*, not her, but *it*, he reminded himself, and promptly forgot again). In a shabby gray cubicle with a single smoky light.

He stank of sweat and sulfur, like all who walked the streets of Skrakky, but there was no help for that. It would be better if he could bathe first, but the room did not have a bath. Just a sink, a double bed with sheets that looked dirty even in the dimness, a corpse.

She lay there naked, staring at nothing, breathing shallow breaths. Her legs were spread; ready. Was she always that way, Trager wondered, or had the man before him arranged her like that? He didn't know. He knew how to do it (he did, he *did*, he'd read the books Cox gave him, and there were films you could see, and all sorts of things), but he didn't know much of anything else. Except maybe how to handle corpses. That he was good at, the youngest handler on Skrakky, but he had to be. They had forced him into the handlers' school when his mother died, and they made him learn, so that was the thing he did. This, this he had never done (but he knew how, yes, yes, he *did*); it was his first time.

He came to the bed slowly and sat to a chorus of creaking springs. He touched her and the flesh was warm. Of course. She was not a corpse, not really, no; the body was alive enough, a heart beat under the heavy white breasts, she breathed. Only the brain was gone, ripped from her, replaced with a deadman's synthabrain. She was meat now, an extra body for a corpse handler to control, just like the crew he worked each day under sulfur skies. She was not a woman. So it did not matter that Trager was just a boy, a jowly frog-faced boy who smelled of Skrakky. She (no, *it*, remember?) would not care, could not care.

Emboldened, aroused and hard, the boy stripped off his corpse handler's clothing and climbed in bed with the female meat. He was very excited; his hands shook as he stroked her, studied her. Her skin was very white, her hair dark and long, but even the boy could not call her pretty. Her face was too flat and wide, her mouth hung open, and her limbs were loose and sagging with fat.

On her huge breasts, all around the fat dark nipples, the last customer had left tooth-marks where he'd chewed her. Trager touched the marks tentatively, traced them with a finger. Then, sheepish about his hesitations, he grabbed one breast, squeezed it hard, pinched the nipple until he imagined a real girl would squeal with pain. The corpse did not move. Still squeezing, he rolled over on her and took the other breast into his mouth.

And the corpse responded.

She thrust up at him, hard, and meaty arms wrapped around his pimpled back to pull him to her. Trager groaned and reached down between her legs. She was hot, wet, excited. He trembled. How did they do that? Could she really get excited without a mind, or did they have lubricating tubes stuck into her, or what?

Then he stopped caring. He fumbled, found his penis, put it into her, thrust. The corpse hooked her legs around him and thrust back. It felt good, real good, better than anything he'd ever done to himself, and in some obscure way he felt proud that she was so wet and so excited.

It only took a few more strokes; he was too new, too young, too eager to last long. A few strokes was all he needed—but it was all she needed too. They came together, a red flush washing over her skin as she arched against him and shook soundlessly.

Afterwards she lay again like a corpse.

Trager was drained and satisfied, but he had more time left, and he was determined to get his money's worth. He explored her thoroughly, sticking his fingers everywhere they would go, touching her everywhere, rolling it over, looking at everything. The corpse moved like dead meat.

He left her as he'd found her, lying face up on the bed with her legs apart. Meathouse courtesy.

The horizon was a wall of factories, all factories, vast belching factories that sent red shadows to flick against the sulfur-dark skies. The boy saw but hardly noticed. He was strapped in place high atop his automill, two stories up on a monster machine of corroding yellow-painted metal with savage teeth of diamond and duralloy, and his eyes were blurred with triple images. Clear and strong and hard he saw the control panel before him, the wheel, the fuel-feed, the bright handle of the ore-scoops, the banks of light that would tell of trouble in the refinery under his feet, the brake and emergency brake. But that was not all he saw. Dimly, faintly, there were echoes; overlaid images of two other control cabs, almost identical to his, where corpse hands moved clumsily over the instruments.

Trager moved those hands, slow and careful, while another part of his mind held his own hands, his real hands, very still. The corpse controller hummed thinly on his belt.

On either side of him, the other two automills moved into flanking positions. The corpse hands squeezed the brakes; the machines rumbled to a halt. On the edge of the great sloping pit, they stood in a row, shabby pitted juggernauts ready to descend into the gloom. The pit was growing steadily larger, each day new layers of rock and ore were stripped away.

Once a mountain range had stood here, but Trager did not remember that.

The rest was easy. The automills were aligned now. To move the crew in unison was a cinch, any decent handler could do *that*. It was only when you had to keep several corpses busy at several different tasks that things got tricky. But a good corpse-handler could do that, too. Eight-crews were not unknown to veterans; eight bodies linked to a single corpse controller moved by a single mind and eight synthabrains. The deadmen were each tuned to one controller, and only one; the handler who wore that controller and thought corpse-thoughts in its proximity field could move those deadmen like secondary bodies. Or like his own body. If he was good enough.

Trager checked his filtermask and earplugs quickly, then touched the fuel-feed, engaged, flicked on the laser-knives and the drills. His corpses echoed his moves, and pulses of light spit through the twilight of Skrakky. Even through his plugs he could hear the awful whine as the ore-scoops revved up and lowered. The rock-eating maw of an automill was even wider than the machine was tall.

Rumbling and screeching, in perfect formation, Trager and his corpse crew descended into the pit. Before they reached the factories on the far side of the plain, tons of metal would have been torn from the earth, melted and refined and processed, while the worthless rock was reduced to powder and blown out into the already-unbreathable air. He would deliver finished steel at dusk, on the horizon.

He was a good handler, Trager thought as the automills started down. But the handler in the meathouse—now she must be an artist. He imagined her down in the cellar somewhere, watching each of her corpses through holos and psi circuits, humping them all to please her patrons. Was it just a fluke then, that his fuck had been so perfect? Or was she always that good? But how, *how*, to move a dozen corpses without even being near them, to have them doing different things, to keep them all excited, to match the needs and rhythm of each customer so exactly?

The air behind him was black and choked by rock-dust, his ears were full of screams, and the far horizon was a glowering red wall beneath which yellow ants crawled and ate rock. But Trager kept his hard-on all across the plain as the automill shook beneath him.

The corpses were company-owned; they stayed in the company deadman depot. But Trager had a room, a slice of the space that was his own in a steel-and-concrete warehouse with a thousand other slices. He only knew a handful of his neighbors, but he knew all of them too; they were corpse handlers. It was a world of silent shadowed corridors and endless closed doors. The lobby-lounge, all air and plastic, was a dusty deserted place where none of the tenants ever gathered.

The evenings were long there, the nights eternal. Trager had bought extra light-panels for his particular cube, and when all of them were on they burned so bright that his infrequent visitors blinked and complained about the glare. But always there came a time when he could read no more, and then he had to turn them out, and the darkness returned once more.

His father, long gone and barely remembered, had left a wealth of books and tapes, and Trager kept them still. The room was lined with them, and others stood in great piles against the foot of the bed and on either side of the bathroom door. Infrequently he went out with Cox and the others, to drink and joke and prowl for real women. He imitated them as best he could, but he always felt out of place. So most of his nights were spent at home, reading and listening to the music, remembering and thinking.

That week he thought long after he'd faded his light panels into black, and his thoughts were a frightened jumble. Payday was coming again, and Cox would be after him to return to the meathouse, and yes, yes, he wanted to. It had been good, exciting; for once he had felt confident and virile. But it was so easy, cheap, *dirty*. There had to be more, didn't there? Love, whatever that was? It had to be better with a real woman, had to, and he wouldn't find one of those in a meathouse. He'd never found one outside, either, but then he'd never really had the courage to try. But he had to try, *had* to, or what sort of life would he ever have?

Beneath the covers he masturbated, hardly thinking of it, while he resolved not to return to the meathouse.

But a few days later, Cox laughed at him and he had to go along. Somehow he felt it would prove something.

A different room this time, a different corpse. Fat and black, with bright orange hair, less attractive than his first, if that was possible. But Trager came to her ready and eager, and this time he lasted longer. Again, the performance was superb. Her rhythm matched his stroke for stroke, she came with him, she seemed to know exactly what he wanted.

Other visits; two of them, four, six. He was a regular now at the meathouse, along with the others, and he had stopped worrying about it. Cox and the others accepted him in a strange half-hearted way, but his dislike of them had grown, if anything. He was better than they were, he thought. He could hold his own in a meathouse, he could run his corpses and his automills as good as any of them, and he still thought and dreamed. In time he'd leave them all behind, leave Skrakky, be something. They would be meathouse men as long as they would live, but Trager knew he could do better. He believed. He would find love.

He found none in the meathouse, but the sex got better and better, though it was perfect to begin with. In bed with the corpses, Trager was never dissatisfied; he did everything he'd ever read about, heard about, dreamed about. The corpses knew his needs before he did. When he needed it slow, they were slow. When he wanted to have it hard and quick and brutal, they gave it to him that way, perfectly. He used every orifice they had; they always knew which one to present to him.

His admiration of the meathouse handler grew steadily for months, until it was almost worship. Perhaps somehow he could meet her, he thought at last. Still a boy, still hopelessly naive, he was sure he would love her. Then he would take her away from the meathouse to a clean corpseless world where they could be happy together.

One day, in a moment of weakness, he told Cox and the others. Cox looked at him, shook his head, grinned. Somebody else snickered. Then they all began to laugh. "What an *ass* you are, Trager," Cox said at last. "There is no fucking *handler!* Don't tell me you never heard of a feedback circuit?"

He explained it all, to laughter; explained how each corpse was tuned to a controller built into its bed, explained how each customer handled his own meat, explained why non-handlers found meathouse women dead and still. And the boy realized suddenly why the sex was always perfect. He was a better handler than even he had thought.

That night, alone in his room with all the lights burning white and hot, Trager faced himself. And turned away, sickened. He was good at his job, he was proud of that, but the rest . . .

It was the meathouse, he decided. There was a trap there in the meathouse, a trap that could ruin him, destroy life and dreams and hope. He would not go back; it was too easy. He would show Cox, show all of them. He could take the hard way, take the risks, feel the pain if he had to. And maybe the joy, maybe the love. He'd gone the other way too long.

Trager did not go back to the meathouse. Feeling strong and decisive and superior, he went back to his room. There, as years passed, he read and dreamed and waited for life to begin.

(1) WHEN I WAS ONE-AND-TWENTY

Josie was the first.

She was beautiful, had always been beautiful, knew she was beautiful; all that had shaped her, made her what she was. She was a free spirit. She was aggressive, confident, conquering. Like Trager, she was only twenty when they met, but she had lived more than he had, and she seemed to have the answers. He loved her from the first.

And Trager? Trager before Josie, but years beyond the meat-house? He was taller now, broad and heavy with both muscle and fat, often moody, silent and self-contained. He ran a full five-crew in the ore-fields, more than Cox, more than any of them. At night, he read books; sometimes in his room, sometimes in the lobby. He had long since forgotten that he went there to meet someone. Stable, solid, unemotional; that was Trager. He touched no one, and no one touched him. Even the tortures had stopped, though the scars remained *inside*. Trager hardly knew they were there; he never looked at them.

He fit in well now. With his corpses.

Yet—not completely. Inside, the dream. Something believed, something hungered, something yearned. It was strong enough to keep him away from the meathouse, from the vegetable life the others had all chosen. And sometimes, on bleak lonely nights, it would grow stronger still. Then Trager would rise from his empty bed, dress, and walk the corridors for hours with his hands shoved deep into his pockets while something twisted clawed and whimpered in his gut. Always, before his walks were over, he would resolve to do something, to change his life tomorrow.

But when tomorrow came, the silent gray corridors were half forgotten, the demons had faded, and he had six roaring, shaking automills to drive across the pit. He would lose himself in routine, and it would be long months before the feelings came again.

Then Josie. They met like this:

It was a new field, rich and unmined, a vast expanse of broken rock and rubble that filled the plain. Low hills a few weeks ago, but the company skimmers had leveled the area with systematic nuclear blast mining, and now the automills were moving in. Trager's five-crew had been one of the first, and the change had been exhilarating at first. The old pit had been just about worked out; here there was a new terrain to contend with, boulders and jagged rock fragments, baseball-sized fists of stone that came shrieking at you on the dusty wind. It all seemed exciting, dangerous. Trager, wearing a leather jacket and filtermask and goggles and earplugs, drove his six machines and six bodies with a fierce pride, reducing boulders to powder, clearing a path for the later machines, fighting his way yard by yard to get whatever ore he could.

And one day, suddenly, one of the eye echoes suddenly caught his attention. A light flashed red on a corpse-driven automill. Trager reached, with his hands, with his mind, with five sets of corpse-hands. Six machines stopped, but still another light went red. Then another, and another. Then the whole board, all twelve. One of his automills was out. Cursing, he looked across the rock field toward the machine in question, used his corpse to give it a kick. The lights stayed red. He beamed out for a tech.

By the time she got there—in a one-man skimmer that looked like a tear drop of pitted black metal—Trager had unstrapped, climbed down the metal rungs on the side of the automill, walked across the rocks to where the dead machine stopped. He was just starting to climb up when Josie arrived; they met at the foot of the yellow-metal mountain, in the shadow of its treads.

She was field-wise, he knew at once. She wore a handler's coverall, earplugs, heavy goggles, and her face was smeared with grease to prevent dust abrasion. But still she was beautiful. Her hair was short, light brown, cut in a shag that was jumbled by the wind; her eyes, when she lifted the goggles, were bright green. She took charge immediately.

All business, she introduced herself, asked him a few questions, then opened a repair bay and crawled inside, into the guts of the drive and the ore-smelt and the refinery. It didn't take her long; ten minutes, maybe, and she was back outside.

"Don't go in there," she said, tossing her hair from out in front of her goggles with a flick of her head. "You've got a damper failure. The nukes are running away."

"Oh," said Trager. His mind was hardly on the automill, but he had to make an impression, made to say something intelligent. "Is it going to blow up?" he asked, and as soon as he said it he knew that *that* hadn't been intelligent at all. Of course it wasn't going to blow up; runaway nuclear reactors didn't work that way, he knew that.

But Josie seemed amused. She smiled—the first time he saw her distinctive flashing grin—and seem to see him, *him*, Trager, not just a corpsehandler. "No," she said. "It will just melt itself down. Won't even get hot out here, since you've got shields built into the walls. Just don't go in there."

"All right." Pause. What could he say now? "What do I do?"

"Work the rest of your crew, I guess. This machine'll have to be scrapped. It should have been overhauled a long time ago. From the looks of it, there's been a lot of patching done in the past. Stupid. It breaks down, it breaks down, it breaks down, and they keep sending it out. Should realize that something is wrong. After that many failures, it's sheer self-delusion to think the thing's going to work right next time out."

"I guess," Trager said. Josie smiled at him again, sealed up the panel, and started to turn.

"Wait," he said. It came out before he could stop it, almost in spite of himself. Josie turned, cocked her head, looked at him questioningly. And Trager drew a sudden strength from the steel and the stone and the wind; under the sulfur skies, his dreams seemed less impossible. Maybe, he thought. Maybe.

"Uh. I'm Greg Trager. Will I see you again?"

Josie grinned. "Sure. Come tonight." She gave him the address.

He climbed back into his automill after she had left, exulting in his six strong bodies, all fire and life, and he chewed up rock with something near to joy. The dark red glow in the distance looked almost like a sunrise.

When he got to Josie's, he found four other people there, friends of hers. It was a party of sorts. Josie threw a lot of parties and Trager—from that night on—went to all of them. Josie talked to him, laughed with him, *liked* him, and suddenly his life was no longer the same.

With Josie, he saw parts of Skrakky he had never seen before, did things he had never done:

: he stood with her in the crowds that gathered on the streets at night, stood in the dusty wind and sickly yellow light between the windowless concrete buildings, stood and bet and cheered himself hoarse while grease-stained mechs raced yellow rumbly tractor-trucks up and down and down and up.

: he walked with her through the strangely silent and white and clean underground Offices, and sealed air-conditioned corridors where off-worlders and paper-shufflers and company executives lived and worked.

: he prowled the rec-malls with her, those huge low buildings so like a warehouse from the outside, but full of colored lights and game rooms and cafeterias and tape shops and endless bars where handlers made their rounds.

: he went with her to dormitory gyms, where they watched handlers less skillful than himself send their corpses against each other with clumsy fists.

: he sat with her and her friends, and they woke dark quiet taverns with their talk and with their laughter, and once Trager saw someone looking much like Cox staring at him from across the room, and then he smiled and leaned a bit closer to Josie.

He hardly noticed the other people, the crowds that Josie surrounded herself with; when they went out on one of her wild jaunts, six of them or eight or ten, Trager would tell himself that he and Josie were going out, and that some others had come along with them.

Once in a great while, things would work out so they were alone together, at her place, or his. Then they would talk. Of distant worlds, of politics, of corpses and life on Skrakky, of the books they both consumed, of sports or games or friends they had in common. They shared a good deal. Trager talked a lot with Josie. And never said a word.

He loved her, of course. He suspected it the first month, and soon he was convinced of it. He loved her. This was the real thing, the thing he had been waiting for, and it had happened just as he knew it would.

But with his love: agony. He could not tell her. A dozen times he tried; the words would never come. What if she did not love him back?

His nights were still alone, in the small room with the white lights and the books and the pain. He was more alone than ever now; the peace of his routine, of his half-life with his corpses, was gone, stripped from him. By day he rode the great automills, moved his corpses, smashed rock and melted ore, and in his head rehearsed the words he'd say to Josie. And dreamed of those that she'd speak back. She was trapped too, he thought. She'd had men, of course, but she didn't love them, she loved him. But she couldn't tell him, any more than he could tell her. When he broke through, when he found the words and the courage, then everything would be all right. Each day he said that to himself, and dug swift and deep into the earth.

But back home, the sureness faded. Then, with awful despair, he knew that he was kidding himself. He was a friend to her, nothing more, never would be more. Why did he lie to himself? He'd had hints enough. They had never been lovers, never would be; on the few times he'd worked up the courage to touch her, she would smile, move away on some pretext, so he was never quite sure that he was being rejected. But he got the idea, and in the dark it tore at him. He walked the corridors weekly now, sullen, desperate, wanting to talk to someone without knowing how. And all the old scars woke up to bleed again.

Until the next day. When he would return to his machines, and believe again. He must believe in himself, he knew that, he shouted it out loud. He must stop feeling sorry for himself. He must do something. He must tell Josie. He would

And she would love him, cried the day.

And she would laugh, the nights replied.

Trager chased her for a year, a year of pain and promise, the first year that he had ever *lived*. On that the night-fears and the day-voice agreed; he was alive now. He would never return to the emptiness of his time before Josie; he would never go back to the meathouse. That far, at least, he had come. He could change, and someday he would be strong enough to tell her.

Josie and two friends dropped by his room that night, but the friends had to leave early. For an hour or so they were alone, talking about nothing. Finally she had to go. Trager said he'd walk her home.

He kept his arm around her down the long corridors, and he watched her face, watched the play of light and shadow on her cheeks as they walked from light to darkness. "Josie," he started. He felt so fine, so good, so warm, and it came out. "I love you."

And she stopped, pulling away from him, stepped back. Her mouth opened, just a little, and something flickered in her eyes. "Oh, Greg," she said. Softly. Sadly. "No, Greg, no, don't, don't." And she shook her head.

Trembling slightly, mouthing silent words, Trager held out his hand. Josie did not take it. He touched her cheek, gently, and wordless she spun away from him.

Then, for the first time ever, Trager shook. And the tears came.

Josie took him to her room. There, sitting across from each other on the floor, never touching, they talked.

J: . . . known it for a long time . . . tried to discourage you,

Greg, but I didn't just want to come right out and . . . I never wanted to hurt you . . . a good person . . . don't worry . . .

T: . . . knew it all along . . . that it would never . . . lied to myself . . . wanted to believe, even if it wasn't true . . . I'm sorry, Josie, I'm sorry, I'm sorry, I'm sorryimsorryimsorry . . .

J: . . . afraid you would go back to what you were . . . don't, Greg, promise me . . . can't give up . . . have to believe . . .

T: why? . . .

J: . . . stop believing, then you have nothing . . . dead . . . you can do better . . . a good handler . . . get off Skrakky, find something . . . no life here . . . someone . . . you will, you will, just believe, keep on believing . . .

T: . . . you . . . love you forever, Josie . . . forever . . . how can I find someone . . . never anyone like you, never . . . special . . .

J: . . . oh, Greg . . . lots of people . . . just look . . . open

T: (laughter) . . . open? . . . first time I ever talked to anyone . . .

J: . . . talk to me again, if you have to . . . I can talk to you . . . had enough lovers, everyone wants to get to bed with me, better just to be friends . . .

T: . . . friends . . . (laughter) . . . (tears) . . .

(II) PROMISES OF SOMEDAY

The fire had burned out long ago, and Stevens and the forester had retired, but Trager and Donelly still sat around the ashes on the edge of the clear zone. They talked softly, so as not to wake the others, yet their words hung long in the restless night air. The uncut forest, standing dark behind them, was dead still; the wildlife of Vendalia had all fled the noise that the fleet of buzztrucks made during the day.

". . . a full six-crew, running buzztrucks, I know enough to know that's not easy," Donelly was saying. He was a pale, timid youth, likeable but self-conscious about everything he did. Trager heard echoes of himself in Donelly's stiff words. "You'd do well in the arena."

Trager nodded, thoughtful, his eyes on the ashes as he moved them with a stick. "I came to Vendalia with that in mind. Went to the gladiatorials once, only once. That was enough to change my mind. I could take them, I guess, but the whole idea made me sick. Out here, well, the money doesn't even match what I was getting on Skrakky, but the work is, well, clean. You know?"

"Sort of," said Donelly. "Still, you know, it isn't like they were real people out there in the arena. Only meat. All you can do is make the bodies as dead as the minds. That's the logical way to look at it."

Trager chuckled. "You're too logical, Don. You ought to *feel* more. Listen, next time you're in Gidyon, go to the gladiatorials and take a look. It's ugly, *ugly*. Corpses stumbling around with axes and swords and morningstars, hacking and hewing at each other. Butchery, that's all it is. And the audience, the way they cheer at each blow. And *laugh*. They *laugh*, Don! No." He shook his head, sharply. "No."

Donelly never abandoned an argument. "But why not? I don't understand, Greg. You'd be good at it, the best. I've seen the way you work your crew."

Trager looked up, studied Donelly briefly while the youth sat quietly, waiting. Josie's word came back; open, be open. The old Trager, the Trager who lived friendless and alone and closed inside a Skrakky handlers' dorm, was gone. He had grown, changed.

"There was a girl," he said, slowly, with measured words. Opening. "Back on Skrakky, Don, there was a girl I loved. It, well, it didn't work out. That's why I'm here, I guess. I'm looking for someone else, for something better. That's all part of it, you see." He stopped, paused, tried to think his words out. "This girl, Josie, I wanted her to love me. You know?" The words came hard. "Admire me, all that stuff. Now, yeah, sure, I could do good running corpses in the arena. But Josie could never love someone who had a job like *that*. She's gone now, of course, but still . . . the kind of person I'm looking for, I couldn't find them as an arena corpsemaster." He stood up, abruptly. "I don't know. That's what's important, though, to me. Josie, somebody like her, someday. Soon, I hope."

Donelly sat quiet in the moonlight, chewing his lip, not looking at Trager, his logic suddenly useless. While Trager, his corridors long gone, walked off alone into the woods.

They had a tight-knit group; three handlers, a forester, thirteen corpses. Each day they drove the forest back, with Trager in the forefront. Against the Vendalian wilderness, against the black-briars and the hard gray ironspike trees and the bulbous rubbery snaplimbs, against the tangled hostile forest, he would throw his six-crew and their buzztrucks. Smaller than the automills he'd run on Skrakky, fast and airborne, complex and demanding, those were buzztrucks. Trager ran six of them with corpse hands, a seventh with his own. Before his screaming blades and laser knives, the wall of wilderness fell each day. Donelly came behind him, pushing three of the mountain-sized rolling mills, to turn the fallen trees into lumber for Gidyon and other cities of Vendalia. Then Stevens, the third handler, with a flame-cannon to burn down stumps and melt rocks, and the soilpumps that would ready the fresh clear land for farming. The forester was their foreman. The procedure was a science.

Clean, hard, demanding work; Trager thrived on it by day. He grew lean, almost athletic; the lines of his face tightened and tanned, he grew steadily browner under Vendalia's hot bright sun. His corpses were almost part of him, so easily did he move them, fly their buzztrucks. As an ordinary man might move a hand, a foot. Sometimes his control grew so firm, the echoes so clear and strong, that Trager felt he was not a handler working a crew at all, but rather a man with seven bodies. Seven strong bodies that rode the sultry forest winds. He exulted in their sweat.

And the evenings, after work ceased, they were good too. Trager found a sort of peace there, a sense of belonging he had never known on Skrakky. The Vendalian foresters, rotated back and forth from Gidyon, were decent enough, and friendly. Stevens was a hearty slab of a man who seldom stopped joking long enough to talk about anything serious. Trager always found him amusing. And Donelly, the self-conscious youth, the quiet logical voice, he became a friend. He was a good listener, empathetic, compassionate, and the new open Trager was a good talker. Something close to envy shone in Donelly's eyes when Trager spoke of Josie and exorcised his soul. And Trager knew, or thought he knew, that Donelly was himself, the old Trager, the one before Josie who could not find the words.

In time, though, after days and weeks of talking, Donelly found his words. Then Trager listened, and shared another's pain. And he felt good about it. He was helping; he was lending strength; he was needed.

Each night around the ashes, the two men traded dreams. And wove a hopeful tapestry of promises and lies.

Yet still the nights would come.

Those were the worst times, as always; those were the hours

of Trager's long lonely walks. If Josie had given Trager much, she had taken something too, she had taken the curious deadness he had once had, the trick of not-thinking, the pain-blotter of his mind. On Skrakky, he had walked the corridors infrequently; the forest knew him far more often.

After the talking all had stopped, after Donelly had gone to bed, that was when it would happen, when Josie would come to him in the loneliness of his tent. A thousand nights he lay there with his hands hooked behind his head, staring at the plastic tent film while he relived the night he'd told her. A thousand times he touched her cheek, and saw her spin away.

He would think of it, and fight it, and lose. Then, restless, he would rise and go outside. He would walk across the clear area, into the silent looming forest, brushing aside low branches and tripping on the underbrush; he would walk until he found water. Then he would sit down, by a scum-choked lake or a gurgling stream that ran swift and oily in the moonlight. He would fling rocks into the water, hurl them hard and flat into the night to hear them when they splashed.

He would sit for hours, throwing rocks and thinking, till finally he could convince himself the sun would rise.

Gidyon; the city; the heart of Vendalia, and through it of Slagg and Skrakky and New Pittsburg and all the other corpseworlds, the harsh ugly places where men would not work and corpses had to. Great towers of black and silver metal, floating aerial sculpture that flashed in the sunlight and shone softly at night, the vast bustling spaceport where freighters rose and fell on invisible firewands, malls where the pavement was polished, ironspike wood that gleamed a gentle gray; Gidyon.

The city with the rot. The corpse city. The meatmart.

For the freighters carried cargoes of men, criminals and derelicts and troublemakers from a dozen worlds bought with hard Vendalian cash (and there were darker rumors, of liners that had vanished mysteriously on routine tourist hops). And the soaring towers were hospitals and corpseyards, where men and women died and deadmen were born to walk anew. And all along the ironspike boardwalks were corpse-sellers' shops and meathouses.

The meathouses of Vendalia were far-famed. The corpses were guaranteed beautiful.

Trager sat across from one, on the other side of the wide gray avenue, under the umbrella of an outdoor cafe. He sipped a bittersweet wine, thought about how his leave had evaporated too quickly, and tried to keep his eyes from wandering across the street. The wine was warm on his tongue, and his eyes were very restless.

Up and down the avenue, between him and the meathouse, strangers moved. Dark-faced corpse handlers from Vendalia, Skrakky, Slagg, pudgy merchants, gawking tourists from the Clean Worlds like Old Earth and Zephyr, and dozens of question marks whose names and occupations and errands Trager would never know. Sitting there, drinking his wine and watching, Trager felt utterly cut off. He could not touch these people, could not reach them; he didn't know how, it wasn't possible, it wouldn't work. He could rise and walk out into the street and grab one, and still they would not touch. The stranger would only pull free and run. All his leave like that, all of it; he'd run through all the bars of Gidyon, forced a thousand contacts, and nothing had clicked.

His wine was gone. Trager looked at the glass dully, turning it in his hands, blinking. Then, abruptly, he stood up and paid his bill. His hands trembled.

It had been so many years, he thought as he started across the street. Josie, he thought, forgive me.

Trager returned to the wilderness camp, and his corpses flew their buzztrucks like men gone wild. But he was strangely silent around the campfire, and he did not talk to Donelly at night. Until finally, hurt and puzzled, Donelly followed him into the forest. And found him by a languid death-dark stream, sitting on the bank with a pile of throwing stones at his feet.

T: . . . went in . . . after all I said, all I promised . . . still I went in . . .

D: . . . nothing to worry . . . remember what you told me . . . keep on believing . . .

T: . . . did believe, DID . . . no difficulties . . . Josie . . .

D: . . . you say I shouldn't give up, you better not . . . repeat everything you told me, everything Josie told you . . . everybody finds someone . . . if they keep looking . . . give up, dead . . . all you need . . . openness . . . courage to look . . . stop feeling sorry for yourself . . . told me that a hundred times . . .

T: . . . fucking lot easier to tell you than do it myself . . .

D: . . . Greg . . . not a meathouse man . . . a dreamer . . . better than they are . . .

T: (sighing) . . . yeah . . . hard, though . . . why do I do this to myself? . . .

D: . . . rather be like you were? . . . not hurting, not living? . . . like me? . . .

T: . . . no . . . no . . . you're right . . .

(2) THE PILGRIM, UP AND DOWN

Her name was Laurel. She was nothing like Josie, save in one thing alone. Trager loved her.

Pretty? Trager didn't think so, not at first. She was too tall, a half foot taller than he was, and she was a bit on the heavy side, and more than a bit on the awkward side. Her hair was her best feature, her hair that was red-brown in winter and glowing blond in summer, that fell long and straight down past her shoulders and did wild beautiful things in the wind. But she was not beautiful, not the way Josie had been beautiful. Although, oddly, she grew more beautiful with time, and maybe that was because she was losing weight, and maybe that was because Trager was falling in love with her and seeing her through kinder eyes, and maybe that was because he *told* her she was pretty and the very telling made it so. Just as Laurel told him he was wise, and her belief gave him wisdom. Whatever the reason, Laurel was very beautiful indeed after he had known her for a time.

She was five years younger than he, clean scrubbed and innocent, shy where Josie had been assertive. She was intelligent, romantic, a dreamer; she was wonderously fresh and eager; she was painfully insecure, and full of hungry need.

She was new to Gidyon, fresh from the Vendalian outback, a student forester. Trager, on leave again, was visiting the forestry college to say hello to a teacher who'd once worked with his crew. They met in the teacher's office. Trager had two weeks free in a city of strangers and meathouses; Laurel was alone. He showed her the glittering decadence of Gidyon, feeling smooth and sophisticated, and she was suitably impressed.

Two weeks went quickly. They came to the last night. Trager, suddenly afraid, took her to the park by the river that ran through Gidyon and they sat together on the low stone wall by the water's edge. Close, not touching.

"Time runs too fast," he said. He had a stone in his hand. He flicked it out over the water, flat and hard. Thoughtfully, he watched it splash and sink. Then he looked at her. "I'm nervous," he said, laughing. "I—Laurel. I don't want to leave."

Her face was unreadable (wary?). "The city is nice," she agreed.

Trager shook his head violently. "No. *No!* Not the city, you. Laurel, I think I . . .well . . ."

Laurel smiled for him. Her eyes were bright, very happy. "I know," she said.

Trager could hardly believe. He reached out, touched her cheek. She turned her head and kissed his hand. They smiled at each other.

He flew back to the forest camp to quit. "Don, *Don*, you've got to meet her," he shouted. "See, you can do it, *I* did it, just keep believing, keep trying, I feel so goddamn good it's obscene."

Donelly, stiff and logical, smiled for him, at a loss as how to handle such a flood of happiness. "What will you do?" he asked, a little awkwardly. "The arena?"

Trager laughed. "Hardly, you know how I feel. But something like that. There's a theatre near the spaceport, puts on pantomime with corpse actors. I've got a job there. The pay is rotten, but I'll be near Laurel. That's all that matters."

They hardly slept at night. Instead they talked and cuddled and made love. The lovemaking was a joy, a game, a glorious discovery; never as good technically as the meathouse, but Trager hardly cared. He taught her to be open. He told her every secret he had, and wished he had more secrets.

"Poor Josie," Laurel would often say at night, her body warm against his. "She doesn't know what she missed. I'm lucky. There couldn't be anyone else like you."

"No," said Trager, "*I'm* lucky."

They would argue about it, laughing.

Donelly came to Gidyon and joined the theatre. Without Trager, the forest work had been no fun, he said. The three of them spent a lot of time together, and Trager glowed. He wanted to share his friends with Laurel, and he'd already mentioned Donelly a lot. And he wanted Donelly to see how happy he'd become, to see what belief could accomplish.

"I like her," Donelly said, smiling, the first night after Laurel had left.

"Good," Trager replied, nodding.

"No," said Donelly. "Greg, I *really* like her."

They spent a *lot* of time together.

"Greg," Laurel said one night in bed. "I think that Don is . . . well, after me. You know."

Trager rolled over and propped his head up on his elbow. "God," he said. He sounded concerned.

"I don't know how to handle it."

"Carefully," Trager said. "He's very vulnerable. You're probably the first woman he's ever been interested in. Don't be too hard on him. He shouldn't have to go through the stuff I went through, you know?"

The sex was never as good as a meathouse. And, after a while, Laurel began to close. More and more nights now she went to sleep after they made love; the days when they talked till dawn were gone. Perhaps they had nothing left to say. Trager had noticed that she had a tendency to finish his stories for him. It was nearly impossible to come up with one he hadn't already told her.

"He said *that?*" Trager got out of bed, turned on a light, and sat down frowning. Laurel pulled the covers up to her chin.

"Well, what did *you* say?"

She hesitated. "I can't tell you. It's between Don and me. He said it wasn't fair, the way I turn around and tell you everything that goes on between us, and he's right."

"*Right!* But I tell you everything. Don't you remember what we . . ."

"I know, but . . ."

Trager shook his head. His voice lost some of its anger. "What's going on, Laurel, huh? I'm scared, all of a sudden. I love you, remember? How can everything change so fast?"

Her face softened. She sat up, and held out her arms, and the covers fell back from full soft breasts. "Oh, Greg," she said. "Don't worry. I love you, I always will, but it's just that I love him too, I guess. You know?"

Trager, mollified, came into her arms, and kissed her with fervor. Then, suddenly, he broke off. "Hey," he said, with mock sternness to hide the trembling in his voice, "who do you love *more?*"

"You, of course, always you."

Smiling, he returned to the kiss.

"I know you know," Donelly said. "I guess we have to talk about it."

Trager nodded. They were backstage in the theatre. Three of his corpses walked up behind him, and stood arms crossed, like a guard. "All right." He looked straight at Donelly, and his face—smiling until the other's words—was suddenly stern. "Laurel asked me to pretend I didn't know anything. She said you felt guilty. But pretending was quite a strain, Don. I guess it's time we got everything out into the open."

Donelly's pale blue eyes shifted to the floor, and he stuck his hands into his pockets. "I don't want to hurt you," he said.

"Then don't."

"But I'm not going to pretend I'm dead, either. I'm not. I love her too."

"You're supposed to be my friend, Don. Love someone else. You're just going to get yourself hurt this way."

"I have more in common with her than you do."

Trager just stared.

Donelly looked up at him. Then, abashed, back down again. "I don't know. Oh, Greg. She loves you more anyway, she said so. I never should have expected anything else. I feel like I've stabbed you in the back. I . . ."

Trager watched him. Finally, he laughed softly. "Oh, shit, I can't take this. Look, Don, you haven't stabbed me, c'mon, don't talk like that. I guess, if you love her, this is the way it's got to be, you know. I just hope everything comes out all right."

Later that night, in bed with Laurel; "I'm worried about him," he told her.

* * *

His face, once tanned, now ashen. "Laurel?" he said. Not believing.

"I don't love you anymore. I'm sorry. I don't. It seemed real at the time, but now it's almost like a dream. I don't even know if I ever loved you, really."

"Don," he said woodenly.

Laurel flushed. "Don't say anything bad about Don. I'm tired of hearing you run him down. He never says anything except good about you."

"Oh, Laurel. Don't you *remember*? The things we said, the way we felt? I'm the same person you said those words to."

"But I've grown," Laurel said, hard and tearless, tossing her red-gold hair. "I remember perfectly well, but I just don't feel that way any more."

"Don't," he said. He reached for her.

She stepped back. "Keep your hands off me. I told you, Greg, it's *over*. You have to leave now. Don is coming by."

It was worse than Josie. A thousand times worse.

(III) WANDERINGS

He tried to keep on at the theatre; he enjoyed the work, he had friends there. But it was impossible. Donelly was there every day, smiling and being friendly, and sometimes Laurel came to meet him after the day's show and they went off together, arm in arm. Trager would stand and watch, try not to notice. While the twisted thing inside him shrieked and clawed.

He quit. He would not see them again. He would keep his pride.

The sky was bright with the lights of Gidyon and full of laughter, but it was dark and quiet in the park.

Trager stood stiff against a tree, his eyes on the river, his hands folded tightly against his chest. He was a statue. He hardly seemed to breathe. Not even his eyes moved.

Kneeling near the low wall, the corpse pounded until the stone

was slick with blood and its hands were mangled clots of torn
meat. The sounds of the blows were dull and wet, but for the
infrequent scraping of bone against rock.

They made him pay first, before he could even enter the booth.
Then he sat there for an hour while they found her and punched
through. Finally, though, finally; "Josie."

"Greg," she said, grinning her distinctive grin. "I should have
known. Who else would call all the way from Vendalia? How are
you?"

He told her.

Her grin vanished. "Oh, Greg," she said. "I'm sorry. But don't
let it get to you. Keep going. The next one will work out better.
They always do."

Her words didn't satisfy him. "Josie," he said, "how are things
back there? You miss me?"

"Oh, sure. Things are pretty good. It's still Skrakky, though.
Stay where you are, you're better off." She looked off screen,
then back. "I should go, before your bill gets enormous. Glad
you called, love."

"*Josie*," Trager started. But the screen was already dark.

Sometimes, at night, he couldn't help himself. He would move
to his home screen and ring Laurel. Invariably her eyes would
narrow when she saw who it was. Then she would hang up.

And Trager would sit in a dark room and recall how once the
sound of his voice made her so very, very happy.

The streets of Gidyon are not the best of places for lonely midnight walks. They are brightly lit, even in the darkest hours,
and jammed with men and deadmen. And there are meathouses, all up and down the boulevards and the ironspike boardwalks.

Josie's words had lost their power. In the meathouses, Trager
abandoned dreams and found cheap solace. The sensuous evenings with Laurel and the fumbling sex of his boyhood were things
of yesterday; Trager took his meatmates hard and quick, almost
brutally, fucked them with a wordless savage power to the inevitable perfect orgasm. Sometimes, remembering the theatre,

he would have them act out short erotic playlets to get him in the mood.

In the night. Agony.

He was in the corridors again, the low dim corridors of the corpse handlers' dorm on Skrakky, but now the corridors were twisted and torturous and Trager had long since lost his way. The air was thick with a rotting gray haze, and growing thicker. Soon, he feared, he would be all but blind.

Around and around he walked, up and down, but always there was more corridor, and all of them led nowhere. The doors were grim black rectangles, knobless, locked to him forever, he passed them by without thinking, most of them. Once or twice, though, he paused, before doors where light leaked around the frame. He would listen, and inside there were sounds, and then he would begin to knock wildly. But no one ever answered.

So he would move on, through the haze that got darker and thicker and seemed to burn his skin, past door after door after door, until he was weeping and his feet were tired and bloody. And then, off aways, down a long long corridor that loomed straight before him, he would see an open door. From it came light so hot and white it hurt the eyes, and music bright and joyful, and the sounds of people laughing. Then Trager would run, though his feet were raw bundles of pain and his lungs burned with the haze he was breathing. He would run and run until he reached the room with the open door.

Only when he got there, it was his room, and it was empty.

Once, in the middle of their brief time together, they'd gone out into the wilderness and made love under the stars. Afterwards she had snuggled hard against him, and he stroked her gently. "What are you thinking?" he asked.

"About us," Laurel said. She shivered. The wind was brisk and cold. "Sometimes I get scared, Greg. I'm so afraid something will happen to us, something that will ruin it. I don't ever want you to leave me." "Don't worry," he told her. "I won't."

Now, each night before sleep came, he tortured himself with her words. The good memories left him with ashes and tears; the bad ones with a wordless rage.

He slept with a ghost beside him, a supernaturally beautiful ghost, the husk of a dead dream. He woke to her each morning.

He hated them. He hated himself for hating.

(3) DUVALIER'S DREAM

Her name does not matter. Her looks are not important. All that counts is that she *was*, that Trager tried again, that he forced himself on and made himself believe and didn't give up. He *tried*.

But something was missing. Magic?

The words were the same.

How many times can you speak them, Trager wondered, *speak them and believe them, like you believed them the first time you said them? Once? Twice? Three times, maybe? Or a hundred? And the people who say it a hundred times, are they really so much better at loving? Or only at fooling themselves? Aren't they really people who long ago abandoned the dream, who use its name for something else?*

He said the words, holding her, cradling her and kissing her. He said the words, with a knowledge that was surer and heavier and more dead than any belief. He said the words and *tried*, but no longer could he mean them.

And she said the words back, and Trager realized that they meant nothing to him. Over and over again they said the things each wanted to hear, and both of them knew they were pretending.

They tried *hard*. But when he reached out, like an actor caught in his role, doomed to play out the same part over and over again, when he reached out his hand and touched her cheek—the skin was smooth and soft and lovely. And wet with tears.

(IV) ECHOES

"I don't want to hurt you," said Donelly, shuffling and looking guilty, until Trager felt ashamed for having hurt a friend.

He touched her cheek, and she spun away from him.

"I never wanted to hurt you," Josie said, and Trager was sad.

She had given him so much; he'd only made her guilty. Yes, he was hurt, but a stronger man would never have let her know.

He touched her cheek, and she kissed his hand.

"I'm sorry, I don't," Laurel said. And Trager was lost. What had he done, where was his fault, how had he ruined it? She had . been so sure. They had had so much.

He touched her cheek, and she wept.

How many times can you speak them, his voice echoed, *speak them and believe them, like you believed them the first time you said them?*

The wind was dark and dust heavy, the sky throbbed painfully with flickering scarlet flame. In the pit, in the darkness, stood a young woman with goggles and a filtermask and short brown hair and answers. "It breaks down, it breaks down, it breaks down, and they keep sending it out," she said. "Should realize that something is wrong. After that many failures, it's sheer self-delusion to think the thing's going to work right next time out."

(IV) TRAGER, COME OF AGE

The enemy corpse is huge and black, its torso rippling with muscle, a product of months of exercise, the biggest thing that Trager has ever faced. It advances across the sawdust in a slow, clumsy crouch, holding the gleaming broadsword in one hand. Trager watches it come from his chair atop one end of the fighting area. The other corpsemaster is careful, cautious.

His own deadman, a wiry blond, stands and waits, a morningstar trailing down in the blood-soaked arena dust. Trager will move him fast enough and well enough when the time is right. The enemy knows it, and the crowd.

The black corpse suddenly lifts its broadsword and scrambles forward in a run, hoping to use reach and speed to get its kill. But Trager's corpse is no longer there when the enemy's measured blow cuts the air where he had been.

Sitting comfortably above the fighting pit/down in the arena, his feet grimy with blood and sawdust—Trager/the corpse—snaps the command/swings the morningstar—and the great studded ball drifts up and around, almost lazily, almost gracefully. Into the back of the enemy's head, as he tries to recover and turn. A flower of blood and brain blooms swift and sudden, and the crowd cheers.

Trager walks his corpse from the arena, then stands to receive applause. It is his tenth kill. Soon the championship will be his. He is building such a record that they can no longer deny him a match.

She is beautiful, his lady, his love. Her hair is short and blonde, her body very slim, graceful, almost athletic, with trim legs and small hard breasts. Her eyes are bright green, and they always welcome him. And there is a strange erotic innocence in her smile.

She waits for him in bed, waits for his return from the arena, waits for him eager and playful and loving. When he enters, she is sitting up, smiling for him, the covers bunched around her waist. From the door he admires her nipples.

Aware of his eyes, shy, she covers her breasts and blushes. Trager knows it is all false modesty, all playing. He moves to the bedside, sits, reaches out to stroke her cheek. Her skin is very soft; she nuzzles against his hand as it brushes her. Then Trager draws her hands aside, plants one gentle kiss on each breast, and a not-so-gentle kiss on her mouth. She kisses back, with ardor; their tongues dance.

They make love, he and she, slow and sensuous, locked together in a loving embrace that goes on and on. Two bodies move flawlessly in perfect rhythm, each knowing the other's needs. Trager thrusts, and his other body meets the thrusts. He reaches, and her hand is there. They come together (always, *always*, both orgasms triggered by the handler's brain), and a bright red flush burns on her breasts and earlobes. They kiss.

Afterwards, he talks to her, his love, his lady. You should always talk afterwards; he learned that long ago.

"You're lucky," he tells her sometimes, and she snuggles up to him and plants tiny kisses all across his chest. "Very lucky. They lie to you out there, love. They teach you a silly shining dream and they tell you to believe and chase it and they tell you that for you, for everyone, there is someone. But it's all wrong. The universe isn't fair, it never has been, so why do they tell you so? You run after the phantom, and lose, and they tell you next time, but it's all rot, all empty rot. Nobody ever finds the dream at all, they just kid themselves, trick themselves so they can go on believing. It's just a clutching lie that desperate people tell each other, hoping to convince themselves."

But then he can't talk anymore, for her kisses have gone lower and lower, and now she takes him in her mouth. And Trager smiles at his love and gently strokes her hair.

Of all the bright cruel lies they tell you, the cruelest is the one called love.

Reunion Moon

REX
MILLER

Rex Miller, like Clive Barker before him, was virtually unknown until the publication of his first book. *Slob* (1987) introduced the reading public to Jack Eichord, a Chicago homicide detective specializing in psychopaths, one who would reappear as the hero of a continuing series of novels like *Frenzy, Stone Shadow*, and *Slice*.

Slob was an event; no less than Harlan Ellison ("*Slob* really smokes") and Stephen King ("too compelling to put down") raved about the arrival of a major new talent. It was also a crossover; with one explicitly violent/sexual book, Rex Miller took the concerns of splatterpunk horror and fitted them to the police procedural novel.

More important, *Slob* introduced the world to the puppy-loving, four hundred fifty–pound serial killer Daniel "Chaingang" Bunkowski. Rapist, cannibal, and all-around fun guy, Chaingang became an immediate cult sensation, tapping directly into the Freddy Krueger–Jason Voorhies vein. Numerous Chaingang short stories (like "Sweet Pea" and "The Luckiest Man in the World") only fed the fire; now Bunkowski has become so popular that he even has his own comic books (the *Chaingang* series from Northstar Productions); what's more, after killing him off in *Slob*, Miller seems to have had no choice but to resurrect Chaingang in *Slice*.

Yet all this brouhaha has, till now, obscured its creator. As it turns out, Rex Miller is not an overnight sensation. For over twenty years he was a deejay and top-rated radio personality in such cities as St. Louis, Chicago, New York, and Los Angeles. Miller was the national voice of Dodge cars in 1966 and has a long list of blue chip agency/account credits as a free-lance announcer. He has written and produced single recordings for Pat Boone, has had short fiction appear in numerous anthologies and *Alfred Hitchcock's Mystery Magazine*, and has, since 1971, been the owner and operator of Rex Miller's Killer

Collectibles and Vintage Videos, a successful mail-order business specializing in character collectibles and media memorabilia (where you can order everything from *I Walked With a Zombie* to a Captain Midnight Mystic Eye Detector Ring).

Rex Miller has been around.

But he's still primarily known for his Chaingang/Eichord work, fiction that is typically brutal, fast paced, and definitely not for the squeamish. Miller is *not* known for comedy, which is what makes "Reunion Moon" such a treat. During the course of putting *Splatterpunks* together, Rex and I had many hilarious conversations; he's one of the funniest guys you'd ever want to talk to on the telephone. In this story of voodoo, constipation, and high school reunions, Miller proves he can write funny, too.

Prepare yourself for a whole new spin on the term *bathroom humor*.

"The doctor will see you now," the young nurse said, turning away as she said it, motioning him to follow her down the hall. "Would you come this way please, Mr. Bryant?" He put his raggedy *People* magazine down on a stack of *Sports Illustrated*s and obligingly got up and started down the hall of the clinic.

Bubba Bryant was not someone whom women looked at twice. In fact nobody, male or female, spent any more time looking at Bubba than they had to. Bubba had a serious case of the fat and uglies, and he'd had it all his life. He was fifty-seven. And he was still Bubba. Unmarried. Lived with his mother and father until first Papa, then Mama, died, and now he lived alone in the little house.

"You get yourself in here feller," the silvery-haired doctor said with seemingly genuine cordiality. "I haven't seen you in about a hundred years!"

"Yeah, I know it. What do you say, Ronald—I mean, Doctor?"

"Not much, Bubba. Do they still call you Bubba?"

"Uh huh," he said, shyly. Although nobody called him much of anything anymore. He had trouble being social—that's the way his mama always liked to describe it. Bubba was a loner.

"You know . . ." The doctor took a clipboard from the nurse and wrote on a form as he talked. "I was looking at the appointment book this morning and saw Bubba Bryant and I thought of the coach, you know, and then I realized—*Bubba* Bryant? The Bubba I went to school with?" He laughed. "Whatever happened to you?"

"Nothin' much. Lived in town here all my life." He looked down at his big feet.

"How come we never saw you at any of the class reunions? We have a lot of fun. You gotta come this year. Gonna be a big fortieth anniversary. The whole gang's coming. People from New York. California. Jimmy Dale Potter's coming from Hawaii. You got to come, Bubba." They had loved to tease Bubba in school. He had no desire to see the old gang again. He loathed all of them.

"Okay. I'll try."

"Well what's your problem, anyway? Have a seat. Take a load off."

"Thanks. Well, I been constipated real bad for about a week or so."

"Uh huh. All right. Well, we'll get you fixed up."

But Dr. Ronald Ross didn't get Bubba fixed up at all. He prescribed some medicine that cost a lot of money, and he teased him some and charged him for an office call, but it didn't do any good. Forty-eight hours later Bubba still hadn't been able to make potty and he was getting worried.

"Bubba?" The doctor's voice was loud on the telephone. "The dam hasn't burst, eh?"

"Huh?"

"You still haven't been able to have a bowel movement?"

"No, sir."

"Well, Bubba, you get in here—uh, let's see—tomorrow at 3:30, and we'll take some X rays. Sounds to me like a logjam." He laughed unprofessionally. After all, this was Bubba Bryant. "We may have to go in there to break it loose."

"Uh—does it matter what I eat?"

"Not at this point. What has it been—nine days or so? I'd say go ahead and kill the fatted calf if you want to."

The next afternoon Dr. Ross felt Bubba Bryant's colon, he probed the mysteries of his inner recesses, he prodded and poked, took pictures, and finally came to a startling conclusion.

"Bubba, you are not impacted."

"Huh?"

"There is no *phys*iological blockage that we can observe. The conclusion is that you may have a little psychological maladjustment of some kind. And there's always the possibility of a dietary problem at your age. You're also sixty-five pounds overweight, old buddy. We're going to put you on a high-roughage diet. Fibers. Lots of water. I'm going to prescribe the most powerful laxative known. We'll work together, Bubba, and we WILL achieve a breakthrough."

"Okay."

But there was no breakthrough. And thirteen days had passed since his last movement. Bubba Bryant was very concerned. He had taken for granted this year-in and year-out regularity business. And now, for thirteen days, nothing. It was most alarming.

Bubba's evening meal on the thirteenth day consisted of a bran muffin, a quarter cup of cooked spinach, half a baked potato, butter, one-half cup of vegetable soup, one tablespoon of syrup hydrolose with a small glass of water, and two of the powerful pills Ronald Ross called Poopalotz.

He still hadn't felt nature's call by ten o'clock that evening and he was getting angry and extremely frightened. He left the house and found a pizza joint still open. He ordered two extra-super-deluxe combination supremos with triple cheese, quadruple sausage, and everything except anchovies. To go. They came to $29.80 with tax. Bubba stopped at a 7-Eleven and got four quarts of beer to wash the pizza down, went home, and pigged out like it was his last meal. All or nothing.

The next morning, the morning of the fourteenth day, Bubba woke soaking wet—not ill, just totally afraid—and he went out into the sunshine. He felt NOTHING going on inside his large frame. No feelings of tightness. No discomfort. And no urge to go to the bathroom. He wandered aimlessly half the day.

Early afternoon he was in the ghetto and passing a small shop that he'd never seen before. He wandered in, looking around, not knowing what he was doing there but feeling right at home.

"Can I hep ya?" said an old black woman.

"No, ma'am. I'm just—" he wanted to say looking around.

"Looking around?" she suggested.

"Uh huh." He looked down shyly.

"What's the problem?"

"Huh?"

"What ails ya, boy?"

"Nothin." He started out. The sign on the tiny storefront window said MADAME DRU T. GIBB'S CANDLES. It was a candle shop. Black candles. Funny looking roots and things. Small bottles with weird labels.

"Come on back here," she said, and Bubba turned. She crooked her index finger and Bubba timidly complied.

"How much money you got, boy?"

"I dunno," he shrugged.

"Look."

He took his money out and counted it. "About eight dollars and some change."

"That's how much a jar of this is. Eight dollars and some change. Here. Give it to me." He forked his money over and she handed him a small, unmarked jar of a powdery substance.

"Take this. Eat a spoonful every night at midnight. Not two spoons, not a spoon and a half. One exact spoonful, understand?"

"Yes'm."

"Do that every night for three nights." That seemed to be all she had to say, so Bubba put the jar into his pocket and went home.

At twelve midnight he ate a spoonful of the stuff. It tasted like shit and he spit most of it out.

The next two nights he followed the old woman's regimen exactly. The morning of the seventeenth day of constipation Bubba went in and poured the entire jar of powdery stuff into the blender and made himself a chocolate malt with it.

There was a sort of gestation period. The seventeenth, eighteenth, nineteenth, and morning of the twentieth day Bubba mostly stayed in bed. He felt his bodily fluids drying up, thinning, evaporating; felt his vital systems shutting down. He knew he was dying.

Bubba kept the house dark and cool and stayed in bed as much as he could, trying to think about nothing. Keeping his eyes shut. Letting whatever was going to happen take place.

On the afternoon of the twentieth day Bubba woke up from his nap with a pain. No. Not a pain. A discomfort. A feeling in his gut. A pressure. It was such an alien feeling, he wondered whether to call for an ambulance. Was this going to be the big casino? But immediately he identified the feeling. He had to go TO THE BATHROOM. My God! At last. He ran into the bathroom and barely got his drawers down in time. Oh my Lord in high heaven oh sweet Jesus at last at last oh, oh, oh, yes-YES-YES-*Y E S* THIS WAS BETTER THAN SEX AAAAAAHHHHHH HHHHHHHHHHHHHHHHHHHHHHHHHHH-HHHHHHHHHHHHHHHHHHHHHHHHH.

Bubba finally made potty, and it wasn't good, it was spectacular. Bubba rode the brown banana express. Bubba took care of business. Bubba was flushed with success.

Bubba Bryant was a happy man. He had a wonderful day. He phoned the doctor. He *would* be at his class's fortieth reunion

—count on it! He tried to call the lady Madame Gibb but he couldn't find the number. He walked all over the ghetto looking for it, but she apparently had gone out of business. When he finally found the storefront it appeared empty. She had moved on.

Then, don't get ahead of me now, but on the morning of the twenty-first day, after the soundest sleep of his life, he woke with a terrible feeling, as bad as the most severe tummyache he'd ever experienced. It was the sort of thing that would send a kid screaming to Mommy, the kind of pain that usually preceded a ruptured appendix. Bad stomach pain. And again, he just got his jammies down and made it to the commode in time.

Rumble grumble rrrrrrrrrrrrrrruuuuuuuuuuuummmmmmmmmmbbbbbbbblllllllleeee it came, grumbling, roaring, growling up the old chocko highway, the brown banana super chief was ON TIME WWWWWWHOOOOOOOOOOOOOOOOOOOOOOOOOO —WHHHHHHHHHHHOOOOOOOOOOOOOOOOOOOOOOOOO EEEEEEEEEEEEEEEEEEEEEEEEEEEEEEEEEEEEEEE! ALLLLLLLLLLLLLLLLLLLLLLLLLLLLLLLLL ABBBBOOOOOOOOOOAAAAAAAARRRRRRRRRRDDDDDDD! *POW!* it came out in a gurgling squirting squishing avalanche oh my God the size of it huge MONSTROUS THINGS bigger than anything not stool but some awful otherworldly noxious awesome excreta from hell and it was all he could do to raise himself as he went, cramping, roaring, screaming, one hand slapping back to flush as this thing kept coming and he forced himself to twist around and look and almost fainted and fell into it when he saw the thing that he'd blasted loose from inside.

Most of the next day was spent cleaning the bathroom. On the morning of the twenty-second day he crawled out of bed before the alarm and ran several blocks to an overgrown lot where a deserted house stood. He was inside by the time the thing hit. It blew him across the floor and out a window, not a thousand Chiquita Nanners, a brown *mountain* of horror came blowing, flowing, growing, the pain like the birth of a hundred baby porcupines, *WHAM!* He spent the day in the stinking weeds and that night snuck home and hosed himself down.

He slept like a baby again that night. On the morning of the twenty-second day he willed himself not to go. By noon he was waddling like a bowlegged caricature of a cowboy. But somehow he made it to seven that night, and—dressed in his best suit— Bubba arrived at his old high school just in time.

The rumbling could no longer be denied.

It was all he could do to throw open the gymnasium doors and scream to his class, *"Hi everybody, Bubba's here!"*

His face bathed in sweat but wreathed in a huge smile, Bubba spun around, dropped his trousers, and filled the high school gym with his true, innermost feelings for his old classmates.

I Spit in Your Face: Films That Bite

CHAS.
BALUN

In my essay "Outlaws" I emphasize the critical impact of splatter films on splatterpunk. Such seminal "moist" cinema as *Blood Feast*, *Night of the Living Dead*, *The Texas Chainsaw Massacre*, *Suspiria*, and just about anything by Italian director Lucio Fulci (*Zombie*, *The Beyond*, *The Gates of Hell*) obviously, and irrevocably, influenced the parameters of splat fiction.

But what of those films appearing today, damp stacks of ten-minute reels that are insidiously corrupting a whole new breed of protosplatterpunks?

The hard-core gore film has become a genre unto itself, with an enthusiastic network of specialized conventions (*Fangoria*'s Weekend Of Horrors), professional magazines (*Gorezone*), and fanzines (*Shock Xpress*) avidly lending support to this admittedly crazed subindustry. One of the best journalists mining this crimson wackiness is Chas. Balun, the Joe Bob Briggs of splatter films.

Balun's work first appeared in small fanzines and, later, larger-circulation publications (*Fangoria*). Even from the start he stood out from the pack. Here was someone who not only was well versed in his subject but obviously loved the work. Better still, Balun *rated* the grossness found in each of these cinematic atrocities. We're not talking that pantywaist Four-Star system, either. Sure, Balun appraised a film's overall merit. But in a stroke of demented genius he also invented "The Gore Score" which, as Balun puts it, "concerns itself with *nothing* but the quantity of blood, brains, guts, slime, snot, puke or other assorted precious bodily fluids spilled, slopped or splattered during the course of the film" (under Balun's ratings system, twisted gems like *Doctor Butcher M.D.* get a "10," while *Terms of Endearment* would rate a big "0").

Besides The Gore Score (which appeared as an independently published book and sporadically resurfaces as an ongoing column), Chas. Balun has functioned as editor for both the splatter film fanzine *Deep Red* and its companion book, *The Deep Red Horror Handbook*. He's authored *Horror Holocaust* and the recent splatter novel *Ninth and Hell Streets*.

Despite his seeping subject matter, Chas. Balun is an informed critic, combining both the enthusiasm of a fan and academic enquiry. "I Spit in Your Face" details the newest crop of recommended splatter films, and as such serves as a handy guide for dedicated gorehounds—and their spiritual brethren, the splatterpunks—everywhere.

Every scene looks you straight in the eye—and spits!
—*Africa: Blood & Guts* (1972)

Some films were never meant to entertain an audience. Many were designed along the lines of a Drano enema . . . get inside you, deep into the soft parts, and rip your guts out.

In many instances, the filmmaker is not looking for any new friends or fans; he wants FEAR, LOATHING, REPULSION and REACTION from his audience. He is not asking you to like him or his work. But he is issuing a challenge, perhaps even a warning, to any potential viewer: WATCH THIS FILM AT YOUR OWN RISK!

These are the films that most severely test the parameters of the genre and how far an audience is willing to go before they'll jump ship. Many of these works are deliberately vile, offensive and excruciatingly violent in ways that will almost always guarantee some sort of cult following. These films are too rude and crude to be ignored. They're not tame, domesticated little beasties; they're wild, dangerous and THEY BITE!

Contemporary horror filmmaking, long accustomed to being further pigeonholed into telling categories like Teenkill, Bodycount, Stalk-'n'-Slash, Slice-'n'-Dice, Splatter, etcetera, has also developed another bizarre and ofttimes alarming renegade strain that threatens rape by cinema in the manner of Du Champ— "The Bride Stripped Bare (And Gutted) By Her Bachelors." These derelict, expatriated horror films nearly always succeed in striking a raw nerve. They make no apologies and expect no mercy. Prisoners are not taken.

The filmmakers follow no rules. Cinematic conventions are usually scrapped in favor of a raw-boned cinema vérité look that makes the audience an accomplice to the action. These works are nearly always bleak, minimalist, micro-budgeted efforts that appear as anti-film; they're more of a raging, primal scream made by the filmmakers than a certifiable cinematic "product" that can be hawked on the marketplace.

In many cases, these films can never be released to the general viewing public. Some are simply too extreme, too outrageous, offering up such a frightful parade of human depravity, perversity and sadistic fetishism that none but the bravest or most foolhardy will attempt a defense. Films like *Last House on Dead End Street*, which features prolonged and numbing sequences of whippings, various humiliations and gruesome torture/deaths, can expect very little sympathy from audiences weaned on safe and sane splatter films like *Friday the 13th*, *Nightmare on Elm Street*, and even *Dawn of the Dead* or *The Evil Dead*.

There is a notorious sequence in *Last House on Dead End Street* that quite nearly defies any form of critical commentary.

After a victim has been taunted, humiliated repeatedly and beaten, he is forced to kneel before a semi-nude woman who has a doe's foot protruding from the zipper of her jeans. Behind her stands some other freakozoid who's framing her head with another pair of deer legs that he's positioned like a devil's horns. That scene alone is enough to punch open your eyeballs and drop your jaw until . . . the guy is forced to orally copulate the hoof from hell in a most particularly disgusting manner. It gets worse after that.

These filmmakers are, most certainly, not the type that are ever invited to weekend seminars with aspiring collegiate film talent and asked to lecture on "Blow Job as Metaphor." These be dangerous folk, my friends.

Ofttimes, though, the most immediate and universal audience response to such nose-thumbing frankness and deliberate provocation is the "Why-Am-I-Watching-This Syndrome?" In fact, many of these nihilistic nasties have forced even the most adamant genre aficionado to reexamine his moral universe. Perhaps the most notable contributions of such films as *I Spit on Your Grave*, *Maniac*, *I Hate Your Guts* or *Henry: Portrait of a Serial Killer* is that they provoke an examination of conscience and force you to reveal your hand . . . and then they cut it off. These films always elicit a highly charged response from the audience, whether vehemently opposed or reluctantly defensive. Viewers are forced into confrontation with many powerfully felt, though often ambivalent, feelings towards the actual intent and purpose of genre filmmaking.

Because horror films can be made so cheaply with minimal trappings, bargain basement FX, no-name stars and inexperienced crews, filmmakers are often given the opportunity to do whatever they want as long as they can get and keep an audience's attention. Many are encouraged to load up their films with a plethora of titillations and incitefully offensive subject matter in order to avoid the worst crime any exploitation film can commit in a business-conscious media: to be ignored. Be blasphemous, perverse, ungodly violent and break some taboos, but for God's sake, DON'T BE BORING.

Many young, ambitious filmmakers, who would later resurface as successful mainstream auteurs, took up the challenge with their first few efforts and presented some very raw, uncompromising and prickly material that was destined to be both hailed and harangued, championed and vilified, but never ignored. People, indeed, were shocked and disturbed by such films as *The Last House on the Left*, *The Texas Chainsaw Massacre* and *I Spit on Your Grave*—but they never forgot the film. Even the rabidly negative, virulent reviews given to such films often backfire, eventually serving only to increase audience awareness and curiosity, stimulate word-of-mouth, heighten the film's media profile and improve its marketing potential. *The Texas Chainsaw Massacre*, *I Spit on Your Grave* and *Basket Case* all enjoyed revivals on home video thanks to some particularly vilifying, though highly quotable, remarks made by various media critics. When Rex Reed called Frank Henenlotter's delightfully bent *Basket Case* "the sickest film I've ever seen," he certainly had not intended it as a rallying cry, a call-to-arms to be breathlessly slung across video boxes and film posters as a major selling point. Superstar film snipes like Gene Siskel and Roger Ebert should even be entitled to video sales profits for their unintentional promotion for such films as *Last House on the Left*, *I Spit on Your Grave* and *Friday the 13th*. Remember the rules, though, THOU SHALT NOT BE IGNORED.

However, it may ultimately prove to be for the best that such films as *I Hate Your Guts*, *Last House on Dead End Street*, *Roadkill: The Last Days of John Martin* or *Nekromantik* never fall into the wrong hands. There is that chance, however slight, that gore-bashing critics might just get the wrong idea about the film, the genre and its fans.

Troubling films like John McNaughton's *Henry: Portrait of a Serial Killer* (1986) pose a moral conundrum to both critic and fan alike with an unblinking and non-judgmental approach to violent death. Murder is presented in rather prosaic, matter-of-fact terms; kind of like a part-time job that's seamlessly integrated into the rest of your lifestyle. And the film's titular character, despite being a combustible psychotic and ruthless killer, is, nonetheless, portrayed as the film's de facto hero. Sure, he tortures and kills women, but he's really a nice guy who can always spare a moment to compliment a self-effacing waitress and offer both a friendly game of cards and a willing, sympathetic ear to those less fortunate than himself. He's fiercely loyal, unusually generous and really rather timid and well mannered; that is, when he's not killing somebody. *Henry* is, indeed, almost an anomaly in this much-maligned subgenre. It's a great-looking film, full of crafty, gliding camera work, punctuated by cunning editing, haunting music and sound effects, and propelled by a taut, compelling script. The acting is unusually good, many times volcanic, and Michael Rooker's riveting lead performance is all too chillingly believable. *Henry* is, by most counts, a deeply disturbing, dangerous piece of genre filmmaking.

Though most films rarely approach the high level of craft evident in a work like *Henry*, few suffer from the lack of technical expertise. In fact, this is one level of filmmaking that allows, and can even benefit from, an amateur, minimalist approach. Most directors need not be warned that they must operate within the strict confines of conventional filmmaking and many are openly encouraged to deliberately "go beyond" the usual genre conventions. Because most of these films are budgeted at well under a few hundred thousand dollars, the risk is minimal; so many producers allow their crews to follow their instincts, secretly hoping that the ferret-eyed maniac behind the camera can deliver yet another "cult classic" or "midnight hit." However, many of these efforts seemed destined for a far more mundane fate, lost somewhere in the twilight zone between the distributor and the marketplace. Many cautious distributors fear the reputation they may accrue by actively trumpeting a film whose acknowledged high points include the degradation of women, fetishist torture, animal mutilations, sexual deviancy and unrepentant, sociopathic thrill killers.

Clever producers and marketing specialists have nimbly sidestepped many of the "unsavory" or unacceptable elements of their product by mounting ad campaigns that are either keenly manipulative, downright deceptive or patently false. Jerry Gross and Hallmark Productions are two outfits that have often turned adversity into advantage. When no one paid attention to a stiff little clunker by the name of *Day of the Woman*, Gross retitled it *I Spit on Your Grave* and cloaked the film in a misleading ad campaign that screamed "an act of revenge" and promised that "FIVE men" would be "cut, chopped, broken, and burned beyond recognition." No matter that there were only four and that nobody ever got "broken or burned," because nobody seemed to notice and the video version became a monster success. Gross is also responsible for other memorable genre heists, including the pairing of the pedestrian black-and-white snorefest *Voodoo Blood Bath* (1964), retitled *I Eat Your Skin*, with *I Drink Your Blood* (1972) as "TWO GREAT BLOOD HORRORS TO RIP OUT YOUR GUTS!" Gross also surgically removed huge sections of Jacopetti and Prosperi's ambitious and award-winning documentary *Africa Addio* (1967) and turned it into the aforementioned film that spits in one's eye. "This is Africa like it is! Where Black is Beautiful! Black is Ugly! Black is Brutal."

Hallmark also promised to deliver the goods with several effective campaigns that screeched: "Can a movie go TOO FAR?" "POSITIVELY THE MOST HORRIFYING FILM EVER MADE" and "THE FIRST FILM RATED 'V' FOR VIOLENCE." Hallmark also scored points with their inspired inclusion of a barf bag for audiences of *Mark of the Devil*, a film experience they guaranteed would "upset your stomach."

Despite the apparent cleverness of these hyperbolic campaigns, Hallmark was really only recycling several concepts that others had already employed. Herschell Gordon Lewis' *Color Me Blood Red* (1964) warned that "You must keep reminding yourself it's just a motion picture." Hallmark apparently thought they were REALLY onto something there and so "To avoid fainting . . . keep repeating . . . it's only a movie . . ." appeared on two of their "house movies," *Last House on the Left* (1972) and *The House That Vanished* (1974), and then showed up again on Hallmark's poster for *Don't Open the Window*, their retitled American cut of Jorge Grau's *Let Sleeping Corpses Lie/Living Dead at the Manchester Morgue*.

Well and good. Barf bags, warnings of faintings and stomach distress, "V" ratings and audience challenges have proved effective in the past, but with today's current crop of in-your-face, hard-core nasties, a most difficult promotional problem arises. Just how do you go about selling/cajoling/enticing an audience to see Jorg Buttgereit's *Nekromantik* (1988), a seriously twisted, monstrous tale of corpse-fucking, bunny-killing degenerates that make Ed Gein look like Pee Wee Herman?

STAY AWAY FROM THAT HOUSE BY A LAKE NEAR THE PARK ON THE DEAD END STREET

Most of today's more disturbing films owe at least a cursory nod to *Last House on the Left*, which, in turn, owes at least that and then so much more to Ingmar Bergman's Academy Award–winning *The Virgin Spring* (1960). *Last House* provided both the model and the inspiration for legions of micro-budgeted mavens who apishly reprised the humiliation-rape-revenge scenario that worked so well in Craven's film.

Throughout the decade that followed, lots of bad things were happening in houses all over the place.

Last House on the Left II was soon unleashed, but was related to the original in name only. It was actually a not-so-clever ploy to disguise Mario Bava's seminal body-count bonanza *Twitch of the Death Nerve* (1972, aka *Carnage*, *Bay of Blood*) for xenophobic American audiences.

The New House on the Left (1977, aka *The Night Train Murders*), again no relation to the original, was a German knock-off that featured a murdering rapist tormenting and torturing while on board a train.

House by the Lake (1977), a Canadian production, proved a rather effective rape-revenge potboiler that was directed by genre workhorse William (*Funeral Home*, *Spasms*) Fruet. Brenda Vaccaro (she of the sandpaper, rocky-road croak) beats off a sleazy troupe of drooling morons led by the irrepressible Don Stroud while her wimpy cry-baby boyfriend cowers in pants-wetting fear.

One of the most frightening entries in the hell-in-house sweepstakes is, undoubtedly, the deeply disturbing, wildly misanthropic *Last House on Dead End Street* (1977). Directed by a young New York film student named Roger Watkins under the pseudonymous moniker "Victor Janos," this *Last House* is a real hellraiser. Also known briefly as *The Fun House*, this film delivers a mule kick to the old nugget sack with a loathsome, virulent fury. A bitter and angry Terry Hawkins, fresh from a year in the slammer for a petty drug offense, wants to be a filmmaker. "I wanna make some films here," he says, "some really weird films. I'm ready for something nobody ever dreamed of. I'll show 'em; I'll show them all what Terry Hawkins can do." And he makes good on that threat, too. The sleazeophiles in the porn business with whom he's been dealing are also ready for something new. They're tired of the boring, boner-abating loops he's been providing them and demand "something really different." Terry comes up with that really different "something," too— snuff films—though he is careful to disguise his real intentions from both crew and potential "snuffee," part of his promise to "show them all something nobody ever dreamed of." What follows is a detailed and intense cavalcade of cruelty including savage whippings, strangulations, stabbings, dissections, drillings and simulated sex with animal hooves. In one of the most harrowing sequences, a truly horrific, nightmarish set piece, a woman is bound to an ersatz operating table and repeatedly abused by a whole crew of sniggering low lifes in masks and gowns. Her face is repeatedly slashed with a scalpel, her legs are severed by hacksaw, and then she's gutted with tin snips, her glistening, shimmering viscera held up high for all to admire and applaud.

The film ends with the prolonged humiliation and torturous death of the hoof sucker, who finally receives a Black and Decker lobotomy as a coup de grace.

With just the right touch of suppressed moral outrage, a studied, somber voiceover adds this postscript: "Terence Hawkins (and others) were all later apprehended and are now serving 999 year sentences in the state penitentiary." Right up until that point, though, the film shows absolutely no sense of moral equilibrium whatsoever.

Last House on Dead End Street proves especially unsettling in the manner in which it blurs the lines between recording, inciting and participating in an act of violence. Other films, such as Michael and Roberta Findlay's *Snuff*, Dusty Nelson's *Effects* (1980), Larry Cohen's *Special Effects* and David Cronenberg's *Videodrome* (1983), have similarly broached the subject, but none have been so alarmingly forthright and as worrisome as is *Last House on Dead End Street*.

Don't Go in the House (1980), released amidst a flurry of Don't Answer/Look/or Open movies, distinguished itself by being, perhaps, the sickest of the lot. The film is unusually well made, sometimes even striking, and slickly directed by Joseph Ellison. It could have proved somewhat of a minor cult hit had it steered clear of the sordid, ugly undercurrent of child abuse that repeatedly oozes forth from the film. A sick-fuck mother repeatedly punishes her child by holding his arms over a gas burner, and you know what? He grows up to be one sick-fuck of a fry-baby who delights in torching girls in his steel-paneled bedroom crematorium. Many of the gruelling, tortured deaths are presented in loving, lingering detail; although our incendiary anti-hero receives his comeuppance at the end (à la *Manaic*), the sense of biblical justice is fleeting. The film's postscript features yet another child being mistreated, threatening to begin the whole cycle once again. Despite its technical sheen, chilling mise-en-scènes and creepy makeup FX, it's simply too hard to admit taking a liking to a film that takes its cynical inspiration from chronic child abuse.

Davis Hess, certainly one of the most memorable screen thugs in *House* history, raises hell in yet another domicile in Ruggero Deodato's *House at the Edge of the Park*. Deodato deserves credit for a bit of a casting coup here; the teaming of Italian Sleaze King John ("The Cannibal Man") Morghen with Hess creates a slice of social pathology that's hard to resist. Morghen's a gibbering retard this time and Hess just continues to do what he does best, making you awfully glad it's only a movie . . . only a movie.

By the mid-80's, it became apparent that people had done about all the nasty things they were capable of in a house and the sub-genre received its termination notice in the form of two gutless and trivial yawners presented by Sean Cunningham, the "original" *House* and its pathetic sequel *House 2: The Second Story*.

HORROR HEROES FOR THE HATE GENERATION

A certain handful of cinematic psychopaths, especially those from the Annihilating Automation School of Serial Killing like Michael Meyers or Jason Voorhees, have managed to attract a worldwide following of loyal fans who respect the reptilian logic of a kill-first/question-later kind of guy. Freddy Krueger, once a loathsome, murderous pedophile, is now a horror institution unto himself and the world's most famous Stand-up Killer Comic. Krueger is adored and venerated by millions and easily able to generate healthy eight-figure returns on a variety of film, video, TV, book, record, poster, doll, glove, mask, hat, and bubble gum—card deals. Truly, a Psycho-Icon for the '80's.

While Krueger and the others have shown what it takes to elevate serial killing into a national pastime, other screen psychos will never have to worry about appointing a treasurer for their fan clubs. Ever.

Robert A. Endelson's violent, inflammatory, racist fantasy, *I Hate Your Guts* (1977) (not to be confused with Roger Corman's 1961 feature, aka *The Intruder*), presents a trio of Black-baiting escaped convicts whose antics make you wonder how this film ever saw the light of a projector's beam . . . anywhere . . . at any time. Deceptively well made, it plays like a particularly lurid AIP potboiler until the taboos start crumbling under the force of a nonstop barrage of the most virulent, inciteful, degrading racist commentary ever committed to celluloid. The stinging epithets aren't limited to the Black family held hostage either, because among the trio of convicts is both an Asian and a Hispanic, conveniently giving vent to a racial hatred that knows no bounds.

Besides the crude, ear-burning dialog, *I Hate Your Guts* stomps on even more toes when it features the graphic, skull-cracking demise of a young boy whose death throes are filmed right up to the last twitch. Despite the fact that the film concludes with an obvious bit of cheap, moral posturing (the police surround the house, but let the besieged family enjoy their revenge), *I Hate Your Guts* remains a risible, nearly indefensible piece of exploitation filmmaking.

Abel Ferrara's *The Driller Killer* (1979) features an uncharismatic, brooding and self-absorbed New York painter (played by Ferrara under the alias "Jimmy Laine") who handily manages to piss off nearly everyone he knows—girlfriend, landlord, neighbors, art agent, audience—and then, for thrills, he drills. Occasionally bloody but rarely explicit, it gained more notoriety in the United Kingdom during a splatter-bashing purge of "video nasties" when it was vilified by limp-dick wankers almost as often as *I Spit on Your Grave*.

Veteran character actor Joe Spinell attempted an angst-ridden portrait of a snivelling sleazoid who scalps hookers in *Maniac* (1980), but the lurid, unrelenting butchery and blubbery, misogynistic ramblings quickly derailed many potential fans. Despite Spinell's shortcomings as an auteur (he co-scripted, produced and starred), the film does contain several hauntingly effective sequences packed with an undeniable, perverse power.

Though there was little interest expressed by either fans or producers for a sequel, Spinell made several failed attempts to resurrect his beloved wormbag character, that irrepressibly dandy degenerate Frank Zito. After all, here was a guy who could garrot-stab-slice-'n'-scalp by day and then effortlessly land a date with a sultry sex bomb (Caroline Munro) by night. Truly a Maniac for all Seasons.

Spinell later produced *Mister Robbie: Maniac 2*, a short promotional reel directed by Buddy (*Combat Shock*) Giovinazzo that bore striking similarities to *The Psychopath*, a 1974 nodfest about a tormented twink of a kiddie-show host that sought revenge against parents who'd been abusing their children.

The idea never caught fire, but Spinell refused to yield. Years later, as production was finally scheduled to begin on Lone-Star Maniac, a quasi-legitimate sequel Spinell had been developing with young Texas filmmaker Tom Rainone, big Joe bought the farm. Just three days before his triumphant sleaze reprise, too. Life is cruel.

Many other filmmakers turned away from the cinematic psycho mythology of murder and instead drew their inspiration by scouring newspapers and magazines for headlines that screamed: "Mom Kills Kids, Self," "Beaten Boy Put In Oven," and "Bizarre Hiway Suicide."

Director Buddy Giovinazzo had already assembled a thick sheath of press clippings chronicling the tragic plights of many Vietnam era vets long before his cult hit, *Combat Shock*, went before the cameras. Giovinazzo, a fiercely independent and enterprising filmmaker, became very dismayed over newspaper reports like "Vietnam Vet Kills Wife, Kids," or "Six Dead After Viet Vet's Rampage" and decided to do something about it. "These stories," Giovinazzo has said, "seem so trivial. We learn nothing about why these things happened, nothing about these people."

Giovinazzo wrote, produced and directed *American Nightmares* in response and offered the film as his graduate thesis at the College of Staten Island. Troma later acquired the film, re-edited it, and released the truncated version as *Combat Shock*. Both prints offer a festering, bleak and hopeless scenario in which a jobless vet (convincingly played by Buddy's brother, Ricky) violently self-destructs during a punishing, unforgettable climax that includes a notorious baby-baking sequence, toned down by Troma in order to secure an "R" rating.

Giovinazzo's film remains a vivid, gruelling and exhausting experience that'll have you on the ropes long before the final shot is fired. It is also a unique and highly charged vision, a poignant cry against war and its remembrance, and a shattering glimpse at familial apocalypse.

Though Troma chose to either downplay or simply ignore many of the film's real strengths by pushing it as an "action-adventure thriller" (featuring nonexistent Rambo-esque scenes on the poster), Kaufman and crew are to be congratulated on taking a calculated risk with such an uncompromising and totally non-commercial work that had already been thrown out of over fifty film festivals.

Another equally troublesome film, John McNaughton's *Henry: Portrait of a Serial Killer*, had been given the bum's rush by nearly everybody except the film festivals. It gained a degree of both prominence and notoriety when shown at the 1986 Chicago Film Festival and has since appeared only briefly at various midnight shows and specially arranged screenings.

Many potential distributors have been unable to come to terms with its seething blend of homicidal fury, sexual abuse, matricide, incest and torture and have been further repelled by the film's casual and cooly distanced attitude towards its titular anti-hero. And no wonder, compared to the various human flotsam wriggling throughout his neighborhood, Henry is a pretty decent, even charming, fellow. With a few notable exceptions, of course. *Henry* was destined to stir up trouble right from the start. Not only is it very loosely based on the real-life exploits of one Henry Lee Lucas, a gap-toothed, scabrous inbred who claimed to have killed over 300 people during a ten-year spree, but both McNaughton and co-scripter Richard Fire have chosen to add other speculative unpleasantries that further potentiate this explosive mix of fact, fetish and fantasy.

Several distributors, who were initially interested, suddenly balked when the film earned an "X" rating from the MPAA. Usually the MPAA will provide the offending filmmaker with a list of suggestions and proposed cuts to be made, but they were clearly exasperated in the case of *Henry*. The film was rated "X" because of its "general tone" and the MPAA insisted it was impossible to cut the film in order to receive an "R" rating. A clearly frustrated McNaughton explained in later interviews that it was like "every fragment was tainted . . . like a hologram or something." McNaughton appealed the rating, resubmitted the film and was slapped with another "X." McNaughton was reluctantly forced to agree somewhat with the MPAA—the film could not be cut to an "R." After years of wranglings, *Henry* was finally picked up by MPI Home Video who plan to eventually release the film in its original and uncut form.

In actuality, *Henry* is richly deserving of its "X" rating. Much to its credit, it doesn't waltz around and simply flirt with the dreaded "X." It stomps right in and wins it within the first couple of minutes. Few, including its director, will honestly debate the accuracy of the proposed rating. Though most of the violence is presented either offscreen or after-the-fact, both the intensity and the impact of the killings are fully retained. Slow, painfully lingering shots reveal a hideously twisted landscape of human slaughter; victims strangled, stabbed, shot and cut to pieces. Most times, these grisly scenes suggest far worse things than we are shown.

The aftermath of a particularly vicious and grisly murder in the film's opening moments gives fair warning that it's going to be a mighty rough ride. Arguably, then, this is probably the scene that began the film's fall from grace; it's a long drop, too. After presenting a particularly well-photographed and orchestrated montage of past mayhem, the camera slowly glides from one room into another, revealing a stomach-churning scene of unparalleled nastiness. A woman is seated on a toilet, arms and legs spread and bound, underwear in violent disarray, with a jagged soft-drink bottle crammed halfway down her throat. Aural flashbacks are cut into the scene and we hear the woman's last few moments of agony. It is, indeed, a vile scene; you feel sucker punched. It's a nut-busting low blow that forces the bile up and into your throat. From that point on, you'd best be ready for anything . . . and *Henry* relentlessly obliges, time after time.

Though the violence, both implied and explicit, is enough to easily earn the film's "X" certification, other equally combustible elements bubble just beneath the surface at all times. In *Henry*, sex is always equated with violence, abuse and perversion. Nearly every character has experienced some form of sexual assault in their past. Henry's mother dressed him in little girl's clothes and forced him to watch her bang a long line of boyfriends. "She was a whore," Henry explains, "but I don't fault her for that. It ain't what she done, it's how she done it." Whew. Henry's roommate, Otis (Tom Towles), lusts after his own sister who was, in turn, sexually abused by their father. Shee-ishh.

The violence is often exacerbated by these deviant sexual undercurrents, especially in the case of the film's most horrific and bloody attack sequence—the murder of Henry's pal, Otis. Henry returns home to find him in a real rutting mood, on all fours and ready to pork little sister, when the chunky brownies really hit the rotor blades. The stabbing frenzy that follows can only be compared with the prolonged and excruciating knife attack preceding the double murder in Argento's *Suspiria*. *Henry* makes you feel the steel slide beneath your own ribs; the low camera angle practically forces participation in the sequence.

Despite the fact that Henry is repeatedly proven to be a card-carrying psychopath, McNaughton chooses to film from a safe moral distance and withholds judgment, even after he's killed and dismembered his best friend. McNaughton offers no excuses and little in the way of explanation. Even with a double-digit-figure body count under his belt by film's end, you still sorta, well, respect this guy Henry. Perhaps, therein lies the film's greatest danger. McNaughton has crafted an enigmatic and deeply troubling portrait of a vicious, unpredictable murderer who's clearly a menace to everyone, but he continually refuses to indict him.

Henry remains a triumph . . . of sorts. It completely betrays the fact that it was shot in 16mm, in one month and for less than $125,000. Its technical and production values are above reproach and the caliber of acting has been heretofore unseen in a film of this type. And Michael Rooker, who has since gone on to such films as *Eight Men Out* and *Mississippi Burning*, has created the most unforgettable and multi-layered modern portrait of a cinematic psychotic since Roberts Blossom tanned some hides with his Gein-inspired ghoul in the always-underrated and rarely seen *Deranged* (1974).

Henry, the film, is, indeed, a real killer; a drop-dead frontal assault that provokes, rather than patronizes, its audience. Truly, the most dangerous kind of genre film in existence.

Noted English poet/mystic William Blake said that "the road of excess leads to the palace of wisdom." Can't really blame the guy, either. That was nearly two hundred years before German director Jorg Buttgereit made *Nekromantik* (1988). Perhaps Buttgereit's running-sore-of-a-film better fulfills George Bernard Shaw's gentle admonishment that "it's just as unpleasant to get more than you bargain for as to get less."

Either way, *Nekromantik* may well prove the logical and genuine post-modernist successor to such early nihilistic taboo trashers as *Last House on the Left*, *Texas Chainsaw Massacre*, the *Ilsa: She Wolf* series and *Bloodsucking Freaks*. The problem with *Nekromantik*, though, is that it's such a sick-fuck of a film that a passionate defense could be tantamount to endorsing bunny-bashing, corpse-banging and suicidal meat-beating as integral elements of a genre catharsis-in-progress. Buttgereit has fashioned a supremely bleak, desperate film; it's a black yawning maw that threatens to swallow you whole. If some new genre hotshot bellows an update to Stephen King's famous fawnings about Clive Barker being the "future of horror" and concludes with "it is named Jorg Buttgereit" . . . then I quit.

Nekromantik is apparently built upon an awfully simple concept: fuck dead things and you'll end up a self-loathing suicidal wanker with a knife in your gut and a bloody, sticky dick hanging out of your shorts.

Actually, Buttgereit has crafted a tender romance between two potential necrophiles who've had to satisfy themselves with their collection of body parts gleaned from various automobile accidents until the real thing comes along. But then, after finally completing their coveted maggot-fueled menage à trois, the sweet smell of putrescence quickly sours and the girl leaves town with Mr. Wormfood riding shotgun. The boy, riddled by heartache and haunted by loneliness, gamely attempts sex with the living but finds he's no longer up to it. Murder becomes a necessary bit of foreplay thereafter until he ends up a whimpering, self-terminated, masturbatory casualty.

Many of the film's smarmier elements are held somewhat in check by the Play-Doh style makeup FX, while other sequences often resort to more risibly offensive, geek-show theatrics as shown by the pandering, on-screen killing and detailed skinning of a rabbit, shown twice (once in reverse) for maximum revulsion.

Despite the film's black, malevolent tone, Buttgereit exhibits a calculated slyness that manages to keep *Nekromantik* from succumbing to its own sleaziness. During a scene inside a theatre showing some nameless, misogynistic slasher, our little ghoul of a "hero" becomes so upset and repulsed by the action that he quickly exits the theater in disgust. The film is lightened considerably and nearly redeemed by a nifty little sting at the end, too. Long after the last drop of bloodied spunk has dried and crusted on his dead dick, our terminal pud-puller is still unable to rest in peace. The film ends with the haunting image of a woman's high-heeled shoe sinking the blade of a shovel into the fresh gravesite, mutely announcing that, indeed, even "death is just the beginning."

One fears what Buttgereit may do next.

* * *

After *Nekromantik*, even the grisly antics of Jim Van Bebber's possum-chomping urban cannibal in *Roadkill: The Last Days of John Martin* appear positively civilized . . . almost. Van Bebber is a young, ambitious Ohio filmmaker whose feature film debut, *Dead Beat at Dawn*, showed considerable promise along the lines of an early Wes Craven, Tobe Hooper or Sam Raimi. Van Bebber also writes, stars, directs and handles the FX in many of his films; and if the short promotional reels of both *Roadkill: The Last Days of John Martin* and *Charlie's Family* are an indication of his current direction, then this filmmaker will be one to reckon with during the upcoming decade.

Roadkill is a stunning, albeit grisly and demented, fifteen-minute descent into the private hell of a beer-swilling, varmint-scarfing spaz who graduates from possums to people without ever looking back. John Martin lives in a rat-infested, filthy shithole adorned with animal carcasses and human skin face masks, a fridge for his brew and a perpetually blaring television set that is always inciting spittle-spewing soliloquies from a guy who could teach Travis Bickle a thing or two about "morbid self-attention."

The film ends with Martin having progressed from roadkill to fresh kill, dismembering and beheading one victim while cooking the guy's naked girlfriend in a chicken-wire crematorium set atop his stove.

Despite its relatively brief running time, *Roadkill* shows more guts and balls than any other stateside genre effort has in years. It has all the makings necessary to be the *Texas Chainsaw Massacre* of the '90's.

While awaiting completion funds for *Roadkill*, Van Bebber is directing *Charlie's Family*, an insider's look at the Manson clan during that summer of '69 when "Helter Skelter" became more than just another throwaway tune from the Beatles' "White Album." *Charlie's Family* threatens to get up close and personal, venturing into forbidden territory previously ignored in the trivial and disconcerting media hogwash that led to a tepid TV movie that played like *Laverne and Shirley's Haunted Summer*.

Director Van Bebber will be a welcome addition to a genre grown fat and lazy with too many clean and sober splatter films that coddle and patronize their mostly teenaged audiences into a false sense of fright.

* * *

Don't attempt to view any of the aforementioned films while harboring a smug, condescending attitude that you're some rough, tough hipster who's seen it all. You haven't. And if you persist with your cocky delusions, you might just run into something that will kick that sniggering grin right down your throat.

These genre bastards prove that REAL fear is here to stay.

Freaktent

NANCY A.
COLLINS

Nancy A. Collins was born in rural Arkansas in 1959. There wasn't much to do in her hometown except read, watch TV, get knocked-up and/or become a teen-aged alcoholic. She opted for reading.

In 1982 she moved to New Orleans after having spent a year in Memphis, Tennessee. Her first novel, *Sunglasses After Dark*, was published by NAL's Onyx Books in 1989. *Sunglasses* was nominated for the Horror Writers Of America's Bram Stoker Award for First Novel and earned Nancy a spot on the ballot for the 1989 John W. Campbell Award. Her second novel, *Tempter*, will be published by Onyx in the Fall of 1990. She is currently working on the sequel to *Sunglasses*, tentatively titled *In the Blood*. She has recently finished adapting "Freaktent" into a one-act for the Off-Broadway theatrical production *Screamplay*, scheduled to open this October (1990) in New York City. She lives with her husband, Dan; their cat, Funky Butt; and way too much stuff.

She still prefers reading.

That's the biography Nancy Collins sent to me with her submission for *Splatterpunks*. While it certainly hits the high points, there's still room for expansion.

For example, *Sunglasses After Dark* was a hip vampire novel that caused an immediate sensation, both for its inventive narrative curlicues and lines like "The switchblade impaled his right eye, burying itself in the spongy softness of the frontal lobes, severing the left brain from the right." Further, Funky Butt may be the name of a cat, but Funky Butt Hall was also the New Orleans establishment where jazz was born. And finally, Nancy A. Collins currently leads the minuscule brigade of females writing splatterpunk.

Or rather, quasi-splatterpunk. In the cover letter sent with her bio, Collins also wrote: "Regarding whether I consider myself a splatterpunk—I don't, really . . . I guess you could say I subscribe to the same philosophy as Joe Lansdale; I consider myself a writer and let other folks worry about what *kind* of writer I am."

Well and good. But the laudatory buzz currently swirling around Collins—and it's increasing—partially rests on the splashy gore found in *Sunglasses*. This is due to the fact that few women presently write explicit horror, with most of them producing one-shots (Jay Sheckley with "Bargain Cinema," Elizabeth Massie's "Hooked on Buzzer," Nancy Holder's "Cannibal Cats Come Out Tonight"). Yet Collins seems bent on *continually* pushing the envelope. After *In the Blood* and *Tempter* will come "Neocrophiles," a story about death-obsessed junkies (Collins's contribution to Book of the Dead, volume two). And then there's her recent—and totally over the top—short story "Rant" ("Purple-pink entrails unravelled onto the carpet like party streamers").

In any event, Nancy Collins tells me her writing *really* breaks down into two broad categories, "Southern Gothics and the other stuff." Which may trigger fantasies of some weird crossbreed between Flannery O'Connor and *Fangoria*.

Not a bad description of "Freaktent," by the way.

My hobby is sideshow freaks. Some call them "Special People." I used to call them that too, until the Seal-Boy (who was seventy at the time) laughed in my face.

It's taken fifteen years of hanging around mess tents and caravans of the few Podunk carnivals that still tour the rural areas to build enough trust amongst these people so they'd agree to sit for me. They guard their private lives, their *real* selves, jealously. In the carny, there's no such thing as a free peek. You see, I'm a photographer.

. Two summers back I befriended Fallon, a human pincushion turned sideshow boss. Fallon's little family isn't much to write home about. There's the usual dwarf, fat lady, and pickled punk. Their big draw, however, is Rand Holstrum, The World's Ugliest Man.

Rand suffers from acromegaly. It is a disease that twists the bones and the flesh that covers them. It is a disease that makes monsters.

Rand Holstrum was born as normal as any child. He served in Korea and married his high school sweetheart. He fathered two beautiful, perfectly normal children. And then his head began to mutate.

The acromegaly infected the left side of his face, warping the facial bones like untreated pine boards. The flesh on that side of Rand's face resembles a water balloon filled to capacity. The upper forehead bulges like a baby emerging from its mother's cervix, its weight pressing against his bristling browridge. The puffy, bloated flesh of his cheek has long since swallowed the left eye, sealing it behind a wall of bone and meat. His nose was the size and shape of a man's doubled fist, rendering it useless for breathing. His lips are unnaturally thick and perpetually cracked. His lower jaw is seriously malformed and his teeth long since removed. Talking has become increasingly difficult for him. His hair was still dark, although the scalp's surface area had tripled, giving the impression of mange.

But these deformities alone did not make Rand Holstrum the successful freak that he is today. While the left half of his face is a hideously contorted mass of bone and gristle, like a papier-mâché mask made by a disturbed child, the other half is that of a handsome, intelligent man in his late fifties. *That* is what draws the fish. He is one of the most disturbing sights you could ever hope to see.

Had his disease been total, Rand Holstrum would have been just another sideshow performer. But due to the Janus-nature of his affliction, he's become one of the few remaining "celebrity" freaks in a day and age of jaded thrill seekers and Special People.

When I heard Fallon's carny had pulled into town I grabbed my camera and took the day off. The fairground was little more than a cow pasture dotted with aluminum outbuildings that served as exhibition halls. Everything smelled of fresh hay, stale straw, and manure. I was excited the moment I got out of my car.

The AirStream trailers that housed the carnies were located a few hundred feet beyond the faltering neon and grinding machinery of the midway. The rides were silent, their armature folded inward like giant metal birds with their heads tucked under their wings. I recognized Fallon's trailer by the faded Four Star Midways logo on its side.

As I stepped onto the cinderblock that served as the trailer's front stoop the door flew open, knocking me to the ground. An old man dressed in a polyester suit the color of cranberries flew from the interior of the trailer, landing a few feet from where I was sprawled.

"Gawddamn fuckin' *pre-vert!*" Anger and liquor slurred Fallon's voice. "I don't wanna see your face *again*, unnerstand? Go and peddle your monsters somewheres else!"

The old man picked himself up with overstated dignity, dusting his pants with liver-spotted hands. His chin quivered and his lips were compressed into a bloodless line. His dime-store salt-and-pepper toupee slid away from his forehead.

"You'll be sorry 'bout this, Fallon! How much longer you reckon Holstrum'll be around? Once your meal ticket's gone, you'll be coming 'round beggin' for ole Cabrini's help!"

"Not fuckin' likely! Now git 'fore I call the roustabouts!"

The old man looked mad enough to bite the head off a live chicken. He pretended to ignore me, walking in the opposite direction with a peculiar, storklike gait, his knobby hands fisted in his pockets.

"What the hell? . . ." I checked to make sure my light meter had survived the spill.

"Sorry 'bout all that, son. Didn't realize you was on the outside." Fallon stood over me, one scarred hand outstretched to help me up. He was still in his undershirt and baggy khakis, his usual off-hours uniform.

Fallon was in his late fifties but looked older. Thirty-five years in the carnival will do it to you. Especially the kind of work Fallon specialized in. For years he had been a pincushion; running skewers through his own flesh for the amusement of others. The marks of his trade could be glimpsed in the loose skin of his forearms, the flabby wattle of his neck, the webbing between thumb and forefinger, the underside of his tongue, and the cartilage of his ears. His face was long boned and heavily creased about the eyes and mouth, the cheeks marked by the hectic ivy blotches of broken blood vessels. As a younger man his hair had been the color of copper, but the years had leeched away its vitality, leaving it a pale orange. With his bulbous nose and knotty ridge of brow, Fallon would never be mistaken for handsome, but his was the kind of face the camera loves.

Fallon's mouth creases deepened. "Come on inside. I'll tell you all about it."

The interior of Fallon's trailer was a cramped jumble of old papers, dirty laundry, and rumpled bed linen. I sat down on the chair wedged beside the fold-down kitchen table while Fallon busied himself with finding two clean jelly glasses.

"I reckon you'd like to know what that hoo-ha was all about." He tried to sound nonchalant. If I hadn't known him better, I would have been taken in. "Seeing how's you got knocked ass over tea kettle, can't says I blames you." He set a jelly glass in front of me and poured a liberal dose of whiskey. Even though it was well after three in the afternoon, it was breakfast time for Fallon. "What you just saw was none other than Harry Cabrini, one of th' sleaziest items found in the business, which is, believe me, sayin' something!" Fallon drained his glass with a sharp flex of the elbow.

"Who is this Cabrini? What does he do?"

Fallon hissed under his breath and poured another slug into his glass. "He sells freaks."

"Huh?" I put my whiskey down untouched. "What do you mean by 'sells'?"

"Exactly what I meant." Fallon was leaning against the kitchen counter, arms folded. He was almost hugging himself. "How d'ya think they find their way into th' business? They drive out on their own when they hear a circus is in town? Well, some do. But most freaks don't have much say 'bout where they end up. Most get sold by their folks. That's how Smidgen got into show biz. Hasn't seen his folks since Eisenhower was in office. Sometimes they get sold by the doctors that was lookin' after 'em. That's how Rand got into it. Before he was th' World's Ugliest Man, he was laid up in some gawdforsaken V.A. hospital. Then this intern heard about me lookin' for a good headliner and arranged it so's I could meet Rand. I paid him a good hunk'a change for the privilege. Haven't regretted it since. I'm sure he didn't think of it as 'selling.' More like being a talent scout, I reckon."

"And you've—bought—freaks?"

"Don't make it sound like slavery, boy! It's more like payin' a finder's fee. I give my folks decent wages and they're free to come an' go as they see fit! The slave days are long gone. But Cabrini . . . Cabrini is a whole other kettle of fish." Fallon looked as if he'd bitten into a lemon. "Cabrini ain't no agent. He's a slaver . . . at least, that's *my* opinion. Maybe I'm wrong. But the freaks Cabrini comes up with . . . there's something *wrong* about 'em. Most of 'em are feebleminded. Or worse. I made the mistake of buyin' a pickled punk offa him a few years back, and he's been hounding me ever since. Wants me to buy one'a his

live 'uns! Buyin trouble is more like it! Here, look and see for
yourself if I ain't right." Fallon leaned over and plucked a color
Polaroid snapshot out of the tangle of dirty clothes and contracts.
"He left one of his damn pictures behind." He handed it to me
without looking at the photo.

I could understand why. In all the years I'd spent photographing flesh malformed by genetics and disease, nothing had prepared me for the wretched creature trapped inside the picture.
The naked, fishbelly-white freak looked more like a skinned,
mutant ape than anything born from the coupling of man and
woman. Its hairless, undeveloped pudendum marked the unfinished thing as a child.

"Where'd he come up with a freak that young?" Fallon's whisper was tight and throaty. "Most of 'em that age, nowadays, are
either in state homes or special schools. Where's its mama? And
how come he's got more than one of 'em?"

I dropped in on Rand after leaving Fallon's trailer. I always visit
Rand Holstrum when I have a chance. I never know when I might
have another opportunity to photograph him. Rand isn't as young
as he used to be, and his ailment is a temperamental one. He's
been told he could die without any warning. Despite the doctors'
prognosis, he remains as cheerful and life-affirming as ever.

I have dozens of photographs of Rand. They hold a weird
fascination for me. By looking at them in sequence, I can trace
the ravages of his disease. It is as if Rand is a living canvas, a
quintessential work in progress.

Rand was in the freaktent, getting ready for that evening's
show. He was still in his smoking jacket, a present from his
daughter. His wife Sally was with him.

Rand extended a hand in greeting. It was a purely symbolic
gesture. The acromegaly had spread there as well, twisting his
knuckles until his hands were little more than flesh-and-blood
catcher's mitts.

"You remember the wife, don't you?" he gasped.

Sally Holstrum was decent looking, as carny wives go. She
nodded at me while she hammered up the chicken-wire screen
that protected Rand from the crowd while he was on display.
The fish get pretty rowdy at times, and a well-placed beer bottle
could prove fatal to her husband.

Rand fished out his wallet, producing a couple of thumb-
smudged prints for me to admire. Randy, the Holstrums' son,

was dressed in a cap and gown, a diploma clutched in one hand. June, Rand's favorite, stood next to her husband, a toddler in her arms. "Randy's a dentist now . . . Got a practice in . . . Sheboygan . . . Little Dee-Dee can say . . . her ABCs . . ." Rand slurped.

"Time flies," I agreed. "Oh, I happened to run into some guy named Harry Cabrini today . . ."

Sally stopped what she was doing and turned to look at me. "Cabrini's here?"

"He *was* here. Fallon threw him out of his office. I don't know if he's still around or not . . ."

"He *better* not be!" she spat, wagging the claw hammer for emphasis. "If I find that slimeball skulkin' round this tent again, I'll show 'im where monkeys put bad nuts!"

"Now, Sally . . ."

"Don't you 'now Sally' me, Rand Holstrum! The trouble with you is that you're too damn nice! Even to people who don't deserve more'n what you'd give a dog on the street!"

Rand fell silent. He knew better than to argue with Sally.

"You know what I caught that crazy motherfucker doin'?" She resumed her hammering with vigor. "I came back from the Burger King and found that nutcase taking *measurements* of Rand's face!"

"It was . . . nothing . . . I've been measured before, Sal—"

"Yeah, by *doctors*. What business does some screwball like Harry Cabrini have doing shit like that?"

Rand shrugged and his good eye winked at me. Just then one of the roustabouts came into the tent with a take-out sack from one of the local burger joints. The grease from the fast food had already turned the paper bag translucent. "Got yer food, Mr. Holstrum." Rand paid off the roustabout while Sally got out the food processor.

"Go change your clothes, honey. You don't want to get that nice smoker June gave you dirty," Sally said as she dropped the cheeseburgers one by one into the hopper. Rand grunted in agreement and shuffled off to change.

The malformation of his jaw and the loss of his teeth has made chewing a thing of the past for Rand. Everything he eats has to be liquified.

"Uh, I'll see y'all later, Sal . . ."

"Sure, hon. Let me know if you see that Cabrini creep hangin' around."

"Sure thing."

I left just as the stainless steel rotary knives whirred to life, mulching the half-dozen cheeseburgers into a protein-rich soup.

I lied to Sally. I didn't mean to, but I ended up doing it anyway. Twilight arrived at the carnival, and with it, life. The cheesy rides and midway attractions took on a magical aura once the sky darkened from cobalt to indigo and the neon was switched on. The rubes came to gawk and be parted from their hard-earned cash. The air was redolent of cotton candy, corndogs, snow cones, diesel fumes, and vomit. Taped music blared from World War II surplus public-address systems. The motors propelling the death-trap rides roared like captive animals and rattled their chains, yearning to break free.

The exhilarated shriek-laugh of the carnivalgoer echoed from every mouth. I began to feel the same excitement I'd known as a kid. The sights, sounds, and smells of the carnival sparked a surge of nostalgia for days that seemed simpler compared to the life I lived now.

I passed a gaggle of school kids gathered near the Topsy Turvy. They were searching the sawdust for loose change shaken from the pockets of the passengers, although they risked retribution at the hands of the roustabouts and being puked on by the riders. I smiled, remembering how I used to scuttle in the sawdust in search of nickels and dimes.

That's when I saw him.

He was weaving in and out of the crowd like a wading bird searching for minnows. His hands were jammed into his pockets. His toupee slid about on his head like a fried egg on a plate. His suit was a size too big for him, and all that kept him from losing his pants was a wide white patent leather belt. He had loafers to match.

I hesitated a moment, uncertain as to what I should do. He was headed for the parking lot. I wavered. The image of the twisted freak-child rose before my eyes and I followed him.

Cabrini got into a secondhand panel truck that had once belonged to a baked goods chain. The faded outline of a smiling, apple-cheeked little girl with blonde ringlets devouring a slab of white bread slathered in butter could still be glimpsed on the side of the van. It was easy enough to follow Cabrini from the fairground to a decrepit trailer park twenty miles away.

He lived in a fairly large mobile home set in a lot full of chickweed and rotting newspapers. Uncertain as to what I should

do, I opted for the direct approach. I knocked on the trailer's
doorframe.

There was scurrying inside, then the sound of something being
knocked over.

"Who the fuck is it?"

"Mr. Cabrini? Mr. Harry Cabrini?"

"Yeah, I'm Cabrini—what's it t'ya?"

"Mr. Cabrini, my name is Kevin Malone. I was told by a Mr.
Fallon that you had . . . something of interest to me." Silence.
"Mr. Cabrini?"

The door opened the length of its safety chain. Cabrini's face,
up close, was as storklike as his movements. His nose was a great
stabbing beak overshadowing his thin-lipped mouth and flat
cheekbones. The store-bought toupee was gone, revealing a
smooth, liver-blotched scalp and a graying fringe ruff level with
his ears. Cabrini stared at me, then at the camera slung around
my neck. He grunted, more to himself than for my benefit, then
shut the door. A moment later I heard him fumbling with the
chain and the door jerked open. The toupee was back—still
slightly askew—and Cabrini motioned me inside.

"C'mon, dammit. No point in lettin' every dam skeeter in the
county in with you."

The interior of the trailer was hardly what I'd expected. The
front section normally reserved for the living room and kitchen
area had been stripped of all furnishings except for the refrigerator and stove. Gone was the built-in wet bar, pressboard room
divider, imitation oak paneling, and wall-to-wall shag carpeting.
In their place was a small formica table, a couple of Salvation
Army–issue kitchen chairs, and one of the best-equipped work-
benches I've ever seen. The rest was a labyrinth of lumber,
varying from new two-by-fours to piles of sawdust. I noticed a
spartan army cot in the corner next to a mound of polyester
clothes.

"Yer that fella what takes pictures of freaks," he said flatly.
"Flippo the Seal-Boy tol' me 'bout you."

"And Fallon told me about you."

Cabrini's spine stiffened. "Yeah? Well, what d'ya want? I ain't
got all night . . ."

I reached into my jacket and withdrew the Polaroid he'd left
at Fallon's trailer. "A picture. Just one. I'll pay you." It made
me sick to speak to him, but I found myself saying the words
nonetheless. I knew from the moment I saw its picture that I had
to add it to my collection.

He looked into my eyes and it was like being sized up by a snake. He smiled then, and it was all I could do to keep from smashing his stork face into pulp.

"Okay. Hunnert bucks. Otherwise you walk."

My bank balance reeled at the blow, but I fished two fifties out of my wallet. Cabrini palmed them with the ease of a conjurer and motioned for me to follow him down the narrow hallway that led to the back of the trailer.

There were two bedrooms and a bathroom connected by the corridor. I glanced into what would have been the master bedroom and saw four or five small crates stacked in the darkness. Cabrini quickly closed the door, indicating that the second, smaller bedroom was what I wanted.

The room stank of human waste and rotten food. I fought to keep from gagging on the stench. Cabrini shrugged. "What can I do? They're morons. Jest like animals. Don't clean up after themselves. Don't talk. Shit whenever and wherever th' mood strikes 'em."

There were three of them. Two girls and a boy. They sat huddled together on a stained bare mattress on the filthy floor. Their deformities were strikingly similar: humped backs, twisted arms, bowed legs, warped rib cages resting atop their pelvises. Their fingers curled in on themselves, like those of an ape. They were pallid, with eyes so far recessed into their orbits as to resemble blind, cave-dwelling creatures. Their features were those of a wax doll held too close to an open flame. Their hair was filthy and matted with their own waste.

The odd thing was that their limbs, albeit contorted into unnatural angles, were of normal proportions. The stunted children looked like natives of some bizarre heavy-gravity planet, their torsos compressed into half the space necessary for normal growth.

But what truly shocked me was the look of animal fear on their ruined faces. I remember Slotzi the Pinhead; despite her severe imbecility, she enjoyed singing and dancing and was affectionate and curious in a disarmingly childlike way. She was locked into an eternal childhood, her mental development arrested somewhere between three and five years of age. Compared to Cabrini's trio of freak-babies, Slotzi was Nobel prize material. One thing was certain; these monstrously distorted children had never laughed, nor had they known any joy or love in their brief lives. Without really thinking of what I was doing, I adjusted the focus and checked the light. And then I had my picture.

Cabrini closed the door, propelling me back into the hall. I stared at him, trying to make sense of what I had seen.

"Those children . . . are they related?"

Cabrini shook his head, nearly sending his toupee into his face. "Drugs."

"Drugs?"

Cabrini's voice took on the singsong of a barker reciting his spiel. "LSD. Speed. Heroin. Crack. Who knows? Maybe an experimental drug like that thalidomide back in the sixties. They were all born within the same year. Ended up in a home. Until I found them."

We were back in the front room, amongst the lumber and sawdust. Cabrini was looking at me, an unpleasant smile twisting his lips. Averting my eyes, I found myself staring at a pile of papers scattered across the workbench. Amongst them were several detailed sketches of Rand Holstrum's face.

Cabrini brought out a plastic milk jug full of homemade popskull and placed a pair of Dixie cups on the workbench.

"Don't get too many visitors out this way. Reckon you deserve a free drink for yer hunnert bucks." White lightning sloshed into the cups and onto the bench. I half-expected it to eat into the wood, hissing like acid.

As much as I loathed Cabrini and all he represented, I found him perversely intriguing. For fifteen years I'd actively pursued knowledge concerning the secret lives of freaks. I'd listened to stories told by men with too many limbs, women with beards, and creatures that walked the blurred borders of gender. I'd talked shop with people who make their living displaying their difference to the curious for a dollar a head. I was aware that by the end of the century their way of life would be extinct and no one would know their story. Harry Cabrini—seller of freak-babies—comprised an important, if unsavory, portion of that history.

"Y'know, I've run across quite a few of yer kind in this business. Fellers who take pictures."

"Izzat so?" I sipped at the deceptively clear fluid in the paper cup. It scalded my throat on the way down.

"Yeah. Some were doctors or newspaper men. Others were arteests." He smirked. "They was like you. Thought I was dirt, but still paid me for the honor of lookin' at my babies! Y'all treat me like I ain't no more than some kinda brothelkeeper. But what does that make *you*, Mr. Arteest?" He tossed back his head to laugh, nearly dislodging his toupee.

"Where did you find those children?"

He stopped laughing, his eyes sharp and dangerous. "None of yer fuckin' business. All you wants is pictures of freaks. Why you wanna know where they come from? They come from normal, God-fearin' folk. Like they all do. Just like you 'n me." He poured himself a second shot of squeeze. I wondered what Cabrini's guts must look like. "The freak business is dyin' out, y'know. Been dyin' since the war." Cabrini's voice became nostalgic. "People learned more 'bout what makes freaks for real. Used t'think they was th' sins of the parents made flesh. That they didn't have no souls cause of it. That they weren't like real people. Hell, now that there March of Dimes has got rid of most that what used to reel th' fish in. Don't get me wrong. There'll always be people who's willin' to look. I think it makes 'em feel good. No matter how fuckin' awful things might be, at least you can walk down th' street without makin' people sick, right? But who wants to pay an' see dwarfs? Midgets? Fat ladies? Pinheads? Sure they're gross, but you can see 'em for free at th' Wal-Mart any ol' day of the week! No, you gotta have something that really *scares* 'em! Shocks 'em! Repulses 'em! Something that makes 'em forget they're lookin' at another human! Tall order, ain't it?"

"Uh, yeah."

"I got to readin' one time about these here guys back in Europe. During what they called the Dark Ages. These guys was called Freak Masters. Nice ring to it, huh? Anyways, these Freak Masters, when times were tough an' there weren't no good freaks around, they'd kidnap babies . . ."

Something inside me went cold. Cabrini was standing right next to me, but I felt as if I were light-years away.

". . . and they'd put 'em in these here special cages, so that they'd grow up all twisted like. And they'd make 'em wear these special masks so their faces would grow a certain way, what with baby meat being so soft, y'know . . ."

Images of children twisted into tortured, abstract forms like human bonsai trees swam before my eyes. I recognized the expanding bubble in my rib cage as fear. Adrenaline surged through me, its primal message telling me to get the fuck *outta* there. My gaze flickered across the jumble on the workbench. Foul as he was, Cabrini was a genius when it came to working with his hands. I saw the partially completed leather mask nestled amidst the sketches and diagrams; it was a near-exact duplicate of Rand Holstrum's face. Only it was so small. Far too small for an adult to wear . . .

". . . they fed 'em gruel and never talked to 'em, so they came out kinda brain-damaged, those that di'nt die. But the kings an' popes an' shit back then di'nt care. They bought freaks by the truckloads! Pet monsters!" Cabrini laughed again. He was drinking straight from the jug now. "They didn't have freaktents back then. But it don't matter. There's always been freaktents. We carry 'em with us wherever we go." He tapped his temple with one unsteady finger. The toupee fell off and landed on the floor; it lay amidst the sawdust and scraps of leather like a dead tarantula.

That's when he lunged, scything the air with one of the leather-cutting tools he'd snatched from the workbench. There was something feral in his eyes and the show of yellowed teeth. The stork had become a wild dog. I staggered backward, barking my shins on a pile of two-by-fours. I'd just missed having the hooked blade sink into my chest.

Cursing incoherently, Cabrini followed me. The knife sliced within millimeters of my nose. I heard the muffled, anguished cries of the idiot children coming from the other room as I threw the contents of my cup into Cabrini's face. He screamed and let go of his knife, clawing at his eyes. Cabrini reeled backward, knocking over the kitchen table in his blind flailing. I headed for the door, not daring to look back.

I could still hear Cabrini screaming long after I'd made my escape. "Damn you! Goddamn you, you fuckin' lousy *freak*!"

Crucifax Autumn: Chapter 18- The Censored Chapter

RAY GARTON

Ray Garton cannot really be called a splatterpunk, and like Joe R. Lansdale, he actively resists the label. This is a position with which I must agree; both of these writers are so proficient in so many other areas that they *should* refuse to be held captive to a single subgenre (as Garton's latest sex and suspense novel, *Trade Secrets*, amply testifies).

But it's easy to see why Garton initially was lumped in with the rest of The Splat Pack—his two favorite themes were pushing the erotic envelope (a topic he continues to explore) and trashing the Seventh-Day Adventists (although Ray now tells me he's put his "Adventist phase" behind him). These are twin obsessions at which Garton is both arousingly and amusingly proficient, as demonstrated in his excellent 1988 short story "Sinema" (which details the relentless relationship between a murdering pedophilic Sabbath School teacher and a very manipulative nine-year-old boy).

Lately, Garton is an increasingly effective novelist; one of his best-known books is the popular *Live Girls* (1987), wherein a not-so-bright associate editor at a Manhattan publishing house finds himself attracted to a vampire working in a Times Square peep show. But to my mind, *Crucifax Autumn* remains his most mature work.

Crucifax Autumn was first printed as a limited-edition hardcover by Dark Harvest in 1988. Detailing the Charles Manson–Pied Piper-like influence of a charismatic stranger named Mace, who holds sway over a group of very contemporary, very aimless teenagers, *Crucifax Autumn* mixes the supernatural with stinging social commentary. *Autumn*'s final argument is that it is not rock music, or drugs, or TV, but *parents themselves* who are responsible for their children's actions. A simplistic lesson, perhaps, but still a necessary one.

Unfortunately, when *Crucifax Autumn* was released as a mass-market paperback by Pocket Books (also in 1988), not only was the *Autumn* dropped from the cover (leaving the book simply titled *Crucifax*), but a number of graphic sequences also were cut—that is, censored—by the publisher. Here, finally restored, is one such omission. I think it more than highlights Garton's unusually powerful facility at mixing the sick and the sensual. Not incidentally, this suppressed chapter also features a splatterpunk first—cunnilingual abortion.

Jeff and Lily have joined forces to find their friend Nikki who has become deeply involved with a dangerous cult led by a mysterious man named Mace. Nikki is young, pregnant, and in trouble. They travel through the sewers—the only route they know to Mace's stronghold—while Mace drives a special guest back to the lair. . . .

The reverend sat stiffly in the passenger seat of his van as the tires below him screamed around the curves of Beverly Glen. The windshield wipers droned back and forth and, at the wheel, Mace grinned into the night, occasionally glancing at Bainbridge.

The reverend could feel the creatures at his feet, three of them, pressing themselves against his ankles and crawling over his shoes. There were more in the back, squeaking as the van rounded the sharp corners.

Bainbridge's mouth was dry as old felt and he could not stop trembling as he prayed frantically for deliverance from what he was certain was the devil's henchman.

If not the devil himself.

"What . . . what are you going to, to do to me?" he asked, his voice a frog-like croak.

"*Do* to you?" Mace laughed. "Nothing. Just taking you to a party."

"Why me? Why am I being *tried* like this?" He closed his eyes as they shrieked around another curve.

"You're not being tried. I'm sorry you feel that way. Why don't you just think of me as . . . oh, how about a buddy? Not friends yet," he chuckled, "just buddies. But later we'll—"

"You're *evil!* This is a trial, a test of my faith!" The reverend clenched his eyes tighter, wanting to cover his ears, but afraid to move because of the beasts at his feet.

Mace's laugh was deep and rich and he punched the dashboard jovially.

"Black and white," he said. "Everything is black and white to you people, good and evil. You're white and I'm black, all black, evil to the bone, right? But, Reverend, you live in a gray world, don't you know that? There is no black, no white, only gray. You say I'm evil, but those kids are *nuts* about me, Rev; I make them happy. Now, is that evil? Making them happy? Huh? *I* don't think so. Now, *you*. You're supposed to be good, all white, but *you*'ve been sneaking around with somebody's little girl and now she's pregnant and *you* won't let her do what she wants with the baby that's growing in *her* belly. Hah! That's *goodness*? You see? We're all gray. Some are blacker than others, maybe a few are *all* black, but I can promise you one thing, Reverend. Nobody . . . *nobody* is all white."

Taking in a deep, unsteady breath, Bainbridge said, "Satan uses the truth to tell lies and, and, we're told he can, can fool the, the very elite, and I will *not* listen to—"

"I'm. Not. Satan." His tone was very serious now, almost threatening. "I'm not from hell or heaven. I'm from . . . *no*-where. And you brought me *here*. You. Your fellow clergy. All the many, many moms and dads here in this Valley." He drove in silence for a while, then said, "There is no place in this universe for gaps, Reverend. I've come to fill the gaps that you have made."

Bainbridge clenched his fists in his lap and continued to pray. . . .

The hand pulled Jeff's head back hard as a ragged voice cried, "Leave us alone! Leave us *alone*!" Jeff saw the bat lift high over his face, saw it stop before swinging down again, and he slammed his arm up, knocking the hand away, felt Lily grab his coat as they dashed away from the opening, avoiding the bat by inches as they moved on down the walkway in a staggering, swaying run, their hands slapping the wall, their feet scraping over the grimy cement.

"Get away!" the voice cried as the bat smacked against the wall once, twice, again. Footsteps followed them a few feet, then stopped.

They didn't look back, kept moving, passed another intersection and another, their gasps echoing in the darkness. The sewer veered left, then right as their feet clanged over another metal plank.

"Wait, wait!" Lily panted, pulling on Jeff's coat.

When he turned and shined the light on her, he saw her tears and she stepped into the crook of his arm.

"What . . . what *was* that?" she asked.

"I don't know. A bum, I guess. I hear a lot of them live down here."

"But what was that room in the —"

"Sh!"

In the silence, water dripped and pattered and sewage gushed. And somewhere in the darkness, music played.

"What?" Lily asked.

"Hear that?"

She listened a moment. "Where's it coming from?"

Jeff faced the opposite wall and listened intently. Mingled with the music were distant, garbled voices, laughter; they were coming from his right, from the direction in which they'd been walking.

"C'mon," he said, taking her hand and leading her along the walkway, the flashlight shining before him. Up ahead, he saw a couple of rats that quickly skittered out of sight before Lily saw them.

As they pressed on, the music grew louder, the voices and laughter more distinct, although they were still faint, ghostly.

"Sounds like a party," Jeff whispered.

The closer they got, the clearer and louder the voices became; the music was replaced by a loud, fast-talking voice that Jeff recognized as a radio disc jockey. Someone was listening to the radio.

"—c'mere before you—"

"—ha-*haaaah*—"

"—me another one of those—"

The music began again: Robert Palmer.

The louder they became, the more difficult it was to tell exactly from where the voices and music were coming.

Until they found the hole.

He could tell the hole had been knocked in the wall fairly recently because there were still bits of rubble and a few bricks scattered around on the walkway beneath it.

"In here," Jeff breathed, shining the light through the rough-edged hole.

"What is it?"

The light fell on dark, wet walls, stacks of boxes, twisting pipes connected by fluttering cobwebs, and a steep metal staircase.

There was a soft, shimmering glow coming from the top of the stairs.

Jeff leaned close to Lily's ear and whispered, "Be very quiet."

He carefully pulled himself through the hole, then angled the light so Lily could see her way through. With Jeff a step ahead, they made their way slowly and silently to the staircase, where Jeff turned off the flashlight; the glow from above gave them enough light to see their way. As they carefully climbed the stairs, trying to keep their footsteps from sounding on the metal steps, the voices crystallized, became clear and distinct.

A male voice: "Did you hear that?"

A female voice: "Yeah, it came from up there."

Another male voice: "The door? Is Mace here?"

They hunkered down as they reached the top of the stairs and something clattered loudly on the next floor: footsteps on metal stairs.

"I'm back!" The voice was loud, deep, booming: it was Mace.

A chorus of greetings replied and Jeff was surprised by the number of people he heard.

He climbed the remaining steps on his hands and knees, peering over the top of the staircase. There had once been a door there, but only hinges remained now. The room he looked into was large and appeared to have once been two rooms; the remaining portion of a wall jutted three quarters of the way across the middle of the room, then ended in a jagged, broken edge where it had been torn away. Bricks and chunks of broken plaster littered the floor. There were three holes in the torn-away wall; bars of soft light shined through from the other side, cutting the dusty, smoky darkness.

Beyond the wall, Jeff could make out some movement in the hazy light. He saw a couple of kerosene lanterns on wooden crates. Murmuring voices were occasionally punctuated by a burst of laughter or a passionate cry.

Reverend Bainbridge was coming down a spiral staircase; Mace was one step behind him, holding a lantern.

"And I have a visitor," Mace said.

Once they were off the stairs, Mace stood beside the reverend and lifted his lantern, illuminating the little man's face.

"This is Reverend James Bainbridge," Mace said. "Some of you may already know him. C'mon in, Reverend."

Bainbridge looked terrified and moved like a bird as he followed Mace deeper into the room, disappearing behind the wall.

A scuttling noise came from the spiral staircase and Jeff's mouth closed over the terrified groan that rose from his chest when his eyes followed the sound.

The creatures that had chased him from the abandoned health club were milling around the bottom of the staircase, sniffing the floor, their eyes glinting in the lantern light.

Jeff's throat suddenly seemed filled with cotton and he reflexively put his hand over Lily's, needing to touch someone, to reassure himself that he was not alone.

"Take your coat off, Reverend," Mace said congenially. "Get comfortable. We're very informal here."

They were out of sight, hidden by the wall, but Jeff could hear their movements above the music and soft voices.

"Nikki!" Bainbridge wailed as if in pain. "My God, Nikki. . . ." Then, angrily: "What have you *done* to her?"

Lily squeezed Jeff's hand.

"*I* haven't done anything," Mace said.

Jeff felt Lily stiffen beside him, looked to see her staring intently at the wall three yards away.

Mace said, "You're here because you want to be, aren't you, Nikki?"

Faintly: "Yes."

"She's been drugged!" the reverend barked.

"Oh, she may be high, but I can assure you she hasn't been *drugged*, Reverend. No one here has been drugged and no one is here against their will. Nikki . . . why don't you come out of the pool.

"I'm taking her out of here," the reverend said, his voice trembling.

"I don't think she wants to go."

"I'll call the police."

"Reverend, I'd like you to meet three very good friends of mine. Officers Peter Wyatt, Jake Margolin, and Harvey Towne." Deep, male voices, groggy and garbled, greeted the reverend. One of them laughed. "They're off duty right now, but if you feel you need a policeman, I'm sure one of them would be more than happy to help you."

After a long pause, the reverend whispered, "I was right." Something seemed to have left his voice—reason, hope, maybe both—leaving behind a hollow, helpless sound. "You . . . you *are* . . . evil."

Mace laughed and said, "C'mon, Nikki."

The reverend pleaded, "Nikki, Nikki, what are you *doing* here?"

"Tell him, Nikki. Why did you come?"

"Because Mace is . . . gonna help me with my . . . problem."

"Tell him *what* problem."

"My . . . my baby."

"Oh, God, dear God, don't do this, Nikki." Bainbridge sounded near tears.

Lily put a hand over her mouth and squeezed close to Jeff.

"Nikki," the reverend went on, his voice a desperate hiss now, "*think* about it, about what you're doing."

"I can't keep it. I . . . I *can't*. I . . . I haven't finished school. My . . . my mother would . . . my mother. . . ."

"But it's . . . Nikki, it's a-a-a—" He gulped back a sob. "—sin, a horrible *sin*, a moral *crime*!"

"Nikki," Mace said, "did the reverend ever mention that what *he* did to *you* was a sin?"

"Mm-hm. He said God would—" She giggled. "—understand. And forgive."

"Okay, Reverend. God will understand Nikki's reasons and He'll forgive her."

"But this is *murder*!"

"Yeah. And what are the words for what *you* did, Reverend?" Footsteps, rustling movement. "Adultery?" Mace's voice grew softer. "Fornication?" Softer still. "Maybe . . . rape?"

Jeff and Lily turned to one another. He saw the same realization in her eyes that he felt: Reverend Bainbridge was the father of Nikki's baby. Lily put her face in her hands and slowly shook her head.

"Is *this* what you did, Reverend?" Mace whispered. "Did you touch her like this. . . ? Like this?"

Nikki moaned, sighed.

"Did you touch her—no, no; lie down, Nikki—did you touch her here, Reverend?"

Lily's eyes burned with fear for her friend; she looked ready to make a dash across the room and around the wall.

"No!" Bainbridge cried. "Stop! Stop this *now*!"

Mace laughed.

Nikki gasped ecstatically.

The reverend sobbed.

The voices seemed quieter, more attentive to whatever was happening on the other side of the wall.

"Is *this* what you did?" Mace hissed, voice wet, lips smacking. "Is this what it was like?"

"I'm leaving!" Bainbridge shouted, his feet scraping on the cement. "Nikki, if you would only—" Something made a wretched throaty hiss and Bainbridge swallowed his words with a gasp.

Jeff recognized that sound. . . .

Lily started to sit up, but Jeff put a hand on her shoulder and firmly held her down.

There were no lanterns at their end of the room; at the other end, with the exception of a few figures shifting in the hazy darkness, everyone had gone behind the wall. If he were quiet, Jeff thought the lack of light at their end might sufficiently hide him until he got to the wall and could look through one of those holes.

Jeff turned to Lily, laid a finger over his lips, and breathed into her ear, "Stay here."

She frowned at him, cocked her head.

Jeff started across the room, moving in a crouch, his feet crunching softly over the floor, too softly to be heard above the music and the quiet buzz of voices.

As he crept to the wall, Jeff heard Nikki's soft murmurs of pleasure grow steadily louder, more intense, heard Mace whispering, chuckling. Amidst the voices were smacking, slurping noises.

Speaking with malevolent deliberation, Mace whispered, "Is this . . . what you did . . . before you planted . . . your *seed* in her . . . Reverend?"

Nearing the wall, Jeff felt as if a steel band were slowly tightening around his chest, making each breath more difficult, squeezing his heart within his rib cage. The back of his neck was damp with sweat.

When he reached the wall, Jeff cautiously peered over the edge of the hole on the right end, instantly taking in all the details on the other side.

To the right, two guitars were propped against the wall and drums and a keyboard were set up between amplifiers; four of the dark creatures were crawling over the instruments, sniffing curiously. Beyond the instruments in a murky corner, Jeff saw what looked like a generator. About six feet in front of the instruments there was, indeed, a swimming pool in which shapes moved within darkness. To Jeff's left, Mace stood in the shallow end of the pool facing the wall, his tall lean frame rising above the darkness below. Lying before him on two fluffy-looking cushions, her legs spread, naked but for a blue shirt open in front, was Nikki. A lantern shined on each side of her, making her skin look pale. Her nipples were dark and erect and a dark, oddly shaped cross rested between her breasts, attached to a cord that went around her neck. Trails of saliva glistened around her breasts and over her belly.

The reverend stood at her head, several of the creatures huddled between him and Nikki; two of them were standing on their hind legs like guards, teeth bared, eyes threatening.

Mace smiled up at Bainbridge, his lips and chin wet; he passed his hands over Nikki's body, caressing and gently squeezing her full breasts, slipping his fingers between her legs.

"Did you do this, Reverend?" Mace whispered, wrapping his lips around a wet finger and licking off the juices. "Or were you too anxious to *fuck* her?"

Mace leaned forward and slowly, luxuriously, slipped his tongue between the flowery lips of Nikki's vagina and moved his head up and down, up and down, licking his way up to her belly, her breast, sucking loudly. Nikki's breaths were thick with moans of pleasure.

"No!" the reverend snapped, but his voice was weak. "Stop this, stop . . . this . . . now. . . ."

Mace raised his head and purred, "Look familiar, Reverend?" then pressed his face hard into the mound of dark hair between them. Nikki's body stiffened, her head tilted back, surrounded by her shiny brown hair, her mouth opening, closing, then opening again as she looked up at the reverend and slowly smiled, purring, ". . . feels . . . sooo . . . *good*. . . ."

Bainbridge frantically muttered prayers under his breath.

The movement within the pool settled down.

The music played on.

Water dripped around them as Bainbridge whimpered.

Nikki suddenly arched her back, her hands closing over the edges of the cushions beneath her; she made a strangled gurgle in her throat and the pleasure in her face suddenly turned to confusion and fear.

Mace's hands slid up her body, over her stomach; his long fingers cupped her breasts, pinched her nipples as Nikki sucked in a long and desperate breath.

Jeff realized he'd been holding his breath, clenching his teeth until his jaws hurt, and he slowly exhaled.

Something was wrong, very, very wrong. . . .

Nikki lifted her buttocks from the cushion, pressing herself up to Mace as his head twisted and turned, bobbed, twitched, his hair falling over his shoulders and brushing against her thighs. Nikki's tongue protruded stiffly from her mouth and she coughed.

Something crunched behind Jeff and he spun around to see Lily hurrying toward him. Thinking she probably shouldn't see what was happening beyond the wall, he waved for her to go back, but she kept coming, her eyes and mouth wide with fear as she sidled up to him and peered over his shoulder, her hands gripping his sides just above his waist.

Nikki's body convulsed, her head jerked forward and back as Mace's head continued to move between her legs. He made a deep grumbling sound in his chest as she coughed again and again, her right fist pounding the cushion.

Lily clutched Jeff's sides tightly and he heard her breath quicken.

Nikki's stomach moved.

Jeff blinked several times, not sure of what he'd seen.

It moved again, roiled, bulged, then flattened.

The reverend raised his voice: ". . . though I walk through the valley of the *shadow of death*—"

Nikki's entire body quaked.

"—I will fear no evil for thou art *with me*—"

She coughed again and spittle rose from her mouth in a spray and rained back down on her as her stomach rose, lowered, rose again as her fists opened and closed.

"—thy rod and thy staff *they comfort me*—"

Mace's eyes rolled up to stare at the reverend and he pulled his face away from Nikki, chuckling—

"—thou preparest a table before me in the presence of *mine enemies*—"

—but something was strung from his mouth to Nikki's vagina—

"—thou anointest my head with *oil*—"

—something long and thick and wet, with dark streaks of viscous matter dribbling from it as it pulled out farther and farther.

"—my cup runneth over surely g-good-goodness and m-mercy—"

Dark lumps clung to it as it pulled out of Nikki, coated with a slimy film, pulling out . . . out . . . out. . . .

The reverend staggered backward out of Jeff's line of vision, bumping the wall, babbling, "Get thee hence, Satan! Get thee hence, Satan, *get thee hence!*"

Nikki made a horrible belching sound as she sat up on the cushions, then fell back again. With the sound of tearing flesh, Mace's tongue pulled out of Nikki, curling upward like a snake. A quivering black-red gob hung from the tip, dripping and gelatinous, bunched around a small lump that rested on the end of Mace's tongue.

"Oh, God," the reverend gibbered, "dear Jesus, merciful Father in heaven!"

Jeff felt light-headed and dizzy as he watched, felt as if he'd somehow slipped into someone else's nightmare, and he pushed Lily back, tried to keep her away from the wall, but she just stepped forward again.

As the dark clot of viscous matter neared Mace's gaping mouth, it dropped off into the darkness and landed with a wet slap, leaving behind the walnut-sized lump which Mace sucked through his smile, holding it between his teeth as he grinned up at Reverend Bainbridge. He lifted one of the lanterns and held it level with his head, illuminating his face and the small, pale object in his mouth. . . .

Its tiny, slightly bulbous eyes. . . .

The minuscule arms. . . .

Jeff's stomach turned when he realized what the lump was; his throat tensed and he tried to push Lily back again, thinking, *Jesus Christ this isn't happening isn't is not* is not *happening!*

"Nikki?" Lily whispered.

Jeff turned to her and angrily shook his head, trying to tell her to be quiet.

"Nikki?" Her voice was louder, coarse and dry, and Jeff pressed his palm over her mouth, craning his head to watch Mace.

Chuckling, Mace closed his teeth on the small, bubble-like skull of the fetus with a soggy crunch, and dark fluids dribbled down his chin as he began to chew noisily, laughing, stroking Nikki's quivering thighs.

Then several things happened at once:

Jeff heard the reverend's body slide down the wall and plop to the floor with a mournful wail.

Nikki rolled her head to one side and vomited.

Lily pulled away from Jeff and screamed, *Nikkiiii!*"

There was a startled murmur of voices in the pool and Mace lifted his eyes, peering through the hole in the wall and looking directly at Jeff, chin glistening, jaw working.

Jeff pulled away from the wall so suddenly he nearly fell. He spun around and pushed Lily, rasping, "Run!" as he heard the chitter and scrape of small claws on the cement floor coming around the wall. "Run, *run!*"

"But N-Nikki's—"

"Just *go*, goddammit!" He grabbed her arm and pulled her along, stumbling on a chunk of plaster.

As they clambered down the stairs into the sub-basement, Jeff heard the vicious sound of snapping teeth behind them, turned on the flashlight, missed a step, and for an instant, was in the air, limbs sprawled; then he hit the floor with a grunt, a needle-like pain shooting through his shoulder.

Shouting upstairs.

Hurried footsteps.

Another loud cry from Nikki, sounding different now, empty, resigned.

"Get up," Lily cried, grabbing his arm. "Get up, Jesus Christ, *get up!*"

Jeff rolled onto his back; the flashlight beam swept upward and was reflected in a dozen golden eyes skittering down the stairs.

Lily pulled, gasping. "Now, *now*, NOW!" and Jeff struggled onto his hands and knees, half crawling to the hole in the wall, gripping the edge, pulling himself to his feet as Lily crawled through.

Claws scratched over the cement behind him, teeth snapped, and the guttural squawls the creatures made sent slivers of ice through his veins as he fell through the hole, nearly tumbling over the edge of the walkway and into the rushing stream of blackness below.

Lily was before him, pulling on his sleeves, babbling, "Get up c'mon please Jeff get up now get—"

Her eyes turned to the hole behind him, widened, and she screamed as she backed away, and above her scream, above the wet sounds of the sewer, Jeff heard them coming through the hole and began to crawl, the flashlight beam cutting wildly through the darkness as he felt them at his feet.

Kicking his feet, hoping to hit them, Jeff managed to stand, his left hand sliding over the wet wall in search of something to grasp. As he rushed toward Lily, he saw her face twist into a mask of horror as she waved her arms, screaming, "Jesus oh God they're right be-be-behind—"

Jeff spun around and swept a foot over the cement, knocking three of them off the walkway, then swept it back again to kick the others rushing toward him.

One stood on its hind legs, hissed, and dove through the air toward him while his leg was still raised. He tried to hop backward but lost his balance, flailed his arms, and fell, splashing into the stream of sewage.

Lily screamed shrilly.

Jeff thrashed in the waste, gulping air, anchoring his feet on the bottom and gripping the edge of the walkway, trying to keep the flashlight safely above his head.

"Get out of here, Lily!" he shouted. "Find a manhole and get out!"

"No, dammit, give me—"

"*Go!* I'm right behind you!" He put his arms on the walkway and started to pull himself up as Lily's footsteps faded.

The sewage was waist-deep; dark lumps washed around him, clung to his jacket, and the rancid odor filled his nostrils and throat.

Something grabbed onto his jacket and he looked down to see one of the creatures hanging by its teeth from his side, flat nostrils flaring, its teeth tearing into his jacket, and Jeff could not hold back the scream that tore from his chest as he brought the butt of the flashlight down hard, striking the creature between the eyes as he swayed precariously in the strong current.

The animal fell away.

Jeff tried once again to pull himself out and saw two black-booted feet suddenly standing before him.

"Help me!" he blurted without looking up. "Help me, please!"

A big hand took his arm and effortlessly lifted him out of the gutter and onto his feet.

"You're welcome to stay," Mace said pleasantly.

Jeff flinched, backed away from him. Mace's chin was still dark and dripping; meaty specks were stuck between his teeth. Jeff aimed the flashlight at him as if it were a gun.

"Is she dead?" Jeff croaked. "Did you kill her?"

"Nikki? No, no, course not. She's fine. I just did what she wanted."

Another step back.

Three of the creatures were sniffing around behind Mace; one of them rubbed itself against his ankle like a housecat.

"If you stick around," Mace went on, "maybe there's something you want, something I can—"

Jeff took several steps away from him. "What are you?"

Mace's smile was filled with such warmth that Jeff felt confused for a moment, thought that perhaps hurrying away was not the right thing to do, that maybe Mace wasn't so bad after all, because he seemed genuine, sincere. . . .

But there were still dark bloody flecks on his teeth, on his lips, and Jeff quickly remembered what he'd seen inside, what Mace had done. Jeff did not yet understand it, but he remembered. . . .

"What am I?" Mace repeated thoughtfully, wiping his chin with the heel of his hand. "I'm . . . a friend. That's all. Just a friend."

Jeff turned and followed in Lily's direction.

"You remember that," Mace called as Jeff found the open manhole, saw Lily's face peering down from the rainy street above. He grabbed the rungs and began to climb.

"You remember that, because you'll need a friend soon. You'll need a friend." With a hollow, echoing chuckle, Mace added, "Big brother."

Goosebumps

**RICHARD
CHRISTIAN
MATHESON**

What?!? *Another* R. C. Matheson story?

Well . . . since "Red" clocks in at only about 650 words, I thought it prudent to give Richard a second shot, to let him demonstrate what's possible when he stretches a little. Besides, "Red" is basically a serious attempt at blowing you away.

"Goosebumps" is anything but.

Rolling Stone was correct when they called Richard Christian Matheson "one of a handful of resourceful, fear-minded authors helping to create a new sensibility in horror fiction that is as daring, frightening and merciless as the modern world itself." What they apparently didn't know was that R. C. is as recognized for his *comedy* as he is for his horror. In Matheson's ongoing scriptwriting and production duties, he's worked with the likes of megacomics Mel Brooks and Goldie Hawn, exercising a darkly ironic bent which R. C. describes as "character aberration humor, psychological horror which is amusing rather than horrifying."

Whatever. *I'd* call "Goosebumps" a roller-coaster fun ride, with a smidgen of satire.

Hold on tight, now.

And don't worry. Horror stories can't *really* hurt you.

Can they?

. . . and so it was on that foul, moonlit eve, the fetid creature disappeared as inexplicably as it had spawned. And though Mr. Edworthy would never tell the good peoples of Frankshire what manner of obscene anguish he'd suffered, he would never forget.

For in that forgotten hamlet, on the farthest reaches of the

Scottish coast, evil had entered not only the body of a man, but his very soul. Evil, which was finally, thank God, gone.

Or at least Mr. Edworthy thought it was.

Until suddenly, he felt that horrid, famished gnawing. The one he'd come to dread.

And the frightened townsfolk could hear his tortured screams as they lit torches and trod up the dirt road to Edworthy's farm.

But what they found was never spoken about again.

Nightmares were just as soon forgotten.

Andy closed the anthology and shivered.

Not a bad little horror story.

Not bad at all.

Nightfall was a terrific collection with a truly unnerving host of stories, including some of the finest horror he'd ever read. The one about the confessional haunted by the long dead priest had really shaken him. And the one about the circus fat man who ate his curious victims was an appalling fascination. But it was this last one, "Edworthy's Fate," which was beginning to really chill him.

As he slid under the covers, he placed the collection on the nightside table and turned off the light.

Bundling up, he shivered.

Christ, he had honest-to-God goosebumps covering his body.

These horror writers were *amazing*.

They knew precisely what it took to make your skin crawl. And once they had you hooked, their phrases and adjectives were like acids that ate away at your mind. When one of these stories worked, it virtually jumped off the page.

Andy noticed his stomach was on edge and smiled.

What better accolade to the writer of "Edworthy's Fate." Some hapless reader, lying in the dark, wide awake, stomach slashed by nerves.

Strange way to make a living, he thought.

Taking a breath, he tried to empty his mind of the loathsome images created by the story. As he did, he reached down to scratch the back of his left hand and felt something.

Damned mosquitos, he groaned, scratching the bitelike rise directly above his knuckles. Must have gotten in through the bathroom window. He was about to get up and close the window, but as he scratched harder, his eyes suddenly widened.

It was *moving*.

Under his skin, it had crept upward, toward the wrist, like an eye sliding from the bottom of its socket to the top.

He quickly turned on the light and his stomach twisted as he watched the tiny rise moving up his wrist. As it went, it pushed the skin outward, making his forearm swell slightly, as if a stray air bubble were lost in his system.

As it travelled further up Andy's arm, the rise left a red trail, causing his arm hair to stand out.

For a moment, he was too frightened to move; he finally reached for the phone and began to dial his doctor's exchange. But he was stopped by the sensation of the bump racing up his left arm and bolting across his shoulders before hurtling down his right arm into his hand.

Shocked, Andy dropped the receiver and lurched into his dressing area to look in the full length mirror.

He slowly raised his right arm and his mouth went dry. There in the center of his palm was the bump, pulsing slightly, stirring like a trapped animal.

In dead silence, he watched the thing continue to swim about beneath the skin on his palms, coursing from side to side in random patterns.

As if it were waiting impatiently for something.

But for what, he wondered, deciding to try and feel it. He could see how far it was stretching his skin but wasn't sure how large it actually was.

Feeling as though he were losing his mind, he cautiously arced his left hand over and allowed it to hover over the right palm. Taking a deep breath, he lunged down on the bump, trying to grab it with his left hand.

But it had already moved and he watched in panic as the bump began to move up his right arm. As it did, it left an inch-wide track of red, swollen skin in its wake.

Sickened, Andy grabbed at it again as it climbed above his elbow. But it had moved too quickly for him and was now sliding to his shoulder. Hysterically, he slapped at his shoulder, trying to stop the bump from moving any further. But though he could feel the lump of it beneath his hand, it quickly slipped away and began to move across his chest.

And as it did, something new began to happen.

As Andy darted back into his bedroom, thrashing from his pajama top, he felt a squeezing, gnawing agony beginning to cover the tingling areas where the bump had been.

Looking in his bureau mirror, he could see ropy bruises where the strands of inflamed tissue had been. And as the bump crossed over his chest, a torturous burning filled his torso.

The thing seemed to be sawing through his flesh.

He knew there was no way he could drive himself to the emergency hospital. The thing would somehow try to stop him and he shuddered at the thought of what it would do if he tried.

Suddenly, the scalding pain had returned, and the bump raced more savagely through his body.

Gasping, he ran into the kitchen and yanked open a drawer. But as he did, the bump slid around his naked waist like a cinch. In seconds it travelled to his back and settled on the spine where it began to torture anew.

As it moved further up his spine, he could feel it squeezing and tearing at the spongy tissue, trying to get at the nerve braids.

Screaming in pain, Andy threw himself onto the floor and lay on his back, pressing hard, trying to crush the bump. As he did, he could feel it boring further into his spinal sheath, devouring nerves. As the bump continued to gorge through his body, feasting on the pulpy nerve junctions and carving through the skin, just a quarter of an inch under the surface, Andy's face turned bright red.

He was screaming but no sound came.

Sprawled fitfully on the kitchen floor, he looked down to see the bump slowly making its way up his leg toward his internal organs.

His mouth opened in revulsion as the bump stopped for a moment, directly above his appendix and intestines and began to pulse, again.

For the first time, he could see it was getting bigger, as it ingested his living flesh for nourishment.

Andy felt like vomiting.

The bump began to gnaw at his intestines and his scream of dread returned.

For the first time, he now knew what the thing needed to survive.

As it continued to feast upon him, Andy struggled to stand, stumbling for the kitchen drawer, reaching into it.

From its interior, he withdrew a huge butcher knife which glistened under the fluorescent lighting.

But in seconds, as if it had seen, the bump moved.

And this time Andy cried out, clutching his hands to his face and shrieking.

Somehow, the bump had moved to his face and was now causing his features to distort as it made its way under the skin, devouring what it could.

Holding the knife firmly, Andy staggered into the bedroom bathroom and watched himself in the mirror.

On the right cheek was the bump.

Only now it was much bigger; the size of an egg. And as Andy watched spellbound, the bump rotated beneath the surface of the bruised skin, showing something on its opposite side.

The incisors were vague under the quilt of his skin, but there was no doubt they were starting to move.

And as they did, he felt the pain, immediately.

The bump was beginning to consume.

Andy could actually hear the sound of his facial meat being ravaged as the insatiable bump continued to grow with each tearing piece it ate.

And though his screams caused him to tremble, he didn't hesitate.

He held the knife directly at his face, and began stabbing at the monstrosity.

As he did, it averted his slashing lunges, as if anticipating every move.

His face bled profusely from deep gashes, and Andy stared through the wash of red covering his eyes to see where the bump would show next.

He screamed for it to go away, blood spraying from his lips.

But as he howled for it to leave, he suddenly felt something in his mouth, filling it like an inflating bladder.

And though he tried to scream, the bump muffled everything, attaching itself to his tongue.

Andy put the knife to his mouth and opened wide. Peering at himself in the mirror, he began to thrust the knife into his mouth, convulsively, stabbing at the bump and causing it to squirt fluid from itself.

It tasted acrid and sloshed down Andy's throat as he continued to stab.

Then it happened.

Suddenly, the bump was gone and Andy could now see only the raw mutilation of his mouth, dripping its bloody wetness down his shirt.

Searching his body, he couldn't see or feel the bump *anywhere*.

For a moment, all pain stopped.

Inexplicably, the thing had ceased and all was calm.

Or at least Andy thought it was.

Until suddenly pain began in his forehead. Then, horribly, his brow began to inflate outwardly, causing him to resemble some terror-stricken primitive. The brow continued to jut out further and the wrenching pain thickened all around, pile-driving through his skull.

Then, in a blinding insight, he knew what must be happening, as he felt his shrieking brain finally being descended upon.

And though the neighbors could hear his screams echoing over the streets, no one called the police until it was far too late.

It was a warm afternoon and the countryside lolled comfortably under a summer sky. As he snipped lovingly at the carnations, the bell caught his attention.

Yawning, he strolled over toward the mailman's bicycle. The mailman strummed the tiny bell, which was attached to his handlebars, one last time, and smiled.

"Lots for you today, Mr. McCauley."

The old man smiled easily. As he stepped closer, he drew a deep breath, taking in the beautiful flowers which bloomed in abundance before his quaint country home. Insects buzzed around the colorful garden.

"Bills, no doubt," chuckled the old man, accepting the handful of envelopes.

"Think there's one in there from your agent in the States, sir."

The old man's eyebrows lifted with interest, and he sifted through the envelopes. In seconds he'd opened it.

As he read the letter, the mailman looked at him inquisitively.

"Sell that horror novel, did you?"

The old man shook his head, with a relaxed sigh.

"No, those publishers in New York haven't made their final offer yet."

The mailman made a look of disappointment.

The old man peered up at him with a glint.

"There is a bit of good news, though. You know that story of mine you hate so much? It's been requested as a reprint in another anthology."

"How many times is that, now?"

"Over two hundred," answered the man, about to turn and putter up the path to his house.

" 'Edworthy's Fate' just never gave me goosebumps," said the mailman.

"Lucky you," smiled the old man, heading back to his flowers, humming a gentle little song.

Goodbye, Dark Love

ROBERTA LANNES

Unlike many of the other writers in this book, I've never met Roberta Lannes (we've only chatted on the phone). But I did receive a short note from her with the contract allowing me to reprint "Goodbye, Dark Love" (which first appeared in the rewarding 1986 anthology *Cutting Edge*, edited by Dennis Etchison). Lannes had some interesting observations on both her story and splatterpunk fiction; here is an extract from that note, dated January 10, 1990.

"Goodbye, Dark Love" was written before the word "splatterpunk" was coined to describe the genre of horror woven with its own questionable excesses. Granted, the explicit sex and violence in my story qualifies as extreme, but not excessive. Splatterpunk, with its inherent gratuitous blood, guts, gore and graphic sex *intends* to disgust and gratify a reader's lowest self-needs. I choose to use extremes when they can push a story into the fully sensual, the experiental realm. Accurate illustration, used sparingly, succeeds where excess ovewhelms and thus detracts from the body of work. My subject matter in "Goodbye, Dark Love" is poignant, and therefore deserves to be treated as important, rather than a mere vehicle to suck a reader into experiencing the shock value. I choose instead to create the power in my work that only personal experience could otherwise invoke. "Splatterpunker" I am not. Explicitly illustrative stylist, yes. Literary snob, possibly.

Sigh. *Another* contributor who's not a splatterpunk.

Ah, well. Lannes's work also has appeared in the anthologies *Lord John Ten* and *Alien Sex* and the fanzines *Iniquities* and *Fantasy Tales*.

Prior to her genre sales, Lannes published in literary reveiws and specialty press poetry anthologies. She is currently at work on a novel titled *The Glass Tomb*.

I still recall the jolt "Goodbye, Dark Love" gave me while reading it one miserable winter afternoon on the train between Tarrytown and Philadelphia, Pennsylvania. In its own small way (as it's really more a fragment than a fully fleshed piece), "Goodbye" is truly subversive. It manages to make necrophilia arousing (from a woman's point of view!) while satisfactorily resolving the moral outrage Lannes obviously feels toward a particularly primal, and complex, societal taboo.

One last thing—however else Lannes chooses to describe it, "Goodbye, Dark Love" is also, and most indubitably, one diseased little beast.

Marla ran her fingers down to the fold in her chenille robe and parted the front. She leaned into the bed where the body lay, still and very dead.

She let the robe drop from her shoulders. It made a muffled sound, like that of a swan's wing flapping, as it hit the floor. She looked down at her breasts, then at the slowly graying form. Grasping one nipple, she reached with her other hand to the body and the exquisite erection that rose over the wide elastic band. Her hand enveloped the shaft as she manipulated her nipple to hardness. Her breath came in gasps as she jerked the stony cock while kneading, teasing, exciting herself. Her fingers moved down to her crotch, parting the lips, feeling for the nub of flesh. Touching. Tingling. Vibrating with urgency. She felt herself dipping close to climax.

"No, no," she whispered. "Not this way."

She released him, pulled herself, her mind, from the place she had been. She made herself think about the outside, the bus stop where people were waiting for their lives to begin again, exchanging lies and wary glances. She listened to their distant voices. Motor noises. She heard his wristwatch. The radio playing softly in the front room. Music. Playful. Far away. Calming.

A cry. The baby. Mrs. Lopez's baby.

Marla smiled.

So perfect.

So new.

So un . . . —but no.

She grabbed the erection more firmly. Lusting. She could only want. She mounted him. She pushed the beet-colored rod to the mouth of her heat and plunged down on it. Orgasm. Again and again. Driving it in. An icicle unrelenting in its cold against her living warmth.

Suddenly the acrid stench of urine overpowered her. There was no ignoring it now. The memories of rest rooms in parks, in town, on the boardwalk, the bus station. Stinking. Cold. Dark gray walls with white turbans of paper toweling hurled against them, fecal arcs like a mad artist's attempts at a statement. Why there? Why had he always wanted to do it there?

There. Then. The better days. The time he'd taken her to the pike. It was hot, sunny. She wore the new sundress he had bought her. Pink. Scant. He won her a stuffed octopus, bought her a sno-cone, rode on the roller coaster with her. When they ran into two of the men he worked with, he introduced her as "my lady." They smiled at her and told him she was gorgeous. A knockout. He'd looked at her that day. Really looked. Like he was seeing her for the first time. It made her hope things would change. Maybe. Someday.

She saw herself then, grimaced, then saw herself here, now, impaled on his lifeless cock, ecstatic. On her terms for once.

The knock at the front door tore into her.

She froze. Her foot began to cramp. She could hear no voices, no sound but her own ragged breath. Like a shot, another knock. It couldn't be anyone important. There *was* no one. Panic roiled inside her. She clenched her teeth. Then, quietly, footsteps marked the retreat of the stranger, whoever it was.

Marla sighed, relieved.

A soft heartache, a little pain rose up from deep inside, breaking the angry lust, crawling up her throat until a small cry passed her lips. Her friends. Where were they now? He'd once welcomed them, enjoyed their laughter, their warm company. Then, one by one, they were forbidden to her. His friends she never saw. They were a part of his world, a world he told her she was better off not knowing. A world she never allowed herself to be curious about. After all, she had someone who loved her, someone to protect her. Her friends had not. She let him become her world, let herself be whatever part of his world she could.

Then the day came when she knew he had protected her too well.

She pulled herself from him and got up. She paced around the bed, pulling on her robe, looking at him. His face was still handsome in death. Clear blue eyes staring wide. Flared nostrils. Aquiline nose. Lips full, parted. Inviting. She put her face close to his. She could smell the familiar alcohol. Sour. She covered his lips with hers. Her tongue searched for warmth, familiar places. He took her warmth, but did not hold it.

She nuzzled him and felt the five o'clock shadow growing on his cold cheeks.

Murky amber light from drawn old yellowed shades gave the room a dream ambience. Alone now, beside him, she had her dream. The dream she had been too frightened to acknowledge, even to herself, for so long. The dream was of choice. *Another man, anyone but him.*

She didn't know when her love, her lust, her need of him turned. When his arrival made her cringe. When the scent of him made her turn away. When his touch reviled her. But when it changed, so did she. Slowly. Steadily. Finally, irrevocably, completely. What was between them seemed no longer bitter-sweet, electric. She became aware he was waging a battle, she the unwilling enemy. It was he, victorious, sabotaging, cunning, brutal, unrelenting. An army of one in a war without political cause, without provocation, without reason. One day he was playful, toying. The next day he was cruel. And all the days after, until something in her turned her devotion into a grain of anger. The grain multiplied into a handful, a bucket, a barrel, until nothing could contain it all. Until today.

He left her his money, his belongings, but they were unimportant to her now. She wanted someone else. Any man who would love her tenderly, openly, kindly. A man would do. She could choose now. She was leaving the chains behind. His death was the ultimate permission. He left her her own life. That she would cherish.

She looked hard at him. A new power flowed into her.

"You will never again tell me that no one else can have me. And I'll never hear your lie—that no one else but you could make me come."

She stood on her knees near his face, letting the robe fall open. Her fingers went to the slash between her legs, parting the swollen lips, touching the growing bud of skin inside. Her fingers moved quickly, hungrily. Her other hand pushed one breast up to her mouth. Her tongue darted out over her nipple, flicking it until it raged red, hard.

"Watch me . . ." Her voice was a husky whisper. She rocked over her fingers, moaning.

Falling back on the bed, spent, she gasped, choked. It had wasted her. She lay there a few minutes until her breathing slowed.

Then she propped herself up on a pillow and reached for the pack of cigarettes on the nightstand. She lit one. She blew smoke in his face. As she took long drags she played with the small round scars over her stomach and chest. Turning the butt in her fingers, she pressed the lit end into the flesh that fell wrinkled and moist from his jaw. The cigarette went out with a spitting sound.

In that instant, she recalled an evening after a long day on the beach. She was severely sunburned, blistering. He'd been so concerned. He put ointment on her, cool compresses. All night, until she finally fell asleep, he held her hand, held an ice cube to her swollen lips, cooed soothing words. The next morning, before she was fully awake, he was on her, taking what he said was owed him. The pain . . .

"Does it feel good? You told me that pain and pleasure were so close. So close. Does it feel the same to you? You bastard! What did you know? You just wanted to mark me for life so no one else would want me. You made sure, didn't you? You loved it. Hurting me. Knowing I would have to lie to anyone who found them. Knowing the lies would be useless because everyone could tell what they were. Knowing no one would dare suspect you. No. Only weird Marla could do that to herself. Ha!"

She lit another cigarette.

The air-conditioner wheezed, then chugged once before purring again. Its rusty dark bulk in the window allowed street sounds to filter through. She had often imagined that it was a huge radio transmitting the music of the city. The raw beat. The wails. The whistle of the wind. The roar of engines. The pounding of the rain. The sirens. The music only she could understand. He'd called her bizarre, silly. He had never understood anything. She burned his cheek. Hair sizzled. Stank.

She could hear the bus pull up. Brakes screamed. All the liars, the rapists, the cheats, the motherfuckers, the phony assholes, the teasers, the pleasers, the real crazies there. Packed in for rides to their individual hells. Soon more would come. Standing in their rootless anger, littering their disappointments, waving false hope behind TV smiles. After all, what else was there in the world? What?

One by one, she left tiny burns across his chest until a heart began to take shape. The wound, like a distant cat's hiss, soothed her. Pulling back her robe, she looked down at the heart shape long ago tattooed into her stomach. She did not smile. It was not beautiful to her. Nor would it be to anyone else. He'd known that. She put the cigarette out in his navel.

He was beginning to stink. Like shit. Like spoiled canned vegetables. Like mold and piss and sweat and vomit and sickness. She gagged. She turned up the flame on the lighter so that it shot out like a blowtorch. She touched the tip of the flame to one of his eyes. She almost expected it to close in reflex. It sizzled and popped. She held her breath. The flame slowly burned the entire eye away, leaving a deep smoking black pit. She began on the other eye. Gagging, she quit.

It was time. She went into the kitchen and found a large carving knife, a box of scented candles, and six heavy-duty trash bags.

She lit the candles first, scattering them around the room. The odors of him seemed to lessen. She then set about carefully dismembering the body. She tried to be neat. It was much more difficult than she had expected. The knife required her full weight behind it to go through bone.

She filled the six bags with the now simplified body, the bedsheets, and her robe. She knotted the tops. In the kitchen, she washed off the knife and put it back where she found it. She then took a long hot shower, dried off, dressed, packed three suitcases and began to straighten up.

Room by room she went, reminiscing. They were full of memories, many good ones. The curtains he brought her that she just had to have. The sofa and loveseat she saw in the Sears catalogue that *he* just had to have. There was his brush on the sink, still full of his soft graying brown hair. The pair of reading glasses he wore to read the *TV Guide*. She loved watching TV with him.

She went to the phone and called a taxi.

She cursed herself for being too young to drive. In a few months she would be sixteen. Then she would come back and take his car. Until then she would have to be patient.

Lastly she dragged the six bags, one by one, to the back door. She opened the door and set them outside in the alley. She locked the door, staring down at the six neatly tied, shiny black sacks. Wistfully, she turned away.

The taxi horn sounded out front.

"Well, I guess it's time to say goodbye, Daddy. Thanks for everything." She shrugged. "Thanks for nothing."

She let the taxi driver take her suitcases out. She stood at the front door trying to remember what it felt like to love him. She felt nothing.

She locked the door and walked out to the waiting world.

Full Throttle

PHILIP
NUTMAN

During the course of putting this book together, I requested biographical information from my contributors in order to flesh out these introductions. One of the best came from Philip Nutman, whose response I now quote (in full):

> At age 27, *Philip Nutman is Splatterpunks*'s youngest contributor. Born in London, England, he was raised in Bath, the ancient West Country city that is "Full Throttle" 's location, but moved back to London in his late teens where he worked for BBC TV. He began writing at an early age, was first published at 15 and has ten years of journalism under his belt. As British correspondent for *Fangoria* magazine he's interviewed most of the top writers and directors in the genre, spent too much time getting sprayed with blood on movie sets, and has seen more bad movies than he cares to remember. "Full Throttle" is his third anthologized work of fiction. *Wet Work*, a novel based on his "Book of the Dead" short story, will appear from Berkley Books in 1991, and *Heatwave*, a contemporary *film noir* screenplay, is under option in Hollywood. His only regret is he can't sing, can't play guitar, and will never appear as opening act for Aerosmith at Madison Square Garden.

Philip Nutman has a certain laconic intensity (if such a contradiction is possible) that alternately reminds me of English nobility or a Chinese mandarin; maybe this last impression is due to his long, thinning hair, combed straight back. I quite clearly recall our first meeting at the 1986 World Fantasy Convention in Providence, Rhode Island. We'd struck up a conversation in the hotel bar, and the hours rolled by as we chattered on about music, films, Phil's *Fangoria* articles (the first work of his which had caught my attention), and my own once-lustrous career as a film journalist. We've been friends ever since.

One of the few joys of getting older is watching younger talent grow and strengthen. Phil is definitely growing. While Nutman's credentials as a journalist are beyond reproach—incidentally, he would also make a fine sleazoid character actor, an avocation Phil's already fulfilled by performing in low-budget films like *Death Collector*—I predict bigger and better things for him in the fields of fiction.

"Full Throttle" should convince you, as well.

"Throttle" is a deeply serious examination of England's disenfranchised youth. By extention, the exploits of the characters Rivers and Hurst also encompass a very specific area of aimless teenage anomie: I know *I* had nights like this. And intriguingly, Phil claims that the psychic experience depicted herein is actually autobiographical.

I'm glad you're still around to write about it, pal.

Travel is less about a specific destination as a certain state of mind.

Henry Miller

Speed kills and so do I.

Anonymous graffiti

"I want to kill the bastard," Rivers said as he pulled the trigger.

The tall teenager was standing still by the open window, and in that instant it occurred to Hurst that he always thought of Rivers in terms of movement: racing their customized sports bicycles, pushing whatever motorbike he could get his hands on to the limit, or running from the law. It was as if Rivers were afraid of stasis, aware that to stay in one position too long was to invite a state of mind akin to living death. Like his surname, Stafford Rivers flowed, moving ever onward, eroding everything around him with ceaseless energy. It was, Hurst acknowledged, what had attracted him to the working class youth the first day they met, as two eleven year-olds garbed in uncomfortable black school uniforms standing in the playground of Ralph Taylor Comprehensive—like inmates freshly arrived at a maximum security prison. At the time, he'd thought it was Rivers's punch-first-ask-questions-later attitude, but now he had to admit it: the guy *flowed*. There was no other word for him.

Except right now.

"Shit," Rivers said. "Missed."

Hurst got up from the bed to look out into the garden as "Wish You Were Here" came to an end on the cheap stereo system. Rivers hadn't missed, he just hadn't killed the crow with one shot, and the bird lay twitching on the weed-infested ground. He said nothing—Staff was too angry for small talk—and went to change the music.

"That two-timing bitch deserves a smack in the mouth. Fucking slut."

Hurst selected Motorhead's "Overkill" from the untidy pile of albums, deciding it was a more suitable accompaniment to the room's tension than the lush aural hallucinogen of Pink Floyd. Rivers reloaded the .22 air rifle.

"If the cow was going to cheat on me, why pick a prick like Tully?"

The question was unanswerable. Andy Tully *was* a dickhead.

So much for a fun evening. Rivers had learned the truth about Phillippa and Tully on his way home from work, his last day as an apprentice plumber it turned out, fired for habitual lateness. Things always come in threes, Hurst thought as he looked at the Page Three calendar hanging over the bookcase containing several girlie mags and Sven Hassel war novels. Miss September 1979 grinned vacuously while holding her size thirty-eight breasts. What next? Maybe he should have stayed home listening to Jimi Hendrix while getting stoned. Nah, that was no option; Jamie, his snot-nosed younger brother, would be in his room pounding away on his typewriter pretending to be Ernest fucking Hemingway while listening to Rush ad nauseum. No, Friday nights meant one thing—the Rivers and Hurst Hellraising Show, two seventeen year olds on a one-way ticket to oblivion, drinking, smoking dope, crashing parties, boosting a car for a ride, sometimes catching the late show at the cinema if a horror movie was playing, and often committing vandalism as the night's festivities drew to a close.

Rivers began pacing, waving the gun around as the dying autumn sun cast an auburn hue across the room, his breathing deepening as his anger increased. Hurst had never seen Staff so pissed off, not even after losing that fight to Barry Marshall. He'd already punched a hole in the door and the air rifle was making Hurst nervous.

"Take it easy, Staff. You were going to dump her."

"Fuck off." A pause. "Bitch! Tully!" He spat out the name like a wad of phlegm.

Rivers strode to the door and disappeared out into the gloomy hallway. Hurst heard him clatter down the linoleum-covered stairs, his size eleven Doc Martens pounding the creaking wood. When he realized Staff wasn't coming back, he followed.

The Rivers house was an old terraced ruin crying out for repair. Half of the light fixtures were without bulbs, there was no central heating, the dry-rotted front door drooped on its hinges, and the plaster was coated with a layer of dirt. The stairs groaned as he descended, a damp smell leaking from the walls.

"Turn that bleedin' racket down," Mrs. Rivers said as he rounded the corner. If the house needed a ghost to add to its charm, she was it. She seldom left the place and always tried to engage him in conversation, a rare commodity in the slum Staff called home. He smiled as she saw him; Mrs. Rivers, seemingly older than her forty-seven years, had a soft spot for Hurst and was pleased that her son had a friend from the better side of town.

"Hello, Alex, luv, how are yer?"

"Fine, Mrs. R."

She stood in the lounge doorway, a cigarette in her yellowed fingers, pink plastic curlers in her hair. Same old Mrs. R., irredeemably tacky: food stains on her blouse, smudged mascara around her eyes, and cheap whiskey on her breath.

Staff stamped out through the tiny, cluttered kitchen at the hall's end, ignoring his mother as he headed for the garden.

"What are you up to?"

"Shut up, you old cow," he muttered under his breath.

Alex smiled with practiced ease. If Mrs. R. heard her son, she took no notice, returning her attention to her bottle and "Crossroads."

As he emerged from the kitchen door, Staff was bent over the still-moving crow, pulling a lighter from the pocket of his ripped jeans, flicking the Bic as Alex came nearer, burning the bird's feet. The crow cawed in pain, trying to push itself away from the flame. After a minute of this, Staff stood, placed the gun to the bird's head, pulling the trigger with a tight grin on his face, his blue eyes glaring from beneath his mane of long, greasy hair. An off-white liquid left the bird's blasted cranium, splattering the soil like dirty semen flecked with blood.

"What do you want to do?" Staff was calmer now, his attention focused on the crow's corpse.

"Score some weed from Dawson. Have a pint at The Five Bells.

Maybe go see the late show. I think it's *Straw Dogs* tonight. You know, Peckinpah."

Staff snorted, turning to Alex, a leer on his lips. "I've got a better idea." He brought his right foot down on the bird's body, the twiglike bones breaking under the onslaught of the steel-toed Martens as he slowly ground the crow into the frozen soil. "Let's crash Tully's party."

Jamie Hurst looked at the picture of Poe's "The Raven" above his desk for inspiration.

Nothing.

His mind was empty, the unfinished essay on Hardy's *Jude the Obscure* lay in front of him slashed with red ink marks, and the silence in the house did nothing to relieve the tension squeezing him like a Sumo wrestler. Anxiety gouged his concentration. He'd been feeling weird all day since waking cloaked with dread from a nightmare he couldn't clearly recall. Just a sense of speed, of being out of control, the bright orange eyes of a huge beast rushing toward him through blackness. He'd assumed it was an anxiety dream rather than a venting dream, his subconscious responding to preexamination pressures, yet the idea of his life out of control was stupid. The next few years were carefully mapped out and all was going according to plan: get his "O" Levels, then Sixth Form and "A" Levels, leading to university and a degree in English. Beyond that he was confident that a promising career as a journalist lay ahead, and maybe—just maybe—a novel or two. But as he pored over the lit essay, he couldn't dispel the feeling of doom hanging over the room like musty drapes in a gothic mansion.

He shivered.

Stop it.

The only thing wrong was a slight temperature—the start of a cold he'd been fighting all week—and an overactive imagination.

Time for a change of scenery.

He got up from the desk. The mundane activity of putting away groceries might help. Friday was his mother's bridge night and she'd dropped the shopping off in the hallway because she was running late. Friday also signaled Alex's weekend disappearing act with Staff Rivers, whom Jamie distrusted.

There was something unsettling about Rivers's blue eyes. Their slow, suspicious movements indicated the cerulean irises concealed a secret. But the effect Rivers had on his brother bothered Jamie more.

Alex, the distant, erratically dutiful son, turned into a shit in Rivers's company, prompting Jamie to feel like Abel faced with Cain whenever their mother was absent, which was often. Despite a company pension, their late father's only legacy, bringing up two young sons with another about to start university had been a tremendous struggle for their mother. She had sacrificed a social life and borne the burden of two jobs, leaving the boys to spend their after-school hours with neighbors indifferent to their needs. Time alone was nothing new to Jamie; in fact, he preferred it to the sullen presence of Alex, who, as soon as Mother appeared, played upon her sympathies. Like Rivers, there was something cold behind Alex's eyes, a barrier Jamie couldn't penetrate. But right now he wished Alex were home playing Hendrix records loudly in his room. Anything was better than the preternatural silence.

He picked up the bags of groceries in the hall, heading for the tidy kitchen. The silence seemed louder, emptier as he began to unload the food, and he hummed "Draw the Line" to break the terrible sense of nothingness. He wished it wasn't bridge night, wished Mother were home so they could watch TV together. Why, he couldn't rationalize. He was fifteen, for cryin' out loud, not a little kid. A sense of reassurance had warmed him when she returned with the groceries, although she only stayed a moment because Dot Wicking, her bridge partner, waited in the car outside. How could he have told her he was afraid

(of what?)

that he didn't want her to go, couldn't face the night alone? The unnatural feeling in the house rubbed away at his nerves like sandpaper on skin.

"Nobody here but us spooks," he said aloud and forced a laugh as he placed a leg of lamb in the refrigerator.

He picked up a carton of eggs.

And then it happened.

One minute he was standing in the middle of the kitchen, the next he felt cold wind hitting his face and he couldn't see. Blackness. Then a smell of exhaust fumes, a rapid acceleration, and an adrenal rush from a sensation akin to traveling at high speed on his bicycle.

(Push it!)

Cold, dark, exciting.

Dread clutched at his back with the desperation of a drowning man.

(Do it! Yeah, go for it!)

Then it shifted.

Sparks.

Bumping.

Flying sensation through blackness.

Two viewpoints—neither making sense—converging.

He shook his head to clear it.

(What? . . .)

And realized he'd dropped the eggs, a dozen size sixes, all over the floor. Nausea rushed up from his bowels. He stepped over the egg massacre to the sink, retching. Once. Twice. Three times. Nothing came up; he hadn't eaten for hours. Retch number four leapt, hurting his insides, but that wasn't why he gasped. As he looked at the window, his eyes widened at his reflection.

Alex's reflection.

Not his.

Alex stared back at him, his deep-set eyes hooded like a cobra's.

Jamie frowned at the optical illusion.

(No it isn't.)

And then it was his face staring back at him.

Oh, God, I'm cracking up.

He felt the room spin. Then the darkness took him as he fainted.

"Sixteen."

"Inflation," Alex said, "or daylight robbery?"

Staff sat beside him on the bench, disinterest writ large across his ragged face.

"It's a steal at that price," replied Dawson. "Supply and demand. You know how many people have been busted this month? Isn't much about. But if you don't—"

"What d'you think?" Alex turned to Staff. Rivers grunted and lit a Marlboro. He knew too much about getting busted.

"Pay him."

Alex pulled out a fistful of crumpled notes. Dawson took the money as he stood.

"It's good stuff."

Alex took the proffered envelope, looking around as he did so. It was almost dark, twilight's last gleaming hanging onto the horizon by its fingertips. A man walking a dog was on the other side of the rec ground, and what Dawson said was true: too many busts. Best be careful.

"See you next week," Dawson said as he walked off toward his car, a green Morris Minor predating the Ark.

"Monday. History exam." Alex couldn't resist the dig; a month into their first term in Sixth Form and Dawson's grades were slipping. The other teenager smirked, flashing him the finger.

"Wanker," Staff said, holding out his hand as he exhaled smoke. Alex pulled a book of Rizlas from his leather jacket.

"Who's going to Tully's?"

"Pricks from King Edwards. Tarts from the high school," Staff replied, taking the papers. "Who cares? I just want to see the look on his face when we turn up."

Alex chuckled.

"He'll probably be drunk out of his skull by the time we get there."

"Good." Staff belched. "Maybe he'll fall down the fuckin' stairs."

He finished skinning up the joint, passed it to Alex. The flame from his Zippo spluttered in the wind despite the shelter of his cupped hands. He inhaled deeply.

Staff had never liked Tully. No real reason, he just had a bloody-mindedness about some of the kids they'd been to school with—or in Alex's case, still went to school with—and Tully's boarding school accent and wisecracks were enough to mark him out as top turd in Staff's shit stakes. Usually his friend's prejudices were unfounded, a randomness Alex found entertaining. But if Alex were honest, there were a lot of people he didn't like either for no apparent reason, although there were many he hated because of the way they treated him.

He coughed as he passed the joint to Staff. "It's good." The dope washed through his arteries, making his head rush. He smiled contentedly. Smoking alone never quite cut it, but dragging with a mate put all the boring shit into perspective. He looked up the hill toward Ralph Taylor Lower School, its Victorian workhouse exterior standing firm against the darkness as the final strip of sunlight thinned on the horizon. In that head-rush moment, the dope rolling through his mind, he felt time compress, contract, back flip on itself. Yeah, Ralph Taylor Lower School, all gothic grimness, had been the crucible in which their friendship had been forged.

* * *

The first day he started at Ralph Taylor, an all-boys secondary
school with twelve hundred pupils spread over two sites, Alex
found Stafford Rivers—like most things—intimidating. It wasn't
the violent way Staff kicked a football around the playground
or his four-letter vocabulary, it was his ability to jump right into
a scrap and beat the shit out of the other troublemaker that made
Alex—all skinny four feet ten inches of him—mentally sidestep.
But within minutes of laying eyes on Rivers, all flowing control
and assurance as he punted the Webley ball around the yard,
Alex had found he had other people to worry about. Really worry
about.

Like Marc Hougan.

If there was a scale for rating preteen psychos, then Hougan
scored an eight. At age eleven, the black-haired kid with mean
eyes like a whipped Doberman was five five and broad shouldered
with an attitude to match. Hougan was trouble with a capital T.
Alex knew that story, having spent the best part of the previous
six years trying to avoid the other kid's violent temper while they
attended Newbridge Junior School.

But on this bright, sunny September day, Hougan's shadow
suddenly cast a black cloud over his hopes for a better time.
Alex's reputation at Newbridge hadn't been good either: afraid
of certain teachers and wary of the other kids, most of whom
didn't like him, he was a frequent truant. It was either face the
terrors of Mrs. Bergen's math lessons or endure repeated scuffles
with the kids from the Weston housing estates. With at least one
fight a fortnight to his credit he was considered an outcast, making it easier for Hougan to pick on him. Mothers walking their
children home avoided the sullen, unhappy, and ultimately misunderstood boy who was trying to make sense of his father's
death when he turned five and the injustice of peer group rejection. All Alex had wanted was acceptance; all his long-suffering
mother wanted was for him to be like his older brother Julian,
thirteen years his senior and a picture of docile, studious piety,
or his goody-two-shoes little brother Jamie, who never cried and
was popular with teachers and kids alike. The week before Alex
had started secondary school, she'd almost gone down on bended
knee, begging him to wipe the slate clean, avoid trouble, and
behave. Alex, sick of fighting, agreed, wanting to be popular like
that little snot Jamie, but most of all wanting to please his mother.

Yet Hougan, a curse on legs shaped by a brutal father, seemed to be a constant shadow at his heels.

Alex stood in the playground that morning watching Rivers and his mate Evans kicking the ball between them, thinking about Newbridge and how all that was in the past. Then Evans punted the ball to him. Surprised, he stopped it, sending it back with a swift sweep of his foot . . .

. . . only to find himself face down on the tarmac with grazed hands, a scraped knee, and torn trouser leg. He looked up, stunned.

"Hurst." Hougan spoke his name with a grimace, then spat close to his head. Evans and the others laughed. Except Rivers, who looked coldly at the two of them, his eyes narrowing slowly.

"Gimme the ball." Hougan stepped over Alex, whose hands were stinging from the fall, knee bleeding. "The ball."

"No," Rivers said softly. Hougan grinned sardonically, then charged him.

The fight lasted thirty seconds, the two boys pounding each other at full strength, fists, feet, and knees pummeling in a blur of movement before Mr. Palmer, the fey music teacher whose thinness belied his strength, appeared to separate them, whacking Hougan round the ear when he didn't stop. Rivers's nose was bloody but Hougan's top lip was split.

"Names," Palmer demanded.

"Stafford Rivers."

"Stafford Rivers, *Sir*!"

Rivers refused to repeat his name.

"You?"

Hougan was silent.

"Name, boy."

"Marc Hougan," he replied, punctuating it with a bolus of bloody snot aimed at the teacher's feet.

"The infamous Hougan, eh? We've been warned about you." Palmer turned his attention to Hurst. "Get up lad."

Two minutes later, with seconds to go before the day was officially due to start, Alex stood outside the headmaster's office, flanked by Hougan and Rivers. No one spoke or looked at the others. He knew then that nothing would change. It was the same as it had always been and looked likely to get a whole lot worse. If he was going to survive the next five years, he was going to need an ally. Standing in the gray, disinfectant-reeking corridor, his stomach churning with nerves, he decided Rivers would be that ally—regardless of what it took to get him on his side—

unaware that the bond between them was already being woven by the Fates.

After a couple of thickly rolled spliffs Staff was calm. He mangled an empty beer can as he sat in the torn armchair while Alex reclined on the bed, a bottle of Guinness in one hand, a joint in the other. Yeah, Ralph Taylor. What a long, strange trip it's been. Clint Eastwood as Dirty Harry looked down on him from the wall. *Go ahead punk, make my day*. More like make my night, he thought. Staff was hidden in thought, his face carved in sand, his expression shifting as the wind of those thoughts changed the angles of his high cheek bones, his wide mouth. Alex flicked ash on the cracked linoleum. The Floyd were playing again, the strains of "Dark Side of the Moon" this time. Yeah, some night. Staff hadn't spoken for nearly an hour.

"Money" started to play and Alex began playing with his keys, examining them with stoned, languid fascination. The ring was a plastic holder containing two pictures. On one side there was a small photograph of the New York City skyline at night, the Empire State Building looking incomplete without King Kong astride it; the other was a skull and crossbones under which the legend LIVE FAST, DIE YOUNG was inscribed. He wanted to live in New York one day, wanted to taste all it promised. Big cities in Britain seemed insignificant in comparison; even London lacked something when you held it up to the Big Apple he'd read so much about. But then anywhere was better than Bath, he guessed, feeling nothing but scorn for the West Country town he'd spent all his life in; New York appeared as one huge adult Disneyland. Okay, so Bath had over two thousand years of history and culture, but that didn't mean a thing when you were seventeen, you had no money, and the future looked as promisig as an old black-and-white photo you'd kept in your back pocket—faded and crumpled.

Staff startled him by standing suddenly, making for the door. He reappeared awhile later, tossing a black crash helmet to Alex, who spilled Guinness over the leg of his Levi's. Staff laughed. "We're leaving." Held up a set of keys in one hand, a red helmet in the other.

"On Brian's bike? You're bloody crazy. He'll kick the shit out of you when he finds out."

Staff laughed, tersely this time. "He'll never know. The old woman's pissed out of her head and won't hear us start The Bitch

up. Let's go. Ninety down the carriageway'll blow out the cobwebs."

He was gone before Alex could object. Shit, why the hell not?
It was 7:45 already, time to do something. If Staff wanted to risk
a punch-up with his brother, fine, it wasn't his problem. Yeah,
The Bitch, Brian Rivers's bike. A red Kawasaki Z1000—now
you're talking. A thousand cc's of throbbing, rumbling four cyl-
inder, four stroke. It would beat getting the bus to Tully's.

The yellow Capri was six years old and starting to rust around
the wheel arches, but Harry Bledsoe didn't give a shit.

He wasn't happy, though, as he looked at the engine one last
time, wiping his oil-stained hands on a dirty rag, aware that
Gibbons, the Hitler of Carpenter & Sons Fruit & Veg (Whole-
sale), was walking toward him. In fact, Harry wasn't happy full
stop. His youngest kid was down with the measles, his wife,
Kathy, was hair trigger because it was that time of the month,
and the Capri wasn't running properly.

He'd recently had the car in for a service, and the vehicle had
gotten a clean bill of health from the mechanic. A couple of new
spark plugs and a replacement fan belt he could live with, but
despite the mechanic's remark that the engine was in good nick
considering the miles on the clock, the Capri hadn't started efficiently for the last week, producing a consumptive noise every
time he turned the ignition and only jumping to life on the eighth
or ninth attempt. To add insult to injury, Hopkins was off sick
and Harry was working double shifts because the mortgage rate
was up again and he had a family of five to feed. He was tired
and fucked off, and he wanted to go home but couldn't because
it was 7:45 and he had another three hours to go.

Harry hated Mondays and loved Fridays—pub night, the only
time Kathy agreed he could go out and get plastered—but this
one was a sack of shit the size of Big Ben.

He closed the bonnet of the car as Gibbons came up behind
him. He had no idea what was wrong with the bloody thing. More
money to spend.

"Get yer arse moving, Harry. The Bristol delivery should have
gone out an hour ago."

"Yeah, I'm on my way." He tossed the rag to one side as he
turned toward the fully loaded Bedford truck. A trip to Bristol
was the last thing he fancied, and it looked as if his plans for an

early knockoff and a jar or two of Sam Smith's in The Queen's Head before it closed were steadily heading up the old turd track without a four-wheel drive.

"And don't forget the invoice this time."

"No, I won't, George," Bledsoe said as he opened the cab door, adding a silent *Go screw a sheep*.

Staff kick-started the Z1000 and The Bitch roared to life, all 1000 cc's of prime Jap engineering. Alex straddled the big bike, holding firmly onto the pillion bar. Staff turned. "Let's do it!" he shouted, revving the engine.

Staff flipped his visor down and the precisioned beast took off down Landsdown View. As they reached the bottom of the road, he pressed hard on the horn, the noise echoing off brick wall as they shot through the tunnel beneath the railway line, Staff slowing at the last moment as they reached the junction with the Lower Bristol Road, the brakes screeching in protest. The Herman Muller building was opposite, its lights still burning as the cleaners worked on the front offices.

They'd broken into it for a laugh a few weeks back after a late-night drinking spree and stole a couple of chairs from the board room, tossing them into the River Avon flowing behind the factory. Staff always knew what to do if the evening was a dead duck. It had been a laugh, jimmying the men's room window, climbing in, and stumbling around in the dark until they found the offices. Staff had taken a dump on a secretary's chair and he'd pissed in a desk drawer, soaking a pile of personnel files. Yeah, that stunt had capped a boring night nicely. Now this one was shaping up as a riot, the Kawasaki rolling like a mechanized wet dream.

A stream of traffic passed, late commuters heading home for the weekend. As soon as the last vehicle went, Staff put the bike in gear, accelerating with the style of a speedway rider. Within moments they were on the car's tail. The road curved to the right and visibility was limited. That didn't stop him from overtaking, dropping a gear, increasing the engine's roar as he continued to push the speedometer up, then slipping into fourth as they glided past the Hillman Avenger. Alex looked at the alarmed driver, a fat businessman type, flashing the finger as they took off. Yeah, it was going to be a good night. He could feel it all the way from his balls to the top of his head, his body vibrating in concert with the powerful bike. He looked over Staff's shoulder: the speedometer read seventy and they were in a fifty m.p.h zone. Big deal. Staff continued to accelerate, pushing the bike past the other cars. Up ahead the houses gave way to factories on the right and, on the left, the stone wall supporting the British Rail line that connected London to the east and Bristol in the west, the direction in which they were headed. Here the speed limit was sixty; they were up to eighty. Ride that Bitch!

If he could have seen Staff's face he would have seen that his friend was smiling, a grim, mean smile charged with aggression. Staff took the bike up to ninety, tempted to give it full throttle, the cars behind them receding rapidly. There was no oncoming traffic as they reached the city limits. The street lights stopping, plunging them into a stretch of blackness, the railway line disappearing into a long tunnel, the factories replaced by the dark, silent, slow-moving expanse of the Avon on the right. The Bitch's engine purred with almost sexual satisfaction as it cut through the black, a thunderous ravaging red devil from hell.

Stoned on dope and speed, all head-rush perfection and oiled movement, Alex had no worries about Staff's ability to control the bike. He'd been riding motorcycles since he was thirteen, way below the legal age limit, but then legality didn't feature too highly in Staff's worldview: a little dope dealing here, a little breaking and entering there—he was small time in his law breaking but he believed that if you wanted something, you should take it; if there was money to be made, make it whichever way you could; if there was a bike challenging enough to ride, then push it to the max, take it to the red line and beyond. Fuck rules and regulations. Alex felt his amigo lean into the wind and lowered himself as far as he could go. There was no past, no future (God save the Sex Pistols!), only *now*—and that was one huge, throbbing brain scream of speed and dark.

They approached the traffic lights at the point where the Upper and Lower Bristol Roads converged and stretched out in a mile-long expanse of straight dual carriageway. The lights were green, and The Bitch blasted through at one hundred m.p.h. Alex whooped inside his helmet. Yeah, this was it. Go for it. Fast, furious, totally exhilarating. All thoughts of Sixth Form, of essays, tutors, home, and boredom, were gone. There was only the sensation of speed.

And the dark.

* * *

The phone rang as Jamie was finally starting to relax after the panic of the dead faint.

He got up from the couch in the dimly lit lounge, swayed slightly as a residual of the fainting vertigo flared in his head, and reached the receiver on the fifth ring.

The line was dead.

Balls. He hated that, not knowing who was trying to call, the tone mocking with its electrostatic hum. He sat beside the phone, shaking uncontrollably, his heart trip-hammering.

What's wrong with me?

He jumped as the phone rang again, picking up with a knee-jerk reaction in the middle of the second ring.

"Hello?"

Static. An echo of a voice. More static.

"I can't hear you."

It sounded like the voice said "Alex." Then the static faded, followed by a click.

Silence. Marred only by the ticking of the grandfather clock in the hallway. He looked at the peach floral wallpaper and felt sick.

The pattern took on a hypnotic aspect, flowers rotating, blending rhythmically.

The vision came.

It rolled over him with the relentlessness of a tsunami, a devastating sensation that moved up from his chest, pushing air from his lungs as his ribs cried out in agony as he felt them splinter. By the time it reached his head, his world was coming apart, the floral print fragmenting, leaves falling, petals scattering in a whirlwind of motion . . .

and he was flying backward through cold, black air, arms backstroking wildly

(Oh God!)

legs pumping at nothing, he felt himself thrown into the black, up, upward, onward. All he could see was the dark and a smear of orange.

      Then rolling

           tumbling

                  with a bone-jarring crash and something inside him burst something else snapping spine shattering

(Oh my God!!)

skin ripping muscles tearing organs coming apart as he saw
stars constellations galaxies nebulae unfolding in celestial majesty
as his eyesight exploded.
(OH GOD! THE PAIN!!)
in a swirl of pink puce blood dark purple and then—
Nothing.
He heaved in a deep lungful of air
(I can't breathe!)
crying out like a baby taking its first taste of oxygen.
"No!"
His sense of balance went and he collapsed back into the armchair still holding the phone, dragging it from the table, the bell
jingling loudly as it hit the floor.

Rivers sounded The Bitch's horn as they reached the round-
about, a long, loud, blaring burst as he handled the bike with
the tenderness of a lover on a first date, taking her around the
traffic island twice before heading away from Keynsham and back
toward the dull lights of Bath. Fourth gear and they were doing
eighty. Fifth and the speedometer was nudging ninety-five.

The mile of carriageway was eaten up in seconds. Alex saw
that the far set of lights were red as Staff dropped speed, de-
celerating rapidly.

Come on, change.

Seventy . . . sixty . . . fifty . . .

Come on!

The lights turned green.

Yeah, push it.

As if reading his thoughts, Staff twisted hard on the throttle,
The Bitch whining in protest. They cut through the lights at
seventy, veering to the left, taking the humpbacked bridge where
the Upper Bristol Road crossed the Avon in a stomach-lifting
jolt, The Bitch clearing the tarmac a foot and dropping into the
right-hand curve in one smooth-as-silk switch. Before them lay
Lower Weston; on the hill above, Newbridge. Way ahead was
the city center and it looked like that was where Staff was taking
them before heading up to Sion Hill and Tully's.

Alex's eyes narrowed unconsciously at the thought of the
numbnutted dickhead. Phillippa had made the wrong choice
there. Whatever Staff had in mind, it was going to be a party
Tully would never forget.

*   *   *

By 8:50 P.M. Harry Bledsoe was pissed off. The drive from Bath
had taken nearly an hour because of heavy traffic compounded
by a three-car pileup outside Keynsham. But now he was in
Kingswood and he would finally reach the Forbes warehouse in
another ten minutes or so.

He wondered how little Markie was doing. The poor kid had
looked like he was at death's door, the measles at its worst, when
Harry'd left this morning. He'd give Kath a call as soon as he
got to the yard to see how the four year old who looked just like
his mother was doing. Marrying Kath had been the best move
he'd ever made and at that moment, as he sat in the truck at a
set of lights in Kingswood, all he wanted was to be at home with
his woman, seated in front of the TV with his kids asleep in bed,
happy in the knowledge that little Markie was doing fine.

The bus behind him honked its horn and he put the truck in
gear, moving slowly as the road was narrow, the traffic still heavy.

"I'll be home soon, darlin'," he said, smiling.

After an hour riding round the city they pulled into Sion Lane
around 9 o'clock and were met with the sight of a police car
outside Tully's house. Staff idled The Bitch's engine, hesitating,
then killed it.

Loud music rolled out on the chilly night air as Alex lifted the
helmet visor, surveying the street for signs of the Boys in Blue.
Staff popped the bike's stand, removed his helmet, and turned
to Alex with a disgruntled expression. He'd had too many run-
ins with the pigs.

"I'll see what's up."

Alex dismounted, placing his skid lid on the seat. Staff grunted.

As Alex drew near the house the music died, Gabriel's "Sols-
bury Hill" cut in mid-chorus, a faint sound of indignant voices
following a beat of silence. He paused, then continued toward
the detached house, his boot heels clocking along the pavement.
When he was about two hundred yards from the house a second
police car drove up from the other end of the horseshoe-shaped
street. He ducked into the bushes fronting the nearest house,
watching as two cops got out and plodded flat-footed toward the
other cops, who were now emerging from the garden with three
teenagers between them. One of the kids was Alan Birch, from

King Edwards, a dealer who made Dawson look like the amateur
he was in the dope stakes.

He looked back up the road. Staff was nowhere in sight.

The two cops took the guys Alex didn't recognize, roughly frog-
marching them to the car. Tully and a small group of kids,
Phillippa among them, appeared at the garden gate and spoke
with the senior cop, but he couldn't hear what was said. He
hoped Staff couldn't see Phillippa. Words continued to be ex-
changed. Tully looked disturbed. The cop shook his head, placing
a heavy hand on the short teenager's shoulder, gesturing toward
the other car. Phillippa started to protest, a delicate blond bird
who'd suddenly found her wings clipped. Tully turned, took her
hand, said something, then walked off with the cop, the other
teens standing with lost, confused expressions on their faces.

He jumped behind the privet hedge as the patrol cars pulled
away and headed up the hill past the bike. Once they were at
the top, he ventured another look toward the house, but Phillippa
and her crowd were gone.

Staff was nowhere in sight as he ran back to The Bitch.

"Hey," he hissed.

Staff appeared from behind a high garden wall bordering a
large modern house.

"Looks like—"

"Saw it." Staff's face was a mask of frustration. He flipped a
cigarette into the gutter as he walked over to a green Metro
parked nearby. He swung his right foot into the off-side rear
end—once, twice—then switched to the other foot, pounding
dents into the body work.

"Fuck."

He turned to the elm tree near the car, its branches reaching
over the wall to down near the pavement. He leapt, grabbing a
low branch, pulling down with his full weight. It broke with
a dry snap and he swung the limb in an arc at the car's windshield.

Again.

And again.

When the branch did little more than break off a wiper blade,
he threw it to one side, resuming his kicking assault on the paneling.

A light went on inside the house.

"Come on."

Staff was on The Bitch before the words were out of his
mouth, his foot kicking the start in one strong downward

motion. The bike roared into life, Alex's helmet toppling into the gutter as Staff revved the engine. He took off before Alex was securely in place, his friend nearly back flipping with the rapid acceleration.

He didn't stop at the top of the road and Alex nearly lost it again, only managing to stay on by grabbing Staff's shoulders as they turned sharp right. Staff hit fourth as Cavendish Road dropped steeply beside the golf course, Alex holding on tight as The Bitch descended.

They drove to The Hat and Feather down on Walcott Street, Alex guessing where they were heading once they crossed Landsdown Road, nearly hitting a pedestrian as they rumbled down the incline to the end of the Paragon, its row of black monoxide–coated Georgian houses exuding all the charm of firebombed Dresden.

Staff remained silent when they parked The Bitch outside the Hong Kong Garden restaurant, his blue eyes twinkling with barely contained anger as he removed his helmet. Alex tried to grin but Staff turned away, striding toward the battered double doors of the pub.

The Hat was a run-down spit and sawdust bar in an area the city fathers seemed to have forgotten. Only a minute's walk from the stylish shopfronts of Broad Street, Walcot was a dark corner of poverty, drugs, and the occasional prostitute. The Hat was a shit hole, a meeting place for the lost, the outcast, the forgotten, those who didn't fit into Bath's orderly image of civil servants, secretaries, shop assistants, and the wealthy. On any given night you'd find a couple of dealers, a rumble of bikers, groups of hippie throwbacks downing pints, wheeling and dealing, and talking dreams as worn as the bar stools cracking under the weight of professional boozers.

Staff pushed open the doors and disappeared. The Hat was their home away from home. Here they were accepted along with the other disenchanted youth supping beer and listening to the jukebox. The Stranglers, the Pistols, Iggy, the Slits—the jukebox had 'em all. The pub wasn't a nihilistic haven, though; it was the nexus between generations, home to the last hippie tumbleweeds blown by the winds of '67, those who had professed to have the answers, and the blank generation whose credo was *We don't care.* Alex liked it here and felt some of his frustration ease as he entered to the dirty noise of the Stooges' *1969.*

Staff weaved through the landmass of punters, making for the bar. The smell of Flower's Best Bitter, cheap lager, and spirits hung above the regulars like a cloud of halitosis. Staff ordered a pint of Skol and a Guinness while Alex maneuvered into the far corner next to Smokin' Joe, an emaciated Hat regular, mindful not to bump against the group of skinheads next to the window. The bar was the kind of place where the wrong move could earn you a smack in the mouth.

Staff joined him. Seeing his eyes were still glowing with rage, Alex concentrated on the Guinness. Best not to speak until Staff was cool.

Rivers sighed after downing half his pint. "What now?"

Alex lit a cigarette. "See the late show."

"Come on! Piss on watching a bloody movie. There's other things."

"Don't know." It was true, he had no ideas at all other than getting stoned while watching slow-motion violence.

Staff grunted. "We got The Bitch. Think of somewhere to go."

"Bristol?"

"Nah."

"The Motorway?"

"No," Staff said again. "Bitch!"

"Come off it," Alex said, annoyed. "Give it a rest."

"Fuck you, she ain't your girlfriend."

"All right, just—"

"Look, I'm pissed off, right?"

"I know," Alex said after awhile, slapping him on the shoulder. "Forget Tully. He's down the Nick trying to convince the pigs he knew nothing about Birch's drugs, I bet."

Staff nodded, looking at the skinheads.

Alex put his drink down. "I gotta take a leak."

The Gents was at the rear on the opposite side. He started weaving through the crowd, navigating the bodies as deftly as he could, particularly past a cluster of mohawked punks drinking with a couple of members of the Bristol Angels. He stopped suddenly a few yards from the Gents' door. Standing right in front of him was a figure he recognized immediately, although he could only see the guy's back. That figure had haunted his dreams for too many years.

Hougan.

All six feet two of the hardcase was blocking him from the Gents, the black-haired troublemaker talking to a pair of underage girls.

Shit!

Alex froze. There was no way to get to the Gents without touching him, as the punters were packed tightly in this corner. Although he'd not had a run-in with his nemesis for nearly two years, more than a decade of trouble had instilled in him a Pavlovian response: Hougan meant trouble, Hougan meant pain. He unconsciously fingered his jawline, touching the two-inch scar under his chin, a present from Hougan on the Ralph Taylor rugby field. Apprehension grabbed his legs and he lost the desire to piss.

"That was quick," Staff said as he returned. Alex shrugged. "Got an idea." Staff smiled meanly. "Let's drop by The Circle, see what's cooking. Maybe Alison'll be there." Alex shrugged again, picking up his pint. The idea didn't appeal to him, and as for Alison . . .

For two years they'd spent most Friday nights at The Circle, the St. Stephen's Christian Youth Club housed at the church hall, a Victorian nightmare of a building in the no-man's-land of Walcot. They'd gone at the invitation of Adam Gibson, the reverend's son, and after a week or so it became a fixture in their lives. When you were underage and had problems getting served in pubs, what could you do but make your own entertainment? The Circle had become that entertainment.

Once they'd exhausted the main hall's possibilities—skateboardng, football, swinging off the balcony—they'd discovered the dark corners of the building, places other games could be played, like smoking weed in the empty caretaker's flat, throwing water balloons off the roof at people down below, and slipping fingers into the moist, hungry twats of choir girls under the cover of darkness in the cellar. For those with mischievous minds The Circle was a jamboree of teenage temptations.

It was fun then, but now Alex felt he'd grown beyond The Circle's confines, had graduated to the real world of sex, drugs, and rock 'n' roll. Dropping by The Circle would be like digging up an old friend to sift through his bones in search of new ideas. But Staff put down his empty glass and made for the door before Alex could object.

He was a couple of hundred yards down Walcot Street by the time Alex finished his drink and fought his way through the punters, happy to put some space between himself and the specter of Hougan. Since The Circle wasn't far away from the pub, Staff obviously wasn't going to bother with the bike. Alex ran after him.

*   *   *

The cup of tea sat untouched on the table as Jamie sat with his head in his hands.

Unlike the cup, his mind was empty. He had no idea how long he'd sat in the chair holding the phone like a lifeline thrown to a man in troubled waters, but he'd finally found the energy to make it to the kitchen where he'd brewed a pot of tea, thinking a good cuppa would revive him from his stupor. He made it, then lost interest.

Dread lay heavily in his stomach, an undigested sweetmeat. He felt lost.

Alex.

A vague image of his brother, frowning, tense, came to him in the white expanse of thoughtlessness.

Something was wrong.

As he reached out to embrace the vision, to feel it, the image dissipated, danced intangibly into the distance.

It was gone.

He woke with a start when his arm slipped from the table and he realized he'd dozed off. The clock on the mantle said 10:05; he'd been asleep for forty minutes. No, not asleep, somewhere between the two states of consciousness, like that guy in the King book, *The Dead Zone.* He'd been in the Dead Zone, a state of nothingness, swimming on tides outside himself.

He'd felt this way once before when he was a little kid. He couldn't clearly remember, but as he reached out, a lost circuit reactivated, a circuit long dormant, burnt out by an overload of input.

Alex.

Alex was the key.

Alex had climbed onto the roof of the garden shed, showing off. Jamie had been withdrawn all day; then, when Alex had struggled up through the branches of the tree, he'd known his brother was going to fall long before the corrugated metal gave way, throwing Alex into the flower bed below.

He'd known.

How?

He had no idea. Why hadn't he remembered what happened that day? He remembered the rest: Alex taken to hospital by a neighbor; their mother angry and upset—angry at Alex for climbing, upset at not having a car and being dependent on the neighbor; Alex with his leg in plaster for six weeks, Jamie envious because his brother didn't have to go to school.

Instead of relieving the apprehension, the unexpected recall increased his tension, the sweetmeat dread turning into anxious broken glass—sharp, stabbing—as his stomach churned.

The feeling, a gossamer strand of a priori knowledge, came to him again as a set of sensations; smells, textures, sounds—all alien yet terribly familiar.

Darkness.

Dust.

Cold stone.

Echoes. Voices in a cave.

A girl's voice. Giggly. Drunk.

(bored bored bored)

(bitch)

He tried to amplify the sensations.

(. . . n't like you . . .)

He tried to see.

(ibson . . . slut . . .)

But all he could perceive was frustration, traces of feelings, snatches of thought.

(. . . cking waste . . . time . . . Friday . . .)

The sensory input jumped and was replaced by overwhelming blackness, the rushing cold and pain.

(PAIN PAIN PAIN)

The world flying apart.

It was now 10:40 and he felt sick again. He started retching until his throat hurt, forcing him to swallow cold tea to ease the ache.

Something was wrong with Alex. Something worse was going to happen.

(What?)

But how could he find his brother before it

(What?)

was too late?

Alex unscrewed the bottle of cider, took a long pull, then passed it to Staff. Alison Gibson, Adam's sister, was giggling as she sat in the old wheelchair in the middle of the cellar cradling an almost empty half-pint bottle of Bacardi in her lap. He wrinkled his nose in disgust. The girl was nearly out of her skull.

"I'm bored," she said.

"Join the club," Staff replied.

Alex could just make out his face in the cellar's gloom, the only light coming from small windows along the far wall near the ceiling, orange light from the street lamps outside. It was barely enough to see by but dark enough for teenage secrets, of which Alison had many. Some he knew: she'd lost her virginity at thirteen, by sixteen she'd already had three affairs with married men (one a senior member of the church), and she regularly stole cosmetics from department stores. She'd told him most of this the morning he'd sneaked into the vicarage to fuck her stupid right under Reverend Gibson's nose. She'd also given him his first blow job on the roof of the church hall one summer night. They'd gone out for awhile after that—his mother had been delighted that he was dating the reverend's daughter—but he soon grew tired of her unfaithfulness. Alison was a slut, pure and simple. She couldn't get enough, and he'd wanted a steady, monogamous relationship, at least for awhile.

Staff drank deep from the bottle of Bulmers, then passed it back to him. Alison fingered the rum bottle. No one spoke for several beats and he decided it was time to piss. Alex gave Staff the bottle, belching as he left the room for the toilet next door.

As he pissed off a full bladder, he felt light-headed, like he'd smoked another joint, and thought of rolling one when he rejoined Staff. But as he walked in, Alison's excited groans alerted him to the drunken passion before his eyes could adjust to the gloom. Coming nearer, he saw that Staff had the girl's red dress up around her waist, his right hand working inside her knickers as they french kissed. Alison was trying to undo his belt. Alex picked up the cider, belching. Alison moaned.

"Don't be a stranger," she murmured as Staff stopped kissing her mouth, moving to her neck. Alex came closer. She reached out for him, found his cheek, touched him gently. "Kiss me," she said, then groaned again as Staff moved his fingers in and out of her twat. Alex reached her, their tongues entwining. Thoughts from the past—Alison blowing him in the back row of the cinema, spreading her legs for him on the vicarage floor—shot into focus, a mixture of disgust and arousal clashing inside him.

He stepped behind her and she tried to kiss his mouth but couldn't reach. He ran his tongue over her ear, feeling her shiver as he wrapped his arms around her, cupping her breasts in his hands as she leaned back against his chest. Staff removed her knickers, still working his fingers in and out of her body, harder, faster. Alison gasped.

"Slower."

Staff took no notice. His belt undone, she tried to get his cock out. "No, *slowly*," she said. He grunted.

Alex's hands were under her sweater, kneading the large breasts. He grasped hard. Alison squealed like a stuck pig.

"Don't—"

"Sssssshhh."

He saw Staff reach for the cider bottle. Then she cried out as he replaced his fingers with the glass neck. She started to struggle in Alex's arms, but his limbs were immobile. Months of working out with weights had increased both his strength and his size; she couldn't break his grasp.

"No, don't—that *hurts!*"

Staff worked the bottle in.

Out.

In.

Out.

In.

She cried again and Alex felt tears splash the backs of his hands. He felt disgust and frustration. And a glimmer of pleasure.

She was getting what she deserved, the prick-teasing bitch.

That was the booze and the dope talking, not his true self, he realized. His sanity flashed as a sick, secret part of him rose up from a hidden place.

Alison cried freely, mumbling "nonononononononono" over and over.

"The wheelchair," Staff said, removing the bottle.

Alex hesitated.

This is wrong.

But his dark half countered the thought, throwing up all the years he'd been snubbed by girls; the ones at Newbridge who constantly made fun of him; the ones in his early teenage years: a torrent of rejection and humiliation. Frances Clarke, daughter of the teacher who'd made his days at Newbridge such a misery, ratting on him for stealing a library book, her upper-class accent ringing in his ears.

Hurst took the book.

Frances and her stuck-up friend Melanie the fat pig laughing at him, telling him he'd never be anything, that he was worthless, no girl would—

"The wheelchair," Staff said forcefully.

Alex complied.

He felt like Alex the Droog from *A Clockwork Orange* about to do the old in-out-in-out.

He manhandled Alison over to the chair as Staff led the way.

"NO!"

"Shut the fuck up,"

Alex stumbled to the front, holding her hands down as Staff moved behind her, Alison's arse pulled up over the back of the chair. Staff tugged his jeans down, his prick emerging, pointing like a divining rod in the gloom, searching blind for her hole.

Alex's anger stretched like an elastic band about to break— then snapped back with a pull of sanity.

This is . . . wrong.

His thoughts cleared. He wanted no part of this . . . this brutality. He felt sick with fear as Staff picked up the Bacardi bottle.

"Staff, don't—"

"Hold her!"

Unable to see, alerted by their exchange, Alison struggled with new strength. Staff leaned over her, clamping a hand to her mouth, stifling her cries.

"Staff, no, this is—"

"What?"

"Wrong."

Staff paused. "You turning into a faggot?"

"No! It's—it's not right!"

"Fuck you."

Staff dropped the bottle, grasping Alison's hips, ready to penetrate her.

The fear became a new creature. Alex couldn't —wouldn't— help his friend. The creature was defiant and he let go of her hands. She thrashed around and Staff lost his balance. When he raised his arm to hit her, Alex leapt forward.

"Don't!"

He caught Staff's arm, pushing his friend back. They struggled for a brief moment, then Staff shrugged him off.

"Okay. Okay."

Alex reached for his arm.

"I said okay, damn you!"

Alison lay crumpled by the chair, sobbing hoarse, deep sobs, pulling her skirt around her legs.

Alex looked at Staff, the taller youth glaring at him, the meager light from the windows illuminating lines of tension around his mouth.

"Okay," he said with unexpected softness, his arm going limp. "You're right." Alex let go, unconvinced by the mood swing. Then Staff's face cracked like crazy paving, his mouth widening into a broad smile.

"You're right." He pulled up his jeans, pushing his erection inside with difficulty, the cock pointing like an accusatory finger.

"Let's go," he said.

Alison sobbed loudly.

Jamie was at the bottom of West Lea Road when the nausea hit him.

He staggered to a low wall for support as the sensation rushed up from the pit of his stomach to double him over. Nothing came up—there wasn't anything to come up.

(Alex . . . don't)

The sensation stopped as suddenly as it had started, but he waited until he was sure he could walk straight.

He had to find Alex.

Alex was in danger.

(Where?)

(. . . wrong . . .)

Jamie didn't have a clue. All he'd known was he had to get out of the house.

With the slow gait of a somnambulist he continued walking, heading for Newbridge Hill as if gravitational force were pulling him toward the river. It was irrational to be walking away from the road that would take him to Rivers's house, the only place he thought he might find Alex, but nothing seemed rational. Instinct took his hand and he quickened his pace.

Elfman placed his hand on Bledsoe's arm.

"Thanks for waiting, Harry."

"Sure." Bledsoe took the invoice from the warehouse foreman.

It was 11:07, and somewhere nearby a police siren cut through the Bristol night. He wanted to be at home, a beer in hand, his feet warming in front of the gas fire, not standing around sixteen miles from Bath. But at least the work was done. Home beckoned.

"See you next week," Elfman said.

He smelled beer on the foreman's breath and thought, At least you got one in tonight. Still, there was a bottle of Pils waiting in the fridge and Kath always had a plate of sandwiches ready for his return.

Bledsoe swung himself up into the cab, starting the engine as Elfman waved.

Broad Street was deserted as they headed for The Paragon, calm now after their confrontation. Staff hadn't spoken for half an hour, seemingly ashamed of his behavior. Alex had made sure Alison was coherent enough to understand his threat before they left The Circle.

If you say anything I'll make sure your father gets the photos.

Fucking as many guys as she could get her hands on was not enough for Alison. She had to keep a visual record, photographing them postorgasm with a Polaroid. But even this hadn't satisfied her. Tired of her organ gallery, she'd started using the self-timer to record liaisons with herself as the star of the show. But like a secret journal, written with the perverse hope that someone will read it, such a confessional only became valid when shared with another. She'd made a mistake when she showed Alex her works of art, though. It had been the nail scratch that drew blood; he stopped going out with her the following week, though not before he'd stolen several prize pictures to show around at school—including one clandestine shot of Mr. Dixon, the church warden, masturbating on the couch in the vicarage.

Satisfied she'd say nothing, they left, an uneasy silence between the three of them. When they exited the hall, Staff started off in the direction of the abbey and city center, attempting to walk off his rage, frustration, and guilt, coming to his senses as the haze of dope and alcohol dissolved.

Alex knew him well enough to realize that Staff was no rapist. He felt sympathy for his amigo, walking with his head down, shoulders rounded as if under a tremendous weight. They were bonded by a hopeless boredom and the unspoken knowledge that the future held little in store for them. Especially Staff. An alcoholic mother, a distant father. Worthless qualifications. Now he had no job, little money and no girlfriend. Although Alex was studying for his "A" Levels so he could go to university, he had no desire to go to another small town to study for another three years. Then what? A career? As what—an accountant? A civil servant? Yeah, with a three-bedroom house, a heavy mortgage,

a wife and three kids. Great. He'd wake up one morning to find
he was fifty, an overweight businessman like all the rest. Staff
would be living in a council house with a wife, kids, and a criminal
record. That's if you live that long, he thought. Staff made him
think of "My Generation"—hope I die before I get old. Prison,
death, or a council house. Was there any difference between
them?

When they reached the top of Broad Street Staff turned.

"Thanks. I was out of order."

"Forget it." Alex lit a cigarette.

They came to the alleyway that cut through The Paragon, its
steep steps reminding him of the ones in *The Exorcist* on which
the priest dies struggling with the demon and his crisis of faith.

Alex had no faith in anything. His life was one long, straight
road, neither yellow brick nor paved with gold, just a brain-
numbing expanse of flat black tarmac measured out in birth,
school, work, death. Bath was ancient, would stand for hundreds
of years. But he would be long gone, either dead in his fifties of
a heart attack or dead of boredom long before then. Thackeray
may have written "As for Bath, all history went and bathed and
drank there," but Alex felt he was drowning under its cultural
weight, a culture in which he had no place. Defoe was right when
he described the city as a place conducive to committing the worst
of all murders—killing time.

There is no God, no point, Alex thought as they descended the
steps. He frowned as Staff stopped on the pavement.

"What's—"

Staff gave him a terse wave. "Catch this."

Five hundred yards away, almost hidden by the shadows cast
by the abandoned bakery, two figures scuffled in and out of the
light from the street lamps like drunken dancers.

"This could be interesting," Staff said.

He moved along, watching closely.

Alex held his ground. The two opponents were mismatched—
one tall, broad, powerful, the other around five three, of light
build, and paying for it. The tall bloke was pushing the smaller,
toying with him, keeping him at bay with his longer reach. The
small guy tried to kick out, provoking a punch in return, which
slammed him against the bakery.

Alex drew a breath through clenched teeth.

Hougan.

"Staff," he said.

He turned, nodding. "Got it."

Alex felt anger rise from the depths of his gut like heartburn. The same old song and dance: a song of fists, a dance of pain. Hougan had the smaller guy—it was always a smaller guy, he thought—in the palm of his hand, trapped, angry, caution thrown to the wind. It was always the same: ride someone's case till they responded, cause enough hurt for the other to lose control, then move in for the kill. Hougan was slamming the small guy against the doors, the sound of the guy's head hitting wood loud enough for Alex to hear.

Painful memories came with each blow:

Hougan punching him unexpectedly in the face at Newbridge.

Hougan ambushing him one rain-splashed day as he walked home.

Hougan suspended for smashing an older kid's head on the playground.

Hougan tripping him on the rugby pitch, kicking him in the face, making out it was an accident.

Alex taken to the hospital: ten stitches and a shot for his shattered teeth.

Hougan swung a roundhouse into the bloke's head. There was a whack as fist connected with face, the smaller guy rebounding off the wall as blood poured from his pulped nose; a punch to the guts and the opponent went down fast.

Alex looked at Staff, his expression hard. "Let's do the bastard."

Staff nodded.

Hougan stood over the slumped body, ready to lash out his foot. The other youth, barely conscious, raised an ineffectual hand. Hougan pulled his foot back with deliberate slowness, savoring every wrinkle of fear on the bloke's face, unaware of Alex and Staff approaching from the other side of the road. Seeing that he was about to kick the guy's head, they rushed him.

Hougan turned as Staff plowed into him, taking them both down as his right fist connected with Hougan's sternum. Hougan tripped over the downed youth's legs, pulling Staff with him but not able to twist away as Staff's full weight landed on his body. Staff punched his stomach but Hougan retaliated with his left fist, catching Staff on the side of the head. Staff saw stars, pain racing down his neck. Hougan growled with the fury of an enraged bear, heaving Staff off as Alex came in.

Alex hesitated. A mistake. Hougan scissored his legs, taking Alex beneath the knees, sending him over to land heavily on his left shoulder, his skid lid flying. He cried out. Staff, despite the bells ringing in his head, backhanded Hougan across the face. Hougan grunted. Alex shouted "fuck," kicking with his right foot at Hougan's balls. He missed, his foot scraping hip bone. Staff stumbled to his feet and kicked. His foot hit Hougan's chest, snapping the youth back, slamming his head to the pavement.

"He's mine!" Alex screamed, diving as he brought his right fist down like a piston, spreading Hougan's nose across his face.

The pain in his left arm was intense, but not as intense as the raging anger exploding his reason. The frightened, wounded animal inside him emerged with teeth bared, claws drawn, as years of fear and hurt rushed out in a flood of adrenaline.

He punched again.

Again.

And again.

Everything went into a red haze and he didn't feel or hear Hougan's jaw break or his teeth shatter. Nor did he hear Staff shouting at him to stop.

He brought his fist down a fifth time, catching Hougan on his left cheek and sending his head over at an unnatural angle, the neck snapping. Deep inside Alex, in that sick, secret place, a voice began to laugh with insane hysteria. He screamed "you fucking bastard you fucking bastard" as Staff slapped him hard, displacing him from the saddle of Hougan's chest.

Alex leapt to his feet, his mind caught on some mad wavelength, waving his fist.

"You want some of this? Come on fucker!"

Staff, his head throbbing, looked at Alex as if for the first time.

Alex went to kick Hougan and Staff grabbed him.

"He's dead!"

He slapped Alex a second time. Alex froze a beat, then shook his head.

"What?"

"He's dead. You broke his neck. Jesus, Alex, he's fuckin' dead."

He looked down at Hougan. The face looked like several pounds of dog meat.

"God . . . God, oh Jesus God . . . nononono God no, Jesus."

He started to rock back and forth, his voice dropping.

Staff looked up the street. A car approached from the Beaufort Hotel end.

"Come on," Staff said, "help me."

He started dragging the body into the dark alleyway beside the bakery. Alex was still rocking, his arms cradling his chest. The semiconscious youth groaned.

"Do it!"

Alex stumbled.

"Shit." Staff pulled Hougan's body out of the light.

The car was closer.

"Alex!"

Alex moved slowly.

"The other one!"

Alex looked blank.

Staff went to the beaten youth. "Come on you stupid fuck!"

The car was almost on them.

Staff grabbed the semiconscious bloke, heaving him from the doorway. Alex understood now, panic replacing shock. He reached down, taking the youth's legs, and helped his friend haul the dazed youth into the darkness as the car passed.

The youth groaned again.

"What do we—"

"Get the hell out," Staff snapped, taking Alex by the arm as he stooped to pick up their helmets. The car hadn't stopped.

Alex hesitated as Staff gave him the red one. He looked at the alley with the expression of a confused child.

"Move."

He took the helmet.

Jamie was down on the Upper Bristol Road near the river when his left arm started tingling, pins and needles running from shoulder to wrist. He stopped.

The road was deeply dark here; the only light was that cast by the high orange lamps on the other side of the river where the Lower Bristol Road turned into carriageway. A gravelike stillness hung over the open fields and boatyard, yet he felt the air dance electrically. He sat on the wall massaging his limb.

(out of here)

He'd been following an internal compass with the blind faith of a sightless pilgrim, his mind tabula rasa, free of conscious direction. Now the compass spun wildly, a vertiginous spiral of confusion.

(move)

The thought was faint, his limbs leaden. He knew his journey was almost over. Whatever uncharted road he was traveling, his destination was on the other side of the river, and he had no control over whatever events were in motion. He was a sailor adrift on a psychic sea in a rudderless boat, at present suspended on a tidal change. Then the compass stopped spinning and he continued.

Staff rolled The Bitch down Queen Square, carefully observing the speed limit. To Alex it seemed they were moving at a snail's pace.

Hougan was dead.

He felt nothing.

No remorse, panic, no residue of the nausea he'd felt as they walked back to the bike, when his stomach had suddenly performed a forward roll, expelling Guinness and cider over the pavement in a hot rush.

Empty.

His head was unnaturally light and clear.

He'd killed him.

Alex laughed silently as Staff headed down toward the Lower Bristol Road.

The clock in the cab said 11:35 as Harry took a wide curve. From his high seat he could see the mile-long carriageway lit up like a neon strip across the uneven hedgerows and dark farmland.

The lights were green as he came out of the curve and he accelerated, willing them to stay that way.

He yawned.

Damn it, he'd drive the truck home. If he took it back to the depot he wouldn't get home till midnight—if the bloody Capri would take him there. The last thing he needed right now was to spend time under the bonnet trying to get it going if it wouldn't start.

Home.

Beer and sandwiches.

Screw it, he was going to take the Lower Bristol Road. That way he'd be in front of the fire within ten minutes.

Alex lifted his visor and tapped Staff on the back. He was still taking it slow and their pace was irritating Alex.

"Head for Bristol," he shouted.

Staff nodded.

Staff's home held little appeal to Alex and his mother's house seemed light years away.

You can't go home again.

He'd left the safe, boring confines of middle-class suburbia, in mind if not in body. He was no longer Alex Hurst, he was Alex the Droog. He'd tasted the rare delicacy of the old ultra violence and was reborn. Nothing could touch him. Hougan was gone and so were the old fears. He sensed a change in Staff, too. They'd been into the fire and had emerged unscathed.

He put his fist in front of Staff's face, making a revving motion. He nodded with enthusiasm.

Full throttle.

The bond between them, two spirits mismatched by social class yet emotionally joined, a pair of empathetic siamese twins, was stronger now, unbreakable.

Staff took The Bitch up to seventy-five and Alex smiled.

Nothing mattered. Only speed, men, and machine moulded into a ménage à trois of rumbling, accelerating motion.

The houses gave way to factories and soon the factories would give way to the long, black stretch before the carriageway.

He felt elated. What was that line from that James Cagney movie?

"Top of the world."

Yeah. Top of the world, Ma.

Alex laughed.

Jamie's consciousness fractured as he set foot on the humpbacked bridge.

One moment he was looking ahead, the next he was paradoxically looking down on himself from a great height, a small figure almost eaten up by the dark, and looking up over the brow of the short bridge toward the traffic lights. His split vision lasted a second, an eternity, then he felt himself dropping out of the sky, descending at an incredible speed, his own body rushing toward him. He heard the rustle of huge leathery wings rippling through the night sky, ancient, unworldly wings not touched by time.

He cried out as something swept into his body, a high-pitched whine shrieking through his ears for an instant.

Silence. Total. Still. Heavy with a strange promise.

Dread and anxiety departed, the stillness a sensation hereto-
fore unimaginable, touching every nerve ending, every molecule.
It was about to end.

Harry rubbed a hand over his tired eyes as he plowed down the
carriageway at eighty-five.

Sleepiness was creeping up his shoulders. He yawned.

Half a mile to the second set of lights, then the Lower Bristol
road. The lights were red. He braked, hoping they would change.

Jamie saw the Beford truck coming down the carriageway as he
heard the loud rumble of a motorbike behind him, a ways off
but growing louder with every second.

The lights went green and the truck accelerated.

The motorbike's rumble increased.

Harry saw the bike approaching at what seemed Warp Factor
Five. One second its headlamp was a small yellow cyclopean orb;
the next, much larger.

The crazy bastard must be doing a hundred, he thought, stifling a yawn.

The light suddenly wobbled. A trace of sparks flew up like
crazed fireflies. The lamp angled toward the truck.

Before he could cry out, Harry was thrown against his seatbelt,
his head whiplashing as the bike impacted into the truck's engine.

Harry screamed.

Jamie's eyes widened. The night exploded with the deafening
sound of 250 pounds of bike melting into the front of one and a
half tons of truck.

The Bitch was doing 113 as it hit; the truck 89, a total impact
speed of 202 m.p.h.

High speed switched to slow motion and he saw every body-
pulping detail with unnatural clarity.

The pillion rider lifted up over the head of the driver and
came apart in a spray of red, like an overripe tomato hurled
against a wall. Strands of muscle, fragments of limb spreading
outward, the body's impact smashed the windscreen. The bike
crumpled in on itself as the engine grill seemed to eat it whole,

smiling a big bad wolf grin as man and machine became muscle and metal, innards and engine.

The truck continued for ninety feet at a skewed angle, riding up the pavement to Jamie's left, heading for the wall as metal scraped on tarmac, gouging furrows in the earth's dark flesh before coming to a stop only feet from the stone, sparks vapor-trailing its movement.

Silence suddenly descended with the finality of a theater curtain bringing the last act to a close.

September 19, 1980.

There had been a severe frost the night before and the flowers on the graves were dying.

Jamie pulled his coat belt tight around his waist, blowing on his hands, wishing he'd brought his gloves. The cemetery was deserted, although it was midday. Even the birds in the trees were quiet; the only noise was a faint rumble of trucks on Rush Hill.

"Well, Alex, how does it feel?"

His words floated on the autumn air and he felt self-conscious. If this were a Brian de Palma movie, he thought, Alex would come bursting forth from the grave in front of him.

But that was impossible.

When the police and ambulance crew arrived at the scene, there had been no body: Alex had ceased to exist, his mortal remains spread over a wide area by the force of the crash. If not for the fact Stafford Rivers had been recognizable—albeit impacted into the engine block with such force that it took the medics three hours to cut out his mangled corpse—it would have taken the police days to identify the pillion passenger. Alex had become a pathologist's nightmare, a minute jigsaw of humanity. Nothing fitted together. The largest part of his body was a section of rib cage and spinal column, but what could it be attached to? There were no limbs. Only fragments of bone, tatters of skin, traces of muscle, a handful of teeth, and pieces of cranium. His brother had been vaporized. There hadn't been enough to bury, and what little was left filled only two small plastic bags. Alex wouldn't become worm food, even the morsels that remained; he'd been cremated, all fifteen pounds of him. But their mother insisted on a gravestone, his testament, to be laid beside the plot inhabited by their father.

Jamie was surprised by his reaction to Alex's death. He'd felt nothing then and felt nothing now, staring at the gray concrete slab with Alex's name on it. Perhaps in years to come he might —at least that's what his doctor said. But he doubted it. Though he'd loved his brother in the unspoken manner of male siblings, he'd experienced a great relief after the funeral chaos had subsided. He'd expected the house to be gloomy after the ceremony; instead it appeared as if the three-bedroom semi had been rebuilt.

He, Jamie Hurst, had been reborn.

Alex, he realized, had cast a shadow over their lives, and with his passing the storm clouds broke up, floating away as a new sun shone forth. The shadow, however, still cloaked their mother. Jamie didn't think it would ever leave. She'd become too used to wearing black to change her wardrobe. A year to the day and she was still on tranquilizers, despite Julian returning to live with them, having quit his job on a North Sea oil rig. Jamie, on the other hand, had gone from strength to strength. He'd passed his exams with flying colors and was on the way to a place at Oxford. He'd sold his first short story to a prestigious literary magazine in January and was halfway through the first draft of a novel, two hundred pages written in a white heat this summer.

Life made new sense now. He understood how Saul must have felt on the road to Damascus: he'd been blind and now he could see, though not with the eyes of a seventeen year old. No, he saw the world through the eyes of an ancient touched by arcane knowledge. Once he'd felt eclipsed by the darkness his brother drew around himself; now he felt bathed in light, baptised by a grace unimaginable before the accident, untouched by the slings and arrows of adolescence.

Alex had lived his dark dream—live fast, die young—and now it was Jamie's turn. Where his brother had failed—or succeeded, depending on your viewpoint—he would succeed on his terms.

Only one doubt assailed him, a question perhaps best left unanswered.

What had happened that night, and why?

When the bike had hit the truck, he'd stood for an aeon—in reality less than a minute—then walked away, not experiencing any feeling akin to those we should feel at the instance of violent death: shock, horror, loss. Of course, there was no way he could have known it was Alex. In fact, he had not known—that terrible, liberating knowledge came later. Yet Jamie *had known* on some deeper level, a primitive, reptilian level of consciousness.

He'd walked away unaware that there was a blind man trapped in the cab screaming silently in mute agony, his vocal chords severed by the shattered windscreen, and as Jamie crossed the river, he felt some part of him—innocence, perhaps—depart on eldritch wings, heard leathery membrane flap and rustle up into the black sky. The only sensation wrapped around his heart was an indescribable peace. When he reached home, still in a somnambulist state, he'd gone straight to bed, falling into a dreamless sleep, the quiet repose of a baby untouched by earthly fears and the dread of adult consciousness. He awoke the following morning to the sound of the doorbell and, seconds later, his mother's scream.

Jamie's world had changed.

Alex had lived a lie, a falsehood woven by those who were imprisoned by their own frightened isolation. So long as the lawn was neatly mowed, the floral print curtains hung correctly, and the checks didn't bounce, there was no teenage suicide, no incest, alcoholism, rape, drug abuse, famine, or war—except in the newspapers. The middle class were too smart and too stupid to let those ills touch them. But Jamie would explore the lie, try on its masks through the role-playing of fiction, seek the truth, however ugly. And if there was a price to pay, when the time came he would freely give the ferryman his coinage and cross the river one last time, secure in the understanding that he'd traveled roads known only by a select few: the dreamers, the mad, the restless.

He sneezed. He was coming down with his usual winter cold and the September chill didn't encourage lingering in the open.

"Good-bye, Alex." Jamie's voice was loud against the cemetery's tranquility.

As he turned he noticed a crow watching him from high up in the branches of an old oak. The bird cawed, rustling its feathers.

His last respects paid in full, Jamie walked up the steep incline toward Rush Hill and school. When he was but a dot on the landscape the crow took flight, arcing up into the clear sky, its wings a black apostrophe on the vast, impersonal cerulean expanse.

For: Piers Locke, with thanks for the Newcastle Brown
     Alice Cooper for "Under My Wheels" and "I'm Eighteen"
     and
     Kitty, with love.

The scariest part of this story is that it's true—in a manner of speaking.

The old ghosts are gone—long live the new demons.

London
January 1990

City of Angels

J. S.
RUSSELL

J. S. Russell doesn't exist. Is it any wonder, then, that he gets the shortest introduction in this book?

Actually, "J. S. Russell" is the pseudonym for a young southern Californian who writes nonfiction professionally under another name. "City of Angels," which first appeared in the Fall 1990 issue of *Midnight Graffiti*, is his first professional *fiction* sale.

At the moment, Russell has a number of other submissions circulating among the various horror magazines, so it may well be that by the time *Splatterpunks* is published, his name will already be familiar to you. If not, "City of Angels" should brand the Russell nom de plume deep into your forebrain. Permanently. For here's a story that takes the moldiest of science fiction clichés—the post-holocaust tale—and deconstructs it into the grisliest form imaginable.

By the way, this story made me laugh. Out loud. More than once.

On the other hand, don't forget your vomit bag. If there's one story in *Splatterpunks* which crystallizes the controversy, this is it.

In fact, here's a cute idea.

You know that obstinate person in your life, the absolute knucklehead who *refuses* to be convinced anything good will ever come from splatterpunk?

Hand them "City of Angels." Sweetly say it's a sober look at a *very serious topic*. Once they start reading, smile a lot.

Then sit back and watch the fun.

"I'm gonna chew me a new asshole," Porquah was mumbling.

He'd been repeating the line for hours, ever since Demodisk got the big laugh with it over by the crumbling shell of the observatory. Demo tried to correct him at first—"Chew *you* a new asshole, asshole. Chew *you*. *You*."—but Porquah's shit-eating grin just got a little wider and he thumped himself on the chest with that big, meaty thumb of his and said it again: "Gonna chew *me* a new asshole!"

Once Porquah gets an idea in his head there ain't no turning him away. Like just the other day with the baby. We was up around the old Hollywood sign, 'cept all that's left of it is the H-O-L-Y, and we find this little black girl and her baby living in the remains of a DWP shack hidden in the trees. Viridiana, she don't cotton much to dark meat, so she slits the girl from cunt to tits before Demo and me can even get our dicks hard. Well, Demo, he says he ain't real particular and figures insides is insides so he sort of mashes her together and goes to plugging that new slit. I thought about doing her mouth, but I seen her teeth were crooked and sort of blackish and fuck me if rotten teeth ain't a fierce turn-off.

So I leave Demo to his belly fucking and see Porqy and Viridiana tussling over the baby. It's a scrawny brown thing, but its making a screeching and a wailing like a rocket coming 'cross the sky. Porqy's got the thing by the feet and Viridiana's holding it by the head and they're like to playing a mean game of tug-o-war. I walk on over and grab hold of the midsection like to take charge and damned if, just for spite, Viridiana don't twist that screaming head so's we hear a clean, crisp snap.

Viridiana, she's acting all contrite and sorry, but I can see the smiling in her eyes down underneath. Porquah, he's all upset and ready to cut Viridiana in half with that 9 mm Needler he's always waving around, but just then Demo walks back over all smiling and humming to himself, stuffing his bloody dick back in his pants, and he says, "Let's cook 'em," and everybody settles down.

Porqy, he's got this thing about the nuts and how they're the "bestest part," which is fine because none of the rest of us ever developed a real hankerin for 'em. Old Porqy's been talking about baby nuts for days, just bitching and whining 'bout how he's gotta have some.

"I figure," he says, "they got to be more tender. Tastier, like lamb or baby corn."

Like I say, once the Porqmeister gets himself an idea in that bullet-shaped head of his, there ain't no living with him till he acts on it. So 'fore I can even set a pot of water to boiling, old Porq he rips them nuts right off that dead little sucker. Pops 'em in his mouth like wet jelly beans. They're tiny goobers, they are, and raw, but Porq, he's chewing on 'em real slow, savoring every bite. A little line of dark fluid is oozing down his chin, but Porq just dabs at it with that tiny brown scrotum and smacks his lips.

"Well fuck my mommy bloody," he says. "They's even tastier than titty tips."

Demo, meanwhile, he's been scrunched over the momma, grunting and puffing and slashing with that monster blade of his, and while Viridiana's hacking up the wee one he tosses something pink and hairy and dripping red onto the ground between us.

"Anybody want to eat a little pussy?" he says and screeches with laughter. Well that Demo he's a card, ain't no doubt, and Porqy and me start rolling on the floor, howling like horny dogs. But Viridiana, she just gets all offended or something and clucks her tongue, like *she's* never eaten pussy before or things one hell of a lot worse. Then Demo, he picks up that flap of flesh and slaps it over his mouth and starts a yammering through them hairy lips, calling himself a chatterbox. Well that's too much even for frosty old Viridiana and she starts to laughing with the rest of us. So we slice up the meat and cook us some dinner and settle in for the night, 'cause the day's fading like an old pair of jeans.

We were sitting all quiet just watching the sky go purple like a big old lilac growing out of the rubble of the city. Demo and Viridiana and Porquah may be like family now, but sleeping's still a funny thing. I've slept on my back and waked up to Viridiana and Demo reaching for my Johnson, and sleeping on your stomach is practically an open invite for Porqy to fuck you up the ass.

So I stayed up, waiting for the others to doze off first. I knew Porqy'd been thinking 'cause he hadn't said a word since dinner and he was scratching at his head and staring off even blanker than usual. Finally, I guess, he hit a brick wall in that little brain of his 'cause he started spouting some damn funny talk about pregnant ladies and unborn babies and such.

After awhile Demo just got sick of it and he said, "Elvis-on-the-cross, Porquah, just tell us what you're driving at here."

Porqy gets all quiet for a minute and stares down at the dirt. "I was just wondering," he says. "If them nuts on that baby was so tender, wouldn't they be even better fresh out the oven?"

I looked at Demo, heard Viridiana cluck again.

"I mean," Porqy went on, "if we could just find us a pregnant lady, we could rip that young 'un right out her belly and I bet you there's nothing that would taste any finer than those tiny baby balls."

Porqy looked up at us like a little boy who'd just peed his pants and didn't know what was coming as a result. Viridiana had been leaning back against a tree sort of dozing, her arms folded tightly against that big chest of hers. She opened her eyes and leaned forward, mussed Porqy's thinning hair with her three-fingered hand. "What the hell's wrong with you, Porqy," she said, pulling out that patronizing tone. "Where in the name of Ronald Reagan are we gonna find a pregnant lady?"

Porqy nodded and looked kind of sheepish, but for two days after that all we heard from him was talk of baby balls. So in a way it was kind of refreshing when he started talking about chewing himself a new asshole. But after a day and a half of that, I was almost missing all that chatter about nuts.

Always did like talking about food.

The Docworker told us for sure but I already knew we was getting worse. Porqy's face was all puffy and red, the skin peeling off his cheeks and arms in long shiny strips. He was complaining about his knees, too, how they was crunching and grinding with every step and it sure enough sounded like a bunch of marbles rolling around in there, bouncing off each other.

Viridiana, now, was oozing from every which way. Them pustules on her face and neck was dripping gray and white and that big red stain on her crotch seemed to spread a littler bigger and smell a lot raunchier every day. Finally, I see her standing off to the side of the camp with her shirt rolled up over her chest and she's prodding and poking those giant boobs of hers and cursing like a sailor with the clap. I called her name and when she turned around I saw she was dabbing at some thick, sticky-looking fluid running out of her nipples. I ain't never seen nothing that color come out a human being before, but I didn't say nothing to her. She looked up at me with kind of sad, hound-dog eyes and I could see she wanted like to cry but she was always trying to show how she's stronger than the rest of us. I couldn't think of nothing else to do, so I just walked away.

I'd gone kind of runny in some damned funny places myself, and truth is it was more 'n a mite unpleasant. Only Demo still looked good, but I knew it was hurting him too, mostly inside. He was acting more squirrelly all the time, talking in nonsense or forgetting our names or even what to call the grass or the sky. His eyes would go a little wild now and again and he'd take to eating the dead rotted things that were always underfoot. But then he'd come back to himself and be the same old joker that kept us going so well.

Anyways, the Docworker—he didn't look so good neither, what with gunk running out of that empty eye socket—he used that scanner of his and told us it was probably just a matter of days now. The others, I believe, knew it too, but old Porqy didn't want to admit it. He was still talking about chewing assholes when he grabbed the Doc and went like to bite away a piece of the man's belly. He only got a tiny chunk of flesh 'fore we pulled him off, and the Doc didn't hold it against him.

"Us Angelinos got to stick together," he said hopping back into his little golf cart, "These are interesting times for us all."

Viridiana was steamed as hell and said it was time to *do* Porqy, but Demo and me talked her out of it. We just agreed that we'd have to take what Porqy said a little more literally from now on.

We decided that come morning we'd head down into the heart of it. Figured it didn't make no difference now anyways so we might as well see what it looked like in the center of the old city. I tried to remember from before, but it was all hazy and distant. I thought about the freeways and the stores and the pretty people and the noise and the Mexicans selling oranges and peanuts on the street corners and all that was gone. I pictured them tall, skinny palm trees what I always meant to learn the proper name for, but never did and reckon now I never will.

I remembered back to that day and the awful, bright flash and the searing winds. It was funny how when it came it seemed so natural, so inevitable. I remember how before I used to think about it, abstract like, trying to imagine the *after*, thinking it would be all romantic and adventurous, like in some of them neat old movies with crashing cars and fancy leather clothes.

I can't believe, sometimes, when I make myself think back, that it ain't hardly been two years. It seems like decades or centuries and I feel like I must be the oldest man in the history of the earth. And then I fish out that old California driver's license and look at that stranger's picture and remind myself: that's me.

I realize that I'm thirty years old and ain't never gonna see thirty-one. And sometimes at night, when I'm not really asleep but like in a dream, I see my Janey's face. I wish more than anything that I could feel her again, bucking on top of me, or just look at her while she laughed at one of her TV programs. I can't believe how much I miss those dopey old shows now that they're gone.

Then I see that gang-bang all around her in our kitchen and I hear her scream as they get inside her from every which way. And then they're cutting her into little bits with that electric carving knife, laughing and dancing in the blood like Gene Kelly in the rain.

And I think, *when things change, they change and that's all there is to it. Ain't no sense or reason and tears is just so much salty water. There's no going back, no unringing a bell, no living for the dead.*

And I'm glad it's just a matter of days.

Wouldn't you know that screwy idea about baby balls would be the death of Porqy.

We could tell from the shadows on the ground that we was close to the center. I'd always heard about them, but never had believed it before. They were everywhere, though, them blackened silhouettes of people who was standing right around ground-zero, their bodies vaporized, their shadows burned forever into the cracked concrete.

Demo, silly as ever, pulled out his flashlight and did hand shadows, making like the silhouettes had dicks and tits and talked like Mickey Mouse. It was funny, I have to admit, but no one did much laughing. The end was too close and we was all feeling it real bad. My skin was itching so's I felt like ants or roaches was crawling over every inch of me, biting and stinging as they marched. Parts of me had gone kind of mushy, too, and I was afraid I'd bust right open like an old tomato if anyone pressed too hard.

Porqy was running like an ice-cream cone in the desert sun. The skin on his face and arms was all peeled off and the pink muscles and tendons glistened like liver in a butcher's window. He was breathing real hard and walking like a three-legged dog with a hangnail, ranting and raving about preggo women.

We turned down what might once have been Sunset Boulevard when Porqy saw her lying on the ground in a pool of Elvis-only-knows-what. I could hear the bones snapping in his legs as he ran toward her. I made to stop him but Viridiana held me back and shook her head. I watched as Porqy flipped the bloated corpse over and dug into the bulging belly with them scaly claws of his.

There was a low ripping sound, like an enormous passing of wind as his fingers broke the blackened flesh and released the gurgling gasses within. A thin geyser of murky magenta spewed out of the decaying husk dousing Porquah's flayed cheeks. Porqy seemed not to notice, though, and scooped out handfuls of brackish grue from the torso, sifting the corrupt tissue, I reckon, for some sign of a fetus. He grasped a small, roundish object—a shriveled kidney, maybe—and shoveled it into his mouth, chewing happily.

"Balls," I heard him say through a mouthful of gray, "Baby balls, yum-yum."

Suddenly, his eyes suddenly went all wide and he started to gag with a noise that sounded like a backed-up drain. Then he went quiet and pitched over face-first into the messy corpse. That body just splattered like a rotten pumpkin as soon as Porqy fell into it, and we knew old Porq was dead as could be.

I figured to just leave him lying there with his nose buried in what once might have been a sweet patch of bush, but Viridiana, of all people, had a fine idea for a memorial. Demo sliced Porqy's balls off and we boiled them over a small fire. Demo and I split one and left the other for Viridiana. We ate in that unnatural silence, and I thought, wherever he was, Porquah would be right touched.

My eyes felt ready to burst out of my head and my tongue was like a hunk of splintery wood in my mouth. We found a patch of mutant wildflowers and marveled at the flowing, surreal colors that glowed in the setting sunlight. The thin clouds looked like paisley against the silky, mauve sky and for a flash I thought I remembered something about what beauty was.

Demo was off on one of his crazy jags, but it hardly mattered now. I looked over at Viridiana and I don't know what it was—maybe the dimming light, maybe just the way she cocked her head—but for a minute I thought I saw just how she must of looked as a little girl, all pretty and bright and full of dreams.

I walked over to her and put my hands on her shoulders, felt the bones grind under my touch. She looked real wary for a second, but then stared into my eyes and seemed to understand.

We took off our clothes, trying to hold on to as much of our skins as we could, and laid down in that bed of soft colors. She was a goopy, dripping mess and I don't suppose I looked a whole lot better, but she opened her legs and I laid on top of her and got inside. I slipped in a little further than seemed right or natural and I didn't much care for the slushy noises we both was making, but it was good and it felt right, in the way that it always had and ever should be. Viridiana was making some mewling sounds and I think they was happy noises. Myself, I've always been sort of a Silent Sam in the sack, but I was liking it too.

At the end, I closed my eyes and I thought about Janey and what had been and I do believe it was the best I ever felt.

I rolled off of her just as Demo strolled over to us, something bulky in his hands. He stood right over Viridiana's head, looking at her all upside down with that toothy smile of his, and fired two tenpenny nails square through her eyes from some sort of pneumatic gun. It must of been battery powered and Elvis alone knows where Demo found it.

Viridiana didn't make a sound when it happened. She just sort of stopped breathing as crimson tears flowed out of the sockets and ran down her cheeks.

I looked at Demo, but he just grinned a little wider. I got up and slapped him playfully on the back of the head and he giggled, but I felt something shift inside his skull so I didn't do it again.

"I guess we both nailed her, huh?" he said.

I laughed and we walked off in the direction of the ocean, toward the setting, decaying sun.

That Demo is a pistol, I tell you.

Outlaws

PAUL M.
SAMMON

Writing about yourself is always a dicey proposition. So permit me to reprint a bio-blurb created by (of all things) the Houston Association of Film and Television. It's part of an informational newsletter passed around by that organization to local professionals while I was in Houston working on *Robocop 2*:

Paul M. Sammon is a media rarity—not only a much published writer, but also (and simultaneously) a professional filmmaker. As a journalist, Sammon has written hundreds of articles on film history, as well as film criticism for such diverse publications as *Omni, The Los Angeles Times, The American Cinematographer, Cahiers Du Cinema,* and *Cinefantastique.* His short fiction has appeared in *The Twilight Zone Magazine* and *The Year's Best Horror Stories, Series XIV.* Sammon also has two upcoming books on tap—*Blood and Rockets,* the definitive guide to the best science fiction, fantasy, and horror films available on videotape, and *Splatterpunks,* a collection of "extreme" horror stories.

As a filmmaker, Sammon has written/produced/edited/directed dozens of promotional films, commercials, and documentaries through his own company, Awesome Productions Inc.; clients included such films as *Platoon, Dune,* and *Robocop.* Additionally, Sammon has worked as a unit publicist and/or promotional consultant for virtually all the major Hollywood studios, traveling the world to give lectures and public appearances on productions like *Blue Velvet, F/X,* and *Conan the Barbarian.* Sammon's latest film effort takes place right here in Houston; he is the Computer Graphics Supervisor and Unit Publicist for *Robocop 2,* and will appear oncamera in a number of cameos throughout this production.

Paul Sammon also functions as the American coproducer of the Tokyo-based television series "Hello! Movies," the most popular entertainment program of its type in Japan, now in its fourth season on the TV Asahi Broadcasting Network. Finally, Sammon recently cowrote the screenplay for the short film *Stereotypes*. Shot in Moscow, where Sammon spent three weeks cowriting the scenario with a Russian collaborator, *Stereotypes* has the historic distinction of being the first Soviet-American coproduction of an animated film.

So now you know. Probably more than you wanted to.

Anyway, "Outlaws" is my attempt at producing the first major overview of splatterpunk. I've tried to thoroughly document splat's roots, superstars, and important works.

It's up to you to decide whether I've succeeded.

And by the way—Paul M. (for Michael) Sammon may well be a "media rarity," but he is also, and most emphatically—

A splatterpunk.

1. THE SPLATTERPUNKS

It's been said that the moment you name something, you kill it.

That's why, despite everything you're about to read, keep one thought in mind:

What follows is not a definition.

Examination, yes. Appreciation, most certainly.

But not a coffin-shaped box.

Having settled that, let's begin with a statement:

Over the past few years, it's become clear that splatterpunk occupies a major and important position within the genre of horror fiction.

Splatterpunk? What the *hell* is splatterpunk?

Well . . . first remove the limits society and so-called good taste impose on fiction. *All* the limits. Add a healthy dose of shock as well as the influence of schlock movies, late-night TV, and the screaming guitar licks of the world's greatest heavy-metal band.

Finally, stir in a strong awareness of pop culture. Season with a no-bullshit attitude. Serve up some of the best *writing* in the field today.

And never, ever flinch.

The writers who comprise *Splatterpunks* haven't just brought horror up to date; they've brought literature up to date. By bringing in the influences of other media, by fearlessly emphasizing honesty and courage and quality, the best splatterpunk not only creates prose that is immediate (fiction for now) but prose that is enduring (fiction for tomorrow).

Think of this, then, as a sort of stop-action photo, freezing a moment in time. A splatterpunk pit stop, if you will. One designed so that those watching the race can pause for a moment to assess the progress of those comprising the field.

You are about to meet the rule breakers, the trailblazers committed to stepping far beyond the barriers.

Artists alone on the rim, at a time when society actively discourages anything outside the norm.

These are *not* "acceptable" writers.

They are, in a word—

Outlaws.

2. SEEDS OF REVOLT

By the time the word *splatterpunk* was coined in 1986 to describe a certain brand of aggressively explicit fiction, the horror community was already in an uproar. And splatterpunk, at least as it currently defines itself, was already over a dozen years old.

Since the appearance in 1971 of William Peter Blatty's novel *The Exorcist* (with its profanity, vomiting, and little girls masturbating with crucifixes), horror fiction had been exponentially growing in critical acceptance and mainstream popularity. The 1974 publication of Stephen King's *Carrie* (and his subsequent, unprecedented career) kicked horror into overdrive; now everywhere, it seemed, there were new horror novels (mostly bad ones). In the related field of the horror film, psychopaths, zombies, and big guys in hockey masks were collectively butchering America's psyche.

And the increasingly graphic nature of horror films was corresponding to an opening up of horror *literature*. In 1971 Richard Matheson's *Hell House* depicted a small band of ghost hunters falling prey to an orgy of explicitly carnal desires. 1975's *The Fog*, by best-selling British author James Herbert, clinically detailed numerous atrocities as escaping government nerve gas reduced the population of a small English town to homicidal hysteria. Stephen King made the film/fiction linkage even more explicit by including a scene of thousands of cockroaches bursting forth from the mouth of an evil tycoon in his script for the 1982 George Romero–directed *Creepshow*.

However, despite these ominous rumblings, the traditional horror establishment (typified by mood-oriented novelist/editor Charles L. Grant) refused to acknowledge the obvious, and continued to preach restraint. Good horror literature, they insisted, was to be modeled on the efforts of Poe and Blackwood and Lovecraft, writers whose trademarks were ellipticism and suggestibility. Anything else was sensationalistic garbage, pandering of the lowest order.

Then came the appearance of such works as *Clive Barker's* 1984 *Books of Blood*, and John Skipp and Craig Spector's 1986 novel *The Light at the End*; with them arrived the embodiment of traditional horror's worst nightmares. Here was horror fiction that was inescapably confrontational; it was visceral in the extreme, contained explicit sex and violence, centered on grotesque set pieces. Take this example from Barker's story, "The Midnight Meat Train," to be found in Volume One of *Books of Blood*:

> The carcass closest to him was the remains of the pimply youth he'd seen in Car One. The body hung upside-down, swinging back and forth to the rhythm of the train, in unison with its three fellows; an obscene dance macabre. Its arms dangled loosely from the shoulder joints, into which gashes an inch or two deep had been made, so the bodies would hang more neatly.
>
> Every part of the dead kid's anatomy was swaying hypnotically. The tongue, hanging from the open mouth. The head, lolling on its slit neck. Even the youth's penis flapped from side to side on his plucked groin. The head wound and the open jugular still pulsed blood into a black bucket. There was an elegance about the whole sight; the sign of a job well-done. . . .
>
> He was not prepared for this last horror.
>
> The meat of [the woman's] back had been entirely cleft open from neck to buttock and the muscle had been peeled back to expose the glistening vertebrae. It was the final triumph of The Butcher's craft. (p. 38, Berkley Books, 1986)

Despite Barker's microscopic examination of abused flesh, fair-minded readers of the *Books of Blood* soon realized that an eloquent new voice had been raised in the field of horror, one capable of existential analysis, dark humor, and deft, stylistic prose. Above all, Barker's vision was ruthlessly, relentlessly honest; story by story, one recognized that the shocking scenes of sex and brutality found in the *Books of Blood* (*and* in *The Light at the End*) actually were fueled by an absolute refusal to flinch from the truth.

Even when it hurt.

Very few people seemed to notice. Quality or intent wasn't the issue here; explicitness was. The controversy raised by the *Books of Blood* (and there was an immediate underground buzz associated with these works) became the catalyst which finally ruptured the long-tenuous alliance between horror's opposing camps of conservatism and candor. Endless divisive debates on the inherent incompatibility between "quiet" and "explicit" horror boiled over from weekend convention panels to the letter pages of the national press. Specialized publications like *Fangoria*, originally conceived to focus on the still-burgeoning field of hardcore gore films, added fuel to the fire by reviewing and encouraging like-minded explicit horror novels. Eventually the issue became politicized, with outraged old-guard horror pros closing ranks against those (typically younger) writers who preferred to chart truly unknown waters.

So by the time a rising young writer named David J. Schow came up with the term *splatterpunk* to taxonomize horror fiction's most outrageous (and courageous) form of expression, the battle, and the battle lines, already were clearly drawn.

Yet within the smoke and fury lay a considerable amount of ignorance and doubt. What was splatterpunk—what was it *really*? Who was practicing it? Was there a manifesto? What were the essential works? There had to be *something* to explain all of this—after all, there was a whole splatterpunk *movement* out there!

Wasn't there?

3. NOT A MOVEMENT
AND
PROBLEMS WITH THE BOOK

The most interesting thing about the splatterpunk movement is that there isn't one.

Not that you'd know it from browsing through various essays on the subject. For instance, in a wry *Village Voice* article titled "More Gore: Splatterpunk Leaves Its Mark," writer Richard

Gehr tells us that: "Included in the s-punk lineup are gory boys John Skipp, Craig Spector, Joe R. Landsdale, Ray Garton, Rex Miller, David J. Schow, Robert R. McCammon, and others, with Clive Barker as their patron saint" (February 6, 1990, p. 57).

Oh, really? Gehr didn't make the same calls I did.

First came the surprises. For example, David J. Schow (the man who invented the term) declined an offer to be included in *Splatterpunks*. His decision arrived in the form of a note enumerating a number of reasons for turning me down; none, to my mind, seemed particularly deal breaking.

In any event, I do regret David J. Schow's absence from *Splatterpunks*. Yet soon after crossing his name off the list of potential contributors, this disappointment was drowned out by a repeated litany that I was hearing from a number of *other* writers, ones who'd *agreed* to be in the book.

Here was the problem: while editing *Splatterpunks* and talking with various potential contributors, most (but not all) of the "gory boys" mentioned by Gehr in his *Village Voice* article kept responding with something like this; "Sure, you can reprint [insert title]. But that's just a story I wrote, okay? I want it made perfectly clear that I'm *not* a splatterpunk. I do a *lot* of other things. I think being labeled a splatterpunk is *very dangerous*. Sure, that story is extreme, but I've done *others* that *aren't*—

And so on.

Here's a more specific example, sent to me by Roberta Lannes, author of "Goodbye, Dark Love," a powerful short story dealing with incest, necrophilia, and revenge:

> "Goodbye, Dark Love" was written before the word "splatterpunk" was coined to describe the genre of horror woven with its own questionable excesses. Granted, the explicit sex and violence in my story qualifies as extreme, but not excessive. Splatterpunk, with its inherent gratuitous blood, guts, gore and graphic sex intends to disgust and gratify a reader's lowest self-needs. I choose to use extremes when they can push a story into the fully sensual, the experiential realm. Accurate illustration, used sparingly, succeeds where excess overwhelms and thus detracts from the body of work. . . . "Splatterpunker" I am not.

Lannes's comments typify, in one sense, everything that is misunderstood about splatterpunk. Here is basically the splatterpunk-as-dirty-word argument, which includes observations that traditionally have sprung from an academic/conservative school of thought, pronouncements which routinely proclaim splatterpunk to be cheap, illiterate trash.

Don't misunderstand; Lannes is obviously entitled to her opinion, just as the overall quality of writing in *Splatterpunks* obviously refutes it. But Roberta's response is only one aspect of the passions the word *splatterpunk* stirs up, leading us to the first inquiry on our quest to understand it:

Who *are* the splatterpunks?

Well, after many phone calls, it soon became clear who *are not* (for the record, the only four "official" splatterpunks are Clive Barker —and he's a marginal case—John Skipp, Craig Spector, and David J. Schow; more on these guys later). Despite their protests, however, an interesting equivocation lay couched within the uneasiness many writers felt on being included in *Splatterpunks*. They didn't mind having their more explicit work labeled splatterpunk as long as they themselves weren't *called* splatterpunks. In other words, one could write a splatterpunk*like* story without *being* a splatterpunk.

Why did they insist on this distinction?

Because the primary emotion splatterpunk first elicits is not revulsion—as one might expect—but *fear*. Not just the charmingly antiquated fear of Lovecraft's Lurker on the Threshold, either. We're talking primal, essentially *societal* fears. Fears that can get you in trouble in the real world, right away, right now.

Fear of offending. Fear of *being* offended. Fear of language; fear of sex. Fear of our bodies; fear of our own deaths.

Obviously, any art form that manages to arouse such emotions carries a potent charge. And this is splatterpunk's true worth; it's managed to resensitize the horror genre in ways that Lovecraft and Poe and King never even *dreamed* of.

Oh, yeah; I forgot to mention the one germane fear most associated with this I'm-not-a-splatterpunk syndrome:

Fear of making a bad career move.

Splatterpunk has a reputation of being a literature of illiteracy, a nauseatingly offensive clash of sound and fury signifying nothing. This is, to put it mildly, an incorrect reading of the field; worse, it suggests the same attitude found in those who didn't have to see *The Last Temptation of Christ* to know it was blasphemous. Yet a reasoned appraisal of such short stories as Skipp and Spector's "Gentlemen" or Lansdale's "Night They Missed the Horror Show" quickly uncovers the complexity, maturity, and deeply felt morality which characterize these works.

Yet the myth persists; splatterpunk is cheap trash. Therefore, the uneasiness many of my *Splatterpunks* contributors felt is at least understandable. After all, what professional writer would want to be associated with the kind of work that cuts through so many taboos, that supposedly panders to the lowest common denominator, that's riddled with words like *fuck* and *shit* and positively revels in carnage and fornication?

Who, indeed? Well, as the contents of *Splatterpunks* attest, simply some of the most exciting writers practicing fiction today (incidentally, even Gehr's *Village Voice* article eventually worked its way up to a pretty nifty description of splatterpunk: "abject fiction"). As it turns out, there *are* a handful of fearless scribes out there who realize that what's loosely pegged as "splatterpunk" is much more than farting at the dinner table. These are a clutch of like-minded individuals with genuine talent and vision, uncensored artists who don't mind reflecting, through the dark mirror of their fiction, what their individual psychic radars have picked up as the *genuine* human condition—one that's not a pretty sight. Splatterpunk's so-called transgressions obviously pale beside what we do to one another in, say, the name of politics—witness the atrocities committed by the Khmer Rouge.

But we'll get to these individual writers later. As I've already said, there are only a handful of true splatterpunks anyway: Clive Barker, John Skipp, Craig Spector, David J. Schow. All the rest sometimes write splatterpunk–like stories. What's important here is an understanding that there is no true splatterpunk movement, that this fiction has deeply divided the horror community, and that much confusion still exists as to—

4. WHAT IT IS

Splatterpunk is controversial, and visceral, and not really very polite.

It is also achingly honest, and fearless, and truly subversive —though its detractors insist that splatterpunk is only viscera and sex(ism), with attitude.

But let's listen to Clive Barker as he describes his artistic intent during an interview with the recommended filmzine *Film Threat*:

"I am not writing horror or making horror movies to produce a mild [frisson] which can be shrugged off, so people can move on to make their cocoon and go to bed. I am writing horror and making horror movies to genuinely disturb people. . . . Subvert them, throw over their ideas about the status quo, throw over their ideas about sexuality, throw over their ideas about death." (June–July 1989, p. 19)

Craig Spector puts this subversion idea on the table much more succinctly: "I want people to be upset by what I write."

What's vital about splatterpunk is the juices it gets going, both in and out of the publishing business; how it stimulates a dialogue. What's interesting is that this daring, quintessentially liberal literary beast flowered during the mindless, monstrous conformity of the Nixon/Reagan decades. And what's relevant is its courage and clarity.

High-sounding statements for a literature primarily known for its lack of restraint. But the simple fact is that splatterpunk is one of the most misunderstood forms of writing today, consistently misrepresented or misunderstood, usually by mainstream critics or traditionalist horror writers.

There's much, *much* more going on here.

The appeal of splatterpunk to its core audience works on two different levels. Obviously, splat's sexual and physical excesses satisfy the unsophisticated or adolescent hunger for forbidden fruit. This is splatterpunk as most critics see it, naked and unadorned, catering to the child—some say animal—within us all. (Of course, these same critics miss the point. Splatterpunk isn't about gore and sex; gore and sex are simply two tools used to express splatterpunk ideation.)

Yet even on the simplistic level of "gross," splatterpunk allows the primal satisfaction of actively defying the parental authority figure; this is the archetype who has traditionally warned us that sex is bad, that saying "fuck" will land us in hell, that vicariously enjoying scenes of violence (whether in print or on the screen) will make us "sick." At its best, this Level-One splatterpunk can be cathartic (or, for the more sophisticated, simply amusing). At its worst, Level-One Splat can be twisted into the schlock mentality which produces such one-dimensional dreck as the *Friday the 13th* film series, where the sole rationale of each film is to invent creative homicides (which, lately, are so censored by the Motion Picture Association of America that the filmmakers shouldn't have bothered in the first place).

Unfortunately, the Guardians of Morality who condemn Level-One splatterpunk's predilection toward catering to the dark fantasies of its audience simultaneously ignore the everyday realities of that audience. For it is obvious that the bulk of most people's lives are in direct contradiction to their fantasies. We *know*, from experience, that watching or reading about sex usually culminates in arousal, masturbation, or lovemaking, not rape or dismemberment; that reading about or watching explicit violence usually results in nervous laughter or simple disgust. Obviously, most of us do not respond to a story like "Night They Missed the Horror Show" by aping its narrative in real life. After all, when was the last time *you* raped the next door neighbor or cut somebody's throat after reading a horror story?

So—the true function of Level-One splatterpunk is to rough up your imagination a little. Past that, you can simply put down the story and walk away (knowing horror fans, though, they're more likely to *share* this dreadful experience by recommending that selfsame story to a friend).

Splat's second level of appeal is far more complex, working as it does with profound social and philosophical contexts. At its best, splatterpunk is a literature of confrontation, anger, and despair, sometimes flirting with nihilism but always aware that it is using materials from the real world as its fabric. In this arena, splat become political and cautionary; there *are* horrors out there, within and without you, and *they really can hurt you.* So *do* something about them, dammit!

This Second-Level splatterpunk, is, to me, the literature's greatest asset. By introducing the most uncomfortable aspects of the real world into traditional horror structures, Level-Two splatterpunk challenges the reader with a multitude of credible concerns. This quality of conscience can appear as social satire (via David J. Schow's "Jerry's Kids Meet Wormboy," with its Jerry Falwell–like minister commanding a literal army of mindless zombies), as a rejection of sexual abuse (John Skipp's solo short story "Film at Eleven"), or a deeply felt moral disgust at religious hypocrisy (Ray Garton's "Sinema," in which a Sabbath School teacher is really a homicidal pedophile).

So much for the hard-core fans. To those coming fresh to splatterpunk, know that it offers unfettered imagination, and energy, and a fascinating pop-culture mix—as well as philosophy, point of view, excess, and freedom—all tied up with explicit sex and violence.

But as I've already noted, it would be a mistake to call splat a *movement.* Splatterpunk is a *subgenre*, one particularly brave and interesting tile in the overarching wall of fantastic fiction. One could go further and venture to say that splatterpunks are a loose coalition of like-minded anarchists fueled by an all-pervasive popular culture, writers who found themselves caught up in a simultaneous case of literary spontaneous combustion.

One *could* say that, but—

Naah.

Let's leave it to Clive Barker. He said it best, in the ad copy for *Hellraiser*, his first film:

"There are no limits."

5. HOW IT GOT ITS NAME
AND
WHAT STEPHEN KING THINKS ABOUT IT

The term *splatterpunk* was invented by writer David J. Schow during a party in 1986, after Schow (*The Kill Riff, Silver Scream, Lost Angels*) and a number of other authors had participated in a panel discussion on "quiet vs. explicit" horror at the World Fantasy Convention in Providence, Rhode Island. It was a partly serious, partly facetious taxonomy applied to the extremely explicit (and growing) body of work being practiced by Schow and others. And initially this explicitness gave such practitioners of "quiet horror" as Charles Grant—who is still in the forefront of the antisplat movement—a massive case of the aesthetic heebie-jeebies (parenthetically, Grant is a skilled novelist—he wrote *The Pet*—as well as the editor of the excellent *Shadows* anthologies).

Let's examine what the traditional horror establishment has to say about splatterpunk. Stephen King indicates that splatterpunk is "the most vital and visceral horror coalition operating today." Peter Straub (*Ghost Story, Mystery, Koko*), in a recent telephone interview I conducted with him, opined that: "As long as the writing is okay, I enjoy it. Part of splatterpunk's intent is to deliberately violate the reader, to be deliberately offensive. To outrage. This has always been the underlying point of horror, and it's one of splatterpunk's greatest strengths."

But as previously noted, not everyone involved with traditional horror tolerates splatterpunk. Berkley Books editor Susan Allison (who works with such best-selling horror authors as Dean R. Koontz and F. Paul Wilson) was quoted in the magazine *Mystery Scene* as saying: "It [splatterpunk] frequently seems misogynistic to me, and I prefer not to publish it if I don't have to" (vol. 25, 1990, p. 102).

One certainly can't fault Allison's aversion to misogyny but her statement sounds suspiciously like a hasty generalization. Yes, it is true that the female characters found in splatterpunk are occasionally thrust into threatening situations (so, by the way, are men—lots of them). Sometimes these women die. Or worse (again, so do the fellas). But there are two basic errors at work in Allison's claim of misogyny.

For one, the arts are riddled with women in threatening situations. These scenarios are constantly played out in detective fiction. In romances. In westerns. Even in Stephen King novels. So it seems a bit unfair to single out splatterpunk for this tendency. And rather than place herself at the risk of not being able to publish *anything*, the more critical issue Allison should be addressing is not misogyny, but drama's ongoing damsel-in-distress syndrome.

Now here's a fairy tale we've carted around for millennia. Yes, it's still a potent fictional device—but it's also one writers shouldn't so lazily, and misogynistically, fall back on, time and again. While there's probably a grain of truth to Allison's statement—after all, we are dealing with human personalities here, and no one in their right mind would insist that all splat writers are capable of empathic or enlightened responses when it comes to women—the best splatterpunk seeks creative ways of leaping *over* these clichés.

Which leads to some examples to back up that last statement, as well as the second implicit error in Allison's aversion. Quite plainly, Susan Allison's use of the word *misogynistic* suggests a basic unfamiliarity with the field. Perhaps Allison (and others who, without a thorough grounding in splatterpunk, consistently trot out this knee-jerk response) hasn't read such hard-core *anti*misogynistic works as the novella "Gentlemen" or the novel *The Scream*, both by Skipp and Spector. Here the majority of the female characters are not only fully rounded and sympathetic (particularly *The Scream*'s Jesse Malloy), but they are placed in situations with morally complex, painfully *empathic* ties to the real world (one harrowing example is Malloy's emotionally agonized visit to a supposedly genuine abortion clinic, one revealed to actually be staffed by pro-life activists).

Misogynistic also ignores the fiction of Edward Bryant. Though personally unwilling to accept the label himself, Bryant nevertheless has written such splatterpunklike works as "A Sad Last Love at the Diner of the Damned" and "While She Was Out."

And both of these stories come down hard on the side of women everywhere.

These are not isolated examples of splatterpunk's sensitivity toward women; how about David J. Schow's "Pamela's Get," a knowing, intensive study of female friendship? Then again, misogyny is not the only negative that's been tossed at splatterpunk by the horror community.

In a recent phoner (media slang for a telephone interview) I did with Charlie Grant, he passed on this up-to-the-minute response:

> The splatterpunk movement isn't doing anything that hasn't been done before; they're just being more graphic about it. What differentiates splatterpunks is their energy, and what they do with it. And what's good about splatterpunk will eventually be absorbed; the lousy stuff will be jettisoned.
>
> Incidentally, their technique of injecting the same kind of violent explicitness found in the movies has really failed; most publishers have found that people who go to graphic films like *Friday the 13th* don't read books anyway, and that putting this kind of violence in books really turns readers off. So it's a self-defeating technique.
>
> But things are changing. Around 1989 Skipp and Spector and I sat down together and decided that this quiet horror—explicit horror thing was getting out of hand. We all decided it was an artificial issue. But splatterpunk is pure hype, anyway.

Well . . . to get the opposing viewpoint, I also interviewed Craig Spector, reading him Grant's remarks. Spector's reply?

> It just irritates me to no end that Charlie would say that we all sat down and agreed that splatterpunk is all hype. We didn't, and it's not. Basically, I think Charlie wishes that splatterpunk would just dry up and go away.
>
> On the other hand, it's obvious that an element of splatterpunk—*the word*—is hype. But the overall aesthetic, the color of the palette of splatterpunk, is not. In any event, this loud versus quiet horror argument isn't the real issue at all; the real issue is, are you a *traditionalist*, or not?

Spector's final comment hits this debate right on its head. Grant's implicit rejection of splatterpunk's rude qualities, and

Spector's equally passionate embrace of them, is a perfect example of the generational divisions within art. The simple chron-
ological difference between Grant and Skipp and Spector
(approximately a dozen years; S & S, in their early thirties, are
younger than Grant) speaks more eloquently than a filing cabinet
full of theorems.

Outlaw art (a sobriquet under which splatterpunk clearly falls)
is usually the province of the young and the young at heart. The
tools of outlaw art have always been challenge, rebellion, and
change. And nowhere has change been more apparent than in
the swirling currents of American pop culture, pre– and post–
World War II; just a scant dozen years between artists, then,
can spell the difference between being hip and being self-calcified.

Other than the obvious generational factor, what else explains
this initial quiet–explicit horror debate? Well, while most would
assume that successful practitioners of a field of literature that
indulges in terror, violence, and imagination would be of the
utmost liberal stripe, the exact opposite holds true. The horror
establishment, like its science fictional counterpart, is basically
conservative. Science fiction and horror fans are notoriously
resistant to change; Spock *can't* die, Jason *must* wear a hockey
mask, and so on. So it's not surprising that the reaction by the
horror establishment to splatterpunk was, at best, one of pained
silence (and to a certain extent, it continues to be so). At its
worst, this reaction is one of loudly vocal revulsion. (Incidentally,
my feeling is that this quiet-versus-explicit debate is a tumorous
old creature that should be shot on sight. After all, the field is
so big that there's plenty of room for both armies to camp on it;
anyway, most horror falls between these extremes).

But let's get back to the origins of the "S" word.

Besides being an outgrowth of the quiet-explicit debate, the
word *splatterpunk* was obviously Schow's reference to the then-
trendy "cyberpunk" cult, created in the novels and short stories
of such science fiction writers as William Gibson (*Neuromancer*)
and Bruce Sterling (editor of *Mirrorshades*). Cyberpunk usually
featured highly skilled yet disaffected urban youths acting out
complex power plays against a decaying, intricately realized fu-
turistic/film noir backdrop. These characters also flirted with
nihilism; they were world-weary and despairing and took an
inordinate amount of exotic drugs. Casual sex and violence were
a given (though never as well detailed as in splatterpunk works).

Most important, cyberpunks adopted a revolutionary stance,

screening their disgust with the political, ethical, and interpersonal corruption of the eighties through a mesh of computer-ridden high-tech science fiction. In its combination of youthful agitprop with an examination of spiritual and social malaise, in its obsession with pop culture, cyberpunk most resembles splatterpunk; in just about every other way, it does not.

In any event, this Schow-cyberpunk story has become the unofficial party line on the creation of the word *splatterpunk*. But the *real* influence on this word and splatterpunk's concerns have more to do with broader-based elements of American popular culture; *splatterpunk* is *not* just beholden to William Gibson's sullen romanticism.

Might I suggest that there could—or should—have been three other influences in Schow's mind, three other equally potent stimulants to the term *splatterpunk*?

One such influence must have been the "splatter film" genre, a term coined in 1984 by writer John McCarty to describe a group of movies that began with the likes of H. G. Lewis's *Blood Feast* and Romero's *Night of the Living Dead* and soon would include everything from Dario Argento's *Suspiria* and Lucio Fulci's *The Beyond* to Ruggero Deodato's *Cannibal Holocaust* (lots of Italians, there . . .).

Splatter films sustain an enthusiastic subculture. This group has its own publications (*Shock Xpress, Psychotronic Video, Gorezone*), conventions (*Fangoria*'s Weekend of Horrors), theme anthologies (David J. Schow's *Silver Scream*), and latest *causes célèbres* (films like *Nekromantik, Street Trash*, and *Henry: Portrait of a Serial Killer*).

Not coincidentally, splatter films are currently displaying an interesting Ping-Pong effect. Barker has written and directed *Hellraiser* and *Nightbreed*. Skipp & Spector provided a screenplay for *A Nightmare on Elm Street 5: The Dream Child* and did a polish on the *Class of 1999*. Schow wrote *Leatherface: The Texas Chainsaw Massacre III*. Obviously, splatterpunk has veered from filmic influence to the printed page and back to film again. This not only underscores the fact that splatterpunk is a multimedia phenomenon but clarifies that, in certain instances, splatter films *are* splatterpunk.

And what about punk rock, the second influence?

Through the mid to late seventies, a musical movement called punk rock exploded in England. Mirroring the despair many British youth felt toward England's moral and economic stagnation, punk soon spread to America. It was led by such bands as the Sex Pistols and (the late lamented) Fear and was experienced through such audience-participation rites as slam dancing and shared fashion statements (torn T-shirts, mohawk haircuts, safety pins through the nose, ear, or chest). Punk rock was an angry howl of protest sheathed in a very specific philosophy. *There is no future*, punk said. The old rock music is pointless, bland, co-opted. Sex is ridiculous, and the world is run by powerful, unbeatable old assholes who've left us no options. All we can see, punkers said, is a gray void of economic, racial, and artistic repression. So *fuck you*, mate!

Punk was noisy and rude, invested itself with tons of attitude, and drew a lot of attention to itself—just like splatterpunk. Of course, punk's pretty much dead now. And rock 'n' roll *in general* is actually the larger splatterpunk influence (interestingly, however, there are now splatter *bands*; in 1989 groups like Gwar showed up onstage wearing horror masks and performing spewing eviscerations as part of their set—yet another example of the splatter culture folding in on itself).

Finally—and I may catch some flack for this—the third cultural splatterpunk influence is video pornography.

Consider; there have always been stroke books, but it took movies like *Deep Throat* and the relaxed social attitudes of the seventies to allow large groups of people easy access to filmed fucking. And by the early 1980s, when porn moved out of theaters and into living rooms via video tapes and VCRs, adult films had gained such a fiscal ascendancy that they're still the most profitable genre in video rental stores.

This type of economic clout means that a *lot* of people are watching other people screwing, whether they'll admit to it or not. So the question is transformed, what with video porn's pervasiveness, from *Why does splatterpunk have to include explicit sex?* to *How could explicit sex not creep into splatterpunk?*

Finally, there's a subversive allure in explicity sexuality; splatterpunk is nothing if not subversive. And, interestingly, there have been crossovers in the opposite direction. A recent underground video movement has, through such short films as R. Kern's *Fingered* or Nick Zedd's *Thrust in Me*, fused explicit sex and violence into a whole new subgenre: splatterporn.

Thus were the word, and informed concerns, of splatterpunk born—through cyberpunk, splatter films, punk rock, and adult videos.

6. ARTIFACTS & INFLUENCES

When you get right down to it, splatterpunk is really just a new word for an old attitude, one which knows no restraints, bows to no god, recognizes no boundaries. Which logically leads us to splatterpunk's deepest roots.

In the second section of this essay, I fixed the birth of splatterpunk in 1971, with the publication of *The Exorcist*. This may seem surprising, as the term itself was coined in the late eighties and its most highly visible authors hit their strides within that same decade. However, *The Exorcist* (the novel) was everything splatterpunk is today: explicit, adult, confrontational, and unafraid (whether or not it was literature is another issue). Most important, America had never seen any best seller like it, and *The Exorcist*'s influence on pop culture throughout the rest of the seventies was overwhelming. Therefore, as a handy line of demarcation, this marking of 1971 as the birth of splatterpunk seems demonstrably correct. (One could go back three years earlier to the furor raised by *Rosemary's Baby*, but even there, despite the satanic rape sequence, Polanski generally opted for suggestion over frankness).

On the other hand, in the sense that there has always been outlaw art, there also have always been splatterpunks.

As Clive Barker has pointed out, splatterpunk is subversion. It actively seeks to *do* something to you, to shake you out of your complacency. It does this with a great deal of energy, and explicitness, and glee (one shouldn't forget this "fun factor." Joyfully grossing out the reader is splatterpunk's most controversial—and endearing—trait).

Yet, excess and subversion have always been with us. In the ninth century B.C., Homer's *Odyssey* depicted not only an entire island of drug addicts (the lotus-eaters), but also one-eyed giant monsters who like to eat people (the Cyclops). In the fourteenth century, Dante (in *The Divine Comedy*) wasn't satisfied with putting his political enemies in hell; he dropped them into boiling pools of shit. Horace Walpole's 1764 *The Castle of Otranto*, the first gothic novel, and M. G. Lewis's 1796 *The Monk*, are two famous examples of eighteenth century artistic aberration.

And let's not forget the Bible.

This game could go on, of course. Shall we narrow our focus? The twentieth century has had no end of extreme artistic movements and personalities; why should horror, or science fiction, or fantasy, be any different?

Following the traumatic cataclysm of World War I, German expressionism reinvented the use of *chiaroscuro*; there was also Dada, surrealism, and Man Ray. The thirties saw Celine, Dali, Buñuel; the forties reacted against World War II with film noir.

By the fifties, the influences that culminated in splatterpunk really started cookin'. William Burroughs is usually left out of any splatterpunk discussion, but the man who created *Naked Lunch* (1959) and Dr. Benway ("And once I was caught short without instrument one and removed a uterine tumor with my teeth.") shouldn't be. William Gaines and E. C. Comics are usually left *in* splat histories, and with good reason—it's easy to see how E. C. Comics were a key influence, what with their gleeful, over-the-top, explicit *comtes cruel* masquerading as morality tales.

Then there's Robert Bloch, forever known as the "author of *Psycho*." Bloch's cornball humor never completely masked a fascination with aberrant psychology and lurid true-crime epistemology. And it was Bob Bloch who spectacularly merged the mystery novel with the still-mind-boggling pathology of splatterpunk inspiration Ed Gein (rhymes with "mean"). *Psycho*'s influence on splat, both through Bloch's book and Hitchcock's film, has been incalculable.

Then came the sixties . . . *whew*!

Drugs, politics, rock 'n' roll. Interpersonal relationships. Standing up for what you believe in. The Vietnam War. And television, television, television. If the fifties gave splatterpunk its raw materials, the sixties invested them with credibility. With its alternate life-styles and do-your-own-thing credo, there's more than a distant echo of the sixties counterculture in nineties splatterpunk (not to forget the influence of sixties literature. For example, the 1964 Hubert Selby, Jr., novel *Last Exit to Brooklyn* is fiercely energetic and uncompromisingly realistic. It portrays thugs, homosexuals, and hookers in scenes of graphic urban violence and degradation; who could forget Tra-La-La's massive gang rape?).

The sixties were also a Golden Age of International Cinema, and I've already noted the extreme influence of film on splat. Remember, this decade not only introduced many Americans to Fellini and Bergman and Godard, it also gave them *Night of the Living Dead* and *Blood Feast*, and Mario Bava's *Black Sunday*, as well. These last were low-budget wonders that decided to throw away the rule book; mirroring the carnage being brought into everyone's living room by the Vietnam War via television, Bava and his cohorts dropped those entrails right in our laps.

Then there's the literary front. Most splatterpunk detractors fail to recognize that those tilling this particularly gory field just possibly might have had a working knowledge of horror fiction's history. Obviously, splatterpunk did not gestate in a vacuum. The legacy of Poe, Hawthorne, Blackwood, Hodgson, Lovecraft, Smith, Howard, Derleth, and so forth is quite well known by many splat writers and, in some cases, is used by them.

It's just that splatterpunks feel this tradition has outlived its usefulness. Take this quote from David J. Schow in Jessie Horsting's article "The Splat Pack: Horror's Young Writers Spill Their Guts," published in the June 1988 issue of *Midnight Graffiti*:

> "A surprising number of horror writers are academicians. . . . Stephen King was a teacher, as were Peter Straub and Dennis Etchison. Charlie Grant was a teacher. Alan Ryan taught English for nine years. T. E. D. Klein—they have an entirely different tradition than we do. Clive Barker said his whole problem with the genre was that the writers never went far enough. And evidently that is now true for many people. It's not enough to see the shadow behind the door—people want to see what's making the shadow, what it looks like and how it comes apart.
>
> "But we wouldn't be trashing the classroom if they hadn't built the school" (pp. 32–33).

By the 1960s there were any number of writers trashing the classroom. Supreme among them were the funny, furious Harlan Ellison. In such stories as "I Have No Mouth, and I Must Scream" as well as "A Boy and His Dog," Ellison quite consciously took the entire genteel heritage of horror and science fiction and pulled it kicking and screaming into the "relevant" sixties. In fact, with his wildly inventive anger, explicitness, and courage, his insistent incorporation of the current cultural mulch into fiction that was soaring and scathing, Harlan Ellison truly can be called the spiritual godfather of splatterpunk.

Then came the seventies. Besides books like *The Exorcist* and *The Fog*, there were real-life mass murderers, like John Wayne Gacy. Or films like *Taxi Driver*. The Reverend Jim Jones. Underground comics like *Skull* and *Death Rattle*. *Dawn of the Dead* (Romero's second zombie film and an undeniable masterpiece of de-resensitization). *The Texas Chainsaw Massacre*. David Cronenberg. Bava's 1972 *Twitch of the Death Nerve* (the original template for the serial-killing genre typified by *Friday the 13th*). And always, over everything, the persistent shadow of Stephen King (suffice it to say that King not only made horror literature legitimate, he made it *popular*—and lucrative).

By the 1980s, with the explosion of mainstream horror fiction as a bankable commodity, with a revitalized rock music scene, with the widespread availability of previously difficult-to-see trash films via the new medium of videotape, with an unparalleled opportunity to experience and synthesize the full range of human art, history, and experience, splatterpunk was an inevitable accident just waiting to happen.

Even if, as we've seen, there always had been some preexisting form of the splatterpunk mentality in the first place.

7. CLIVE BARKER

Like surrealism before it, splatterpunk was a specific revolt against an artistic establishment—in our case, the traditional, meekly suggestive horror story. In a broader sense splat can also be seen as yet another example of anarchy erupting through (and because of) a period of social repression, specifically, the vicious conservatism of Ronald Reagan and Margaret Thatcher.

Enter Clive Barker, stage left.

Obviously goaded by the commercial success of Stephen King (and not so obviously influenced by the Liverpool-based fiction of Ramsey Campbell) Englishman Clive Barker, interestingly, arrived on the horror scene at the very moment that Maggie Thatcher was tightening her stranglehold on his country. As for why Barker was noticed . . . well, to put it crudely, it was sex and violence. Yet included in these excesses were Barker's broad-based knowledge of classical literature mixed with an even more evident love of trash movies and traditional theatrical techniques; the results were *Clive Barker's Books of Blood, Volumes One–Three* (1984).

I still remember the sense of queasy complicity I felt on first reading such Barkerian classics as "Rawhead Rex" (in which an ancient monster eats kids) and "Son of Celluloid" (a talking tumor goes to the movies); I was sickened, but I was *thrilled*. Here, finally, was a writer who turned on all the lights. And he did it with style, wit, and a peculiarly European sense of grace.

On a more superficial level, the *Books of Blood* were not only, well, *bloodier* than much of what had gone before, they also were packed with a veritable catalog of delectable diversions—hideous creatures pissing down the throats of clergymen ("Rawhead Rex"), bizzare creatures gang banging willing women ("The Skins of the Fathers"), glistening eyeballs being slipped into the cunt of Marilyn Monroe ("Son of Celluloid").

Yet if Clive Barker's only major talent lay in being epically gross, he would have been as easily dismissed as such fellow countrymen as Shaun Hutson (*Slugs*) or Guy N. Smith (*The Sucking Pit*). What truly elevated the *Books of Blood* were a vigorous imagination, a fierce intelligence, a sophisticated (and bleak) worldview, and a truly radical sexuality.

Not enough has been made of this last trait. Barker's obvious fascination with homosexuality, S&M, golden showers, and so on—indeed, with almost any form of sexual "perversion"—reoccurs in his fiction often enough to suggest a hidden manifesto. Just as prominently featured as his scenes of explicit physical carnage, this rampant sexuality is an ongoing concern, from the gay male lovers of "In the Hills, the Cities" (one of Barker's finest works) to the necrophilic S&M zombies of the films *Hellraiser* and *Hellbound* (and its companion story "The Hellbound Heart").

An example which combines both Barker's palpable sense of flesh and his surreal libido is "Jacqueline Ess: Her Will and Testament." Beautifully written, "Ess" has undertow as well as flash; its perfectly realized encapsulation of contemporary female rage provides a sturdy substructure to support its excesses.

Jacqueline Ess is a despairing housewife—bored, frustrated, furious at the male condescension she see everywhere around her—who awakens from a suicide attempt to find that whatever she thinks, becomes reality. This newfound power is exercised in ways as diverse as crushing her wayward husband (without laying a finger on him) to forming female breasts on a patronizing male physician. Finally, Jacqueline literally kills herself with tenderness:

> He lay down beside her, and the feel of his body against hers was not unpleasant.
> She touched his head. Her joints were stiff, the movements painful, but she wanted to draw his face up to hers. He came, smiling, into her sight, and they exchanged kisses.
> My God, she thought, we are together.
> And thinking they were together, her will was made flesh.

Under his lips her features dissolved, becoming the red sea he'd dreamt of, and washing up over his face, that was itself dissolving; common waters made of thought and bone.

Her keen breasts pricked him like arrows; his erection, sharpened by her thought, killed her in return with his only thrust. Tangled in a wash of love they thought themselves extinguished, and were. (In *Books of Blood*, Vol. Two, p. 116, Berkley Books, 1986.)

The above not only exhibits Barker's poetic gifts, it puts to sleep the cliché that splatterpunk is worthless juvenile ejaculation. There's an evocative, first-rate talent at work here, one aware of nuance and subtlety; Barker can *write*. (Commendably, he also routinely creates strong female characters.)

But there are always downsides, of course. The *Books of Blood* and subsequent Barkerian efforts, such as *Cabal, Hellraiser, Hellbound, Weaveworld, Nightbreed*, and *The Great and Secret Show*, occasionally display a distressing inclination toward thin characterizations. Perhaps this is a byproduct of Barker's furious creative pace; he is nothing if not prolific.

Yet Barker's best fiction exhibits a technical sophistication and virtuosity that lend comparisons to the work of such countrymen as John Le Carre and Graham Greene. Density, maturity, complex and knowing morality—all are Barker/Le Carre/Greene trademarks. There are other, less noticeable parallels, too. For instance, Graham Greene has always clearly marked his work as "entertainment" or "novel," classifications indicating fiction that is to be read for either enjoyment or edification. Barker himself once told me he makes this distinction in his own work; "The Midnight Meat Train," for example, is clearly an entertainment. "Jacqueline Ess," just as clearly, is not.

The *Books of Blood*, then, deserved their success. But who could have foreseen the consequences? It's an interesting commentary on the immediacy of current world media (and a testament to Barker's industry) to realize that Barker went from cult personality to international celebrity in the space of six short years. Stephen King's classic quote, "I have seen the future of horror, and its name is Clive Barker," was only the opening salvo in the ongoing barrage of shooting the latest Barker offering right to your local bookstore/theater/mailbox.

For make no mistake; Clive Barker is now the most commercially successful writer utilizing splatterpunk techniques. In fact, much like Stephen King, he has become something of a brand name, with each novel or story or film topping the previous effort in recognition and revenue.

The Damnation Game (1985), which followed the *Books of Blood* and was Barker's first novel, is a Faustian tale of a wealthy industrialist's attempts to elude a soul snatcher. Yet despite its commendable scope, ambition, and Barkerian flourishes (including a hallucinatory, atmostphere-drenched prologue set in a post–World War II Warsaw), *The Damnation Game*'s total effect was less than the sum of its parts. Barker then took the horror community off guard with *Weaveworld* (1987), a larger, more coherent, and satisfying novel. Concerned with an entire world hidden within the loom of an ordinary rug, *Weaveworld* nevertheless (and in spite of its grotesque touches) fell more into the epic fantasy genre popularized by J. R. R. Tolkien than the straight horror novel, confounding the expectations of those anticipating another exploration of the gleeful carnographic landscapes mapped out by the *Books of Blood*.

Barker's popularity continued its ascendancy with a concurrent broadening into other media. At this point in his career he moved into film, writing, producing, and/or directing *Hellraiser* (1987), *Hellbound* (1988), and *Nightbreed* (1990), projects described as "Hammer Films Meet the Marquis de Sade." Since then Barker has kept his literary hand in, writing the novella "The Hellbound Heart" (1987) and the novel *Cabal* (1988). His recent, more substantive *The Great and Secret Show* (1989) is a fantasy/horror story/love fable concerning, as Barker puts it, "Hollywood, sex and Armageddon."

Despite his ever-increasing celebrity and signs that he may be spreading himself thin, Clive Barker remains an artist of intimidating resources. Quite simply, he is one of the finest horror writers ever to grace the genre; informed, witty, technically superior, disciplined, and imaginative. Not to mention relentless. And Barker was clearly the next logical step on the ladder supporting Stephen King. For where King is essentially a literary conservative, stressing nuclear families and all other manner of American middle-class virtues (including a near-reactionary fondness for such horror fiction clichés as *The Shining*'s haunted house and *Thinner*'s gypsy curse), Barker is an artistic revolutionary, drawn to the outcast (Boone in *Cabal*), the fringe figure (Marty Strauss in *The Damnation Game*), and the outlaw (Ezra Garvey in "The Madonna"). Yes, Stephen King may lead his readers right to the edge of the contemporary horror pit; Barker, cackling, tosses them in.

So—here was a writer who went the full nine yards (and then some!), and managed to do it with wit and style and intelligence. Not only that, Barker managed to get filthy rich in the process.

What an irresistible combination!

Other exciting talents were on their way.

8. JOHN SKIPP AND CRAIG SPECTOR

It's just not accurate to contend that splatterpunk began with Clive Barker, or that those who since have been dubbed splatterpunks merely springboarded off Barker's success. Indeed, such seminal splatterpunkian works as Joe R. Lansdale's *The Nightrunners* (1987) or Skipp and Spector's *The Light at the End* (1986) either were written long before or were already in gestation prior to Barker's emergence. But since the word *splatterpunk* was coined *after* Barker became a household word, there's been a tendency in the popular press toward labeling those who've arrived since the *Books of Blood* as obvious Barker wannabes.

Nothing could be farther from the truth. These people would have come into their own under any circumstances.

Chief among these post-*Blood* talents are John Skipp and Craig Spector, collectively known as "The Boys." Intense and articulate, ready to go to the mat for their principles, Skipp and Spector are, next to Clive Barker, the most highly successful, high-profile members of The Splat Pack.

But one of the dangers of assuming a label like splatterpunk is that it constricts as well as categorizes. Speaking in the British horror film fanzine *Samhain* (June–July 1989), Spector has this to say about the S word: "It's just a label that's useful for making people aware of us. There aren't any rigid definitions . . . because that would be limiting. We're just a bunch of guys doing shit and talking to each other" (p. 10).

Throughout their fiction, Skipp and Spector have been doing much more than just talking to each other. Their first novel was 1986's *The Light at the End*, and like the *Books of Blood*, it seemed to have come out of nowhere (although The Boys had actually already been writing a number of short stories well before this—works such as the 1982 story "The Long Ride," which was collected with other S & S stories and tied together with a new framing device in *Dead Lines*, published in 1989). Fast, furious, and funny—while technically more than a bit shaky— *The Light at the End* detailed a very contemporary vampire named Rudy Pasko. He haunts the subways of New York, a vain, egotistical creature who ultimately is eradicated by a motley group of Manhattanites.

Once one penetrated the stylistic crudeness, it became dramatically clear that *The Light at the End* was out to systematically update the vampire myth, primarily by refusing to indulge in the slightly musty formalism that has always dogged this particular symbol (recreating the nineteenth-century drawing-room elegance of *Dracula*'s Bram Stoker is still a going concern, however; witness Anne Rice's Vampire Lestat novels). The more one read, the clearer it became that *The Light* was after something other than stakes and crucifixes.

Skipp and Spector zeroed in on Manhattan's working class; no counts or aristocrats here, only credible Everymen. *The Light* took a clear stance against crime, urban angst, and desensitization, never flinched at violence, and rejected any form of hypocrisy. In the process, The Boys also created a gritty, most authentic vision of New York hell. The way its story was told— energetically and profanely, with a suffusion of flashy cinematic techniques—one finished with the impression that *The Light at the End* was printed with amphetamines, not ink.

Next up for Skipp and Spector was a novelized tie-in to the (also vampire-oriented) film *Fright Night*. But for their second original book, *The Cleanup* (1987), The Boys returned to Manhattan. And it quickly became evident that not only had the general quality of their writing greatly improved, but the stylistic techniques and moral concerns of *The Light* weren't contrived by one-shot wonders. In other words, it was now clear that The Boys possessed an authentic voice.

Much like Barker's "Jacqueline Ess," *The Cleanup* centers on primal wish fulfillment. Billy Rowe, its central character, is an aging rock musician down on his luck and coming up against his own mortality. Suddenly granted enormous paranormal powers by a mysterious stranger named Christopher, Rowe begins a one-man crusade against crime; his holy mission is "the cleanup" of Manhattan's mean streets.

Both *The Light at the End* and *The Cleanup* are large, sprawling books populated by a believable host of characters and revealing an excitingly *alive* portrait of New York's underbelly. By their third novel, *The Scream* (1988), concerning a satanic rock band, The Boys cemented a growing reputation as splatterpunk's premier rock 'n' rollers. There was a demonstrable beat to their fiction; you could dance to it, and if you listened to the lyrics, you just might come away with something to think about.

The fact that both Skipp and Spector actually *are* rock musicians certainly has something to do with the energy, style, and attitudes of their work:

> "I love rock 'n' roll," Skipp mentions in the *Samhain* interview, "and it's not intrinsically bad or good, it's a neutral force. A band's rhetoric isn't as important to me as what they do. Personally, I don't care how much a band talks about sacrificing groupies to the devil and sucking out their eyeballs, it's when they actually do it that I have a problem" (p. 10).

Skipp's clear delineation between a music's message and how one acts on it is a critical key to understanding his and Spector's work. Much as they may feel uncomfortable with the tag, The Boys are clearly the most *moral* of the splatterpunks; beneath the heat and jangle of their prose lies a dead seriousness of intent, a fiction rich with moral choices, and a cumulative celebration of the life principle. This is a Very Good Thing, for like Barker and his kinky explicitness before them, if all The Boys had brought to the splatterpunk party were Fender guitars and Pig-Nose amplifiers, they quickly would have been forgotten.

This rockin' splatterpunk quality was perhaps best explained in the finest critical article yet published on Skipp and Spector's work, a critique which appeared in the now-defunct fanzine *The Horror Show* (a fanzine being a small press, privately published magazine). The article, "Extreme Measures: The Fiction of John Skipp and Craig Spector," was authored by R. S. Hadji, who conjures up a host of incisive insights, among them this consideration of The Boys' stylistic methods:

> Dissonance can be found throughout Skipp and Spector's writings, producing a seeming cacophony which actually represents the unharmonized music of life. Rather than impose an orderly world-view, they prefer to let natural rhythms shape the fiction, embracing variations, contradictions and ambiguities. This celebration of diversity threatens sensory overload and the energies released are so intense as to elevate their reality to what could be more accurately described as a hyperreality. (p. 19)

You can also get something like this in the writings of Skipp and Spector; the appearance of a massive demon at a heavy metal concert:

> The face was here.
> It emerged the size of a weather balloon, with a skin about as thick, growing thicker by the second. Its head wasn't coated in slime, its face *was* the slime, as viscous as the skin of a soap bubble. It was an enormous outline, filling itself in; translucent, swirling, mutating a million times a second like some humongous claymation creation, boiling and spitting and laughing insane howling rage as it became zygote, then fetus, then baby, then toddler child teen adult ancient twisted inhuman mockery of the world it was struggling to gain hold of. (*The Scream*, p. 402)

The Scream was The Boys' third novel and is generally regarded to be one of their lesser efforts. I disagree; this is the book Skipp and Spector were born to write. The dramatic canvas is writ large, the thematic concerns are multilayered and commendable, and the technical quality is light-years ahead of *The Light at the End* (in fact, by this point Skipp and Spector had cemented an enviable, multisensory style very much their own).

Focusing on a primal good-versus-evil conflict symbolized by contrasting rock groups (the Jake Hamer Band being the semi fucked up but demonstrably human Good band; the Scream being the totally fucked, barely human, very *Bad* band), *The Scream* is Skipp and Spector's most ambitious work to date. Its sprawling cast of characters struggles over drugs, teleevangelism, parental responsibility, abortion, and the First Amendment . . . all the while immersing the reader in a sensual, skull-pounding, truly *right* re-creation of basic rock 'n' roll and the arena concert experience. (*The Scream*'s primary error is structural; fully two-thirds of the book builds to a carefully orchestrated outbreak of violence at a Rock Aid concert before downshifting and building to a *second* cataclysmic musical event. One would have sufficed.)

Skipp and Spector's next effort was originally titled *Nightmare New York* but ultimately was published (in early 1989) as *Deadlines*. It was their first short story collection. That same year also saw *Book of the Dead*, one of 1989's finest original horror anthologies.

This time working as editors for others' material, The Boys took the "shared universe" concept so familiar to fantasy anthologies and gave it a radical twist; *Book of the Dead* is based on George Romero's *Living Dead* films, and it allows any number of authors (from Stephen King to Joe R. Lansdale) to build upon, reinvent, and otherwise pay homage to the zombie mythos first put forth in Romero's trilogy. Expectedly explicit, but surprisingly well balanced and with the emphasis on excellence, *Book of the Dead* points The Boys in gratifying new directions; one anticipates their next editorial effort.

Dead also contains one of the best summations yet written of Skipp and Spector's goals and techniques; not surprisingly, it was penned by The Boys themselves. Titled "On Going Too Far; or Flesh-Eating Fiction: New Hope for the Future," this general introduction to *Book of the Dead* touches on Skipp and Spector's influences and reveals their thoughts on film, television, and violence. "Going Too Far" also contains well-considered, thoughtful explications on the artistic relevance of explicit violence. I've already written of Level-One splatterpunk (pure effect) and Level Two (real-world concerns); let me now introduce you to Level Three (resensitization):

> . . . the third level: the level of gestalt, of fusion and reintegration. At this point, you can no longer detach; the unknown has become tangible and all too real, beyond cheapening on the one hand or denial on the other. You can see the wet hole and the charred stump, yes; but beyond that—and in vital, visceral conjunction—you can know how it feels to be a part of it. ("On Going Too Far," in *Book of the Dead*, p. 10)

The Bridge is The Boys' upcoming novel. It is generally concerned with ecology. Specifically, I'm sure it will address the perennial splatterpunk's concern of going too far.

9. THEY'RE NOT THE SAME

The myth that all splatterpunk stories embrace the same techniques, subtexts, and concerns dies hard. The fiction of John Skipp and Craig Spector, Clive Barker, David J. Schow, Joe R. Lansdale, Ray Garton, and so on, is still often and indiscriminately lumped together; undue emphasis is placed on their shared kineticism and unyielding explicitness (which would be a valid point, if it weren't the *only* point that most critics can come up with).

Yet even the most casual reading of what's loosely deemed splatterpunk displays clearly marked dissimilarities in style and intent among its various practitioners. Perhaps the best way to clarify the complex and clearly individualistic approaches of writers working within this area is to contrast the work of splatterpunk's most successful practitioners, the three men I've just cited: Barker and Skipp and Spector.

All three may subscribe to a clinical (some may say forensic) love of detail, and all three may invoke the same pure gonzo rush you feel when you *know* the roller-coaster car is gonna shoot off its tracks.

After that, the comparisons end.

First, take point of view. As Lawrence Person writes in his *Nova Express* article "The Splatterpunks: The Young Turks at Horror's Cutting Edge" (one of the handiest overviews on this subject): "Though Barker's prose is as sharp as a knife, it is frequently as cold" (p. 19).

Cold? Well, "warmth" certainly isn't a quality one associates with Clive Barker. (Still, his best fiction is refreshingly free of bogus sentiment.) Perhaps a more rewarding critical inquiry may be aimed at Barker's fundamental outlook, for in spite of his spectacularly warped imagery, deadpan black comedy, and morbidly fetishistic sexuality, Clive Barker is essentially a nihilist. As Lacey (a teenage boy whose soul is transferred to a pig's) says in "Pig Blood Blues": "This is the state of the beast—to eat and be eaten" (in *Books of Blood*, Vol. One, p. 121, Berkley Books, 1986).

Throughout the *Books of Blood* (and, by extension, most of Barker's other works), characters are fundamentally motivated by appetite: power (Whitehead in *The Damnation Game*), sex (Jerome in "The Age of Desire"), greed (Shadwell in *Weaveworld*). Inevitably, weakness consumes. Innocence is no defense, either; witness the devoured children of "Rawhead Rex." This notion of life as a simple snack on the cosmic food chain, of personality inevitably digested by nothingness, clearly reflects Barker's fascination with negation. In his quasi-Calvinistic universe, Evil not only triumphs, it's *meant* to triumph.

Now contrast Barker's nihilism with the surprisingly traditional moral universe of Skipp and Spector. From *The Light at the End* to *The Scream*, Skipp and Spector's ethics remain consistently Judeo-Christian—good conquers evil, and love conquers all (a simplified reduction of The Boys' more complex philosophy, to be sure, but still a valid one).

Skipp and Spector's preference for classic religious myth lies in marked contrast to Barker's wholehearted embrace of the heart of darkness. Whereas the climax of Barker's "The Hellbound Heart" (and its cinematic adaption *Hellraiser*) sees the character of Frank torn to pieces by the Cenobites, the disparate group protagonist of Skipp and Spector's *Light at the End* (concentration camp survivor, young messenger, weak-willed boyfriend/girlfriend, and so on) vanquishes the vampiric Rudy Pasko through the strength of their communal friendship. Where Barker's *The Damnation Game* has the dangerous multimillionaire Joseph Whitehead constantly reiterate that *"Nothing* is essential," the ultimately doomed David of Skipp and Spector's "Gentlemen" still can declare passionately:

> Part of my heart sincerely believed that she would wake up one day with the realization that no one would ever love her like I did. No one else could be so tender, so compassionate, so understanding. No one else would bear with her through her tragedies and madness, devote themselves so selflessly and so completely to her needs. (In *Dead Lines*, p. 189, 1989.)

Whatever else you think about that passage, it's definitely not the work of nihilists.

Then there's characterization.

Barker's approach to his human creations is that they're fundamentally less interesting than the baleful creatures with which they inevitably will interact. Typically it is the *monster* (within and without) who is Barker's true protagonist. As Barker told interviewer Tim Caldwell in *Film Threat*, "I like the idea of giving monsters heroic status." (No. 19, p. 19).

This preoccupation finds its fullest flowering in Barker's film *Nightbreed* (1990; based on his 1988 novel *Cabal*). Here the usual symbols of social stability (psychiatrist, priest, policeman) are shown to be hopelessly and insanely corrupt. Only the fascinatingly grotesque inhabitants of the charnel city of Midean are invested with attractive human traits—and to become a citizen there, you have to die first.

As invigorating as this inversion of the classical hero can be (and Barker knows his classics; witness his recurring fondness for Jacobean revenge tragedies), the danger lies in fleshing out your monsters at the expense of your people. Unfortunately, Barker occasionally commits the sin of two-dimensionality. Nowhere is this more apparent than in his films *Hellraiser* and

Nightbreed; does anyone remember the *human* protagonists here? Nope—most of us recall Pinhead and the Breed.

Overall, then, Barker's characters are more acted on than actors, walking targets stumbling toward the pit. And since his fiction frequently seems more inventive than moving, imagistic rather than empathic, it's fair to say that Barker's art primarily springs from his fertile intellect and enviable imagination. (As I've said before—here it comes again!—none of the other splatterpunks can touch Barker's astonishing gift for truly breathtaking weirdness. And did I mention he's also the most obviously urbane and sophisticated writer in this group?)

Skipp and Spector, however, write from their hearts. Fortunately, their intellects are keen, and The Boys' ability to portray believable characters set against instantly recognizable urban landscapes is matched only by Stephen King. In fact, King seems to be one of their seminal influences. As Skipp told *Samhain* (in a somewhat misquoted context; with Skipp's input, I've corrected the transcriptional errors originally attendant to this piece):

> "It was the Maine Man who inspired [me] to start thinking seriously about being a writer.
>
> "One day while I was writing a political novel, my good friend Leslie Sternbergh came in and tried to convince me to read *The Stand.* I was saying, 'Nah, this guy's a best-selling author, he can't be any good . . . just another asshole.' I was that snobbish. But Leslie insisted, saying, 'No. You should read this. You're a lot alike.' Eventually I gave in and of course she was right, I loved it, discovered that King and I could shatter the same taboos . . . and I thought, 'I can do that!' Now I'm really proud of King, I adore him." (So much so that The Boys apparently share King's fondness for traditional horror devices; vampires in *The Light at the End*, wish-fulfillment in *The Cleanup*, demons in *The Scream*.) (June–July 1989, p. 10)

King-like, a great deal of Skipp and Spector's success comes from the fictional characters they create in their own work. From the vulnerable physical-abuse victim LeeAnn in "Gentlemen" to the confused rock musician Pete in *The Scream*, Skipp and Spector continue to assemble some of the most textured, recognizably human characters in splatterpunk. Despite a persistent fascination with the idea of evil as an immortal, transcendent spirit (a concern that begins with *The Light at the End* and continues in a straight line to The Boys' abortive first-draft screenplay for

A Nightmare on Elm Street 5: The Dream Child), Skipp and
Spector clearly identify with their human characters. They in-
tend their readers to identify with them as well.

Yet, the clearest line of demarcation between Barker and Skipp
and Spector is political.

The main plank of Barker's agenda seems to be radical sexuality, with a recurrent examination of the practices of homosexuality and S&M. Such sadomasochistic or homoerotic icons
as fellatio, golden showers, public defecation, and bondage regularly appear in works like *The Damnation Game*, "Sex, Death
and Starshine," "Rawhead Rex," and "The Hellbound Heart."
So-called normal heterosexual activity is certainly not absent
from Barker's work (after all, it is heterosexual passion which
fuels *Hellraiser*), but it is just as certainly not uppermost in his
mind; when male-female sex arises in a Clive Barker story, more
often than not it takes the form of someone getting a blowjob
from a corpse ("Sex, Death and Starshine," again).

Intriguingly, these "deviant" preoccupations also have influenced Barker's sense of graphic design. By way of explanation,
I refer to the fact that Barker is an artist as well as a writer,
with particular talents for sketching, painting, and drawing (Barker himself illustrated the British hardcover dust jackets for the
Books of Blood). And in the Film Threat interview mentioned
earlier, Barker told Caldwell: "My favorite reviews of HELL-
RAISER have been the alternate reviews. There have been some
wonderful S & M magazines that have done great reviews of
it . . . in fact . . . specialized magazines [that is, S&M ones]
were highly influential in the design of the Cenobites" (p. 18).

Skipp and Spector's concerns likewise include an endorsement
of freer sexuality. But their politics are complex, with an overall
agenda that mirrors a late-sixties-like liberalism. The Boys embrace feminism, drugs, racial harmony, and social tolerance toward the unusual, the eccentric, the strange. Basically, then, and
in contrast to Barker, Skipp and Spector's general concern seems
to be one of functional humanism.

Interestingly, they often couch this humanism in multiple viewpoints. Skipp and Spector present so many disparate points of
view in their books that the end effect is one of multiple options.
It's as if The Boys were saying, Look, you may have decided
what *we're* all about, but just remember—there are lots of
choices out there.

The Scream clearly demonstrates this tactic. This novel's supernatural locus may well be a rock band capable of calling up

demons and making eyeless zombies out of its audience, but its *focus* is on its sprawling cast of human characters (everyone from disenfranchised Vietnam vets to a drugged-out groupie who, in a typical Skipp and Spector now-we're-gonna-mess-with-your-preconceptions ploy, is saved from a poolside massacre through the Divine Intervention of none other than Jesus H. Christ). Each *Scream* character is clearly given their due, whether right or wrong, good or evil. This multiplicity of belief not only echoes the real world, of course, but allows for the reader's own choice of moral focus.

Or, as R. S. Hadji writes in "Extreme Measures":

> To their credit, Skipp and Spector refrain from providing the "right" answers. Or "left." They practice what they preach and leave all options open. Even assholes get their say. . . . And why not? Skipp and Spector are those same men who dedicated *Light* to "The Creator, Who gives us the Light by which we more clearly see the Darkness."
>
> And meant every word. Their God is a god of ambiguity and contradiction, and His covenant is personal (p. 18).

In his own "Splatterpunks" article, Lawrence Person concludes with these comparisons:

> Where Barker's work is grim, Skipp and Spector's is droll, where Barker's characterization is shaky, Skipp and Spector's is vibrant. And where the S Guys insert recognizable terrors into the fabric of everyday life (vampires, demons, etc.), Barker creates Brave New Horrors and landscapes that far surpass most people's wildest imaginations (*Nova Express*, p. 23).

You could also say that The Boys are heavily into life, whereas Barker is heavily into death.

Not that either is necessarily the better approach, particularly regarding the infinite warp and variety of contemporary art.

But they *are* radically different forms of splatterpunk.

Just as there are radically different kinds of splatterpunk writers.

10. DAVID J. SCHOW

The cover blurb on David J. Schow's *Lost Angels* (a 1990 collection of his short stories) trumpets "Five Dark Tales From

The Father Of Splatterpunk." One certainly can't argue with this claim to splatterpunk's paternity, since, as we've seen, he invented the word. And as the term *splatterpunk* is short, catchy, and definitely marketable, Schow obviously knows a good promotional tool when he sees one.

He certainly *seems* media savvy. It was Schow who continually appeared at the initial photo sessions highlighting splatterpunk writers, Schow who fired off articles to *Fangoria* on the making of his *Leatherface* film, Schow who explained the splatterpunk philosophy to *Midnight Graffiti*, Schow who was interviewed in the "Special David J. Schow Issue!" of *Weird Tales*, Schow who was dubbed "The Father Of Splatterpunk."

Yet a flair for self-promotion can breed certain dangers. Despite a varied and impressive body of work, David J. Schow is probably better known—as Lawrence Person described him on page 25 of his *Nova Express* article—as splatterpunk's "chief polemist." This is a shame, for he's actually one of explicit fiction's most gifted authors.

Schow's shrewd media familiarity apparently springs from the hard-won experience of his early career. This phase included writing film criticism for magazines like *Cinefantastique*, doing anonymous rewrites for science fiction film books, and delivering novelized tie-ins to television shows like "Miami Vice." In the field of splatterpunk, Schow has given us one novel (*The Kill Riff*, in 1988), two collections of short stories and novellas (*Seeing Red* and *Lost Angels*, in 1990), one edited anthology (*Silver Scream* in 1988), and one screenplay (*Leatherface: The Texas Chainsaw Massacre III*, in 1989). Schow also has placed numerous short stories in magazines like *Midnight Graffiti*, and the defunct *Twilight Zone*, as well as anthologies like *Book of the Dead*. He's even cowritten, with Jeffrey Frentzen, a television history book titled *The Outer Limits Companion* (could this acclaimed TV series have been an early splatterpunkian influence?).

Stylistically, Schow's fiction is studded with dense, layered prose that mercurially shifts between balls-to-the-walls explicitness and achingly tender sentiment; overall, his work is surprisingly protean. Story by story, you simply don't know what to expect next.

There's thematic diversity, rigorous plotting, precise attention to language. Unexpected sweetness. Resentment, ambition, darkness, dread. All of these qualities teem through Schow's work; for someone who's been labeled The Father Of Splatterpunk, Schow also seems intent on confounding audience expectations

by writing quality fiction that refuses to restrict itself to superficial exercises in carnographic explicitness. (Allow a short digres-
sion here. The word *carnographic* first cropped up in the late
eighties in various essays on splatter films and splatterpunks. It
signifies explicit violence in the same way *pornographic* signifies
explicit sex. It's a word I love, and in the best of all possible
worlds, even Dan Quayle would use it. Incorrectly, probably.)

The Kill Riff, Schow's first—and so far only—novel, is a good
example of his mutant complexity. Superficially it resembles *The
Scream* without the supernatural element. *The Kill Riff* also
seems to be (incorrectly, once you read it) an antirock screed
ghostwritten by Tipper Gore; when a young girl is crushed underfoot at Whip Hand's heavy metal rock concert, her father
Lucas Ellington begins to systematically pick off Whip Hand's
band members, one by one.

The setup here seems obvious. Yet Schow so consistently shifts
his tones and attitudes that, as Richard Gehr points out in his
article "More Gore," "For a writing so full of rock 'n' roll attitude, the new horror is often curiously ambivalent, or ironic,
regarding the music's morality. . . . [In *The Kill Riff*] Schow goes
out of his way to detail a certain backstage glamour and decadence, then has his incest-impassioned father bring it all down"
(*The Village Voice*, February 6, 1990, p. 57).

Yet, despite its subject matter (or perhaps because of its less-
than-stereotypical treatment), *The Kill Riff* was not a smash
success. The novel's relatively lukewarm reception did not stop
Schow from forging forward, however, or from constantly shifting emotional gears within the overall framework of his work.

Contrast this nasty bit from "Jerry's Kids Meet Wormboy":

> A long, gray-green rope of intestine had paid out behind the
> geek. It gawped with dull hunger, then did an absurd little push-
> up in order to bite it. Teeth crunched through geek-gut and gelid
> black paste evacuated with a blatting fart noise. Sploot! (In *Book
> of the Dead*, p. 360.)

with the sly irony involved in a deranged ex-teleevangelist naming
his undead congregation of flesh-eating zombies after the Three
Stooges (also from "Jerry's Kids"):

> Back in the days before it had become synonymous with smut,
> the Right Reverend Jerry had enjoyed comedy. Upon his name-
> less deacons he had bestowed the names of famous funnymen.

As the ramrods wore out or were retired, Jerry's list of names dwindled. Just now, the deacons in charge were Moe, Curly, W.C., and Fatty (p. 366).

But just when you think Schow's all about satire and hip zombie wit, he'll do the seemingly impossible, executing a beautifully stylistic 180-degree right turn. The antithesis of "Jerry's Kids" is to be found in the splatter-free (and deeply affecting) "Monster Movies," an unbashed love song to late-night Creature Features, childhood nostalgia, and contemporary romance—not to mention the personal epiphanies inherent in having your first letter printed in a magazine called *Famous Monsters of Filmland*:

At the Hilltop Liquors magazine rack, Jason discovered that his long-ago fan letter to FAMOUS MONSTERS had proven worthy of print. His legs shook and turned unreliable; this was literally the first time in his short life that anything this enormous had coalesced into printed history around *him*. He was ultimately forced to walk his bike partway home, pausing at every intersection to page back to where his name was writ large in bold black and savor his own words, inscribed with monkish patience months before, over and over, until what he had to say on his college-ruled paper was purged of the tiniest error. (In *Lost Angels*, pp. 226–227.)

This is splatterpunk as shared memory, inscribed with love and lyricism, refuting the notion that this particular brand of writing is merely a literature of illiteracy and effect.

Moving on to a quick overview of Schow's corpus reveals two recurring motifs. One is an ongoing fascination with the dubious moral landscapes of Hollywood (including its lowlife losers), resulting in such well-observed short stories as "Pamela's Get," "The Falling Man," and "Graffiti" (this isn't this story's title, by the way; I've chosen to call it "Graffiti" because this novella is headed only by a graphic resembling spray-painted graffiti). The aforementioned "Monster Movies," "Red Light," and "Brass" indicate a second, more sentimental concern: a near-obsessional belief in the redemptive powers of romantic heterosexual love.

Yet, predictably, Schow seems to be most closely identified with his occasional forays into explicitness; having been dubbed The Father Of Splatterpunk may have something to do with that. (Unfortunately, it's also predictable that too much has been made of splat's fondness for frankness, when unbridled *enthusiasm* is splatterpunk's truly common trait; Schow, Barker, and the rest *love* what they're doing.) However, the fluctuating emotional and stylistic tonalities of Schow's fiction should underscore the fact that his candidness is simply another tool—albeit a very sharp one—in an impressively large box of tricks.

So, right next to Schow's graphic descriptions of zombies munching on their own entrails is a wicked sense of wit. Hand-in-glove with his relentless depiction of chainsaw massacres goes a uniquely passionate tenderness (one lurking behind even his most confrontational work). And among his more important accomplishments are the 1987 World Fantasy Award–winning short story "Red Light," sort of a modern-day variant on Fritz Leiber's "The Girl With the Hungry Eyes," wherein a beautiful young model finds her soul being sucked away by the very media that nourishes it. Schow also edited the stellar *Silver Scream* (1988), still the best motion picture/horror story theme anthology ever put together. Period.

David J. Schow is currently working on a second novel, *The Shaft*. As one of the most wide ranging and surprisingly romantic of the splatterpunks, his multifaceted, multimedia talents probably will catapult him far beyond the usual rank and file of mundane horror writers. They'd better; Schow writes likes an angel.

11. THE USUAL SUSPECTS

The actual number of writers who unabashedly embrace the splatterpunk label is quite small. Most of what routinely passes for splatterpunk today is generated by a larger group of writers whose occasional splatterpunk story or novel is a deviant by-product of their daily output. These works may clearly reflect the splatterpunk attitude, but their authors still vehemently resist the splatterpunk label.

For reasons of clarity, true splatterpunks have dubbed themselves "The Splat Pack" (a satiric reference to Hollywood's "Brat Pack," composed of such young, undertalented, overpaid, and overexposed actors as Charlie Sheen and Rob Lowe). At the core of The Splat Pack are really only Schow and Skipp and Spector (Clive Barker has never officially aligned himself with this group). As I have shown, these three writers explicitly apply splatterpunk techniques to film, literature, and music.

However, a number of other authors have drifted in and out of the splatterpunk sphere of influence, some intentionally, some kicking and screaming. Writers who occasionally are tagged with the splatterpunk label—and vociferously deny same—include Joe R. Lansdale, Ray Garton, and Richard Christian Matheson.

In any event, for your clarification and edification, the following is a quick compendium of borderline and don't-wannabe splatterpunks. Plus a few surprises.

MARK ARNOLD Mark Arnold's contribution to Schow's movie-themed *Silver Scream*, "Pilgrims to the Cathedral," is a long, sometimes rambling, but cumulatively powerful novella with strong echoes of Lansdale's *The Drive-In*. In Arnold's story, the Zone is a derelict, remote drive-in theater, first refurbished before slowly acquiring its own sentience. Initially this emerging intelligence takes the form of the Zone's screens magically creating such unknown masterpieces as the sixteen-hour Alejandro Jadorowsky–David Lynch collaboration of *Dune*; lucky Zone attendees also get to see Roman Polanski's version of *The Shining* and an adaptation of *Cleopatra* by Ed Wood, Jr. But as the national attitude of America shifts inward and begins to consume itself (via Reaganomics, among other things), the Zone turns nasty, resulting in a spectacular orgy of splat.

This cinematic-sociopolitical fable packs enough power to make it an instant classic. Other works by Arnold include a story for the upcoming *Book of the Dead 2* (yep, the sequel), and, with Laura Simpson, a splatterpunk comedy-novella titled "Zooey and Koala Blue." "Zooey's" main characters are (among others), David J. Schow, Clive Barker, John Skipp, and Craig Spector, all involved in a wild chase through nightime Los Angeles (incidentally, "Zooey" was an original submission that just missed being included in *Splatterpunks*).

Mark Arnold first made his mark as an editor of such books as *Elsewhere* (volumes one through three; volume one won a World Fantasy Award in 1982) and *Borderland*. He was calling himself Mark Alan Arnold then. His nonfiction has appeared in the *New York Daily News*, *Omni*, and the late *Twilight Zone Magazine*.

A social realist with a keen eye for pop culture and the semi-losers who drift along the edges of the American Dream, Arnold will surely continue to be heard from in the future.

J. G. BALLARD   A British writer who became associated with New Wave science fiction in the late sixties, J(ames) G(raham) Ballard is thus only tangentially aligned to splatterpunk. But his literature has subsequently crossed over into a number of different genres (mainstream, horror, biography, the avant-garde); further, his obsessional concerns with insanity and apparent reality (and the manner in which technology and the media have warped those perceptions) shows him to be at least a kindred spirit of the splatterpunk. If not a first cousin.

"The Assassination of John F. Kennedy Considered as a Downhill Motor Race," Ballard's 1967 short story, kaleidoscopically fractured national despair into a barrage of seemingly random imagery. His 1973 novel *Crash!* remains a cult favorite; it's the story of a recovering automobile accident victim who develops a bizarre sexual fetish for the twisted geometry of car crashes (here's a book begging to be filmed by David Cronenberg).

Ballard's most splatterpunkian work is his 1975 novel *High Rise*. This societal fable of class and privilege illustrates, step by downward step, a group descent into utter barbarism. What's unnerving is that this regression is never explained; what's shocking is that it happens to the very ordinary tenants of a self-contained high-rise luxury apartment complex (speaking of Cronenberg, his 1975 film *They Came From Within*, released the same year as *High Rise*, features much the same plot).

Ballard went on to see his fictionalized memoir *Empire of the Sun* filmed by Steven Spielberg.

Read *High Rise* instead.

CHAS. BALUN   Throughout "Outlaws," I've repeatedly emphasized the crucial impact of splatter films on splatterpunk. Well, since the mid-1980s, Chas. Balun has prolifically, and enthusiastically, become one of the two film critics most associated with this genre (the other is John McCarty).

A bearlike Viking of a man, Balun initially caught my attention with a small, self-published book (self-illustrated, too; Chas. is a commercial artist) titled *The Connoisseur's Handbook of Horror*. Then came *The Gore Score*, one of the first splatter film compendiums to deal exclusively with that genre. And what distinguished this little book was a rating system based not only on a film's overall merits but on how "moist" it was (Fulci's *Gates of Hell*, for example, rated a "10"). Balun then began popping up in small fanzines and, later, larger-circulation publications like *Fangoria*. Other Balun efforts include his own splatter film fanzine *Deep Red* and its companion book, *The Deep Red Horror Handbook*. He's authored *Horror Holocaust* and the recent splatter novel *Ninth and Hell Street* (Westminster, CA: Chunkblow Press, 1989).

Chas. Balun is thoroughly knowledgeable on his subject, and his criticism displays an interesting mixture of a fan's wholehearted enthusiasm tempered by a critic's awareness of just how low such films can sink. Currently, like many before him, Balun is trying to make the jump into screenplay writing. However, Chas.'s criticism always will find a soft spot in my heart, particularly for popularizing the word *chunkblower* and the ultimate phrase of critical scorn:

"Sucks the farts out of dead cats."

ROBERT BLOCH   A seminal splatterpunk influence.

Robert Bloch is to splatterpunk and the fifties what Harlan Ellison is to the sixties and James Herbert is to the seventies. Most of today's splatterpunks either were raised on or developed a true affection for Bloch's countless novels, short stories, and screenplays; very few, I'm sure, have not been influenced by him.

Originally a 1930s disciple of H. P. Lovecraft, Bloch primarily wrote old-school horror until *Psycho*—probably the keystone of the entire school of splatterpunk—cemented his reputation as a master of psychological horror. But from the beginnings of his career, Bloch always enjoyed trashing taboos; his first short story, "The Feast in the Abbey," made waves because of how it dealt with cannibalism (needless to say, the public wasn't ready for this in 1934!).

Bloch's fiction usually ends with a grisly little stinger, twist, or pun; many of his short stories, in fact, read like sick jokes. "Yours Truly, Jack the Ripper" is a perennial favorite, as is "A Toy for Juliette"; both deal with variations on the Springheel Jack theme, a recurring Blochian concern.

Interestingly, although everyone and their mother's mother has written about the profound influence *Psycho* exerts on current film entertainment, very few critics seem to have noticed the equally profound influence Bloch's *other* movie projects have had on *splatter* films. Actually, that influence is twofold.

First came talented hack director William Castle, who blatantly aped and amplified *Psycho* in a number of early 1960s shockers. Guess who wrote two scripts for him? Robert Bloch, whose *The Night Walker* had creepy dream sequences and grotesque burn makeup. But in the Joan Crawford vehicle *Strait-jacket*, Castle's exploitative gusto and Bloch's cheery gruesomeness met their perfect match. And anyone fortunate enough to have caught *Strait-jacket*'s initial run in 1963 will recall that the film was a minor sensation, primarily due to an axe-murder scene in which George Kennedy's head is hacked off over a deep freeze.

Second, in the late sixties and early seventies, Bloch scripted a number of anthology films for the England-based Amicus company. Titles like *The House That Dripped Blood*, *Asylum*, and *Torture Garden* routinely featured stabbings, strangulations, burnings, defenestrations, beheadings, and so on (and on). The fact that these were all essentially low-budget B-pictures kept the censors away; simultaneously, movie by movie, script by script, Robert Bloch was slowly shouldering open the door of cinematic permissiveness.

For his influential fiction, then, as well as his graphic film work, Robert Bloch is hereby inducted into the Honorary Splatterpunk Hall of Fame. Perversely, Bloch *hates* the current cinema's use of explicit violence. Well, hey, Bob . . . where do you think they got the idea in the first place?

EDWARD BRYANT   Edward Bryant's recent inclusion of horror in a career that primarily spotlighted science fiction marks a welcome addition to the fold.

Ed began as a protégé of Harlan Ellison. He first coauthored (with Ellison) the book *Phoenix Without Ashes*, a novelization of an Ellison-based pilot for the long-forgotten (and dreadful) Canadian science fiction television show "The Starlost." Bryant later contributed to the Ellison-edited anthology *Again, Dangerous Visions*. He later emerged from under Ellison's wing as the author of nine other books and hundreds of short stories and articles, usually with an SF flavor. Lately Bryant has gained a certain notoriety as a probing literary critic for such publication as *Locus*.

While Bryant insists he's not a splatterpunk, his novella "A Sad Last Love at the Diner of the Damned," found in Skipp and

Spector's *Book of the Dead*, is one of the best offerings in that excellent anthology. Set inside a small southern Colorado eatery, "Diner of the Damned" focuses on beautiful waitress Martha Malinowski as she becomes an object of desire for both the living rednecks within and the living dead without. Arch, exciting, and cinematic, "Diner" is potent stuff. Bryant first presents a large and well-drawn cast of characters, then laces his narrative with vicious black humor and lacerating attacks on the macho ethic before winding it up with a jet-black climax. It's an ending that manages to be simultaneously despairing and hilariously over the top. "A Sad Last Love" would make a wicked motion picture; I thought long and hard about including it in *Splatterpunks*.

But that honor finally befell "While She Was Out," a witty, committed repudiation of horror's insulting stereotype of woman as victim ("While She Was Out" further resembles Bryant's grave and terrifying story, "The Transfer," found in Etchison's anthology *Cutting Edge*). Superficially, "While She Was Out" plays as a clever upending of a traditional slasher movie. A harried young housewife is pursued from a shopping mall by a clutch of criminals intent on rape and murder; dealing rather permanently with them herself, she returns home to confront her real problem—a boneheaded husband.

Beneath Bryant's droll scenario is an acutely rendered sense of frustration and restricted choices, one that any sensitive woman must feel regarding our violent, obsessive American society. With "While She Was Out," "Diner of the Damned," and "The Transfer," Ed Bryant is building a reputation as the best kind of woman's writer. The fact that such feminist fiction is being written by a male piques my sense of irony and tickles me to no end—particularly because splatterpunk is constantly accused of being only written by agitating, low-foreheaded, sex-obsessed young men.

WILLIAM BURROUGHS   While I have tried throughout this essay to keep my sights on those authors loosely known as "horror writers," it's pretty hard to ignore the influence of certain authors *outside* the realm of splatterpunk, ones who definitely have left their mark on the field.

Writers like William Burroughs.

Depending on whom you listen to, William Seward Burroughs is either a self-indulgent asshole or one of the major forces in

American literature. Me, I'll pick number two. From his first novel *Junk* (written in 1954 under the name William Lee) to such later books as *Queer* and *Mind Wars* (both published in 1985), Burroughs has, sequentially: been one of the pivotal figures of the Beat Movement of the late 1950s; influenced countless rock 'n' rollers, from Patti Smith to Lou Reed; invaded world cinema (Burroughs has a supporting performance in the 1989 movie *Drugstore Cowboy*, narrated the otherwise silent film *Witchcraft Through the Ages*, and provided David Cronenberg with the source material for that director's upcoming adaptation of Burrough's controversial 1959 novel *Naked Lunch*).

William Burroughs is perhaps best known artistically for his "collage" technique of random cut-up paragraphs. He was also among the first serious American writers to avidly incorporate the pop aspects of film, television, and rock into his work (not to mention being a junkie for fifteen years and accidently killing his wife while drunkenly attempting to emulate William Tell). Additionally, Burroughs energetically did away with any and all taboos; his books teem with physical abuse, crime, and twisted sexuality.

Among Burrough's more splatterpunklike works are *Nova Express* (1964), a mix of science fiction and realistic horror, and *Cities of the Red Night* (1980), a mind-boggling bit of surrealism wherein the world suffers a mysterious plague; one of its by-products is the telescoping of time.

NANCY A. COLLINS   With the publication in 1989 of her debut novel *Sunglasses After Dark*, Nancy A. Collins leaps to the forefront of women writing splatterpunklike work.

Concerning a part-vampire, part-vampire hunter named Sonja Blue who tracks down and destroys those who vampirized her, *Sunglasses* displays a visceral, imagistic talent; this first novel is sensual, kinky, and exciting. Collins also shares the energy and imagination typical of the best splat fiction; she dives right into the down 'n' dirty. As David Kuehls writes in *Fangoria*, "This book is weird with a capital W and raw with a capital OUCH!" (May 1990, p. 57).

Rumor has it that Collins is writing a sequel to *Sunglasses* titled *In The Blood*. She also recently contributed a story to the spring 1990 "Psychos" issue of *Midnight Graffiti* (titled "Rant," it concerns a madman's first-person narration; he's planning a knife-induced cesarean section). And Collins will be represented in *Book of the Dead*, volume two, with "Necrophiles"—this one's about death-obsessed junkies.

Keep your eyes on this writer.

DIRECTORS   Some film directors just seem to palpitate when they're pushing the envelope. Those whose works have reflected various elements of the splatterpunk ethic include:

David Cronenberg (*Dead Ringers, Videodrome, The Fly*); David Lynch (*Blue Velvet, Wild at Heart, Eraserhead*); Tobe Hooper (*The Texas Chainsaw Massacre*); George Romero (*Dawn of the Dead*); Dario Argento (*Inferno, Suspiria*); Lucio Fulci (*Zombie, The Beyond, The Gates of Hell*); Wes Craven (*Last House on the Left, The Hills Have Eyes, A Nightmare on Elm Street*); Herschell Gordon Lewis (*Blood Feast*); Mario Bava (*Blood and Black Lace, Black Sunday, Twitch of the Death Nerve*); Ruggero Deodato (*Cannibal Holocaust*); John Waters (*Pink Flamingos*); Russ Meyer (*Faster, Pussycat! Kill! Kill!, Beyond the Valley of the Dolls*); Sam Raimi (*Evil Dead I* and *II*); Stuart Gordon (H. P. Lovecraft's *Re-animator*); Brian De Palma (*Sisters, Dressed to Kill, Casualties of War*); Paul Verhoeven (*Robocop, The Fourth Man, Flesh and Blood*); Alfred Hitchcock (*Psycho, Frenzy*); Chuck Russell (*The Blob, A Nightmare on Elm Street 3: The Dream Warriors*); Kathryn Bigelow (*Near Dark, Blue Steel*); Umberto Lenzi (*Make Them Die Slowly*); Clive Barker (*Hellraiser, Nightbreed*); John Carpenter (*Halloween, The Thing, The Fog*); James Cameron (*The Terminator, Aliens*); Lamberto Bava (*Demons*); Ridley Scott (*Alien*); Frank Henenlotter (*Basket Case, Brain Damage, Basket Case 2*); Luis Buñuel (*Un Chien Andalou*); Pier Paolo Pasolini (*Salo*); Pedro Almodovar (*Matador*); and Roman Polanski (*Repulsion*).

EDITORS WHO HAVE ACCEPTED OR HELPED GIVE EXPOSURE TO SPLATTERPUNK   A number of professional editors have, directly or indirectly, displayed something of a preference for splatterpunk fiction, publishing seminal splat works. In the course of their acceptance, they've helped raise the overall splat profile. These personages and their respective magazines have included: Jessie Horsting and Jim Van Hise of

Midnight Graffiti; Alan Rodgers of *Night Cry* (now defunct); Tappan King of *The Twilight Zone Magazine* (also defunct); David B. Silva of *The Horror Show* (ditto—defunct); Ellen Datlow, fiction editor for *Omni*; Richard Chizmar of *Cemetery Dance*; and Ed Gorman of *Mystery Scene*.

HARLAN ELLISON   A prolific writer of essays, short stories, and screenplays, Harlan Ellison is the godfather of splatterpunk. Outrageous and outspoken, Ellison first came to national prominence in the 1960s, a decade that perfectly matched his revolutionary zeal for honesty and learned confrontation. The winner of seven Hugo Awards, three Nebulas, and one Edgar (at last count, anyway), many of Ellison's stories are laced with science fiction trappings. In reality, however, Ellison is a moralist and a fantasist whose best work is often grim, dark, and uncompromisingly adult.

Stylistically Ellison frequently employs cinematic techniques and (particularly in his 1960s period) fuses extreme sex and violence with white-hot anger. Of particular splatterpunkian notice are such works as "I Have No Mouth, and I Must Scream" (1967), about a group of humans trapped and inventively tortured by a malevolent computer; "The Prowler in the City at the Edge of the World" (1967) a story of Jack the Ripper in the future; "A Boy and His Dog" (1969), about postholocaust teenage gangs; "Along the Scenic Route" (1969), in which everyday commuters are locked in mortal freeway combat; and "The Whimper of Whipped Dogs" (1973), the urban nightmare explained as demonically influenced. Ellison is also an acute (and hilarious) social critic; some of his best essays can be found in *The Glass Teat* (1970), essays on television; and *Sleepless Nights in the Procrustean Bed: Essays* (1984), essays on everything else.

Harlan Ellison's impact on splatterpunk is incalculable. A self-made man in the most positive sense, he was also one of the first genre writers to recognize the importance of self-promotion and the myriad ways in which the media could be bent to best serve his own purposes. With his colorful, fearless, and often flamboyant personality, and with his extremely high profile and creative overspill into such media as television anthology programs (Ellison generally is acknowledged as having written the best scripts for two of genre TV's most influential programs, "Star

Trek" and "The Outer Limits"), it was nearly impossible for nascent writers of the sixties and seventies not to have been exposed to—and, by inference, influenced by—Harlan Ellison. Ellison is still active today—still writing, still angry, still fighting the good fight (one of his latest collections is *Angry Candy* published in 1988). May he continue to do so into the 21st century.

And beyond.

RAY GARTON Like Joe R. Lansdale, Ray Garton cannot really be called a splatterpunk. What initially put him in this category were such books as *Live Girls* (1987), with vampires in a peep-show off Times Square, and *Crucifax Autumn* (1988), one of the best examinations of modern teenage angst to come out of the horror field.

In both of these novels the violence is intense and the sex graphic (a continuing concern; Garton is one of the few horror writers today who understands the difference between explicitness and eroticism). And at the start of his career Garton waged a scathingly amusing one-man crusade against the Seventh-Day Adventists, personal retribution for certain hometown actions Ray feels the Adventists directed at him. (For further details, read the illuminating Garton interview in the fall 1988 issue of *Midnight Graffiti*.)

Two of these Adventist stories are "Sinema" and "Punishments," and the satire therein reaches near-Swiftian levels (I'm almost saddened to have to tell you that recently Ray has put this crusade behind him). And Garton is well aware of the effect he has on his audience. He also has misgivings about both being labeled a splatterpunk and the counterproductive one-upmanship games splatterpunks can play on one another. In the magazine *Gauntlet* Garton explains,

> I do censor myself. . . . It's more as a result of the Splatterpunk movement, in which I have so often been included. In fact, I *welcomed* the inclusion at first, but then took a few steps back and thought about it a little. I began to think that a lot of writers—myself included—were throwing in a lot of graphic sex and violence just for the hell of it, just to outdo their last book, or somebody *else's* book, and it was getting pretty disgusting (premier issue, 1990, p. 29)

Splatterpunk or not, Ray Garton's talents are developing at an astonishing rate. Recent suspense novels like *Trade Secrets* (published in 1990 by Mark V. Ziesing) indicate a confident command of narrative, character, and plot; the backgrounds are believable, the motivations clean, and the rough stuff very, *very* rough. And Garton's still only in his late twenties!

Ray's other novels include *Seductions*, concerning a modern succubus. Upcoming works are the novella "Lot Lizards," about truck-stop vampire hookers, and *Dark Channel*, a new age horror novel due out from Bantam Books in 1991.

Lawrence Person, in his *Nova Express* article, said this about Ray: "Garton is undoubtedly going to be one of the most important horror writers of the next decade" (p. 21).

I agree.

JAMES HERBERT   Yet another seminal splat influence, James Herbert surpasses only Clive Barker as England's most popular horror writer. His first novel, *The Rats* (1974), used the symbol of mutated rats pouring out of London's East End to stand for the neglect and dismissal of an entire lower class of English society. But with *The Fog* (1975), Herbert not only echoed *The Exorcist* in savage explicitness but set a standard for the splatterpunk mode that was to find clear reverberations in the eighties and nineties. In this truly gut-wrenching work, a nerve gas slowly sweeps across England, leaving death, madness, and savage carnage in its wake.

Other splatlike Herbert horror novels include *The Survivor* (1976) in which the restless souls of an airline disaster wreak havoc on the surrounding countryside, *The Spear* (1978), *The Dark* (1980), *The Jonah* (1981), and *Domain* (1984), a sequel to *The Rats*, this time set against the background of a nuclear holocaust.

As with Harlan Ellison, Herbert commands a high media profile (at least in his native England); one cannot but wonder as to his early influence on Clive Barker. And like Stephen King, Herbert couches his prose in everyday language and situations, assuring the widest possible audience.

Fellow English novelist Ramsey Campbell makes an interesting observation in his essay on Herbert in *The Penguin Encyclopedia of Horror and the Supernatural*. According to Campbell, Herbert shares a unique gift with Italian splatter filmmaker Dario

Argento (*Suspiria, Inferno, Opera*): "His images of violence are powerful because they are painful" (p. 201).

If Harlan Ellison was the protosplatterpunk of the sixties, then James Herbert was the splat king of the seventies.

ROBERTA LANNES   Roberta Lannes, a fine artist and graphics designer, has variously taught English, art, journalism, creative writing, and photography. Her short story "Goodbye, Dark Love" first appeared in Dennis Etchison's sophisticated 1986 horror anthology *Cutting Edge*; it will, I think, persist as a certifiable splatterpunk miniclassic, even though it's really not a short story at all.

More anecdotal than dramatic, sketchy in character and background development, "Goodbye, Dark Love" nevertheless resonates with profound emotional impact. Its "plot" describes a fifteen-year-old incest victim as she methodically mocks, mutilates, and has sex with the corpse of her recently deceased father. Through these rituals the teenager reenacts the abuses she's suffered, purging herself on the man's cooling, helpless flesh.

This fragment of necrophilic retribution hums with immediacy and sensual power. Morally, "Goodbye, Dark Love" could be justified as therapeutic exorcism, wish fulfillment for the powerless. But with its overlay of sexually explicit detail (the kind usually reserved for "BeeLine 3-in-1 Adult Novels"), its frank examination of incest, and its emotional ambiguity (the young protagonist can still remember, after all, when Daddy was just Daddy), "Goodbye, Dark Love" works best as an exploration of the outer limits of human sexual response.

And as splatterpunk with a social conscience.

JOE R. LANSDALE   If Mark Twain had marched in Selma, Alabama and then caught *The Texas Chainsaw Massacre* at his local drive-in, he could have grown up to be Joe R. Lansdale.

Lansdale is a true original, a regional American writer (eastern Texas) with an authentically individualistic voice. While splatterpunk has been categorized as dealing wtih disaffected urban youth, Lansdale's characters inhabit the dusty main streets of small town U.S.A., isolated backwaters where ignorance is the norm and casual brutality the interactive method of choice.

Although he resists the label, Lansdale's fiction (for me, anyway) displays all that's right about splatterpunk. There's lean and economical prose, an adult concern with social issues (including a characteristic willingness to tackle racism head-on), and some of the best dialogue of *any* genre.

Not to mention Joe's astoundingly warped sense of bad taste.

Lansdale's primary literary influences have been Flannery O'-Connor and Chester Himes (the black Harlem and Paris-based author who wrote *All Shot Up* and other Coffin Ed–Gravedigger Jones adventures). And, a-yup, Joe *will* make you laugh; he has the most genuinely funny sense of humor in horror fiction. But again, Joe's no splatterpunk. While some of Lansdale's stories reflect a hard-core splatterpunk attitude ("On the Far Side of the Cadillac Desert With Dead Folks"), he's equally adept at westerns (*The Magic Wagon*), science fiction ("Tight Little Stitches in a Dead Man's Back"), and mysteries (*Cold in July*).

Still, Lansdale has produced a number of deeply disturbing stories and novels that clearly belong to the splatterpunk school of thought. "Night They Missed the Horror Show" begins as a deceptively simple tale of bored rednecks on a Saturday night and quickly escalates through so many levels of racism, sexism, and murder that the cumulative effect is like being kicked in the stomach by a steel-toed boot. Graphically intense, *The Nightrunners* (1987) follows a young couple trying to recover from the effects of a vicious gang rape—and coming straight up against the bizarre God Of The Razor. *Dead in the West* (1986) is Lansdale's zombie western novel.

Lansdale's most compact and truly inspired book (to date) is 1988's *The Drive-In (A B-Movie With Blood and Popcorn, Made in Texas)*, in which thousands of just-plain folks flock to the Orbit Drive-In to catch the Friday All-Night Horror Show . . . and find that they can't get out. This hallucinatory, very cinematic combination of *The Exterminating Angel* and *Lord of the Flies* was followed by *The Drive-In 2 (Not Just One of Them Sequels)* in 1989; Lansdale promises a third *Drive-In* volume soon.

Immediately grab anything with Joe's name on it. You won't be disappointed. As he likes to say, Lansdale is his *own* genre.

RICHARD LAYMON   A writer only now being identified with the splatterpunks (probably because of his grisly "Mess Hall," which appeared in *Book of the Dead*), Richard Laymon actually has already written over a dozen novels and fifty short stories in the mystery, romance, western, and juvenile genres (many under pseudonyms).

His first splatlike novel was the unrelentingly horrific and downbeat *The Cellar* (1980). In fact, Laymon has earned a certain reputation for producing work in which very few survive . . . and those who do would have been better off dead. His other novels include *The Woods Are Dark, Night Show, Flesh, Resurrection Dreams, The Stake,* and 1990's *Funland* (in which Laymon invents a bizarre new wrinkle on the blood-brother ritual: a vengeful girl cuts her labia with a razor and urges a bloody-handed boy to slip his fingers inside her to seal their oath).

Laymon is also a hard-and-fast fan of splatter cinema; this influence can be seen most clearly not only in "Mess Hall" but in "Mop Up" (found in *Night Visions* 7), a novella clearly influenced by *Night of the Living Dead.*

As squarely as he sits within the splatterpunk tradition, however, Laymon is clearly ambiguous about the terminology. In an interview with horror historian Stanley Wiater printed in *Fangoria*, Laymon had this to say:

> I don't like the "punk" part of it, because you picture people with spiked hair and razor blades in their ears. Now, if you want to call it "rock n' roll horror," I might go along with that. My real problem with some of the splatterpunks is that their main characters often seem to be the real punks. . . . But I don't want to be identified with a group, anyway. Especially not that one. (May 1990, p. 15)

RICHARD CHRISTIAN MATHESON   Son of famed writer and screenwriter Richard Matheson (*The Incredible Shrinking Man*), Richard Christian Matheson is a unique talent in his own right. Writing of R. C. Matheson in *The Twilight Zone Magazine*, Edward Bryant dubbed him "a multiple artistic threat, a bit in the same tradition as Clive Barker." Indeed—like Barker, Matheson is a recognized force in contemporary films, television, and literature. Unlike Clive, however, RC also has garnered a considerable reputation as a master of the potent, punchy short-short story.

Though not a splatterpunk (more on this in a moment), Matheson effortlessly glides among the various media that have influenced it. A charming, strikingly handsome young man, Matheson is primarily a television and film writer and producer—with over three-hundred produced prime-time credits. At age twenty he was also the youngest television writer ever placed under contract at Universal Studios. R. C. Matheson has written screenplays for such films as *Three O'clock High* (produced in 1987 by Steven Spielberg) and the United Artists feature *it Takes Two* (1988).

But it's probably his short (*very* short) fiction which has secured Matheson's position as one of the premiere writers tilling today's horror field. Typically lean and compressed (averaging three to five pages apiece), RC's stories periodically address traditional horror elements before twisting them into contemporary shapes. Usually, though, he writes from the inside out. As *Fangoria* puts it, "Matheson is primarily interested in the monster inside the human mind, rather than the bogeyman supposedly lurking under the bed."

A 1987 hardcover collection of these short-shorts, *Scars* (originally published by specialty house Scream/Press and later reprinted as a Tor paperback), showcases Matheson's dexterity. *Scars* contains such noteworthy stories as "Conversation Piece," "Dust," and "Goosebumps" (an over-the-top black comedy invested with a screeching, nails-on-a-blackboard physicality). "Where There's a Will," written in conjunction with RC's father, Richard Matheson, Sr., was dubbed by Lawrence Person in *Nova Express* as "his best and most splatterpunk-like story" (p. 24). (I disagree.) More conventional than RC's usual fare, "Where There's a Will" has a man waking up in a coffin, clawing his way out, and—after finding a mirror—wishing he hadn't.

Personally, I feel that "Goosebumps" is Matheson's most ostensibly splatterpunklike tale (a rogue lump crawls around under a young boy's skin, wreaking the most personal kind of havoc). However, his story "Red" is *subtle* splatterpunk (if that's not an oxymoron) and still my all-around favorite of RC's shorter works.

"Red" follows an emotionally blasted man as he staggers down a highway, weeping, picking things up off the pavement. Only in the last few sentences do we understand that this is a grieving father who has accidently killed his young daughter in an auto mishap; the "things" he's scooping up are her various body parts. Suggestive rather than explicit, capped by one hell of a retroactive kick, "Red" ranks among Matheson's most emotionally devasting works.

NEWS FLASH!!! Richard Christian Matheson's first novel is

scheduled to be released by Bantam Books in early 1992. Titled *Created By*, this is a psychological horror story set in Hollywood; it's a milieu RC knows well, and I look forward to his own informed take on the rigorous, loony film industry (as do others; Clive Barker, who's had an advance look at the manuscript, calls *Created By* a "masterly fable"). As for his other film projects, Matheson is currently writing Kim Basinger's new feature for Warner Brothers, has two other scripts about to go into production (one for director Richard Donner, the other for megaproducer Joel Silver), and soon will begin a new film with Steven Spielberg.

Oh—about the splatterpunk tag. RC originally was lumped together with the splatterpunks at about the same time that David J. Schow invented the term. But according to recent conversations I've had with him, Matheson never really thought of himself as a splatterpunk in the first place; today, RC says definitely, "I'm still not one." Perhaps this misidentification arose in splatterpunk's early days, when the term itself was being thrown around much more loosely (more as a lark than anything else) and RC posed in some Splat Pack group photos. Or perhaps it's his friendship with David J. Schow.

In any event, the bad news is that Richard Christian Matheson is not a splatterpunk. The good news is that his first novel is coming out and that RC's success in the film market is continually expanding. One can expect to see more major motion pictures from him in the not-so-distant future.

Maybe even a splatterpunk epic in 70 mm, with wall-to-wall Dolby?

ROBERT R. McCAMMON   Like Richard Christian Matheson, Robert R. McCammon was identified as a splatterpunk right around 1986 or 1987. Like Matheson, McCammon posed in a few of the group shots. And like Matheson, he's not a splatterpunk.

A native of Birmingham, Alabama, McCammon *is* someone who occasionally writes splatterpunklike stories (he's also a best-selling author). *Book of the Dead*'s "Eat Me" is a comic yet poetic effort involving cannibalism, zombies, and terminal oral sex. "Best Friends," from *Night Visions 4*, is usually singled out as McCammon's most overtly splat effort. It's not hard to see why; a young boy's inner demons really *are* internalized, and in the climax they burst out of his body and savage a hospital ward.

But to my way of thinking, it's "Nightcrawlers" which is really McCammon's premiere splatterpunk entry (it first appeared in J. N. Williamson's 1984 anthology *Masques* and later was reprinted in *Blue World*, a 1990 collection of McCammon's own stories). "Nightcrawlers" concerns a Vietnam vet named Price who was chemically altered during the war, a man who now hallucinates so vividly that his visions actually come alive. Unfortunately, Price's hallucinations center on the dead platoon he left back in the 'Nam . . . and now a little piece of the war is about to come home . . .

On one level this story is simply another example of the projection of inner demons; on another it's an uncomfortable metaphor for the overwhelming American guilt engendered by our disastrous involvement in Southeast Asia. Incidentally, "Nightcrawlers" was adapted for TV in 1985. Directed by William Friedkin (*The Exorcist*) as a continuous twenty-minute segment for CBS's new "Twilight Zone" series (and first aired with no commercials), "Nightcrawlers" was elaborately produced. Shot like a feature film, swiftly paced and stunningly choreographed, it remains one of the best film or television horror adaptations of the 1980s (remember that line, "Charlie's in the light!"?). The fact that "Nightcrawlers" is not yet available on videotape is a criminal one.

Other McCammon novels include *Swan Song* (a post-Holocaust story that someone really should do as a TV miniseries) and *The Wolf's Hour* (werewolves in Nazi Germany). His borderline splat work includes the epic novel *They Thirst* (vampires in Los Angeles), which I highly recommend; the short story "He'll Come Knocking at Your Door" (a Halloween-themed tale involving the price one family pays for success); and "Something Passed By" (an end-of-the-world science fiction offering in which literally *anything* can happen).

JOHN MCCARTY   John McCarty occupies a unique position in film criticism, for it is he who coined the phrase *splatter movies*. Where Chas. Balun tends to be more folksy and informal in his splatter critiques, McCarty is "the John Simon, the Leonard Maltin, the Siskel and Ebert of carnography," as Edward Bryant has labeled him.

McCarty first coined the term in his 1984 book *Splatter Movies: Breaking the Last Taboo of the Screen*. This volume was a pioneering effort, one that attempted to define and corral an up-till-then maverick film genre. As McCarty himself pointed out in the introduction to his later (1989) *The Official Splatter Movie Guide* (an essential compendium of more than four hundred cap-sule reviews of "the goriest, grossest, most outrageous movies ever made"):

> A number of years ago, I published a book called *Splatter Movies: Breaking the Last Taboo of the Screen.* One of my purposes in writing the book was to give what I saw to be a clearly evolving genre an appropriate and definitive *name* that I and other critics could use so that we (and our readers) would all recognize what we were talking about—similar to *film noir.* Prior to the book's appearance, no one (save George Romero, on *one* occasion) used the term. Today, everyone does—from the *New York Times*'s Vincent Canby to Siskel and Ebert to *Fangoria* magazine, the splatter buff's bible. Congratulations, John. Mission accomplished. (p. ix)

And *Bravo!* as well; it's not every day that a critic introduces a term with such far-ranging impact and appeal. As someone who's also managed to consistently offer valuable commentary on splatterpunk's primary influence *as well as* becoming partly responsible for the very origins of the word, McCarty's position within the history of splatterpunk is secure.

REX MILLER   The outlaw tradition in art, of which splatterpunk is a subset, has also spilled over into the genres of detective and crime fiction. Writers like James Ellroy (*The Big Nowhere, The Black Dahlia*), Jim Thompson (*The Killer Inside Me*), and Andrew Vachss (*Flood, Blue Belle*) have turned mystery novels inside out with their unflinching focus on the seamy, the sordid, and the pathological.

Rex Miller belongs in this category; he's also one of the most uninhibited of the group. Miller's first novel, *Slob* (1987), which was greeted with wild enthusiasm, chronicled the brutal exploits of the puppy-loving, four-hundred-fifty-pound serial killer Daniel "Chaingang" Bunkowski. A monstrous representation of primal id, Chaingang raped and maimed and killed with frightening abandon, until finally being stopped by ex-alcoholic Chicago detective Jack Eichord. And although Miller killed off Chaingang at the climax of *Slob*, such was the character's popularity that Miller resurrected him in the 1990 novel *Slice*, in such short stories as "Sweet Pea" and "The Luckiest Man in the World," *and* in a limited run edition of Chaingang comic books from Northstar Productions.

Since *Slob*, Miller also has sustained the exploits of Jack Eichord, who specializes in psychopaths; Eichord has appeared as the hero of a continuing series of novels, such as *Frenzy* and *Stone Shadow*.

Miller began writing later in life; up until the eighties, he supported himself primarily as a radio announcer and as the owner and operator of Rex Miller's Killer Collectibles and Vintage Videos, a successful mail-order business specializing in character collectibles and media memorabilia. His horror output per se has been small, although the Eichord books definitely contain horrific overtones. Nevertheless, the horror community has embraced Miller as one of their own.

Rex Miller typically writes stripped-down, brutal prose obviously influenced by Hemingway; just as obviously, he has a good time seeing what he can get away with, especially in the sex and violence department. "Reunion Moon," in which Miller deals with the uneasiness attached to high school reunions by shitting all over them, is a voodoo comic fantasy; let's hope he has similar stories in his pen.

PHILIP NUTMAN   Philip Nutman comes primarily from film criticism and film history, where an enthusiasm for splatter films was his most evident trait. Although Nutman's first professional job was with the BBC, this young (twenty-seven-year-old) Englishman initially drew attention with his numerous articles, interviews, and on-set reports in such magazines as *Fangoria* and *Shock Xpress*. Nutman seems to have interviewed just about everybody. After a few years of these and similar pursuits (including acting stints in such low-budget films as *Death Collector* [1990], available from Raedon Video), Nutman turned to fiction. His first short story, "Wet Work," which appeared in *Book of the Dead*, posited a paramilitary hit squad that in reality turned out to be composed of intelligent zombies.

Nutman's "Full Throttle" is his first published novella, but it represents a remarkable broadening of literary scope. Set in the staid, listless English town of Bath, "Throttle" combines the paranormal with the drab as two brothers experience a psychic link, leaving one dead and the other irrevocably (and positively) altered. What differentiates "Full Throttle" from "Wet Work" is the fact that its supernatural element is slight (and that its paranormal event was based on Nutman's own experience). Further, "Throttle" is an accurate, depressing, enraged depiction of the hopelessness forced upon much of contemporary Britain's youth.

In its moving delineation of teenage angst and aimlessness, "Full Throttle" continues a curiously English heritage begun with the late-fifties work of "angry young man" John Osborne, one which mutated into the late-seventies punk rock attitudes of rage and despair. Specific splatterpunk elements of "Throttle" include a drunken group sex/bottle rape scene that is all the more shocking for its uncomfortable plausibility; anyone who's had a "wild youth" (this author included) will be able to pinpoint this and other moments in "Full Throttle" as uneasy reminders of those moments in our own early lives when we, too, could have gone—or *did* go—much too far.

Nutman is currently working on expanding "Wet Work" into a novel. His film noir screenplay *Heatwave* is currently making the rounds of studios in Hollywood, looking for a home.

J. K. POTTER   J. K. Potter was mistaken as a splatterpunk early on due to his prolific contributions of cover and interior artwork to various efforts linked with the splatterpunk field. These included bygone magazines like *Night Cry* (which had an open-door policy toward splat fiction), Scream/Press specialty books, and hardcover collections of stories by Clive Barker and Joe R. Lansdale.

In reality, Jeff Potter is more a mainstream graphic artist who, as part of his overall commissions, has supplied a prodigious amount of horror and splatterpunk illustrations. Potter is one of the best fine artists in the field, and it's easy to see why he remains in such high demand.

Potter's singular photocollage-airbrush technique and obvious education in photographic history (one sees traces of Diane Arbus in his work) is coupled with a truly surreal imagination. Potter loves to twist the human form, and one of my favorite JK creations shows a long-legged woman topped by a head. No torso, no arms . . . only a head.

Not a splatterpunk, but consistently polished and rewarding.

J. S. RUSSELL   It's ridiculous to recommend a new talent on the strength of a single story, and a first story at that. But if J. S. Russell can continue in the direction of his "City of Angels," then splatterpunk may be soon graced with a distinctively deranged voice.

"City of Angels" takes place in a nuked Los Angeles two years after the bombs have dropped . . . but don't expect your typical post-holocaust fable. By minutely dwelling on the grossest physical and mental aftereffects of nuclear warfare, Russell has broken through the stale surface of that old "atomic war survivors pulling together to build a clean new society" myth and exposed the raw, cancerous ooze lurking beneath. Believe me, this is *strong* stuff.

It's also hilarious. Russell uses near-redneck dialogue and ultra-black humor in the same way, say, Joe R. Lansdale does; in the process, Russell totally skews our perceptions of what is, or shouldn't be, funny.

"J. S. Russell" is a pseudonym, by the way. But who cares what the real name is when, first time off the block, a writer can produce an instant splatterpunk classic like "City of Angels."

WAYNE ALLEN SALLEE   Primarily a poet (with more than seven hundred published poems so far!), Wayne Allen Sallee is also a prolific contributor to small press magazines (including *Grue*, *New Blood*, *Portents*, and others). Holder of numerous real-life jobs in the underbelly of Chicago (skip tracer and crime reporter), Sallee has written a number of angry, uncompromising short stories which sharply prick the splatterpunk vein.

Among these is "Rapid Transit" (1985), Sallee's first piece of fiction; after witnessing a stabbing on a subway platform, a young man named Dennis Cassady begins to tip over into psychosis. "Take the A-Train" (1986), a sequel to "Rapid Transit," concludes Cassady's descent into madness. "Bleeding Between the Lines" was published in 1989, is directly related to "Rapid Transit" and "Take the A-Train," and rounds off what Sallee calls the "Dennis Cassady trilogy" ("Bleeding Between the Lines" has absolutely no explicit sex and violence, though; it's basically a discourse between a writer and his psychiatrist).

In Lawrence Person's *Nova Express* splatterpunk article, he dubs Sallee's style "uncompromising" and likens him to Harlan Ellison. It remains to be seen if Sallee's future fictional and novelistic output matches Person's comparison. In the meantime, it's a measure of Sallee's talents (and impact—there's a cockroach-in-the-crotch scene in "Rapid Transit" that's particularly unnerving) that he's made such a broad impression from within the relatively restricting confines of the small press.

Sallee's collection of short stories, *Running Inside My Skin*, is scheduled to be published by Mark V. Ziesing in 1991; a novel, *The Holy Terror*, also will appear from that same company the same year.

DOUGLAS E. WINTER   Douglas E. Winter is a good example of someone aesthetically bridging the gap between suggestive and explicit fiction.

Not a splatterpunk (by the way, I'll gladly give a nickel to anyone who'll count up the number of times I've had to type this), Winter initially gained attention as the first serious critic of Stephen King (*Stephen King: The Art of Darkness*, 1984). He then broadened his critical gaze to produce a book-length overview of new horror writers (*Faces of Fear*, 1985), and has continued to produce numerous essays on this and other subjects (Winter's "Writer's of Today" contribution to *The Penguin Encyclopedia of Horror and the Supernatural* is particularly worthwhile). Doug's interviews and criticism have appeared in such magazines as *Harper's Bazaar* and *Saturday Review*, as well as newspapers like the *Washington Post* and the *Philadelphia Inquirer*. He's also edited an outstanding collection of original horror stories titled *Prime Evil* (1988), with new contributions by the likes of Stephen King, Peter Straub, and Whitley Streiber.

Yet for someone so obviously connected with more traditional horror, Winter is also a dedicated fan of uncensored cinema and quality splatterpunk. His first novella, "Splatter: A Cautionary Tale," was an explicitly anticensorship piece that mixed politics, the witch-hunt mentality, and gore films (each subchapter's heading was the actual title of a splatter movie).

"Less Than Zombie," Winter's next fiction, evidenced a startling creative leap. With its rich, jaded teens coming to life only when one of their own becomes a "zombie," the story functions (on one level) as a perfect parody of Bret Easton Ellis's mininovel *Less Than Zero* (1985). On another level "Less Than Zombie" is pointed social criticism of an increasingly desensitized society *as well as* seeming to be an antisplatterpunk critique; although it employs splat techniques, "Less Than Zombie" implicitly turns these devices against themselves.

Interestingly, Winter resists the idea of splatterpunk being thought of as either a genre or a movement.

> For that matter, I resist the idea of horror itself being a genre. Horror is an emotion. And "Less Than Zombie" was written as an antisplatterpunk story, not in the negative sense, but in the sense that I have used the concept of "Antihorror" as a critique of horror, one which continues the dialogue about the directions that horror should go . . . rather than defining where it's been.

"Antihorror" is Winter's intriguing theory that most of what we now think of as horror has become restrictive; what Antihorror examines and confronts are exactly those same conventions to which the horror story has succumbed. Perhaps he will continue to explore these areas himself; in any event, Winter's burgeoning fictional career is one to anticipate.

12. A SPLATTERPUNK SAMPLER

Throughout this essay, I've mentioned numerous works of splatterpunk, both essential and peripheral. In the true archival spirit, what follows is both a recap and addition to this material. By actually leafing through the works listed in "A Splatterpunk Sampler," a reader will have an immediate understanding of what splatterpunk is all about, much more so than they would by simply rereading "Outlaws."

Some guidelines: Only written works are listed below. I would have cataloged all of the essential splatter films, but in that direction lies madness; anyway, I've tried to keep my focus on the literature.

Works not mentioned in the text of "Outlaws," or only glancingly referred to, are followed by a brief commentary.

Some of these works are in paperback, some are hardcover. Some are limited first editions. Wherever possible, I've tried to include those editions that are either simplest to obtain or most representative of that particular listing. Be forewarned, however; not all of these books and magazines are still in print or easy to find.

Short stories, articles, and essays are all listed individually, as are novels and anthologies.

Finally, not all of the works or authors referred to in "Outlaws" are listed in the sampler. Overall, I've tried to include only those articles, books, and stories that either embody the true splatterpunk spirit or somehow reflect it.

Browse and enjoy.

1. "Along the Scenic Route," by Harlan Ellison. In *The Essential Ellison*, ed. Terry Dowling (Omaha and Kansas City: Nemo Press, 1987).
2. "Best Friends," by Robert R. McCammon. In *Night Visions 4* (Arlington Heights, IL: Dark Harvest, 1987).
3. *Book of the Dead*, ed. John Skipp and Craig Spector (New York: Bantam Books, 1989).

   Includes "Wet Work," by Philip Nutman; "Mess Hall," by Richard Laymon; "On Going Too Far," by Skipp and Spector; "Eat Me," by Robert R. McCammon; "Less Than Zombie," by Douglas E. Winter; "Jerry's Kids Meet Wormboy," by David J. Schow; "On the Far Side of the Cadillac Desert With Dead Folks," by Joe R. Lansdale; and "A Sad Last Love at the Diner of the Damned," by Edward Bryant. *(Whew!)*

   One of the seminal splatterpunk anthologies.
4. "A Boy and His Dog," by Harlan Ellison. In *The Essential Ellison*, ed. Terry Dowling (Omaha and Kansas City: Nemo Press, 1987).
5. *By Bizarre Hands*, by Joe R. Lansdale (Shingletown, CA: Mark V. Ziesing, 1989).

   Included are "Night They Missed the Horror Show," "On the Far Side of the Cadillac Desert With Dead Folks," "Tight Little Stitches in a Dead Man's Back," and "Hell Through a Windshield" (an essay which formed the basis for Lansdale's later novel *The Drive-in*).
6. *Cabal*, by Clive Barker (New York: Poseidon Press, 1988).
7. "Cannibal Cats Come Out Tonight," by Nancy Holder. In *Women of Darkness*, ed. Kathryn Ptacek (New York: Tor Books, 1988).

A young boy is told by his abusive father that it's "A dog-eat-dog world out there, son." The boy takes it literally, growing up to become a repressed homosexual and a cannibalistic rock star particularly fond of female backup singers. The story is essentially a black comedy with serious undercurrents. Holder previously appeared in such Charles Grant anthologies as *Shadows* 8, 9, and 10; let's hope she continues in the "Cannibal Cats" vein as well, for here's a story that's sharp, well written, and fun.

8. *Carrion Comfort*, by Dan Simmons (Arlington Heights, IL: Dark Harvest, 1989).

Simmons's massive second novel (following his popular *Song of Kali*) charts the warfare between a small group of upper-class psychic vampires (working as movie producers, politicians, and businessmen) and middle-class vampire hunters (cops and portrait photographers). The pin connecting them is an elderly Jewish psychiatrist who survived the Nazi death camps. Simmons adroitly balances the real-life horrors of the Holocaust with the ironic mental manipulations of his fictional villains; for instance, one vampire (the producer) uses his power to force beautiful women into having lascivious sex with him, particularly when they've pissed him off.

Borderline splatterpunk, but the jolts keep zinging in from powerful and unexpected directions. I recommend it.

9. *Cemetery Dance* magazine, P.O. Box 858, Edgewood, Maryland 21040.

With the demise of *The Horror Show* magazine, *Cemetery Dance* looks to fill the gap as *the* premiere fanzine for innovative horror fiction. Editor Richard Chizmar has already printed works by the likes of Joe R. Lansdale, David J. Schow, and Richard Christian Matheson; *Dance* looks to be a publication, like *Midnight Graffiti*, where splatterpunk will find a home.

And in a nod to the spirit of P. T. Barnum, be aware that Paul M. Sammon will soon be contributing a regular film column to *Cemetery Dance*, tentatively titled "Rough Cuts."

10. "City of Angels," by J. S. Russell. In *Midnight Graffiti*, Fall 1990.

11. *The Cleanup*, by John Skipp and Craig Spector (New York: Bantam Books, 1986).

12. *Clive Barker's Books of Blood*, Vols. One–Three and Four–Six, by Clive Barker (London: Sphere Books, 1984, 1985). Volumes one–three also available from Berkley Books, New York, 1986.

Absolutely essential volumes for the splatterpunk library.

13. *Connoisseur's Guide to the Contemporary Horror Film*, by Chas. Balun (Westminster, CA: (Self-published, 1983).

14. *Crucifax Autumn*, by Ray Garton (Arlington Heights, IL: Dark Harvest, 1988).

15. *Cutting Edge*, ed. Dennis Etchison (New York: Doubleday, 1986).

Besides Lannes's "Goodbye, Dark Love," other splatlike stories in this exceptional anthology include "Muzak for Torso Murders," by Marc Laidlaw, and "They're Coming for You," by Les Daniels.

16. *The Damnation Game*, by Clive Barker (London: Weidenfeld & Nicolson, 1985).

17. *Dead in the West*, by Joe R. Lansdale (New York: Space & Time, 1986).

18. *Dead Lines*, by John Skipp and Craig Spector (New York: Bantam Books, 1989).

19. *The Deep Red Horror Handbook*, ed. Chas. Balun (Albany, NY: Fantaco Books, 1989).

Includes "I Spit in Your Face: Films That Bite."

20. *The Drive-in*, by Joe R. Lansdale (New York: Bantam Books, 1988).

21. *The Drive-in 2*, by Joe R. Lansdale (New York: Bantam Books, 1989.)

22. "Eat Me," by Robert R. McCammon. In *Book of the Dead*, ed. John Skipp and Craig Spector (New York: Bantam Books, 1989).

23. "Emerald City Blues," by Steven R. Boyett. In *Midnight Graffiti*, Fall 1988, pp. 16–24.

An F-18 pilot, hauling a bellyful of atomic weapons, passes through a dimensional warp and reappears before the Emerald City of Oz. Bye-bye, Tin Man.

An angry, cautionary, exceptionally well-researched fable on the horrors of nuclear warfare. In Boyett's hands, the destruction of such an innocent, pristine childhood symbol as Oz is a masterstroke.

Highly recommended; Boyett also has contributed "Like Pavlov's Dogs" to *Book of the Dead* and "The Answer Tree" to *Silver Scream*.

24. *The Essential Ellison*, ed. Terry Dowling (Omaha and Kansas City: Nemo Press, 1987).

  Included are "A Boy and His Dog," "Along the Scenic Route," "I Have No Mouth and I Must Scream," "The Prowler in the City at the Edge of the World," and "The Whimper of Whipped Dogs."

  An invaluable historical overview of prime Ellisonia.

25. *The Exorcist*, by William Peter Blatty (New York: Bantam Books, 1972).

26. "Extreme Measures: The Fiction of John Skipp and Craig Spector," by R. S. Hadji. In *The Horror Show* magazine, Fall 1988, pp. 17–20.

27. *Fangoria* magazine, 475 Park Avenue South, New York, New York 10016.

28. "Film at Eleven," by John Skipp. In *Silver Scream*, ed. David J. Schow (New York: Tor Books, 1988).

29. *Film Threat* magazine, P.O. Box 951, Royal Oak, Michigan 48068.

  The July 1989 issue has a Clive Barker interview by Tim Caldwell.

30. *The Fog*, by James Herbert (New York: New American Library, 1975).

31. "Freaktent," by Nancy A. Collins. In *The Horror Show* magazine, Spring 1990.

32. *Gauntlet* magazine, Department GA2, 309 Powell Road, Springfield, Pennsylvania 19064. The magazine premiered in 1990.

  Gauntlet's subtitle is "Exploring The Limits Of Free Expression," and that's precisely the function of this new and recommended publication. Published only once a year (as of this writing), *Gauntlet* also has produced only one issue—but it's an excellent forecast of things to come. With the explicit aim of both defending First Amendment rights and exposing attempts to destroy same (certainly one of splatterpunk's primary concerns), *Gauntlet* includes far-reaching articles, fiction, and critiques by the likes of Ray Bradbury ("More Than One Way to Burn a Book"), Harlan Ellison ("Nackles"), George Carlin ("The FCC Cracks Down on Filthy Words"), Rex Miller ("Nasty Times"), and Dan Simmons ("Determine Your Censorship Quotient").

  Mixing mainstream arts and generic material, *Gauntlet*'s first issue also includes an interview with photographer Andres Serrano, whose "Piss Christ" (along with a traveling exhibit of fellow photographer Robert Mapplethorpe) so incensed Senator Jesse Helms that Helms led a widespread effort to emasculate the National Endowment for the Arts.

My favorite *Gauntlet* pieces thus far, however, include two frightening exposés on the ultraconservative, politically powerful, power-hungry Donald Wildmon. Wildmon's American Family Association has managed to pressure Pepsi Cola into not running a Madonna commercial, kept certain 7-Eleven stores from stocking *Playboy*, and generally made life hell for any Tupelo, Mississippi, citizen (where the AFA is based) daring to contradict Wildmon's fundamentalist beliefs.

I also loved "Let the Darkness In," by Steve Rasnic Tem, which cogently examines America's squeamishness about bodily functions, among other things.

Gauntlet's publisher and editor, Barry Hoffman, strikes me as a true American patriot. We need more of them.

33. "Gentlemen," by John Skipp and Craig Spector. In *The Architecture of Fear*, ed. Kathryn Cramer and Peter D. Pautz (New York: William Morrow, 1987); also found in *Dead Lines* (New York: Bantam Books, 1989).

To my way of thinking, this is Skipp and Spector's best piece of short fiction. A novella centering on physical abuse toward women, "Gentlemen" primarily takes place in the saloon and men's bathroom of a seedy Manhattan bar. The atmosphere is smoky, the characters complex, and the moral imperative deadly serious; those who accuse splatterpunk of misogyny should be force-fed this story one paragraph at a time.

The Boys are really onto something here. In the process, they've come up with one of their angriest and most compassionate efforts. "Gentlemen" takes a close, brutal look at a particularly repellent testicular trait, one long overdue for immediate castration. And the central metaphor is furious, hilarious, and absolutely brilliant: the macho ethic conceptualized as a literal piece of shit.

34. "Goodbye, Dark Love," by Roberta Lannes. In *Cutting Edge*, ed. Dennis Etchison (New York: Doubleday, 1986).

35. *The Gore Score*, by Chas. Balun. (Self-published, 1985).

36. "Graffiti," by David J. Schow. In *Midnight Graffiti*, June 1988, pp. 36–47; also found in *Seeing Red* (New York: Tor Books, 1990).

One of Schow's finest novellas.

A group of aimless Hollywood punks find themselves haunted by their dead friend, the pumpkin-crazed Jocko. Detailed, sharp, believable—the Hollyweird milieu is particularly well invoked.

Once again, the word *Graffiti* is only a visual approximation of Schow's purely graphic heading; there is no actual word used for a title.

37. *Hellbound: Hellraiser II*. 1988, directed by Tony Randel, story by Clive Barker. New World Pictures.

I know, I know—I said there'd be no film titles in this list!

So sue.

Despite its occasionally laughable lapses and fragmentary storyline (the result of last-minute recutting by the studio). *Hellbound* contains one of the toughest splatter endurance tests of the 1980s. This is the scene where a pathetic mental patient repeatedly slashes his body with a straight razor. If you can sit through *this* puppy, you'll have survived one of the indelible moments of carnographic cinema.

Just thought you'd like to know.

38. "The Hellbound Heart," by Clive Barker. In *Night Visions 3* (Arlington Heights, IL: Dark Harvest, 1987).

39. *Hell House*, by Richard Matheson (New York: Viking Press, 1971).

40. "Hooked on Buzzer," by Elizabeth Massie. In *Women of Darkness*, ed. Kathryn Ptacek (New York: Tor Books, 1988).

Intense short fiction melding religious fanaticism, orgasm, and electricity, "Hooked on Buzzer" is one of those stories that somehow slipped through the public-awareness cracks. Recommended.

41. *Horror Holocaust*, by Chas. Balun (Albany, NY: Fantaco Enterprises, 1986).

42. *Hot Blood*, ed. Jeff Gelb and Lonn Friend (New York: Pocket Books, 1989). This volume contains "Punishments," by Ray Garton, "Footsteps," by Harlan Ellison, and others.

This sex-themed horror story anthology is sort of an Americanized companion volume to Ramsey Campbell's *Scared Stiff* (with more contributors). The sexual shenanigans range from coy to explicit; Garton's "Punishments" is the standout contribution.

43. "I Have No Mouth, and I Must Scream," by Harlan Ellison.

In *The Essential Ellison*, ed. Terry Dowling (Omaha and Kansas City: Nemo Press, 1987).

44. "Inside the New Horror," by Philip Nutman. In *The Twilight Zone Magazine*, August 1988.

Nutman's essay is an overview of the emergence of the new attitude in horror fiction as exemplified by splatterpunk; "Inside" was also among the first serious probes into splatterpunk to be published by a professional horror magazine. It is historically important: cites Schow, Skipp and Spector, Douglas Winter, and others. Nutman also has found an invaluable quote from J. G. Ballard, who states that many of us refuse to acknowledge "the immense hold that violence exerts over people. It seems to me that's unhealthy. One should face up to the realities of human nature; that way, one can do something about improving it."

Exactly.

45. "I Spit in Your Face: Films That Bite," by Chas. Balun. In *The Deep Red Horror Handbook*, ed. Chas. Balun (Albany, NY: Fantaco Books, 1989).

46. "Jacqueline Ess: Her Will and Testament," by Clive Barker. In Clive Barker's Books of Blood, vol. two (London: Sphere Books, 1984; New York: Berkley Books, 1986).

47. "John Skipp and Craig Spector in Skipp & Spector's Excellent Adventures," an Interview by John Martin and Angus MacKenzie. In *Samhain*, June–July 1989, pp. 8–11.

This recent interview with The Boys is worth a look for Skipp and Spector's current thoughts on splat. It was conducted at about the time they were appearing as film extras in Barker's *Nightbreed*.

48. "Joy," by Mick Garris. In *Midnight Graffiti*, Spring 1990.

Details the quite deranged but generally benign mind of a madman, who ends his day by burying a baby—while it's still alive.

49. *The Kill Riff*, by David J. Schow (New York: Tor Books, 1988).

50. "Less Than Zombie," by Douglas E. Winter. In *Book of the Dead*, ed. John Skipp and Craig Spector (New York: Bantam Books, 1989).

51. "A Life in the Cinema," by Mick Garris. In *Silver Scream*, ed. David J. Schow (New York: Tor Books, 1988).

Mick Garris is primarily a screenwriter and director these days; his fiction is a fairly recent phenomenon. He's directed *Critters 2* and *Psycho 4* (sounds like a splatterpunk football game to me) and written for television and other films. Based on "A Life in the Cinema" and his film work—which includes *The Fly II*—Mick is obviously sympathetic to splatterpunk attitudes. We'll have to wait and see if this manifests itself in further fiction.

52. *The Light at the End*, by John Skipp and Craig Spector (New York: Bantam Books, 1986).

53. *Live Girls*, by Ray Garton (New York: Pocket Books, 1987).

54. *Lost Angels*, by David J. Schow (New York: Onyx Books, 1990).

Schow's best story collection, thematically unified through love lost, love found. Includes "Brass," "Red Light," "Pamela's Get," "The Falling Man," and "Monster Movies." Character-oriented, tart, and intelligent, these stories are played out before a corrosively etched Los Angeles backdrop. If Skipp and Spector are splatterpunk's best observors of the New York scene, nobody does Los Angeles like David J. Schow.

55. "Meathouse Man," by George R. R. Martin. In *Songs the Dead Men Sing* (London: Sphere Books, 1986).

56. *Midnight Graffiti* magazine, 13101 Sudan Road, Poway, California 92064.

An impressively produced publication, *Midnight Graffiti* continues to regularly feature splatterpunk works.

57. "The Midnight Meat Train," by Clive Barker. In *Clive Barker's Books of Blood*, vol. one (London: Sphere Books, 1984).

58. "Monster Movies," by David J. Schow. In *Lost Angels*, by David J. Schow (New York: Onyx Books, 1990).

59. "Mop Up," by Richard Laymon. In *Night Visions 7* (Arlington Heights, IL: Dark Harvest, 1989).

60. "More Gore: Splatterpunk Leaves Its Mark," by Richard Gehr. In *The Village Voice*, February 6, 1990, pp. 57–58.

61. "The 'New' Horror," by J. N. Williamson. In *Masques III*, ed. J. N. Williamson (New York: St. Martin's Press, 1989).

In this short essay, Williamson (anthologist and a founding member of the Horror Writers of America) sketches in his thoughts on splatterpunk. "At its worst," Williamson observes, " 'new' horror can be choppy, or filled with a certain belligerence; with vulgarity. At its best, it's a marvelous use of American freedom to say or do that which the writer hopes devoutly will make one particular, monstrous social fuck-up leave our griefstricken lives forever" (p. 104).

Despite a seeming unease with profanity (Williamson's line " 'new' horror can be . . . filled with . . . vulgarity" is an obvious tip-off) and splat's use of dope, booze, and "improbable intercourse" (he objects to a gratuitous insertion of these elements—where have we heard *that* before?), Williamson's miniessay arrives at a rather balanced, tolerant assessment of splatterpunk. He does it on aesthetic, freedom-of-choice grounds, too, making "The 'New' Horror" one of the more evenhanded critiques of splatterpunk.

62. "Nightcrawlers," by Robert R. McCammon. In *Blue World* (New York: Pocket Books, 1990.

63. *The Nightrunners*, by Joe R. Lansdale) (Arlington Heights, IL: Dark Harvest, 1987).

64. "Night They Missed the Horror Show," by Joe R. Lansdale. In *Silver Scream*, ed. David J. Schow (Arlington Heights, IL: Dark Harvest, 1987), and in *By Bizarre Hands*, by Joe R. Lansdale (Shingletown, CA): Mark V. Ziesing, 1989).

65. *Nova Express*, P.O. Box 27231, Austin, Texas 78755.

66. *The Official Splatter Movie Guide*, by John McCarty (New York: St. Martin's Press, 1989).

67. "On the Far Side of the Cadillac Desert, With Dead Folks," by Joe R. Lansdale. In *Book of the Dead*, ed. John Skipp and Craig Spector (New York: Bantam Books, 1989), and in *By Bizarre Hands*, by Joe R. Lansdale (Shingletown, CA: Mark V. Ziesing, 1989).

A modern-day zombie western, with bounty hunters, escaped badmen, and carnal nuns. Fast, funny, and evocative. The scene with the cannibalistic, undead woman dancing naked in a run-down topless bar—her hands have been cut off and her mouth muzzled so she can't bite the customers—is a little gem. Nobody but Lansdale could've pulled this one off.

68. *The Penguin Encyclopedia of Horror and the Supernatural*, ed. Jack Sullivan (New York: Viking, 1986). This volume includes "Writers of Today," by Doug Winter.

69. "Pig Blood Blues," by Clive Barker. In *Clive Barker's Books of Blood*, vol. one (London: Sphere Books, 1984; New York: Berkley Books, 1986).

70. "Pilgrims to the Cathedral," by Mark Arnold. In *Silver Scream*, ed. David J. Schow (Arlington Heights, IL: Dark Harvest, 1987).

71. *Prime Evil*, ed. Douglas Winter (New York: New American Library, 1988).

This collection of mostly traditional horror stories contains a number of borderline splatterpunk texts. One is Stephen King's "The Night Flier," with its sated vampire going to a men's room and pissing blood.

But the best splat story is Peter Straub's "The Juniper Tree," a complex, nostalgic, absolutely horrifying restructuring of the famous brothers Grimm fairy tale, one using movie matinees and homosexual child molestation as its central dynamic. This truly is among Straub's strongest, most mature effort.

Very highly recommended.

72. "The Prowler in the City at the Edge of the World," by Harlan Ellison. In *The Essential Ellison*, ed. Terry Dowling (Omaha and Kansas City: Nemo Press, 1987).

73. *Psycho*, by Robert Bloch (New York: Warner Books, 1982).

74. "Punishments," by Ray Garton. In *Hot Blood*, ed. Jeff Gelb and Lonn Friend (New York: Pocket Books, 1989).

Painful, pathetic, and carnal, "Punishments" charts the downwardly spiraling sexual relationship between an innocent young man and a self-loathing older woman. The female character, in particular, leaves a haunting, melancholy mark. Very strong, very real. Part of Garton's anti-Adventist canon, and one of his best shorter works.

75. "Rant," by Nancy A. Collins. In *Midnight Graffiti*, Spring 1990, pp. 44–48.

76. "Rapid Transit," by Wayne Allen Sallee. In *The Year's Best Horror Stories, Series XIV*, ed. Karl Edward Wagner (New York): DAW Books, 1986).

77. "Rawhead Rex," by Clive Barker. In *Clive Barker's Books of Blood*, Vol. Three (London: Sphere Books, 1984; New York: Berkley Books, 1986).

78. "Red Light," by David J. Schow. In *Lost Angels*, by David J. Schow (New York: Onyx Books, 1990).

79. *Samhain* magazine, 19 Elm Grove Road, Topsham, Exeter, Devon, EX3, OEQ, England.

80. *Scared Stiff*, by Ramsey Campbell (Los Angeles: Scream/Press, 1987).

A compendium of Ramsey Campbell's erotic horror fiction—not a genre he's exactly known for.

One of horror's most respected writers, Campbell *is* known for his moody, elliptical tone and relentlessly downbeat atmosphere; such *Stiff* stories as "Stages" and "Loveman's Comeback" combine Campbell's usual effects with hard-core sex scenes. Little known to diehard splatterpunk fans, *Scared Stiff* is worth searching out.

Clive Barker contributes an introduction to *Scared Stiff*, focusing on the classic theme of death and the maiden.

81. *Scars*, by Richard Christian Matheson (Los Angeles: Scream/Press, 1987).

82. "Schow, David J.—Special Issue." In *Weird Tales*, Spring 1990, pp. 14–25.

83. *The Scream*, by John Skipp and Craig Spector (New York: Bantam Books, 1988).

84. *Seeing Red*, by David J. Schow (New York: Tor Books, 1990).

85. *Silver Scream*, ed. David J. Schow (New York: Tor Books, 1988).

Included are "A Life in the Cinema," by Mick Garris; "Sinema," by Ray Garton; "Son of Celluloid," by Clive Barker; "Night They Missed the Horror Show," by Joe Lansdale; "Sirens," by Richard Christian Matheson; "Splatter: A Cautionary Tale," by Douglas E. Winter; "Film at Eleven," by John Skipp; and "Pilgrims to the Cathedral," by Mark Arnold.

Like *Books of Blood* and *Book of the Dead*, *Silver Scream* is another landmark collection in the history of splat.

86. "Sinema," by Ray Garton. In *Silver Scream*, ed. David J. Schow (New York: Tor Books, 1988).

87. *Slice*, by Rex Miller (New York: Onyx Books, 1990).

Chaingang returns in this direct sequel to Miller's popular *Slob*. This time the quarter-ton killer (who survived *Slob*'s hot-lead climax by recuperating in the sewers of Chicago) goes after Jack Eichord, the cop who nearly killed him. More brutal than the first Chaingang novel, *Slice* nevertheless invests Miller's serial killer with a new quality: heart. What's next—*Chaingang in Love?*

88. *Slob*, by Rex Miller (New York: Signet Books, 1987).

89. "Son of Celluloid," by Clive Barker. In *Clive Barker's Books of Blood*, Vol. Three (London: Sphere Books, 1984).

90. "The Splat Pack: Horror's Young Writers Spill Their Guts," by Jessie Horsting. In *Midnight Graffiti*, June 1988, pp. 30–35.

91. "Splatter: A Cautionary Tale," by Douglas E. Winter. In *Silver Scream*, ed. David J. Schow (New York: Tor Books, 1988).

92. *Splatter Movies: Breaking the Last Taboo of the Screen*, by John McCarty (New York: St. Martin's Press, 1984).

93. "The Splatterpunks: The Young Turks at Horror's Cutting Edge," by Lawrence Person. In *Nova Express*, Summer 1988, pp. 17–27.

94. *Sunglasses After Dark*, by Nancy A. Collins (New York: Onyx Books, 1989).

95. "Take the A-Train," by Wayne Allen Sallee. In *The Year's Best Horror Stories, Series XV*, ed. Karl Edward Wagner (New York: DAW Books, 1987).

96. "Threshold," by Wayne Allen Sallee. In *New Blood*, issue 2.

A mutant child is kept locked in a cellar by its parents, who are training it as a bizarre gladiator. Somewhat like the senior Richard Matheson's first short story sale, "Born of Man and Woman"—but with a definite splatterpunk spin.

97. "Waiting for the Barbarians," by Lucius Shepard. In *Journal Wired*, Winter 1989, pp. 107–118.

Shepard has been tagged a "magic realist" and usually is associated with the science fiction community. Whatever the taxonomy, works like *Life During Wartime* and *The Jaguar Hunter* mark Shepard as a relevant, adult presence in the usually socially arrested genre of speculative fiction. (In fact, about all I can stomach in the way of science fiction these days are folks like Shepard and William Gibson; God save me from the deluge of elves, militarists, and "Star Trek" knock-offs dominating current science fiction!)

"Waiting For The Barbarians" is an essay mainly focusing on the cyberpunks; along the way, Shepard touches on the splatterpunks. Despite its brevity, this is still probably the most clear-eyed, truly *critical* look at splat I've run across.

Need I say it's recommended?

Here's a sample: "To write without making it an act of conscience is essentially to become an accomplice in the tragedy of the late Twentieth Century" (p. 117).

98. "The Whimper of Whipped Dogs," by Harlan Ellison. In *The Essential Ellison*, ed. Terry Dowling (Omaha and Kansas City: Nemo Press, 1987).

99. *Women of Darkness*, ed. Kathryn Ptacek (New York: Tor Books, 1988).

This collection includes "Hooked on Buzzer," by Elizabeth Massie, and "Cannibal Cats Come Out Tonight," by Nancy Holder.

100. "The Yattering and Jack," by Clive Barker. In *Clive Barker's Books of Blood*, vol. one (London: Sphere Books, 1984; New York: Berkley Books, 1986).

101. *The Year's Best Horror Stories, Series XIV*, ed. Karl Edward Wagner (New York: DAW Books, 1986).

Included in this volume is "Rapid Transit," by Wayne Allen Sallee.

102. *The Year's Best Horror Stories, Series XV*, ed. Karl Edward Wagner (New York: DAW Books, 1987).

"Take the A-Train," by Wayne Allen Sallee, appears in this volume.

13. IT'S A WRAP

Three final questions.

First—why was Paul Sammon drawn to splatterpunk in the first place?

Well, I could trot out the usual rationales. For instance: I intimately understand the extraordinary delight in the power of transgression, of taking things to the limit.

I was also once a rock musician.

And I possess a deep and lifelong love of and familiarity with the genres of horror and science fiction—not to mention an unashamedly encyclopedic knowledge of film.

The truth of the matter, though, is something much more personal, and much more private.

Generally, my enjoyment of splatterpunk has to do with the accepted notion that evil is of enormous interest to us all. Specifically, I know that evil is not only personified, but random; you see, chaos and terror were my childhood companions.

During my formative years (the late fifties and early sixties), I spent a great deal of time in the Philippines, growing up at a number of U.S. military installations. During some of this time my father worked for military intelligence—the Naval Counterintelligence Support Unit, to be exact—and such a close proximity to this essentially retributive, violent line of work (not to mention daily encounters with the Third World, since I wasn't the kind of kid who stayed home very much) inescapably altered my worldview.

I saw my first corpse before I was eight years old. Watched

forensic examiners pick a suicide's brains out of a baseboard at twelve. Saw firsthand the effects of opium smoking and barbiturate addiction before I was thirteen. Fired a Thompson submachine gun, turned down hookers, touched drowned men's flesh by the age of fifteen.

In those days the Philippines was a wide-open country (it still is), and the topics around our dinner table routinely centered on child prostitution, incest, and accidental electrocution.

Every day I saw the consequences of these acts, mostly for the people involved in them. I smelled their shit, evacuated in fright or death. Heard their lies and screams. Witnessed laughter. Silence. Tears.

Needless to say, when I finally returned to a comfortable middle-class existence in the States, I experienced a wee bit of culture shock. (How come American men didn't check in their firearms at restaurant cloakrooms? Filipinos did.)

Never mind.

Those days in the Philippines have stayed with me, and I'm grateful for them. They taught me early on that the human beast is indeed capable of anything, both squalid and transcendent.

So I've lived my life accordingly. Mere existence is precious to me . . . I know what to carry in the dark.

As does splatterpunk.

That's why I love it.

Second question: why edit a book called *Splatterpunks* or write an essay like "Outlaws" in the first place?

That's an easy one to answer, short 'n' sweet.

My basic intent with "Outlaws" (a title which refers to the anarchic spirit, the willful turning away from the proper bounds of law and order which, to me, is splatterpunk's secret heart), was simply to attempt an informed, informational overview of the subject.

It's long been needed.

I hope I've succeeded.

Finally, is splatterpunk dying, or dead?

Well . . . maybe Charlie Grant is right. Perhaps splatterpunk *is* a dead issue. Or perhaps it will mutate into a new art form, leaving behind its small legacy of pioneering disruption (I'm already noticing the phrase *New horror* where *splatterpunk* used to do).

Conversely, the word *splatterpunk* may enter the public consciousness like a subversive virus. It may continue to attack the *corpus traditionalis*, continue to attract new practitioners, and continue to forge new ground (though it's always been a sure sign in the past that, once a generic term enters the public consciousness, it usually has already been bypassed by the very group that spawned it). *Splatterpunk* may even, someday, be as familiar a label to the general public as the dreaded "sci-fi" is today.

Who knows?

One thing is certain. The powers that fuel the *attitudes* of splatterpunk—courage, energy, joy, explicitness—are about as likely to die as rock 'n' roll. Or honesty. Or humanity itself.

What's wonderful about splatterpunk is that it's constantly *changing*. The best of the splatterpunks—even those who only write splatlike stories—show incredible growth, book to book, story to story. And this brands the myth of splatterpunk tilling a very small field as a total lie. In a real sense, splatterpunk is mutant literature, fiction in a constant state of flux.

This is as it should be. Herbert Read, one of the leading British advocates of the modernist and surrealist movements, has written that "art is never transfixed. Change is the condition of art remaining art."

Which puts a different spin on Grant's argument, don't you think?

And splatterpunk—or whatever it will be called next year—will always be confrontational. One could cite numerous examples, quote chapter and verse, concerning the essentially provocative nature of art. But let's settle for no less a personage than Salman Rushdie, who can begin to edge us toward some final insights on splat. After all, Rushdie is a man well acquainted with the controversial—not to mention life-threatening—aspects of literature.

In this era of Congress trying to withhold federal funds from those artists it fears may be "offensive," in this age of ultraconservative minorities forcing their philosophies on an all-too-passive majority, it's buoying to encounter someone with Rushdie's intellect, balance, and integrity. The following excerpt, delivered by Harold Pinter at the Institute of Contemporary Arts in London on February, 6, 1990 (while Rushdie was still in hiding for fear his life might be taken by zealous Iranians angered at his book *The Satanic Verses*), is from Rushdie's lecture "Is Nothing Sacred?" And while its text specifically addresses the responsibilities of all novels in general, Rushdie might as well have been writing about splatterpunk.

. . . while the novel answers our need for wonderment and understanding, it brings us harsh and unpalatable news as well.

It tells us there are no rules. It hands down no commandments. We have to make up our own rules as best we can, make them up as we go along.

And it tells us there are no answers; or, rather, it tells us that answers are easier to come by, and less reliable, than questions. If religion is an answer, if political ideology is an answer, then literature is an inquiry; great literature, by asking extraordinary questions, opens new doors in our minds.

Splatterpunks have opened a new door in the house of horror fiction.

No—they've *kicked it in*.

And the current owners of that house, the landed gentry who've grown fat and comfortable and secure with their holdings, aren't very happy about it.

They should have known better.

Because there always have been—and there always will be—Outlaws.

The End

Los Angeles
March–May 1990
For Luis Buñuel

ABOUT THE EDITOR

Paul Michael Sammon was born in Philadelphia, Pennsylvania, in 1949. He spent most of the first twenty years of his life in the Philippines and Japan; he now resides in Los Angeles.

Sammon's distinctive career is best described by the film industry expression "hyphenate." As a film critic and historian, his work has appeared in *Omni, The American Cinematographer, Cinefex, The Los Angeles Times, Cahiers du Cinema,* and *Cinefantastique.* Sammon's short fiction has appeared in *The Twilight Zone Magazine* and *The Year's Best Horror Stories* edited by Karl Edward Wagner. He is currently finishing *Blood and Rockets,* the definitive consumer guide to the best science fiction, fantasy, and horror films available on videotape.

Sammon is not only a writer, but a professional filmmaker as well. For the past three years he has served as the American producer of the Tokyo-based television show "Hello! Movies," the most successful entertainment program of its kind in Japan today. Through Sammon's company Awesome Productions (which he founded in 1980), Sammon has produced/edited/directed dozens of documentaries, commercials, and promotional films for all the major Hollywood studios. He has also provided publicity services for films like *Platoon* and *Blue Velvet,* and was recently Computer Graphics Supervisor on *Robocop 2.*

Awesome Productions is currently developing Joe R. Lansdale's novel *The Drive-in* as a major motion picture. Sammon is writing the screenplay, and hopes to direct.